Temper
FOR YOU

BY GENNA RULON

Temper For You
Copyright © 2014
Genna Rulon

The Cataloging-in-Publication Data is on file at Library of Congress
ISBN-13: 9780990777809

Cover design by G. Relyea
© Genna Rulon, 2014

Cover Images Copyright
Used under license from Shutterstock.com

Dedication

To Debbie,
my bestest friend and the sister of my heart

Twenty years of friendship all began with purple nail polish!

Without your encouragement, nudges, and occasional butt-kicking, *Temper For You* would never have been finished.

Thank you for pulling me out of my shell when I 'go turtle' and for standing beside me, no matter what. You know me better than anyone and love me anyway. You are my rock, my cheerleader, and more often than not, my sanity.

So many readers have told me they wish they had an Everleigh or Sam in their lives, but what they really need is a Debbie.

PS- Does this count as a card

tem·per
/ˈtɛm pər/

noun:

1. a particular state of mind or feelings.
2. habit of mind, especially with respect to irritability or patience, outbursts of anger, or the like; disposition: "an even temper."
3. heat of mind or passion, shown in outbursts of anger, resentment, etc.
4. calm disposition; composure: "to lose one's temper."
5. a substance added to modify other properties.
6. the degree of hardness and strength imparted to a metal, as by quenching, or treatment with heat.
7. a middle course; compromise. *(archaic)*

verb:

8. to moderate or mitigate: "to temper justice with mercy."
9. to soften or tone down.
10. to make suitable by/as if by blending.
11. to impart strength or toughness by heating and cooling.
12. to produce internal stresses in by sudden cooling from low heat; toughen.
13. to pacify. *(archaic*

Chapter 1

"We are what we believe we are."
-C. S. Lewis

<u>Meg</u>

"Excuse me, sir, can I ask you a question?"

I opened my eyes to find Sam leaning across the narrow aisle to address my seatmate in 1A. I whispered a silent prayer to a God I no longer believed in that she was not about to do what I *knew* she was about to do.

"Sure," the unsuspecting gentleman replied while he leaned forward to meet Sam's eyes.

I braced for it.

"Have you ever been charged with a violent crime?" Sam inquired in her sweetest voice as if it were a completely routine question from one air traveler to another.

"Um...no. No criminal record," Mr. 1A responded with a mixture of amusement and confusion.

"Do you have a history of drug abuse or mental illness?" Sam continued, clearly pleased with his answer and willingness to accept her bizarre behavior.

"Nope," he responded as the corners of his lips tilted upward.

Sam continued her now familiar inquisition as I pretended to be invisible.

"On a scale of one to ten—one being fumbling idiot, ten being orgasmic virtuoso—how would you rate your sexual prowess?"

I subtly banged my head against the headrest, trying to distract myself from the routine.

Luckily, 1A had a sense of humor and chuckled before playing along, "I'd say I'm a solid eight—with moments of nine...with the right partner, of course."

"Hmm...an eight is acceptable," Sam muttered, before offering him a wink, "but a nine is better. Have you considered joining the 'Mile High Club,' or if you're already a member, would you like to renew your *dues*?"

I groaned my embarrassment, while 1A choked on his surprise.

"Unless the invitation is on behalf of the spectacular example of male perfection to your right, I'll have to decline," Mr. 1A replied suggestively, leaning forward to partake in a thorough examination of the 'male perfection' in question.

Sam's laughter filled the air around us, and I couldn't help but smile. At least she was having fun.

"Love that sound," I heard Griffin whisper to Sam before addressing the less-than-subtle pick-up line. "Sorry, man. The head of the inquisition," he nodded to Sam, "and I have an exclusive club all our own."

"Figures," 1A complained good-naturedly, "all the best ones are taken or straight." He ended his assertion with a defeated sigh.

"Guess I need to add a question about sexual orientation to the list," Sam mused. "Oh well, can't fault a girl for trying. Thanks for playing along. I'm Sam, by the way," she introduced before pointing beside her. "The super-sized sexiness with a side of hot-damn you were coveting is Griffin, and the stunning lady beside you—who is pretending not to know me—is Meg."

"I assume Meg was the prize if I'd answered all the questions correctly," 1A deduced. After sweeping his gaze over me, he added, "Honey, if there was ever any doubt, I can now lay it to rest. Because if my bat won't swing for you, then there is no woman who could ever get me to play. You're stunning."

"And you, Mr. 1A, are a charmer," I said with sincerity.

"While 1A has a certain ring to it, please, call me Stuart," he replied.

"I'm sorry for Sam's interrogation. Her favorite pastime is trying to find a bedmate for me, despite my protests. You, sadly, are only one in a long line of failed attempts."

"Why on earth would you need anyone's help finding a man? Your smile alone must attract a dozen guys, ready to propose."

I rolled my eyes at his over-the-top compliment. It was sweet, regardless of the exaggeration.

"I'm not in the market for anything requiring the exchange of rings—*ever*—or anything in the neighborhood of commitment, for that matter. I'm just interested in a bit of *satisfying* fun, but my track record in selecting partners is less than stellar. Which is why Sam appointed herself my 'screening committee,'" I said while making air quotes. "It keeps her entertained and I couldn't stop her if I tried, so I roll with it," I finished with a shrug, no longer shy in explaining the source of Sam's crazy behavior after nearly a year of similar antics.

"If you can't beat 'em, join 'em?" he commiserated.

"No, more like, if you can't beat 'em, stay the hell out of their way so you don't get steamrolled."

Stuart smiled a sympathetic grin, which led me to believe he had his own 'Sam' to contend with.

After a brief pause, Stuart switched gears, much to my relief. My pathetic sex life—defined by the seemingly endless dry spell I was currently *not* enjoying—was not a topic that gave me the warm fuzzies.

"Were you in LA for business or pleasure?" he asked.

Ah, the quintessential air travel question.

"Actually, LA was a layover on our way home from Hawaii. Our close friends got married in Kona over the weekend," I replied. "We decided to overnight in LA in each direction to break up the trip from New York. Six hours trapped in a tin can is Sam's limit."

"A destination wedding...how romantic. Did you have fun?"

"I'm not generally a fan of weddings—or flying—but I would do anything for Hunter and Everleigh. They're perfect together. Hell, I even got a contact high from their joy." And it was true. I didn't believe in marriage as a rule. I'd even refused to attend weddings in silent protest, but Huntleigh (their couple name, as christened by Sam) were one of only two exceptions...the other being GriffLo (Griffin and Sam's couple name, as christened by me—the result of Griffin's pet name for Sam, 'Lo').

"A woman who hates weddings? I didn't think such a creature existed. There *must* be a story there. We have five hours to kill...regale me!" he ordered.

Despite Stuart's warm, engaging demeanor, I'd known him all of twenty minutes. I didn't share my life story with strangers—or anyone, for that matter. Sam and Everleigh were my most trusted friends, and even they knew only carefully selected pieces of my past—a synopsis, if you will, some of which included less-than-accurate details. Twenty-five years of hard-learned lessons had taught me well; I didn't share the *whole* truth of my past with anyone, and I never would. Some burdens were meant to be borne alone. Why?

I am an apple.

Everyone knew that a rotten apple spoils the bushel if left close to the good apples for too long. But that apple didn't start out rotten...it didn't *ask* to spoil and turn rancid. Climate and environment—circumstances beyond the innocent apple's control—caused the decay. Something made its way inside what was once a perfectly healthy, desirable apple, full of promise, and contaminated its previously unblemished state.

Was it the apple's fault that the Evil Queen's magic caused it to become poisonous? The apple had nothing against Snow White. There was no long-standing Snow/Apple feud filled with backstabbing and prince-stealing. 'Granny Smith' didn't want to harm the fairest in the land. The naïve produce was simply minding its own business, hanging on its tree and sunning itself, when the Evil Queen (or more likely one of her minions, as I doubt royalty— even of the evil variety—personally harvested anything, despite its importance to the nefarious plan) came along and plucked the guileless apple from its home. The apple had no defense. Against its will, the otherwise benign fruit was submerged in a cauldron of black magic, where the malevolence soaked through to its very core and changed the once life-giving flesh into a vile aberration of its former self.

But here's the kicker—the pièce de résistance. The prince, dwarves, Snow White...no one blamed the apple, right? The kingdom wasn't suddenly decorated with apple tree stumps. No one was burning apples in the town square. Nope, the apple wasn't vilified at all, even though it was unquestionably a tool for evil. *But*...I would bet every penny to my name, few though there are, that Snow White *never* ate an apple again. Snow wasn't snacking on apple Danish at breakfast. There were no apple pies at the harvest celebration. She may not have blamed the apple, but there was no way girlfriend ever wanted another bite to cross her ruby red lips. Although blameless, the apple was quietly ostracized and excluded once the truth was revealed.

That's the reality of being a rotten apple...and the reality sucks. Not only was the apple rotting, but it's lonely and forced to choose between rolling beside other rotting apples (an unpleasant prospect to be sure) or coexisting near beautiful, untainted apples, though always on the periphery to minimize the risk of contaminating others with its own foulness.

"Meg...are you still with me?" Stuart asked, pulling me from my Disney-inspired self-realization.

Excusing myself from the one-woman pity party I was hosting, I turned my attention to Stuart and did what I do best...listen and evade.

"We'll get to my wedding aversion, which is a result of various boring clichés, but first you *must* tell me whose text you were hoping to receive when you checked your cell phone no less than a hundred times before takeoff," I deftly dodged the conversation.

With a dramatic sigh, Stuart launched into his life story with an emphasis on Taylor, his 'heart's one true desire.' Each time he attempted to turn the tables back to me, he was easily redirected by my follow-up questions. Genuinely interested in my seatmate's love woes, I was entertained for the duration of the flight. It was clear that Taylor was head-over-heels in love with Stuart and their spat was the result of both men's fear of being hurt. They were entrenched in the uncomfortable transition from casually dating to deeply committed.

When we landed at JFK, Stuart and I parted with a hug. I encouraged him to forgive Taylor for his 'bitch fit' and not allow fear to spoil his happiness. Once his promise was secured, I departed with Sam and Griffin, knowing it was the last I'd see of Stuart. In a different life, I would have exchanged contact information and happily welcomed a new friend into my sphere...but in this life, my attachments were few by necessity. Only four persistent and stubborn individuals managed to breach my guard, and while I was grateful beyond words for their friendship, I knew it was still four too many—at least for their own well-being.

Until the foursome strong-armed their way into my life, I'd never sought the intimacy of friendship. It wasn't because I didn't want it, mind you, but you can't want something you don't believe lasts or will be taken from you. And like love, friendship has never been anything more than an abstract concept or literary device...at least in my experience. The possibility of melting the ice of loneliness encasing a soul was unfathomable to someone who had never felt the warmth of support or care. That warmth was like a drug, and I had to be very careful not to become an addict, mindlessly searching for my next hit of affection. I knew, without a doubt, that I would have to live without it again one day in the not-so-distant future...regardless of how much the thought tore at my heart.

When all was said and done, I was still rotting, and I wouldn't—*couldn't*—contaminate those I'd grown to love.

Chapter 2

*"Sometimes being a friend means mastering
the art of timing. There is a time for silence.
A time to let go and allow people to hurl
themselves into their own destiny.
And a time to prepare to pick up the pieces
when it's all over." -Octavia Butler*

<u>Meg</u>

"Thanks again...for everything," I said to Sam and Griffin as we neared Sam's townhouse, where I've lived for the past seven months.

"Oh god, not again. I'm going to find one of those water cooler jugs and we are going to start a swear jar, but instead of putting money in for cussing, you'll have to put in a dollar every time you say 'thank you' for something ridiculous!" Sam threatened.

This was a threat she may actually follow through with and I'd be broke. Already destitute, I would have to fill the jug with 'I owe yous.'

"Whatever. I'm eternally grateful—deal with it. You just paid for my damn trip to Hawaii! If that isn't worthy of a 'thank you,' then what is?" I argued. "Stop being an overly generous beyatch and I'll stop thanking you," I added with a heavy serving of sass.

A glimpse in the rearview mirror showed Griffin's eyes were smiling at my feisty retort. Sam whipped around to glare at me from the front seat, but she couldn't fully suppress the smile that tugged at the corners of her lips.

My display of cheekiness satisfied Sam more than any words of gratitude ever could. Sam and Everleigh have inspired and encouraged this feistiness in me over the last year and a half. The spark wasn't new per se—I've always had a snarky inner monologue—but their friendship decimated a few barriers.

Ultimately, I gave myself permission to voice the thoughts I had been taught to restrain. I no longer believed expressing myself was shameful or disgraceful—holy hell, it was a relief! The burden of suppressing my natural reactions was debilitatingly heavy, so shrugging off the constraints was a relief I'd never imagined. My entire life, I'd held myself so tightly bound I was little more than a robot. The freedom to just be me was a revelation.

"Megs, you mind if I kidnap Lo? I'd like to pretend we're on vacation for one more night before re-entering the real world," Griffin asked.

"Well, I don't know, Griff. It is a weeknight after all, and you know her curfew is ten pm," I teased. His question was equal parts sweet and lunacy. First, Sam spent at least five nights a week at Griffin's house (he spent the remaining two nights here)—it was expected. Second, Sam was a grown woman and didn't answer to me. Third, I was a grown woman perfectly capable of being alone.

"Wise ass," he retorted as I leaned forward to give them both a kiss on the cheek. "Make sure to lock up and set the alarm."

I smiled as I waved goodbye from the front door while rolling my suitcase into Sam's townhouse, where I re-armed the alarm, grateful for Griffin's never-ceasing concern. Griffin and Sam shared a misguided sense of obligation after I was shot while trying to save Sam from a kidnapper. Who knew being shot would transform my bleak life so drastically? It's probably best that I didn't know gunshot wounds to the stomach were so effective at improving one's quality of life, otherwise I would have launched myself into the line of fire a decade ago. I could imagine myself googling shooting ranges before dressing in head-to-toe black and skulking around between the shooting gallery and targets. Crazy, I know, but given the life I previously led, not as cray-cray as it sounds.

My life has never been easy. In fact, every second of my existence has been the definition of complicated. The nicest way to describe the last ten years would be *messy*. Each milestone brought a new level of cluster-fuck-upedness. Yes, some circumstances were so extreme they required the innovation of new word combinations, and my history has been responsible for countless additions to the American lexicon.

When I awoke after surgery, GriffLo was waiting with a heavy dose of gratitude and responsibility, which kicked their respective caregiver and protector sensibilities into overdrive. Under the pretense of invitation, Sam advised me that I would be staying with her upon my release from the hospital and throughout my recovery. Having no one else to call and in need of assistance, I caved like a poorly excavated mine shaft. A week to recover in the comfort of Sam's home was the answer to un-prayed prayers.

I was relieved...until they requested the keys to my apartment to pack a bag for me. Then I panicked. They *could not* go to my apartment. I protested, offered weak excuses, and finally begged that they forego the visit. I could have swiped a hospital gown before leaving and rocked it for the entire week, possibly even starting a new trend. Infirmary chic—the runways in Milan and Paris might be littered with hospital-inspired gowns next fashion week, all made of luxe fabrics and embellishments.

Unfortunately, Sam had a determined glint in her eye that proved to be stronger than my drug-addled resolve. Reluctantly, I relinquished the keys to my apartment. It was luck (otherwise known as a potty break for Sam) that provided a moment alone with Griffin. I made him swear on his love for Sam that he would not let her visit my apartment alone, and that they would go during daylight, preferably armed with Mace and a stun gun. Griffin studied me with keen eyes before nodding his agreement. When they left for the day, I spent hours dreading the pitying looks and questions their return would bring.

My tiny studio apartment was located in the worst possible neighborhood in a building that should have been condemned twenty years prior. On its best day, the building was a rat-infested shithole that no one, not even those living well below the poverty line, would dare enter. In truth, it was only a step above a crack house, and a tiny step at that. The only 'luxury' the tiny studio boasted was a minuscule bathroom. The premium for this convenience pushed my limited budget to the max, but communal bathrooms in the type of areas I could afford were a considerable safety risk for single females.

It was not 'home sweet home,' but I'd disinfected every square inch with bleach until my skin burned, painted the walls, and added a few touches of color with end-of-day garage sale bargains. I'd scored after one such garage sale when I found a small table and dresser curbside. These were the only furnishings I had other than a futon, which doubled as both a couch and bed. But regardless of how much dollar store make-up you slapped on a pig, it was still a pig. Oink, oink!

Thankfully, GriffLo didn't question the state of my humble abode when they returned, but they wasted no time in shuffling me off to Sam's house. Not long after, Sam invited me to live with her permanently, reassuring me that I would be doing *her* a favor by alleviating her guilt, since I'd incurred my injury in her defense. *Right!* She insisted I live rent-free, which was out of the question, and we eventually agreed that I would pay a very modest rent for the room. The savings increased my budget from $27 per week to a whopping $102, allowing me to sustain myself on something other than Ramen noodles and peanut butter straight from the jar. I was still poor, but I now lived in a luxury townhouse and slept on a top-of-the-line queen pillow top. My diet included consistent calories from healthy sources, and I was able to save a little money each month for my next—still unknown, yet undoubtedly coming—car trouble.

Beyond the improvements to my housing and diet, I also gained a family in Sam, Everleigh, Griffin, and Hunter. That was the most profound change: friendship, family...a connection. They were only on loan. I couldn't keep them—I loved them too much to be *that* selfish—but I treasured every day with them and soaked up their friendship and support like a flower in drought, thirsting for water. Knowing how dismal my life could be, I cherished this gift. It was my season of love and security, but like all seasons, it wouldn't last forever. Winter would return and I would be alone once again.

As I said, had I known being shot would be the impetus to completely transforming my wretched life, I would have painted a giant bull's-eye on my tummy and stood downrange as a volunteer target.

With a smile on my face at the thoughts of my change in fortune, I dragged my suitcase to the laundry room to start my first post-vacation load. After a quick shower to wash away the travel grime, I threw on a pair of black leggings, a moss green tank, and a comfy pair of black Muk Luk slipper-boots. Glancing down at my uber-comfortable attire, I couldn't help but chuckle—this would drive Sam nuts! Ev used to share stories of Sam's intense need to ensure that none of her posse were seen out-and-about in loungewear (the bane of Sam's existence). I thought Ev was exaggerating for maximum impact. Boy, was I wrong.

After seven months of living with Sam, my comfy clothes, which constituted the majority of my wardrobe since they were cheap and—as the name implies—comfy, still regularly disappeared. When asked, Sam always told me that the missing items must have been lost in the move, regardless of the fact that said items were purchased after the move to replace items that had also mysteriously 'disappeared.' It turns out she was every bit the appearance-Nazi Ev accused her of being. I couldn't help but find it hysterical. It may have been less humorous if she hadn't replaced the absconded articles with Sam-approved alternatives, thus preventing me from blowing my meager weekly budget on replenishing the 'missing' cheap clothes with even cheaper alternatives.

My stomach growled as I headed to the kitchen, reinforcing my intent on foraging to find dinner in our bare post-vacation pantry. Luck was on my side when I located a portion of vegetable lasagna in the freezer, which I'd made for GriffLo and myself a few nights before our trip. With Griffin's frequent visits, food rarely survived more than a day. That man could *eat!* Then again, he was the size of a Hummer so it was to be expected.

After a brief defrost in the microwave, I popped my soon-to-be dinner in the toaster oven to finish cooking.

I ran upstairs to snag one of Sam's naughty books to pass the time until dinner was sufficiently warm when I heard the unmistakable sound of grinding metal and an air-break release. Ever the curious kitten, I peeked out the front window to assess the situation. A huge moving van was parked in front of our neighbor's driveway, partially obstructing ours. Oh well, I didn't have anywhere to be, so why complain?

Chapter 3

"Love thy neighbor—and if he happens to be tall, debonair and devastating, it will be that much easier." -Mae West

<u>Meg</u>

I was nearly done with dinner and thoroughly engrossed in my borrowed romance novel—a surprisingly emotional story given the fact that the alpha-male hero spoke in fragments often beginning with 'babe' and ending with 'yeah?'—when the doorbell sounded, startling me. I wasn't expecting anyone. Hunter and Everleigh were still on their honeymoon. Griffin and Sam both had keys. No one should be at the door at seven o'clock.

I fought to calm myself as I quietly crept to the front window. At dusk, it was difficult to see any details about the unexpected visitor, other than it was a man in jeans, a dark, fitted t-shirt, and a baseball cap.

As I debated my best course of action—run, hide, or answer—the doorbell sounded again, and again...and again. Then came the knocking, or more accurately, banging. Well, *that* was rude. Who bangs on a door like they're carrying a portable battering ram unless there's a fire? Or an emergency...what if he was hurt or in trouble? I couldn't ignore him now that the seed had been planted. He could be in desperate need of help.

I scurried to the door, the incessant hammering ramping up my concern with each step. After disarming the alarm, I hastily swung the door open as my concerns tumbled from my lips, "Are you okay? What's wrong? Should I call an ambulance?"

When he didn't reply immediately, I took quick inventory of his body. His face was shadowed by the brim of his hat and the porch light was of little assistance in my assessment, but there were no obvious injuries to be found. His extended silence unnerved me and unease quickly overcame my concern.

Before seeking approval of my brain, more questions poured out, "You aren't a serial killer, are you? I mean, serial killers don't knock and call attention to themselves before committing a crime. No...serial killers are all about the stealth." I nodded to myself, confident in my conclusion. "Okay, you're not a serial killer. So stay right there, sit if you need to. I'll grab my phone and call an ambulance. Don't worry, you are going to be okay. I'm going to help you. Just stay calm," I continued to ramble as my fear waned and my concern for his well-being returned in full force.

A hand grabbed my wrist, derailing my plan to call for medical assistance.

"Calm yourself, beautiful. No reason to get your panties all tangled. I just need the number for the maintenance office. I can't find it online and the movers cracked one of the sprinkler heads in my yard, causing water to pool everywhere. It's a mess," his smooth voice explained.

"Oh, of course. Sorry. The way you were banging on the door, I thought it was life or death," I gently chided, partly because his rude ringing and nonstop knocking were over the top, but also because I was embarrassed by my own worried ramblings. In the spirit of neighborliness, I continued, "However...moving *is* stressful, so I guess your frustration is understandable. Give me a minute and I'll see if we have the number."

I ran to the kitchen and grabbed the small contacts book we kept near the phone. When I approached the front door, I noticed he had taken the liberty of stepping into the foyer during my absence. It was a presumptuous act for any man to invite himself into a woman's home without her permission and it was on the tip of my tongue to tell him as much, but my reprimand was diverted by the view.

Dang! The man's behind was *fiiiine*, with a capital 'F.' I stole a moment to appreciate the fitted denim encasing said fineness. He was tallish, probably six feet two, with a swimmer's build—toned with broad shoulders and a narrow waist, well-muscled but not bulky. Even at five feet nine I could wear heels and he would be taller than me—unless, of course, they were stripper heels. Then again, why the hell would I wear stripper heels? *Hmmm...*

He turned to face me just as my musings drifted from PG-13 to R-rated, allowing the chandelier to illuminate his face. The address book slid from my fingers and fell to the floor as my brain struggled to process the information my eyes were relaying. What the—?

"You!" I accused harshly.

His condescending smirk was the only reply I received.

"What are you doing here, Black? Are you here to threaten Sam again? You better get the hell out of her house before I call Griffin to come and kick your ass."

"I see your temper hasn't improved," he muttered. "Nice to see you again, Meg. I just need the number for the maintenance office and I'll be on my way. And for the record, I never threatened Samantha, I merely...*cautioned.*"

"That's semantics and you know it!" I charged. "You tried to bribe her and then intimidate her from testifying against that piece-of-shit psycho, Heath. The only reason you backed off was because he pissed off a bunch of inmates who decided to relieve him of the burden of breathing."

"Semantics, sweetheart, are my bread and butter. And threatening a witness is a prosecutable offense, which I would never risk. Cautioning a witness of the rigors and trauma of trial is a kindness. Furthermore, what you call a bribe, I call restitution, which Mr. Varbeck would have been ordered to pay if found guilty in a civil court. I was simply trying to expedite the inevitable outcome without all the legal woes and media frenzy," he replied, unperturbed by my hostility.

"Is that the line of bullshit you feed yourself so you can sleep at night? That bullying victims until they are too afraid to seek justice is in their best interests? That money tainted with their own blood will heal the scars on their souls? Lie to yourself, if you want, but don't you *dare* lie to me. Sugarcoated intimidation is still intimidation. You victimized those poor women all over again and left them with one more regret to face in the future. But hey, you billed your hours and bought a sweet new townhouse, so the ends justify the means for you, don't they?" I was breathing heavily as I finished hurling my accusations like knives. Apparently, my aim was stellar, because I caught a glimpse of something akin to pain on his face before he masked it.

"Is it hard to breathe up there? The air must be very thin way up on that high horse," he replied coldly. "As riveting as this debate has been, I have an appointment to watch paint dry that I simply cannot miss. I assume you won't be providing me with the number?"

"Oh, I'll give you the number because—unlike you—I do the right thing, even if the jackasshat doesn't deserve it." With my last dagger thrown, I opened the book, angrily flipping pages until I found the number in question, and rattled it aloud with no small dose of resentment.

He silently headed to the door but paused to look back at me over his broad shoulder.

"Thanks for the number. I'm sure you'll sleep better knowing you did the *right thing*, despite my inferior character. I'm sure that small concession you condescended to make completely offsets the fact that you're a hypocrite. I may be an asshole, but at least I own up to it. You're a judgmental bitch who masquerades as a compassionate do-gooder." Then he left, having thrown a dagger of his own.

I reengaged the alarm after closing the door and stomped to the kitchen.

How dare he? That pompous, slimy, immoral jerkface had the balls to call *me* a hypocrite? Who was I kidding—his balls were big enough even if he'd been skinny-dipping at the North Pole in sub-zero temperatures. Not that I knew from personal experience, but to stand there and call me a judgmental bitch after what he'd put Sam through…those had to be some huge elephant balls.

Westly Black—asshole extraordinaire—the defense attorney who represented the family of Heath Varbeck, the man who raped and beat Sam until she was on the brink of death. How could a person represent the devil's kin and still look at himself in the mirror every day? How could he go to the homes of all the victims—those who survived anyway—and persuade them not to testify in exchange for huge settlements? It was unconscionable.

And yes, some of my anger may also stem from his manipulation of me personally. He invited me to dinner during the ordeal, happily taking advantage of my ignorance, as I had no idea who he was or what he was doing to Sam. I may still be pissed that it was the best date of my life—not that the bar was set very high given my extremely limited dating experience. There may also be residual anger because he gave me the best kiss I ever had, again with very limited comparison. And I may have intended to sleep with him on our next date in my quest to find the fabled orgasm that Sam and Ev assured me did occur in real life. However, after committing myself to riding the Black train to Orgasmville and fantasizing about what his magical mouth could do to the rest of me, I was blindsided to learn he was the scumbag lawyer harassing Sam. So there was definitely history that contributed to my need to remind him that he was a slimy bottom-feeder.

It was this wealth of evidence that I'd assessed before rendering a judgment about his actions. I may have been a bitch in how I delivered my verdict, but I was justified in the defense of my friend and myself. What bothered me most about his barb was that 'judgmental' and 'bitch' were two adjectives no one would ever use to describe me. I strived to be objective and understanding—that was a freaking requirement for my professional aspirations as a sociologist. I also tried to be kind and bring joy to everyone I meet. It was only this specific instance that induced my judgmental bitchiness, and I felt that my uncharacteristic show of temper was completely understandable given the circumstances. Not to mention, I did give the man the number he needed!

After cleaning my dishes, I headed to bed, exhausted from the days of travel and the evening's dramatic exchange. Mr. Sandman, unfortunately, proved elusive. As my mind wandered, his voice emerged with one word repeating—*hypocrite*. Wes' knife had found flesh, because despite my harsh yet accurate summary of his offenses, and regardless of how dirty and vile he may be, I knew—deep down—I was just as vile and offensive as he was...I just hid it better.

Chapter 4

"The meeting of two personalities is like the contact of two chemical substances: if there is any reaction, both are transformed."
-Carl Jung

<u>Westly</u>

Son of a bitch!

I marched back to my house, dodging furniture and movers along the way, not stopping until I reached my home office, where my cell phone and solitude were located.

Son. Of. A. Bitch!

I swore if I ever saw her again I would either: a) pretend I didn't know her, or b) coax her into my bed. Nothing in either plan dictated cursing at her; it was an inexcusable fumble. Dammit! The only good news was that my father wasn't alive to hear me confess my crimes. He would have ripped me a new one for talking to a lady that way, even if the description had been accurate—which unfortunately, it was *not*. Therefore, I couldn't even comfort myself with the knowledge that I'd simply verbalized the truth because Meg was a lot of things, but she was definitely *not* a bitch.

Meg...when she opened the door, it knocked the wind out of me. I'd convinced myself—after she'd unceremoniously kicked me to the curb in the middle of the coffee shop—that my memories were idealized after nine months fantasizing about her. Nope. She was even more stunning than I remembered, and every part of me responded to the sight of her. My brain stalled, deprived of oxygen, as all of the blood in my body detoured southward. While some parts appeared to be stupefied into complete stillness—for example, my mouth, which was apparently unable to form words—another part of me was rising to the occasion and begging for attention. Yes, Little West was pointing due north.

Everything about Meg was complex and captivating. No one could deny her astonishing beauty, one that was wholly her own with no references to famous faces, past or present. Her face held hints of exotic distant locales, tempered by a sweetness that reflected the warmth she exuded. Her bone structure, covered in smooth olive skin, was a sculptor's dream. Her almond-shaped eyes of various shades of green—not unlike the empress marble I'd just installed in my master bath—with a ring of copper around her pupils were captivating. They were expressive and perceptive, but in their depths I could see vague shadows of pain. Pink lips with a slight pout that belied the radiant smile they produced had kept me mesmerized throughout our one-and-only dinner. Her thick, shiny brown hair had been damp when she opened the door, as if she had just showered (that particular observation likely conjuring the graphic images now tormenting my sanity). It was the type of hair a man could grab hold of without causing damage or pain. Her body though...Victoria's Secret models would kill for her body, and I'd known men who would sell their souls to spend a night exploring every God-given curve. She was the perfect balance of fit and curvy, tall but lithe, soft and firm.

She'd captured my attention the first time I saw her, so distracting that I'd nearly forgotten the purpose of my visit. All I'd wanted was to march over and follow her around like an eager puppy. When I finished my conversation with

Samantha that day, I had to haul my ass out of the coffee shop to prevent myself from looking like a fool.

When I'd returned days later, I was better prepared for her impact, ever ready to make my move. I was charmed by her guileless, tongue-tied ramblings. How a woman could be drop-dead sexy and completely adorable at the same time was beyond comprehension. Those two qualities should be mutually exclusive. I was so perplexed by the intoxicating combination, I again missed my opportunity. Never one to give up, I returned two more times until she felt more at ease with me and then I went in for the kill. *Success.*

On our sole date, it became clear that her intellect and passion matched—if not exceeded—her outer beauty. Our conversation remained mostly surface, but I learned she was a twenty-five-year-old graduate student, studying at Hensley University to attain her doctorate in sociology, she lived alone at the time, had no family to speak of, and was only interested in a casual relationship. I nearly indulged in a touchdown dance with the last proclamation.

Following dinner, I also learned that she was a fantastic dancer, while at the end of the night, I discovered her kisses were more effective than any narcotic known to man. I knew it in my gut that if I had pushed, she would have been tangled in my sheets that first night...her eyes were screaming, '*take me.*' I don't know why I didn't accept their invitation, but I'd convinced myself we needed one more date to build anticipation.

Unfortunately, that was our first and last date. Three days later it all imploded when I walked into the café to talk to Samantha and Meg greeted me. Sam was furious at my '*conniving*' and Meg was livid at my '*manipulation,*' promptly canceling our date after declaring me an asshole. Let me state for the record, I had no clue Meg was unaware of my interactions with Sam. In our brief, pre-date conversations, she'd indicated that she knew I was a lawyer. She'd been working at least two of the days when I'd gone to talk to Sam. It wasn't until "dump day" (as I liked to call it) that I came to realize Meg thought I was the assistant

District Attorney for Sam's case. Wasn't that a kick in the head? Five years earlier and it might have been true.

Her rejection burned, especially since she never gave me a chance to offer any explanation. There was no hesitation or consideration—I was dismissed instantaneously for conduct unbecoming.

It should have rolled right off my back. I wasn't invested. There were plenty of beautiful women begging to spend a night in my bed. I'm not cocky, it's simply fact. I'm good-looking, wealthy, and one helluva fuck. There's never been a shortage of hot, willing bodies. Why did I care that *this* girl discarded me so easily?

I had zero interest in any relationship that even verged on committed. It's just not my scene. I wasn't dysfunctional; I tried the relationship route after college, but it wasn't for me. Why stick to one flavor when there were countless options available? Some people needed the co-dependency a relationship provided because they weren't strong enough to stand on their own. They needed a partner beside them to hold their hand or pick up their shit—literally and metaphorically. That's not me. I brought home more than enough to pay someone to pick up my literal crap and had enough of my own metaphorical shit to pick up, thank you very much. I didn't need anyone to hold my hand because—bottom line—I'm not a weak-ass pussy. I had neither the time nor the interest in dealing with someone else's shit. I did it for my Pops when he needed me and because I loved him, but I've taken that trip already and have the frequent flier miles to prove it—no need for a return leg. The only trips I took these days were hassle-free, expectation-free, commitment-free good times that ended with a smile on everyone's faces.

What I couldn't wrap my brain around was why I couldn't shake off the regret of missing *dessert* after my dinner with Meg. Why did my mind still conjure images of her late at night? Why did the mere thought of her make my dick rock hard at the most inopportune times? Okay, the answer to that one was obvious—the girl's body was made for sin, and I was nothing if not a sinner. It must have been the missed opportunity, the rejection, and...and...pheromones! Studies were always talking about how pheromones screwed with the brain, reducing impulse control and overriding established behavior patterns. I blamed the pheromones—pesky little fuckers.

Yet by some miracle, I managed to buy the townhouse adjacent to hers, and thanks to a broken sprinkler head, I finally received my chance at redemption. Did I take advantage of this golden opportunity? No! I screwed the pooch royally, which was completely unlike me. I blew it...not once but twice.

I could have recovered from the first screw-up—I'm a persuasive bastard—but there's no way to recover after my last hatchet job. What the hell happened? I was always cool—the freaking definition of cold calculation—and never ruffled, but something about her set me off-kilter.

As a defense attorney, I made the majority of my obscenely large paycheck from defending parties that were more than likely guilty (not that I ask). But in this case, she was wrong. The Varbecks were not bad people. They were parents desperate to get their son help, and if he was beyond help, contain him permanently for the safety of the public. Their son was Satan—pure evil, no doubt. There was no fixing him, and deep down they knew it and never would have let him loose on the streets. However, they were still parents with two other children who they were frantically trying to protect from the media circus and stigma the trial would bring.

The original plan I proposed was solid: convince the victims that an invasive public trial would reopen fresh wounds and offer them extremely generous restitution for their suffering. Once the victims were no longer willing to testify, strike a plea deal with the district attorney that ensured Heath would spend the rest of his life in a maximum-security mental institution. Do it all under the radar and contain the goddamn media.

The public would be safe, my clients would gain a small measure of peace, and Heath's siblings' lives would not be marred beyond repair by the trial of their depraved brother. Most importantly, the victims would obtain the reassurance that their attacker would never be free *and* enough money to rebuild their lives, pay medical bills, cover future counseling, buy a house...whatever they needed. My plan was an effective and efficient solution to an unparalleled mess of pain and suffering, and best met the needs of everyone involved.

When Heath was killed in prison (thank God for small miracles), I reworked the plan accordingly and persuaded the Varbecks to offer seven-figure restitution to each of the victims, which also helped assuage the family's misplaced guilt. It was brilliant—I was brilliant. I orchestrated the best outcome possible for everyone, in circumstances where no one could ever be deemed a winner.

It was one of the few accomplishments I could honestly be proud of.

When Meg attacked, using her beautiful mouth to throw spiteful words that cut deeper than she will ever know, I lost my composure. Her accusations, in any other case, might have been warranted, but this time I did well and—for once—my conscious was clear. I was actually able to sleep at night without guilt plaguing me. It was such a novel feeling that when she tried to take it away, my composure faltered. I lost my cool, and along with it, my second chance at getting between those long, inviting legs.

Damn pride.

Damn temper.

I was almost positive those assholes cost me the single most memorable night of my life.

Chapter 5

*"Sex without love is a meaningless
experience, but as far as meaningless
experiences go it's pretty damn good."*
-Woody Allen

<u>Meg</u>

Desperate for my morning hit after a restless night's sleep, I stumbled to the kitchen, opened the cabinet that housed the mugs and coffee, and stretched on my tiptoes to reach my stash on the top shelf. I broke off a square of my treasured Lindt Dark Chocolate with Sea Salt and popped it into my mouth with a sigh of pleasure—*ah, that's what I'm talking about.* Everyone I knew required a cup of coffee in the morning to get moving and start their day. Not me....I needed a chocolate fix. After a moment of debate, I broke off a second square—it had been that kind of night.

I may have slept, but I didn't rest. My dreams were plagued by warm caramel eyes that promised endless hours of yet unknown satisfaction. *Damn the man.* He was indisputably the most beautiful creature I had ever seen...devastating, that was the word for him. If the whole sleazebag-lawyer thing didn't work out, there's no doubt Calvin Klein or Armani would be knocking down his door. His defined bone structure with high cheekbones, prominent jaw, and strong brow were *every* woman's fantasy. And his lips...I wanted to bite those full, luscious lips. Add the chocolate brown hair that begged to be pulled while locked in an undulating embrace...irresistible!

What was wrong with me?   I knew he was a conscienceless miscreant. Shouldn't that knowledge work as a sedative to my recently awakened—and usually dormant—sex drive?   But no, my otherwise mute inner hussy jumped up and down, shouting like a drunken sorority girl after losing her third game of flip-cups, every time he entered a room.

It had taken months after I'd learned who he was and what he had done to force him from my mind. I lied to my friends, pretending to dismiss him without a second thought, but I couldn't lie to myself—I still craved him in an unfamiliar and overwhelming fashion.

And now he was going to live next door.

We didn't even have a few feet of lawn separating us...no, he was a narrow flower bed away. I could only wonder what I had done to piss off the bitch known as karma to justify this turn of events.

That's a lie.

I knew what I had done, and I deserved every torturous moment.

Lying alone in my bed last night, I could practically feel his presence seeping through the sheetrock, tormenting me. As my hand slid down my stomach in response, I chided myself before firmly tucking both hands beneath my pillow to ward off any temptation. Subsequently, I spent the next hour debating the merits of moving out before vowing not to let him run me off.

He. Would. Not. Win.

Yep, a double dose of chocolate was necessary this morning.

Seeing the time, I hustled up to my room and threw on pair of skinny jeans, a cream-colored peasant shirt, and tan knee-high riding boots (my Christmas gift from Sam last year). I slid my arms into a cropped leather bomber jacket (another garage-sale bargain), picked up my messenger bag, and headed for the door.

Thankfully, my car—Old Bessie, as Ev called her—started without drama. It was a short drive to Hensley University, where I'd spent two years of undergrad to earn my bachelor's before completing my first year in the Ph.D.

program. Now, halfway through my third semester of grad school, I officially had a master's degree in sociology and approval for my proposed dissertation. With two to three years of studies remaining to complete the requirements for my Ph.D., Hensley would continue to be my scholastic home for quite some time—I hoped.

After three back-to-back classes and countless hours of reading ahead of me, I headed home to crack open some books. Popping another square of chocolatey goodness to fuel my studies, I trudged to my room. Settling on my bed with textbooks and journals surrounding me, I flipped open my Walmart clearance-sale laptop and waited for the sucker to boot up. Eons later, I was finally able to access the desktop and launch my student email to confirm the reading assignments. On a whim, I decided to peek at my personal email account, which I rarely bothered to check as only a handful of people had the address. I sucked a tense breath through my gritted teeth when I saw that there was a message from Jay. Regardless of how much he had done for me, he was still a reminder of the past I struggled to forget. It wasn't his fault, and he'd been incredibly good to me when I needed him, but still...

I steeled myself to face the specters of my past and opened the email.

Hey Hun,

It's been a while since you checked in.
How are you? Keeping out of trouble?
Remember your promise not to jump into any
fires unless I'm there to pull you out!
Things are good here in NC. Same old, same
old for the most part. I met someone.
She's a sweet thing with a body that brings

me to tears. She said she loved me, but
she may just love my *skills* ;-)
Let me know if you're ok. I worry (I know
you just rolled your eyes at me).

Miss you,
Jay

Despite my initial trepidation, I was smiling as I closed the email. The past that Jay represented burned less than it once had. Seven years after leaving him behind in North Carolina, time was finally healing old wounds.

I spent the next two hours reading about the theory and practices for compiling empirical data. *Yawn!* Thankfully, I was saved from bored oblivion by GriffLo's arrival.

"Megalicious, get your butt down here and have some dinner with us," Sam called from downstairs.

After unburying myself from a mountain of books, I headed to the kitchen. Griffin was unloading an insane amount of Chinese food on the table while Sam brought over the drinks.

"I see you guys decided to order one of everything on the menu," I laughed, only partially kidding.

"He's a growing boy," Sam teased, patting Griffin's stomach. "Plus, he needs to build up his energy...I have *big* plans for him," she finished with a salacious grin directed at her man.

Griffin swatted her tush playfully in response. "Your plans for me involve rearranging all the furniture in your bedroom, and not in the way I'd prefer. Food may be the deposit, but that smile better be hinting at settling the remaining balance in more enjoyable ways."

"We'll see how much you complain about the rearranging, then I'll make my decision on any *tips*," Sam said.

"Lo, please...you can't resist me," he said with utter confidence. "But don't worry, I can't resist you either— never could."

I loved seeing them like this. Sam had overcome more obstacles than any single person should ever have to face.

Life may have broken her, but she'd pulled herself back together— with the help of Griffin—and was stronger now than ever before. She was the person I wished I could be: pure and brave, she was goodness personified. I may be three years older than Sam, but I looked up to her, despite the fact that she regularly embarrassed me with her lack of filter and inappropriate over-shares. Sam was Sam, and in her own way she was looking out for me. She'd found her happily ever after, and now she was on a mission to find mine...even if she had to cram it down my throat. I loved her for caring though.

Griffin captured my attention with a nudge and stage whispered, "How much you want to bet that after rearranging the furniture three times, she'll decide to put the pieces back in their original spots?"

"I'll bet you five dollars you can distract her and never wind up lifting a bulging bicep," I countered at full volume.

Sam's eyes narrowed at Griffin.

"Dammit, Meg. Stop foiling my evil schemes. Now she's onto me."

As we passed around the food containers, I was careful to avoid the favorite dishes, only scooping a small helping of each of the 'less-favorites.' Seeing that the restaurant had provided ample white rice, I loaded my plate with the complimentary item.

I was about to dig in when I felt two pairs of eyes boring into me. I heard Griffin's displeased grunt and looked up in time to catch Sam's chin jerk. Before I knew it, Griffin had nabbed my plate and spooned heaping mounds of sesame chicken (my favorite—and Sam's) and orange beef (my other favorite—and Griffin's) without saying a word. Sam plucked a cheese wanton (my absolute favorite) from the bag next to her and dropped it on top before pushing my overflowing dish in front of me.

"Guys, I don't need—" I began but Griffin cut me off.

"Eat."

"You know, if you were getting some, you would have less energy to focus on being a martyr. I guess I'll have to redouble my efforts and find you something to sink your teeth into—or someone," Sam teased...or was that a threat?

I rolled my eyes and popped a bite of sesame chicken into my mouth. *Yum!* Speaking of yummy, an unbidden image of a certain modelesque lawyer reared its ugly head. I glanced at the wall of the great room.

"What's up?" Sam asked.

There was no way to hide the identity of our new neighbor. It was only a matter of time before they ran into each other and Sam needed to be prepared. I just hated to be the one to deliver the news, especially since I fully expected Griffin to launch into alpha-protectinator mode. Aw hell, it needed to be done. I cleared my throat.

"We have a new neighbor," I announced, and they both looked at me expectantly. "He came over to get the number for the maintenance office last night. I didn't realize who it was at first...and then I recognized him."

Sam waved her hand, urging me to finish.

"It was that lawyer...Westly Black," I finished quietly.

I waited, but there was nothing. Crickets might as well have been chirping in the kitchen. *Hmm, not quite the reaction I was expecting.* I had braced myself for fireworks at my announcement. When I looked at Griffin, he was looking at Sam. When I looked at Sam, she appeared to still be processing the information. Finally, she raised one shoulder in a dismissive shrug.

"Oh well, not much we can do about it."

Griffin and I exchanged skeptical looks.

"Really?" I asked in disbelief. "Geeze, even I was shell-shocked when I realized who was at the door."

"That is because he makes your mouth water—along with other parts of your anatomy. You may hate him, but you still want him. I'm not stupid and you don't hide your feelings nearly as well as you think. I knew you were still pining for him months later," Sam replied.

"But he's a lying bottom-feeder! I *can't* want him," I argued.

"Yes and no. I've had nine months to process everything that happened, and I'm not sure he was trying to con you. He looked genuinely shocked and upset when you gave him the epic smack-down. It's possible he thought you knew who he was. Despite his tactics— which were shady, I'll give you that—he never actually *did* anything wrong. We made some assumptions because of the threats I was receiving that proved to be inaccurate."

I was about to argue that his unethical behavior was a direct reflection on his character, but Sam raised a hand to silence me.

"I'm not saying you should marry the guy. He definitely has some dubious personality traits. But there is nothing to say you couldn't use him for a little *hmmuna, hmmuna* and then be on your merry way with no guilt, no strings, and no heartbreak. In a way, he's perfect for what you need. Your moderate disdain would allow you to let it be only about sex. Plus, you don't have to like a man to have sex with him. From the look of him, that is the *only* thing you should ever count on him for...mind-blowing, headboard banging, sweat induc—"

"Ahem," Griffin loudly cleared his throat, interrupting Sam's vivid description. "I'm still sitting here, Lo. And despite a healthy dose of self-confidence, I'd rather my woman not openly recount her fantasies about another man. Call me old-fashioned."

"Oh please, why would I want him when I have all of *that*," she said, gesturing to Griffin's mountainous physique, "at my beck and call? I know where my bread is buttered. I know who greases my wheel. I know who licks my—"

"Okay, we get it," I interrupted, saving myself from a visual I didn't need stored on the hard drive of my brain. "You are an exceptionally satisfied woman, who has no need to use her imagination when real life surpasses it. No need to elaborate further."

"Anyway...my point remains. Westly is *definitely* not relationship material, but he is the epitome of what a one-night stand should be. I actually feel bad that you didn't get to ride that wave," Sam sighed, sounding disheartened. "Then again, he's probably a pro at the love 'em and leave 'em routine. You could still take advantage of his benefits package though, and there wouldn't be any weirdness when you issued his pink slip."

"First of all, I am *not* hooking up with someone who did you wrong. Secondly, any chance he would be receptive is long gone after I verbally assaulted him last night. And finally, I can't start hooking up with him when I'm seeing Mark," I concluded decisively. Surely these observations would mark the end of the conversation.

"*Pssht.* Don't be ridiculous. Using Wes to meet your needs is the perfect payback for him trying to use me to meet his. Furthermore, no man—and you can tell me if I'm wrong, love," she added, looking to Griffin, "is going to turn down a hot piece of ass like you."

Griffin nodded his agreement. "Males are simple creatures and Black doesn't even have the emotional functionality of a preschooler. Even if you could hurt his non-existent feelings, he would still bed you."

"See?" Sam resumed excitedly. "He would definitely still do you. Hell, he'd probably give his left testicle to have a night with you—but I digress. What was your last reason? Oh yeah, Mark. Four so-so dates over the course of six months does not a commitment make. You aren't even into him. Four dates and I'll bet you haven't even considered sliding between the satin with him. He's good-looking and all, but he doesn't smolder like Westly. You are well within your rights to sample an undeniably tasty morsel. You don't owe Mark anything. Do you think he's been celibate for the last six months? No way."

"I'm not interested in Wes, and Mark is a nice guy—I couldn't do that to him. He was wonderful to you when you were preparing for trial, and he's been nothing but a gentleman when we've gone out."

"*Bah.* Gentlemen make good husbands; slick hotshots make good mattress dancers. Don't forget, Mark had his own horse in the race. He wanted me to testify so the DA's office could notch another win in their belt—it wasn't altruistic," she stated, bringing up a solid point. "Just promise me you'll think about it. If the opportunity arises, don't say 'no' right away."

"Whatever. I promise," I lied, knowing Sam wasn't going to let up until I'd complied. Despite my acquiescence, there was no way I was giving Westly a second thought. I was over him and his promise of sexual acrobatics. Really, I was. Not even tempted, not one little bit. Nope.

Okay, I still found him irrationally appealing physically—and kinda-sorta wanted him in a disconcerting way. That didn't mean a damn thing. I was a rational woman. My lady bits would not be making this decision.

Chapter 6

"A house divided against itself cannot stand."
-Abraham Lincoln

Meg

Clearly, my lady bits didn't get the memo about who was running the show, because three days later they attempted a coup d'état. Stupid lady bits!

I was pulling into the driveway after an unusually contentious meeting with my graduate advisor, Dr. Mesina, my frustration level already in the red zone, when I was confronted with the object of my unwelcome desire.

As I exited my car and headed for the front door, my nighttime obsession exited his own abode. We both froze and our eyes locked in a moment that was made for overdramatized romantic movies. Needing to break the awkward tension, I offered a jerky nod before resuming my trajectory, now better classified as my escape route. A mere five steps from the sanctuary of the front door, I was stopped by a hand on my shoulder. I shivered as goosebumps rose on my arms, decorating my flesh with evidence of his nearness. His presence was electric, short-circuiting every nerve in my overcharged body.

Uh-oh, this was *not* good. I didn't want to have this profound physical response to his nearness.

I debated ignoring him, but one clench from my disobedient southern hemisphere persuaded me to turn and greet him, if only to prove who was winning the civil war my body and mind were waging.

"Mr. Black, what can I do for you?" I inquired, emotionless but not rudely. He didn't deserve the expression of such strong emotion. Maybe if he believed his effect on me had dwindled, it would become truth. *Fingers crossed!*

"For a brief time, you called me Wes...I wish you would again," he finished, barely above a whisper, as if telling a secret he never intended to reveal.

"I thought you were a different person then. I thought I knew you. I thought we might—" I trailed off, unwilling to admit the hopes I'd held.

"I'm the exact same person, only your assumption has changed. Now, instead of the do-gooder knight in shining armor, I'm the villain...at least in your narration. But in reality, I am the exact same man you had dinner with nine months ago. The one who enjoyed every second of your company and wanted to see you again more than I've wanted anything in a very long time."

His honesty caught me off-guard, which is the only excuse I could offer for not fleeing after his declaration. Unsure of how to respond, I said nothing. He didn't seem to share my loss for words.

"Do you lie to yourself and pretend it wasn't an amazing night? Have you convinced yourself you didn't want me? Because I know the truth, Meg. I saw it in your eyes and felt it in your kiss," he whispered, leaning in close, until I could smell his cologne and feel his breath against the shell of my ear. "Do you know what your kiss told me? It said you were ready for me, desperate to have me inside you. You craved me as much as I craved you."

His closeness was intoxicating and his words wove a spell around me, causing my breathing to shallow and my thighs to tense.

Dammit! I wanted him and he knew it. No, I didn't want him. I *craved* him...like a drug my addled body believed it was dependent upon.

Steeling my spine, I raised my chin until our eyes met.

"There's no point in lying," I admitted, shrugging dismissively. "Yes, I wanted you. All of me was determined to have my wicked way with all of you. And if you must know, I fully intended to see you again to find out if you could live up to the promise," I said, waving my hand to indicate his alluring body.

"Then I found out the truth," I reminded him. "So while my body may be raring to go, my mind is firmly locked in the 'not with a ten-foot pole' position. I may lust after you, but I don't like you. I don't trust you. And worst of all, I don't respect you. That's not gonna change. So this thing," I said, gesturing between the two of us, "is not going to happen. Not now, not ever. Just give it up."

He *tsked* quietly as he tucked a section of hair behind my ear, allowing his hand to brush against the side of my face as he withdrew. It was an intimate caress, inconsistent with our conversation, like choreography being performed to the wrong track. Yet the gentle touch unbound something deep inside me—the touch more tender than I'd ever received from another person.

He fixed his eyes on mine, searching for something I couldn't identify. With a nod to himself, as if satisfied with his discovery, a Cheshire grin shaped his lips.

"This reminds me of something Abraham Lincoln once said," he said with a chuckle, clearly entertaining himself. "You want to deny me and yourself? I'll give you that play—for now. Let's find out how much persuasion it'll take for your house to fall. What's between us can't be ignored, Meg, and don't forget, persuasion is my bread and butter. Make no mistake, it *will* happen, and when it does, I will enjoy every second. And so will you...All. Night. Long."

After delivering his breath-stealing promise, he brushed his lips against my cheek in a whisper of a kiss and walked away with all the confidence in the world.

Shaken by his tenacity, it took several moments to mobilize my body and make my way inside. My mind protested every word that dripped from his delectable—*no, despicable*—mouth. Unfortunately, the dictator ruling my southern hemisphere was busy throwing in a dollar's worth of her two cents. The sensible, intellectual part of me was screaming 'run for the hills' and 'danger, Will Robinson, danger!' But her royal naughtiness was shouting 'open for business—24/7—Black Light special.'

I desperately needed a prescription-strength dose of common sense...and a cold shower. Did it work for women the way it did for men? I planned to conduct some independent research. Between Sam's encouragement to use and abuse all that Wes' body had to offer, and Wes' promises to make me forget my own name, my resolve was weakening pathetically. As was the pattern of my life, the greatest danger to me was myself. My own self-discipline and judgment couldn't be trusted, and any progress I thought I had made was nothing more than an illusion.

I stepped into the icy spray to cool what remained of my heated libido, but I suspected the realization of my ongoing weakness did far more to squelch the wildfire between my thighs than the water stinging my skin.

Some people had memories that traced back to early childhood—even as early as three—and most had significant recollection from the age of seven onward. My youngest years were deliberately unremarkable and isolated, and therefore I remembered very little of my own childhood—likely because there was little to recall. However, the first significant memory I possessed could never be forgotten, regardless of what age it had occurred.

Then there was the first time I was given a choice. The first occasion where I was acknowledged as anything more than a decoration or something that might one day be of use. Like most young, when given the opportunity to direct my future, I made a bad decision—a very, *very* bad decision. Unfortunately, unlike most children, my choice wasn't something as trivial as whether or not to steal a pack of gum from the local convenience store, or if I should lie about a broken trinket on the mantel. Nope, apparently I was the 'go big or go home' type of screw-up.

At ten years of age, I made a choice that would shape the rest of my life and define who—or more accurately, *what*—I was from that day forward. And I chose wrong. I was foolishly naïve and pliable. There was no little cricket with a top hat and umbrella to climb on my shoulder and whisper words of guidance. Left to my own devices, I was ill-equipped to comprehend the significance of the moment or the decision I was expected to make. Desperate to be acknowledged by someone—*anyone*—I chose to speak the words expected of me to please others. This was my first and biggest mistake, the beginning of my deepest regrets and shame. At ten years old, my judgment proved to be shit, and my second greatest fear was that in the fifteen years since, it had not improved...not fundamentally, and not when it mattered most.

So, regardless of what my body cried for and irrespective of my weakening resolve—or perhaps *because* of both—I was going to do the exact opposite. I would temper my will in fire and water until it was unbreakable.

I would resist Wes.

Chapter 7

"I think I could fall madly in bed with you."
-Author Unknown

Westly

I strode into my office, the only room in my new home with
any semblance of completion, and settled myself into the
oversized armchair, otherwise known as 'solution central.'
I was wrestling with a problem that—for once—wasn't the
facts of a case, the questionable innocence of my client, or
the overzealous ambitions of the prosecution. For the first
time in—well, ever—I had to strategize how to make a
woman want me. No, not *want* me—Meg already wanted
me, that I knew beyond a reasonable doubt. I needed to be
irresistible. *Undeniable.* This proved to be a more a
challenging dilemma than anticipated.

After an hour in contemplation, I was still drawing a
blank. I'd never been forced to persuade a woman to fall
into bed with me. It may be arrogant, but it was also the
truth. Women wanted me...all women. I wasn't husband
material—the very thought made my skin crawl and my
stomach churn—and women knew it, seeing as how I'd
never been particularly subtle in sharing these feelings. I
was, however, made for a night of pleasure that would

wreck a woman for her future husband. They came to me eagerly with nothing more than a look or a nod. Provided they were single, it was game on. It was one of my few—correction, *only*—examples of moral fortitude.

Bottom line: I wanted it, I got it. Simple. The requirement of exerting effort to satiate my hunger was unfamiliar, and frankly, uncomfortable. How did normal guys deal with this crap?

It was time to call in reinforcements...but who? I had no family, I worked in an environment more closely related to *Jaws* than *Finding Nemo*, and I hadn't made the effort to keep in contact with any of my buddies from college. There was only one name in my contacts list I could call a friend, and I felt like shit that the only time I bothered calling him was to ask for advice or help. I was usually too busy to meet him for drinks or return his calls when he made the invite—damn, I was the asshole everyone accused me of being! He wasn't even my ideal candidate for this particular roundtable, seeing as he was a good-looking bastard, too. He might have been my opposite in every possible way, but the ladies still fell at his feet or into his bed as easily as they did mine. But he was all I had, so it was time to suck it up and make the call.

"Hey, asshole. What, you need me to help move some furniture? Borrow my pick-up? Donate an organ?" was the greeting I received. Okay, I deserved it.

"Ry, you're a funny bastard. How the hell are you?"

"Doing good, man. How's the new place working out?" he asked, offering his forgiveness of my shortcomings as quickly as ever.

"Perfect. Thanks for the tip. I'm happy to be out of the old house...too many ghosts," I replied with uncharacteristic honesty.

"Understandable. That much history would fuck with anyone's head. I'm glad you finally decided to get off your ass and make a change. It was time."

"What are you doing tonight? Want to come over and have a beer?"

"Uh-oh, you *do* need me to help move furniture. Lucky for you, my appointment tonight canceled. Do I need to call my brothers to help us move shit?"

"Wiseass. I just want your input on a problem I'm dealing with. No heavy lifting required," I promised.

"That big, devious brain of yours needs help from this dumb tattoo artist?"

"Sell that BS to someone who doesn't know your IQ is north of 170," I replied impatiently. Ry loved to play into every stereotype people expected from a heavily tatted, muscle-bound badass. He was happy to be underestimated—in fact, he courted it. He was an artist and skin was his favorite medium, but the guy's genius wasn't limited to just one aptitude. I didn't get the appeal of hiding his intellectual capabilities, but I didn't judge him for it either.

"I'll be there in thirty. Need anything?" he asked foolishly.

"Yeah, pick up some beer on your way, will you?"

"Asshole," he muttered as he hung up.

An hour later, Ry and I sat on the couch with Sam Adams in hand.

"So, what's the big issue?" Ry asked, cutting to the chase as usual.

"Remember the girl I went out with a while back? The one who blew me off?"

"How the hell could I forget? It was the first time you've struck out since eighth grade," he said, snickering at the memory. "I told you there was no way Julie DiCorzo would say yes, but you wouldn't listen," Ry goaded.

"She would have said yes if you and your brothers weren't standing behind my back making faces like a bunch jackasses."

"Man, she was a junior in high school. You always had game, but those three years might as well have been thirty. You were dead on arrival," he laughed in my face.

"Can we get back to the problem at hand? This fantastic house you were kind enough to give me a heads-up about just happens to be located next door to Meg."

"You're kidding me! Damn, you owe me. If I need a kidney one day, it's your ass that is going under the knife, not one of my siblings, capiche?"

"Yeah, yeah, you have dibs on all my vital organs. Now can we focus? I knocked on my neighbor's door to get the maintenance number and there she was."

"And?" he prompted.

"Let's just say I left my powers of persuasion back here at the house," I admitted.

"What did you do? It can't be insurmountable, not for you."

"I completely fucked it up and insulted her." At his raised eyebrows, I sighed, reluctant to go on but knowing there was no choice at this point. "I called her a bitch and told her to get off her high horse," I confessed, continuing quickly before he could interject, "I know, I know. Not one of my finer moments. It couldn't be further from the truth, but she was pushing all my buttons and I wasn't thinking clearly."

"Wes, we've been friends for-fucking-ever, but that doesn't mean I won't knock you on your ass for talking to a lady like a whore—at least outside the bedroom anyway—*especially* if it's not warranted," Ry threatened with every intent of following through. His parents did right, raising their sons to respect women and their daughters to respect themselves. No one in his family would have tolerated my behavior toward Meg. "What the hell is the matter with you?"

"I don't know. She says things that make me feel like shit, and I react—poorly. Her accusations are completely unfounded, but she doesn't know that. Instead of proving her wrong, I keep reinforcing her negative opinions," I said, frustrated by my own stupidity. "I ran into her again tonight and I can tell she wants me, but she's standing strong. I need to breach her defenses, but I've no idea how to accomplish that particular feat. How the hell do you persuade a woman to let you in her bed?"

"Just an idea, but you might start by not cursing at her and acting like a prick."

"You think?" I said, my patience running low. "I'm being serious. I need to get her beneath me, or over me, or beside me...it doesn't matter where. I need a plan, Ry, and I've got nothing," I admitted, pride be damned.

"Why should I help you get this girl, who by your own account is hotter than anything you've ever seen, sweet, funny, smart, mysterious—shall I go on? You want her for a night. I, on the other hand, would be willing to give a woman like her anything she wants, for as long as she wants. It seems that we should be planning a strategy for me, not you. Plus, I haven't dropped the ball, so I can just head over there now, no plan required," Ry finished as he rose from the couch. I quickly grabbed his arm and hauled his ass back to the cushion.

"You may be my oldest friend, but if you take one step toward the door with the intention of going to Meg's, I'll break your fucking leg," I said, serious as a heart attack. I was mostly certain he was messing with me, but either way it wasn't funny.

"I am the last person who would ever step over that line, man, you *know* that," he said in an anguished tone he usually managed to hide. If I had a heart, it would have broken for him. Gathering himself, he continued, "But that doesn't mean I'm convinced you deserve a shot at this girl. To you, women are disposable...you use them like toilet paper."

"You are forgetting a significant point of our previous conversation. Meg doesn't want a relationship. She shares my allergy to permanence and told me so. It wasn't just the female party line—she meant it. Why the hell do you think I said she was perfect for me?"

"Alright, I'm sold," Ry conceded, "but you have your work cut out for you. I think you should start by not being an asshole."

"That's really helpful," I said, heavy with sarcasm. "How about something a little more constructive, Captain Obvious?"

"Okay...show her you're not the asshole you pretend to be," he countered.

"I don't pretend to be anything. I *am* an asshole."

"You *can* be one, for sure," he chuckled before turning serious. "You insulate yourself to prevent personal attachments, but you're not nearly the prick you pretend to be. You forget, I know you better than anyone. You gave up more than most would ever consider to take care of your dad when he was sick, and you had my back when I needed you most. Hell, you sacrificed a piece of your soul to take care of that joke of a mother—"

"Of course I took care of Pop," I interrupted, "he needed me and there was no one else to step in. I was his son." I hated stating the obvious, but what type of degenerate could abandon their family in a time of need? Oh, that's right...my mother. On that note, "And we're not talking about my mother," I shook my head, "so just drop it."

Why creative types like Ry insisted on examining and expressing their feelings was beyond me, but to each his own. What pissed me off was the assumption that the rest of us should be forced to endure the same introspection.

"Fine, but to weasel your way into Meg's pants, you'll have to show her a bit of the man behind the curtain. From your description, she'll see right through you if you fake it. Just be you. You're an arrogant bastard, but that is only one side of you. Let her see the other side too."

"That's your genius plan?" I asked, disgruntled by the logical simplicity. He made it sound so easy.

"It's a start. Work your mojo, make sure to run into her frequently—wear her down."

"Wear her down...*that* I can do."

Four days after plotting with Ry, I was seriously questioning the wisdom of enlisting his help. I'd spent far more time than I cared to admit sitting at my front window, trying to catch Meg coming or going without success. It was like she knew I was lying in wait. If this was a war, she was clearly winning with her preemptive maneuvers. I was turning into a pathetic lapdog, waiting for his master to return and throw morsels of attention his way.

After painfully long days at Cauldwell, Rueger & Stein— a viper's nest regarded as New York's premier law firm—I spent my nights reevaluating the plan to win Meg. With most women lavish gifts would smooth the way, but my instinct screamed that attempting to buy her attentions would be a third strike—and this time I'd be out.

Inspiration never struck, which left me with Ry's harebrained 'be yourself' strategy—an approach that seemed destined to fail. In regards to purely sexual encounters, women wanted seduction, mystery, and conquest. They were looking to live out the fantasies they indulged in at night alone in bed. What they didn't want was substance which worked for me. I offered an evening of shared pleasure, and that was where it began and ended to the satisfaction of all involved.

Including 'real' in my plan to seduce Meg changed the parameters and established a connection I consciously avoided. I didn't want to confuse our intentions by replacing the fantasy with real. It could get messy, and that was the *last* thing I wanted to invite into my life.

But to have Meg, I was willing to rewrite the script—just a little.

Chapter 8

*"I believe that everything happens for a
reason. People change so that you can
learn to let go, things go wrong so that
you appreciate them when they're right,
you believe lies so you eventually learn to
trust no one but yourself, and sometimes
good things fall apart so better things
can fall together." -Marilyn Monroe*

Meg

I sat on my bed with the door closed and locked, every light
in the house blazing, while I stared at my computer screen.
It was the precise position in which I'd spent the better part
of the last forty-eight hours, going so far as to email a
professor, claiming to be sick. The only time I'd ventured
out was for work, only because I didn't dare call-out while
Ev was on her honeymoon. However, I spent most of the
shift ducking behind the display cases unless it was
absolutely necessary to come out of hiding.

The unread message in my student email account
continued to taunt me, daring me to open Pandora's box
with one click. My hope that—against all odds—the

electronic tormenter would suddenly disappear like a figment of my overactive imagination proved fruitless.

I startled as the heat switched on to warm against the cool fall night. After a quick scan of the room for the umpteenth time to ensure I was alone and secure, I paused to study the blinds, debating if I should adjust them—yet again—in case an outsider could glimpse through the sliver of exposed window.

A deep breath and ten count served to galvanize me to finally muster the courage to open the email.

My heart pounded in an unnatural rhythm that was disconcerting, to say the least. Could fear cause permanent arrhythmia? If so, it was time to visit a cardiologist.

Desperation triumphed as I contorted my hand to reach into the very back of the nightstand drawer, pulling out the disposable cell phone I'd kept for the last seven years in case this day ever came.

With a shaking hand, I dialed the only number stored in the contact list.

"No," Jay's voice declared in greeting, "please tell me you missed me so much you had to hear my voice after seven years of emails. Tell me, babe."

I shook my head in answer before remembering he couldn't see me.

"They found me. Oh god, Jay. How did they find me after all this time? What am I going to do? I've been so careful, and it's been so damn long. I actually started to believe they'd forgotten me. Stupid...so freaking stupid—"

"Shh...relax, sweets. It's going to be okay. I'll help you, you know that. Tell me what happened and we can figure this out together," Jay soothed.

"I logged into my email—"

"Which email? The personal one we use?" he interrupted to clarify.

"No, my student account. It completely blindsided me. I was expecting a message from my advisor, but instead...well, you know."

"What does it say?"

"Not much," I hesitated to finish, not wanting to concern him any more than necessary.

"What does it say, babe?" he repeated, unwilling to let it go.

"Obedience," I shared.

His sharp inhale echoed over the phone line. *Yep, that said it all.*

"I need to leave, as soon as I meet with my advisor and defer my enrollment. Then I have to figure out what to tell Sam and Griffin. I wish Ev and Hunter were back from their honeymoon—I hate to leave without saying goodbye to them. But maybe it's for the best..."

"Hold up. Let's take a minute to think this through before you go running off into the night—again. The email was sent to your student account, which means they know you are associated with a specific university, not where you are precisely."

"True, but how long before they send someone here? One tail from school and they'll know where I live and work," I argued.

"Yes, but that buys you some time, provided you're careful. You don't need to make any rash decisions. The email was an order to return, which means they'll hold off to see if you obey. If you don't, *then* they will come. In fact, I'll bet Malachi already has it planned out...if you don't come willingly, he will announce your impending return on January 3rd, and they will be on your doorstep within a few days. I'd stake my life on it."

"Jay, you are so damn smart. That's exactly the type of thing he would do! " I felt my heart slow as the truth settled in, calming me. "That gives me more than two months to get my life in order. I can even finish this semester and apply for a leave of absence from the Ph.D. program."

"What can I do to help? Do you need me to come to you?" A dry laugh immediately followed the question. "I guess you'd have to tell me where you are for that to happen. Given they've found you, I think it's safe for me to know."

"Yeah, you're right. They have no reason to track you down now that they've found me. It's possible they don't even know you helped me when I first left. I'm in New York at Hensley University, but you can't come see me. I'm not going to put you in danger, regardless of how low the risk might be. As long as they don't know we've been in contact, they have no reason to go after you."

"Hmm," he grumbled, not appreciating my protectiveness. *Men!* "Fine, but if you need me, I'm there. Don't be a martyr."

"I promise. Now enough of this depressing crap, tell me how things are going with your new girl!"

Twenty minutes later and sufficiently distracted by Jay's love life, we said our goodbyes. Jay had been a true friend to me, risking everything to save me when I had nowhere else to turn. He gave me a chance at a new life without conditions or thought of himself. At the time, he harbored hope that something would develop between us, but even after I pointed out the many reasons it was impossible, he continued to support me. I liked to think of him as my guardian angel.

I was glad he'd found someone and was happy. We had shared one night together before I left him in North Carolina, and it was clear to me that we would never be more than friends. He was selfless and caring—good-looking, too—but there was no electricity between us...at least none *I* felt. Thankfully, circumstances and concern for his safety had provided a legitimate excuse to watch him sadly wave goodbye in the review mirror of the old beater car he gave me—the one I still drive today.

Without question, Jay was one of the best men I'd ever met—perhaps the only good man until Hunter and Griffin strong-armed their way into my life. One day I'd find a way to repay them all for their kindness, even if I wasn't here to do so in person.

The thought of leaving everyone, the closest I'd ever come to having a true family, hit me like a sledgehammer and all at once, I was on the verge of uncharacteristic tears. Gahhh! How could I ditch my friends, knowing I wouldn't be able to keep in touch? After all they'd done for me...all they'd meant to me. My heart was breaking and there was no way to console myself.

"Hey, Megalicious!" Sam's voice rang out as she attempted to enter my room, only to find the door locked.

I hastily wiped the moisture from my eyes as I scurried to open the door.

"What's up with the door?" she asked as she studied me. "Have you been crying?"

"Oh, nothing. I caught one of those ghost hunter shows on TV and it spooked me so I locked the door. Then I tried to distract myself with a book, but it ended up being one of those gut-wrenching reads that takes your heart and shoves it in a meat grinder—a crank-handle one like they have in old-school butcher shops—hence, the ophthalmic precipitation."

Sam looked at me as if I'd grown a second head and third eye. I didn't blame her. Lying was most definitely *not* my forte, ironic given it had been my way of life for the past seven years.

"Okaaaay," she said suspiciously. "Maybe you should lay off the tear-jerkers and borrow some of my literary lady porn. I just finished this book about a group of investigators and the main guy was rockin' meat metal. One word, my friend—trifecta! I've spent the last three days promising Griffin all sorts of debauchery if he gets one...well, three."

"Enough! I don't even know what a trifecta is, and now I won't be able to look Griffin in the eye for the next week," I pleaded.

"Fine, but let me just say, I think I'm wearing him down. His mouth says 'no,' but after the promises I made last night, his eyes were singing a different tune," she finished, rubbing her hands together like a vaudeville villain.

"TMI, Sam. There are some things I can't unhear, so quit painting traumatic visuals that will forever haunt me."

"Whatever. If you followed my advice and saved a horse, you would be excited, not traumatized."

"Save a horse?" I questioned, utterly confused.

"Save a horse...ride a cowboy. Geeze, have I taught you nothing?"

"I love you, lady, but you may be a few straws short of a full bale," I teased.

"Huh? What the heck are you talking about?" Sam asked, perplexed.

"It's not funny if I have to explain it. I was following your cowboy-farm theme," I explained. A blank stare greeted me. "Forget it," I said, the moment lost.

"You're being weird—lucky for you, I have the cure for what ails you...girls' night!" Sam said enthusiastically. "Griffin's at The Stop tonight, so shall we drink for free or stay in for facials?"

Any other time I would have voted for girls' night in, but the clock was ticking and in a couple of months, all I would have left were the memories I made now. Plus, we would be safer at The Stop than anywhere else in the state should Jay's prediction prove overly optimistic. Griffin was a behemoth, and God save anyone who dared to threaten Sam. She was a survivor and had already overcome more than even the most overdramatized Lifetime Movie heroine. It was Griffin's lifelong mission to ensure nothing even remotely unpleasant ever touched her again.

Their love was epic, and I envied them without jealousy. Alone in the dark, I sometimes wondered if being witness to the depth of love Huntleigh and GriffLo shared was my penance for the choices I've made. Observing loves so pure and connections so deep, knowing I could never have the same but with only myself to blame, was a cruel punishment. Yep, the universe was meting out some wicked poetic justice. It was almost laughable...most people settled for quasi-happiness because they desired a family and companionship, never fully believing in the existence of the type of love and passion I was surrounded by daily. I had to wonder if those same people would have waited to find their other halves had they known such love existed—or would their impatience and doubt have gotten the better of them?

"Earth to Meg? Come back to us...tell the extraterrestrials to stop their kinky experiments. Unless, of course, you're enjoying all that probing, then feel free to finish up first," Sam interrupted my musings, finishing with a sassy wink.

"Sorry, I got lost in my head for a second. And, ewww, alien sex. That's just nasty," I teased, shaking my head in disapproval but secretly enjoying every second of the vivacious craziness that was Sam. "Let's go to The Stop. I haven't seen Griffin the last few days and it's Thursday, which means live music."

I adored music. It was one of the subjects that Griffin and I bonded about when we first met. Having spent so many years unable to express my own feelings—and barely understanding them anyway—the emotion that music and lyrics evoked was addictive and captivating. The right song at the right time could communicate the multitude of turbulent and complex emotions swirling inside me far better than I ever could. Music was like therapy to me, and searching and finding the perfect song was a ritual that allowed me to process and compartmentalize my frequently riotous thoughts. It was evocative, penetrating, and restorative.

"Sheesh, your spacey today. Get dressed—no yoga pants or leggings," Sam added, accompanied by her sternest, no-nonsense look.

Something told me that tonight was going to be good night—I hoped my gut was right.

Chapter 9

"For women the best aphrodisiacs are words. The G-spot is in the ears. He who looks for it below there is wasting his time."
-Isabel Allende

<u>Westly</u>

"Why did I agree to this?" I groaned to Ry. Despite my desperate need for distraction from window-stalking Meg and countless failed attempts at formulating a sure-fire seduction strategy, *this* was pathetic beyond words.

"Sorry for disturbing your plans to obsessively pine after your neighbor," Ry accurately assessed my alternate plans for the evening.

"We're surrounded by college undergrads. I feel like a lecher," I complained.

"Man, you're twenty-seven, not sixty. You know everyone is over twenty-one, which hardly makes you the creepy old guy. Stop your whining—we're here for Paris. It's her first *big*," he said while making air quotes, "show and as her brother I'm obligated to attend. As my friend, it's your duty to keep me company and applaud if she chokes."

"Where are the rest of clan Mesina? I would've expected them to be here in full force, holding up signs and chanting Paris' name."

"Bingo! She didn't want *anyone* here because she was convinced we would embarrass her," he rolled his eyes as if her concerns were ridiculous, which they totally weren't. "The only way she was able to dissuade the rest from coming was to allow one representative from the family to attend...and she chose me. The girl's always had good taste."

His modesty aside, I was glad Ry was here to support Paris. Regardless of her claims, she would be glad to have a friendly face in the audience as she performed, and a guaranteed round of applause when she finished wouldn't hurt either. Granted, if all seven of the Mesinas showed up, it would have been sensory overload, but Ry's mellow support would be welcome. Not that she really had a choice—there was no way her brothers or father would let her come to a bar alone, twenty-three-year-old woman or not.

I glanced to the right and my eyes clashed with the blond giant behind the bar—Griffin. I'd warned Ry that there was a distinct possibility I would be unceremoniously ejected from the bar before Paris ever sang her first note, which he thought was hilarious—of course he did. After explaining the complicated past I shared with The Stop's owner, as well as the connection to Meg, Ry begged me to come, going so far as to promise me free ink in order to witness my discomfort. He was a twisted bastard.

However, the inevitable threats and expulsion never came. Griffin studied me for a moment before offering a curt nod and then breaking eye contact.

Hmm. That was unexpected—and strange.

Ry nudged me, forcing my attention away from the odd exchange and toward the stage where Paris now stood, looking entirely too close to losing her dinner for my comfort. *Uh-oh, this was not a good sign.*

She reached to adjust the mic, sending shrill feedback throughout the room and I winced, as uncomfortable for her as I was from the sound. Her nervous chuckle carried over the mic, followed by a labored breath.

"You got this, girl," a familiar voice called from behind me.

I looked over my shoulder to see Sam sitting at the bar with Meg by her side. I leaned toward Ry and whispered, "I could kiss you right now."

"Dude, love is love and all that, but I'm just not that into you. I know I'm difficult to resist, but you've got to make the effort."

"Meg's here," I said, ignoring his inflammatory comments.

Before Ry had a chance to look, Paris spoke, redirecting his attention back to the stage.

"Not quite the greeting I intended, but at least I know you're awake. My name is Paris—like the city. And don't worry, it can only get better from here on out...it couldn't get worse," she mumbled to herself but the words were captured by the mic, causing the patrons to laugh. The tension broke and with a small smile, Paris began to finger pick the opening chords of a chipper, quirky song. Thankfully, her voice was mesmerizingly clear and her awkward, off-beat stage presence, appealing. As she played, an unassuming confidence took root and the music seemed to flow through her.

I'd like to say I paid attention to my friend's sister. I tried—honestly I did—but I was too busy assessing Meg, who was too busy watching Paris to notice. By the time Paris' first set was finished, I was itching to make my approach. In a silent show of support, Ry patted my shoulder as I rose from my stool and made my way toward Meg.

Sam saw my approach and offered a smile that nearly caused me to stumble. First, Griffin, now Sam. These people hated me, didn't they? When had we transitioned from threats of bodily injury to smiles and nods?

I reached my destination, standing beside Meg's stool, where she was carefully avoiding my gaze while sending Sam a warning look.

"Hello, Wes—may I call you Wes? Of course I can...you're trying to get under the denim of my girl so being rude to me—again—wouldn't be strategically sound," Sam said, asking and answering her own question. "I'm glad we got that straightened out. How the heck are you? Actually, don't answer that. We have far more important ground to cover first." *We do?*

"By all means, question away—provided I get a turn," I allowed, pleased with my change in luck. Although I had no clue why, it seemed I had an unlikely ally in Sam.

"Griffin," Meg suddenly called out across the bar, "Sam is about to put her life in jeopardy. You may want to do that cool jump-over-the-bar-to-save-the-day move you've perfected. She needs rescuing."

Having quickly assessed the situation and satisfied Sam was in no real danger, Griffin shrugged nonchalantly. "Hunter's been teaching her self-defense moves. She can take him."

"*He's* not the one who's going to throttle her," Meg replied earnestly, but Griffin had already returned his attention to the paying customer.

"Last time I take a bullet for you," Meg whisper-shouted at Sam, who was clearly undeterred by her friend's objections.

"Pssht! No more bullets or knives for me. I've reached my quota of life-threatening situations. Now, where were we—ah, yes, Q&A time. So, Wes, let's be honest here. What are your intentions with the beautiful Megalicious?"

"Once she agrees, I intend to take her out to dinner, then have her for dessert," I answered honestly, following Ry's suggestion.

"I approve," Sam offered, almost too easily, "if—" There it was, I knew there was a contingency. "If you can guarantee a certain level of—how should I say this?— *satisfaction*. Do you have a satisfaction-guaranteed policy, Wes?"

"I do," I said simply.

"Are you sure you're *up* to the challenge? She doesn't need a 'me man,' we're looking for a 'she man.' Hmm...that sounds a little tranny, but you get my drift. Meg needs a man who is willing to make *her* his sole focus for as long as it takes to wear her out. You strike me as a selfish asshole, if I'm being honest, but that doesn't mean you don't have the skills to get the job done. Actually, I think you may be the perfect man for the position. I don't think your ego could handle failure, which virtually guarantees success. What do you say...do you have the equipment and endurance to give my girl what she needs?" she finished with a pointed look at my groin.

As if she had X-ray vision, my package retreated in fear under her keen examination. Hell, at least she was only requiring verbal confirmation and not actual proof. Even Meg seemed to be eyeing my goods surreptitiously, which thankfully brought my boys out of hiding.

"As flattering as I find your character assessment," I began wryly, "you're off base...at least partially. I concede to being an asshole, but I'm not selfish—in or out of bed. When Meg gives in to the inevitable, she won't ever regret it."

Sam nodded, then shoved Meg with enough force to knock her body into mine.

"Megikins, he's the one. It's taken a year, but I've finally found the right candidate—mission accomplished. He'll rock your world with no demands or expectations afterward. Go forth and discover the life-changing capabilities of the big O with my blessing."

Sam leaned toward me, suddenly serious, "If you hurt her—in any way—they will never find your body." After her dramatic pronouncement, she turned on her heel and headed to Griffin at the opposite end of the bar, leaving me alone with Meg. *Finally!*

"Is there anything I could say that would wipe the last five minutes from your memory? Someone in here must have a roofie or training as a hypnotist," Meg rambled.

"No chance in hell. Even drugged, that exchange couldn't be forgotten."

"I was afraid of that," she sighed, adorably discouraged. "Look...Sam is ever-so-slightly insane. It may be a new form of Tourette's, but I'm waiting to hear back from the

Psych department for confirmation. Despite her best intentions, she has an astounding propensity to embarrass me. You are just one in a series of cringeworthy moments so don't think you're anything special, and whatever you do, don't read too much into anything she said. Nothing is going to happen between us."

She was so certain, I almost believed her—*almost*.

I grabbed the edges of her stool and spun until we were face-to-face, the change of position creating the illusion of privacy and removing the deliberate need for her to speak to me over her shoulder. I expected a protest but was pleasantly surprised when the only reaction I received was a raised brow.

"That's better. Now, was Sam telling the truth? Are you interested in a no strings...friendship? Because I promise, I am a *very* accommodating friend. And you won't find anyone less capable of strings than me," I finished with a salacious smile full of carnal promise.

She leaned into me, her body already buying what I was selling. It was a moment of weakness I needed to capitalize on.

Splitting the distance between us, I locked my eyes onto hers, my mouth mere inches from her pouty lips. It was my last chance and I damn well knew it. *Time for the most persuasive closing argument of my life.*

"There aren't many things I'm truly exceptional at. I'll never be husband material. I'm a shit friend most of the time. I believe the ends usually justify the means. My moral fiber is questionable, at best. I will never be the person you call when you're in a bind or need a shoulder to lean on. I don't express my feelings, mostly because I don't have any that aren't shallow. I don't like animals as a general rule, and children—no, just no," I paused, asking myself what the hell I was saying as the same question echoed in her eyes. Too late now—in for a penny, in for a pound. "The only steadfast rule I have is I do not sleep with someone else's woman—*ever*. Other than that one display of principles, I have few redeeming qualities. There are two areas I excel, the law and sex—and when I say I excel, I mean I'm a fucking god. You will forget your own name because all you'll be able to do is scream mine...over and over again. You want no-strings, mind-blowing sex? There is no one better qualified."

Her eyes were wide as saucers and her mouth slightly open, which I took as an invitation. I closed the gap between us, brushing my lips against her silky pink ones. I took advantage of her shock and slid my tongue inside, tasting and teasing. It was a kiss meant to entice, not conquer—that would come later. I gently nipped her plump lower lip with my teeth and was rewarded with a sharp inhale of desire. She was so close to surrender, I could taste it—sweet and hot, with a hint of vanilla and cranberry.

Her resistance collapsed, marked by the alluring breasts suddenly pressed against my chest—*victory*. I grasped her hips, pulling until she was pressed firmly against me and undoubtedly able to feel the steely effect of her kiss. As I subtly rocked my hips against her core, warm fingers twined through my hair, tugging me closer, causing a groan of pained pleasure to escape from my mouth into hers.

Unwilling to continue my exploration with a bar full of witnesses, I attempted to pull away—an attempt met with unintelligible protests. I couldn't risk giving her an opportunity for second thoughts, so I did what any sane man would do. I slid my hands down to cup her lush ass, lifting until her legs wrapped around my waist, and without breaking the kiss, I carried her out of the bar. Perhaps I was more of a gentleman than I'd given myself credit for.

Chapter 10

*"Sex pleasure in woman is a kind of
magic spell; it demands complete abandon;
if words or movements oppose the magic
of caresses, the spell is broken."*
-Simone de Beauvoir

<u>Meg</u>

A fire consumed every nerve in my body until I felt I would fall to the floor as ash. What was this intense and all-encompassing white-hot desire? I'd fully intended to deny him yet again, but his unorthodox monologue entranced me. As he laid his countless flaws and character defects at my feet, the uninhibited honesty gave weight to his promises of pleasure. Why lie about the few skills he claimed to possess when he'd already given me every excuse to turn him away? It was truth, pure and simple. Every word was immediately verified with a kiss that brought me closer to orgasm than any sex I'd ever had, limited though it may be.

He continued to prove himself to be exactly what he claimed—not all of it good, but with Wes I knew precisely what I was getting myself into. And for me, nothing was more essential. There was no hidden agenda or ulterior motives, no skeletons lurking about. He was in your face, this is me, take it or fuck off...and I reveled in it.

With little time remaining in New York and a dismally uncertain future, I wanted this experience...this passion. There may never be another opportunity that could rival his no-strings promises. I wanted this one small indulgence in my life of never-ending denial and restraint. One memory I could turn to through the rest of my solitary life that proved I had lived—just once, I had truly and completely lost my past and escaped my future to live in the moment. Wes was offering me that freedom on a silver platter and I was seizing the chance with both hands, holding on for dear life until the ride ended.

I found myself deposited in the front seat of a posh sports car and watched as he virtually sprinted to the driver's side. Someone was worried I would change my mind. He needn't be—this was happening if I had to club him over the head and drag him back to my cave. He'd awakened my inner cavewoman and the primitive sheanderthal would not be denied.

When he entered the car, it was clear the club would not be necessary. The desire was palpable, an electricity surging until sparks of anticipation and need danced across my skin. Without warning, Wes' hands grasped the back of my head, tugging my mouth against his in a kiss so suggestive it should require protection. As suddenly as it began, it ended, his urgency evident in a reverse-drive maneuver that would make any stuntman proud.

We drove in silence, the only sound our heavy breaths punctuated by the occasional rev as the automatic transmission shifted. While on the verge of screaming, desperate to reach our destination as time dragged endlessly, Wes taught me a valuable lesson: life can become infinitely worse and better in tandem, offering the sweetest torture.

Eyes never leaving the road, he reached over to run the tips of his fingers along the inside of my denim-clad thigh, leisurely climbing closer to the part of me beckoning for attention. Her Royal Horniness decreed he come to her and prove his fealty with a display of skills.

When he reached the apex of my thighs, he continued stroking me with a barely perceivable touch that unraveled what was left of my tattered sanity. The teasing caress slowly transitioned into a purposeful combination of rotating and kneading until my hips arched against his hand, following his tempo but seeking more pressure. My muscles clenched as I reached for my approaching climax, unconcerned with the sounds of demand flowing from my mouth. Almost there...a few more seconds and—

He stopped.

The son-of-a-bitch stopped.

My chest heaved with unquenched lust and searing anger that spread like wildfire when he chuckled.

"Don't hate me. We're here, and given the choice, I prefer you come on my tongue while naked and spread across my bed—not fully clothed in a car like a high school kid chasing a quick release."

Hmm, how about that—we were parked in his garage. Who knew? Still, I was so damn close.

"What about *my* preference?" I retorted, not bothering to mask my irritation. "I was so close."

"It'll be worth the three-minute delay. Let me make this good for you—isn't that the point of this arrangement?"

I couldn't argue his logic. I nodded my agreement, and we exited in silence. He waited as I walked around the car to meet him, and I was surprised when he took my hand and led me into his home. For a moment I was confused by the familiarity of the space before my brain clicked on, reminding me that his townhouse would be the mirror image of Sam's.

"I'm still settling in," he explained, gesturing to the stacks of boxes and askew furniture visible in each room we passed on our way to the stairs.

The unyielding need to strip him bare had receded to manageable levels over the past sixty seconds, but the closer we drew to the master bedroom, the greater my need surged like a tsunami poised to strike. Apparently, I wasn't the only one affected by the room's proximity. No sooner had we crossed the threshold than I found myself anchored against the nearest wall being devoured mercilessly.

The man must have been part octopus. His hands were everywhere: in my hair, kneading my ass, ridding me of my shirt. As if by magic, my top half was bared to him and he greedily sucked my nipples, laving each with equal attention while carrying me to the massive king-size bed. Once positioned in the center, my back gently cradled by the luxurious pillow top, Wes made quick work of my jeans, expertly extricating me until I was unabashedly naked.

Without delay, he nipped his way down my body, stopping when his mouth aligned with the part of me most excited to welcome him home like a long-lost friend. He flattened his palms against my inner thighs, pressing them up and back, opening me fully. His tongue circled my clit as a finger slipped inside me. I found satisfaction in the quiet groan announcing his appreciation for the proof of my desire—I was dripping wet and there was no doubt to whom the credit was due.

He worked my body with every weapon in his arsenal until I was writhing in pleasure so intense every thought fled my mind. There was nothing but him and the sensations he wrung from my body. I teetered on the edge of fulfillment for several minutes, wanting to fall into the fabled bliss awaiting me, but it remained just beyond my reach.

Frustration overtook me and I pushed against Wes' head, indicating I was done. As if in a trance, he ignored my shove, plunging his tongue deep inside me. It felt incredible, a strange new sensation that captivated my body. But like every previous sexual experience—feeble attempts in comparison to the expert ministrations I was currently receiving—I couldn't reach the Promised Land.

My frustration descended into resentment. Resentment directed at those whose influence molded me into a person who couldn't find satisfaction. Resentment toward the first man who took me to his beds but never cared for more than his own gratification. Resentment for the second man to take me to his bed who couldn't be what I needed. Resentment aimed at Wes for possessing all the skills he boasted of, proving with undeniable finality that the problem was *me*. Worst of all, resentment at myself and my failure—I was defective. I would never realize the ecstasy others found so easily in the arms of a lover.

Unable to stand another second of futility, I placed my feet on Wes' shoulders and shoved—hard—finally breaking our connection.

"Enough. I—" My voice broke with my regret and shame. "Thanks, but this was a mistake. It's not you—you're great. Amazing, actually. It's just not going to happen."

I carefully avoided his eyes, but his intense scrutiny pricked my flesh.

"What's going on, Meg? You're calling time-out?"

"No, I'm forfeiting the game. I was hoping things would be different this time, but..." I trailed off, unwilling to disclose my dysfunction. I chanced a look at his face, which was shrouded in confusion and disbelief—*yeah, welcome to my world, buddy*. I almost felt bad for the guy. "Like I said, it's me, not you. I'm gonna head out."

I sat up and scooted to the edge of the bed...only my feet never reached the floor. All of a sudden, I was sideswiped by a hard, muscled body. A series of quick movements found me with my back pressed to Wes' chest, his arms wrapped around me in an odd combination of embrace and restraint.

Okaaay. I hadn't seen that one coming. I wasn't sure if I should fight him or snuggle in close—neither felt quite right. Instead, I lay perfectly still and mute.

"We're going to talk about this. When we've finished our discussion, if you still want to leave, I won't stop you. But no more of the vague BS you just tried to spoon-feed me. I've spent nine months imagining you in my bed—to the point of madness—so if you're walking out, I'd like to understand why."

His request was reasonable and I found it difficult to deny him. *Dammit.* He'd neatly cornered me; if I insisted on leaving without another word, I was nothing more than a bitch or a tease. I nodded with a resigned sigh.

"Good. Now what happened? You were with me, wet and willing one minute and running for the door the next."

"I haven't had many partners," I admitted with a sigh, "two to be exact." His attempt to suppress his shock resulted in a coughing fit. Serves him right. Geeze, what was with people? I'd only had two sexual partners, but everyone acted as if I were a forty-year-old virgin. I jabbed my elbow into his ribs in reprimand before continuing, "Yeah, two partners and I can count the number of times I've had sex on one hand. Neither was able to...close the sale—at least on my end. The first invested no effort and the second...it wasn't mean to be. When Sam found out I'd never...well, thus began her mission to find me the 'orgasm whisperer.' I never believed all the hype about sex, but Sam and Ev assured me the elusive O was more than grown-up fairy tales invented by men to lure women to bed.

"Fast forward to me in your bed. You're everything Sam predicted and you promised to be—still, no matter how skilled a 'whisperer' or how close I come—no pun intended—I can't *get there*. Which is frustrating. Actually, it fucking sucks—big, giant suckballs of suckage. It is the epitome of suckiness. You pretty much forced me to admit that the problem is me, at which point it seemed ridiculous to continue the farce. I'm either not made right or I'm broken...whatever. It's not gonna happen and all I want to do is go home, have a whole bar of chocolate, and listen to songs written by angry women. I've answered your question, your male pride remains intact, and now it's time for me to go."

Only he didn't let me go. Nope. He held tight as I tested the strength of his embrace. *Figures.* Was it too much to ask to limit my humiliation to a single explanation? Apparently, the universe demanded I surrender the few scraps of pride that remained.

"Just to clarify...you've never had an orgasm? Not by your own hand or someone else's? Never with a toy? Never an erotic dream? Never, as in...never?"

I waved goodbye to the remains of my dignity. "That's what I said. Never. And before you require further clarification, Webster's hasn't changed the definition of the word, and there's no urban slang where 'never' actually means 'all the damn time.' Never. *Never, never, never, never!*" I wanted to add one more 'never' for good measure, but I was afraid it might be overkill.

"I accept."

This was Wes' response to my stomach-churning admission?

"You accept what? The definition of 'never'—good for you. Does that mean you'll let me leave now?" I questioned, exasperated by his flippant attitude.

"I accept your challenge. God, this is going to be so much fun. You really are perfect for me—nothing is ever easy with you." The jerk sounded happy, excited even.

Talk about taking joy in the suffering of others.

"So glad I can entertain you, but I don't think you were listening. So pay close attention and read my lips...

I.

Can't.

Come.

I'm physically incapable. You gave it your best shot and nothing happened—not your fault, it's all on me."

"Oh, Meg. Baby, that was my warm-up routine—no bells or whistles—which is usually enough to get the first one out of the way. You need the big finale for your first time— fanfare and fireworks. I refuse to believe you're incapable of climax...your body was more than ready to slip over the edge. Once I overload your body with pleasure and distract your mind, you'll fly. I guarantee it."

"Awfully sure of yourself," I grumbled, still smarting from how much he was relishing my discomfort.

"I've never been more *sure* in my life."

Chapter 11

"An orgasm a day keeps the doctor away."
-Mae West

Meg

"Lie back and relax. Only focus on what you feel in the moment, not where you think you should be," Wes' smooth baritone instructed.

Despite my reservations, his confidence and command were intoxicating, coaxing me to comply. I tried to push all thoughts of my sexual ineptitude from my mind and force my resistant body to relax. He wanted a challenge, not mission impossible.

His hands trailed over my body in feather-light strokes, deliberately avoiding the 'usual suspects' to discover unexpected erogenous zones on my stomach, neck, and arms. He was in no rush, exploring every inch of my body as if it were the sole source of ultimate pleasure. The focus on 'non-sexual' territory enabled me to further relax—there was no pressure to push toward the finish line. All that was expected of me was to lie back and enjoy the experience. By the time his fingertips ghosted across my breasts, my body was covered in goosebumps and I was trembling.

As his fingers circled my rigid nipples, I reflexively opened my eyes.

"Keep them closed," Wes instructed, "just feel."

I obeyed immediately and was rewarded with a hot, wet suction on my left nipple. It was impossible to identify the specific techniques he employed to worship my breasts, since only the overwhelming sensations translated to my foggy brain. Teeth, tongue, hands, lips...they were all invited to the party, equal participants wreaking welcomed havoc. I'd always believed my boobs were nothing more than playtoys for men, of little significance to my enjoyment. Oh, how wrong I'd been. Wes' attentions proved the worth of my girls beyond question, and as a result, I'd never been more aroused or desperate for more.

Wes' mouth left my breast to trail down my stomach, lips dragging sensually across my taut flesh, pausing to nip above my belly button and along my sides. When he settled his broad shoulders between my thighs, he continued to tease me relentlessly, skirting the places screaming for him.

His touch, playful and unhurried, was so different from earlier. Instead of feeling pushed toward a destination, I was being coaxed as if the climax were courting me. It was a seductive persuasion. My fingers gripped the back of his head, silently begging for more, causing a sound of approval to rumble through his chest.

Unable to resist, I opened my eyes to find him staring at me intensely. His gaze was hungry—a starving man before an opulent meal—but there was more. Behind the craving was gleeful amusement, and I could tell he was savoring every minute as much as me. In that moment, a deep and acute connection was created, borne from the raw exposure of my weakness and our joint mission to overcome. It was not love. It was a mixture of empathy and lust, both of us surrendering to the desire that hammered ruthlessly—both understanding that sex was all we had to offer the other, accepting it and wanting nothing more.

Our eyes remained glued to one another as his tongue finally explored my depths. We groaned in tandem, though for different reasons.

"Fuck, you taste amazing," he praised at the same time *'Shit, that feels good'* fell from my mouth—neither of us eloquent in the moment but both honest.

He retained his composure far better than I, continuing his mission to lure my body into submission with deliberate strokes and tantalizing caresses. The pace and intensity progressed slowly, unnoticeable until I was panting, my hips arched against his mouth and fingers. When the first shimmers of euphoria began, I was too consumed to register what was coming. And then it happened...

I shattered.

I fell.

I floated.

I flew.

I found a state of divinity where nothing existed beyond Wes and I in that moment. No past or future. No regrets or guilt. No insecurity or fear. I found my first moment of true bliss—a paradise sought by many through religion, an oblivion promised by drugs. I found it in Wes' head between my thighs.

As the last quivers ebbed, I opened my eyes and returned to reality, where Wes' self-satisfied smile and joy-filled eyes welcomed me back. It was obvious he was pleased with himself, but he was also happy for me.

"That, beautiful girl, was most definitely an orgasm. I believe we can say with confidence you are more than capable of having and enjoying them." Yep, he was smug, but it was strangely endearing—not to mention, well deserved. "There was never anything wrong with you that a change in partners couldn't fix. How do you feel?"

"Amazing? Drained? Like I could do it again," I added cheekily.

"Ironically, I was just thinking our experiment wasn't complete. We've only assessed your ability to have one type of orgasm. Ready to test my efficacy for type B?"

"How very thorough of you."

"I'm nothing if not thorough."

Agreement reached, Wes' lips found my own, sealing the deal. Who needed a handshake? The man kissed like it was his life's calling. He could pioneer a web series offering guidance to the men of the world on the seductive power and proper execution of a kiss. If he needed a volunteer for demonstrative purposes, I'd be first in line.

His tongue stroked mine before dancing away to explore as if it were our first kiss. Nothing was overlooked, no crevice ignored, causing warm tingling to seep through my limbs. I was pliant and willing, drugged by the intoxicating way he made love to my mouth, a foreshadowing of what was to come.

Recognizing I was more than ready, he slowly rose from the bed and stood before me, still fully clothed. *Huh?* How did I not notice all the eye-candy I was missing out on. He unbuttoned his navy dress shirt as if choreographed, allowing the shirt to slide down his shoulders and to the floor.

Wes' body was a work of art. No woman could fault his physique, regardless of personal preference, but to me his body was the quintessence of perfection. A broad chest and muscled shoulders followed by well-defined biceps and triceps. He wasn't bloated with unnatural bulges. Instead, Wes was sculpted as if honed from marble by a renowned artist's hand and impeccably proportioned. His core was equally flawless, a network of defined abdominals inviting exploration. But the superstar of his V-shaped build were the matching bands of chiseled muscle from his abs down past his hips...an arrow pointing the way home.

His hands reached for the belt buckle hugging his trim hips and I salivated—the wait was unbearable. I'd wondered what was hidden beneath the designer denim more than once, and based on the ridged length I'd felt pressed against me tonight, I was a anticipating a very, *very* impressive piece of equipment. The belt was whipped from its loops, the leather clutched in Wes' hand, and he captured my gaze before allowing the strap to drop with a soft thud. Slowly, his hands found the button resting several inches beneath his ridiculously attractive belly button. Seriously, who knew a belly button could be sexy? They were all the same, weren't they? Evidently not. The sound of a descending zipper called me back from my musings.

Finally, the moment of truth.

When the fly gaped, two very important details screamed for attention. First, Wes was going commando—the Hallelujah Chorus swelled in my mind—a fact easily discernible thanks to detail numero dos: a large and extraordinarily swollen cock pointing heavenward, indicating the destination it intended for me. This was no ordinary penis...it was too spectacular to be marginalized in such trite terms. This incomparable member was straight and long, tantalizingly thick, and topped with a substantial, defined head that was begging to be licked.

Standing before me, naked and proud, Wes exceeded my every fantasy. He was sex personified.

"Now you know how I feel when I look at you," he said, breaking into my reverie. "Your body was made for sex, designed to tempt the most principled of men—luckily, I'm a man of few morals and principles."

After reaching into the nightstand, he slowly rolled the condom down his shaft, watching me watch him. He prowled to the bed and covered my body with his own. Braced on his forearms, he lowered his head to whisper in my ear, "Ready?"

Beyond ready. I was embarrassingly close to dropping at his feet in supplication.

He rested his heavy cock against me, sliding against my bare lips until we were both coated in slick desire. Each time the ridge of his head caught my clit, stars exploded behind my eyelids. If he didn't move this along, I was going to come before he ever entered me.

"Wes, please."

"Please what, beautiful?" he teased, clearly wanting me to vocalize my request.

"Please, put it inside me. Make the ache go away. Make me fly."

He obeyed my command, plunging inside before slowly retreating and advancing, inching himself into me while provoking every nerve ending that hugged him tightly. When buried fully, he circled his hips, grinding against my clit. *It. Was. Heaven.* I cried his name in appreciation, praising the feel of him...the fullness.

"Wrap your legs tight around my waist, beautiful."

I clutched him in a vice grip and twined my arms around his neck. Never breaking our connection, he rose on his knees, lifting and lowering me with his hands on my ass.

"Fuck, yes!" Wes groaned, "You are so tight and wet. I can feel you dripping down my cock. I can't get enough of you—it'll never be enough. I want to take you every way possible until I'm all you'll ever feel."

I never understood the appeal of dirty talk. When I read Sam's smutty books, I usually skimmed these sections. But the sound of Wes' voice whispering dirty words about me and how much he enjoyed my body...damn, I couldn't get enough!

All words stopped, however, as he began to drive into me with the force of a freight train. Still clinging, I used what little range of motion was available to me to meet his powerful thrusts, rotating my hips to increase the pleasure for us both.

Moans and incomprehensible utterances filled the room, accompanied by the sound of damp flesh hitting flesh. It was an erotic soundtrack that heightened a primal instinct, taking me further into a jungle of hedonism so dense with carnal delight I could get lost forever and never want to be found.

"Wes...Wes, I'm going to come."

"Wait for me, beautiful," he ordered breathlessly.

"I can't, it's too much," I pleaded for understanding.

"Look at me...I want to watch you come."

I opened my eyes and stared into his caramel depths.

"Now!" he shouted.

It was all I needed to fall over. My body exploded and quaked, rippled and quivered, all while my gaze remained with Wes. I watched his release with the same attentiveness directed at me, each of us absorbed in the pleasure of the other, further increasing our own.

Slowly, he lowered me to the bed, pulling me across his body in a boneless heap.

I didn't know what to say. The gift Wes had given was beyond words of gratitude. So I said nothing. But my mind was at peace and my heart sang with the knowledge that I was not the detached, frigid girl I had always believed.

When morning came, we were still entangled. Throughout the night, Wes had proved with ease that I was capable of any and every type of orgasm in any and every position imaginable. My voice was hoarse from the number of times I'd called out his name, and every muscle in my body ached. Forget CrossFit or Spin class, if we repeated our birthday-suit aerobics every night, I would be on the cover of Fitness magazine in a month.

In between our bouts of erotic gymnastics, we spent time exploring one another's bodies with gentle hands and teasing mouths while we both recuperated. The most surprising time was spent napping, my head on his chest and his arms encircling me. It was unexpectedly intimate, but there was a comfortable familiarity in those sleepy moments.

The night had been everything I never believed existed...and so much more. But now the sun was rising through the uncovered windows, announcing the end of our sexual exploits. It was time to return to reality, regardless of how much I would prefer to steal one more night in Wes' bed.

He was still dozing as I entered the bathroom to dress. I splashed water on my face and used his toothpaste and my finger to dispel the dreaded morning breath. A few minutes later I exited to find Wes awake, reclining against the headboard and staring at me like the baby seal to his shark. An involuntary shiver rippled down my body—dayum, the man was H.O.T, hot! Although his exposed chest beckoned me closer, begging to be worshiped, regretfully, it was time to go.

I sashayed toward him—hey, he deserved a show after his performance last night—placing my knee on the edge of the bed closest to him, leaning in to provide a gentle, close-mouthed kiss.

"Thank   you   for   an   incredible   night.   You were...everything." We smiled at each other, both enjoying a moment of recollection. "I'll let myself out."

"Thanks for an extraordinary evening, Meg."

With a smile and mini-wave, I left him alone in bed.

"Love is the answer, but while you are waiting for the answer, sex raises some pretty good questions." -Woody Allen

Meg

Keys in hand, I dashed the short distance between Wes' and Sam's doors, leaping dramatically over a flowerbed, not wanting to get busted making the walk of shame. Closing the front door as quietly as possible, I headed to my room in the hopes of catching a few hours of sleep before my afternoon shift at Higher Yearning.

Sex may be a stellar workout, but it was hell on a restful night's sleep. Not that the shut-eye I'd sacrificed wasn't *well* worth it.

Slipping into my room, I kicked off my shoes and zombie-walked to my bed, my eyes already closed in anticipation of the rest to come. *Mmm, bed.*

"Well, hello, you raunchy rod rider!" Sam's obscenely chipper voice greeted, scaring me to death. "Spill!" she commanded, either not comprehending or not caring about my desperate need for rest.

"Sleep now. Talk later," I grunted, my voice hoarse from a night of screaming Wes' name.

"Oh, no you don't. You are going to dish every delicious detail right this minute. I hooked you up—you owe me!"

"Sam," I whined, "I'm so tired. I promise to tell you everything later."

"Nuh-uh. I've been waiting all night for this. I plan to live vicariously through you."

"Live vicariously...what? Girl, you have more sex than those guys on that gigolo reality show. You are not in need of vicarious anything in that arena."

"What?! There's a show about gigolos and I don't know about it? Why the hell didn't you tell me? I bet it's hysterical...and sexy."

My momentary hope that I had sufficiently distracted Sam quickly died on the vine.

"Don't answer that, I'll look it up later. We have far more important info to cover now."

I sighed heavily. There was no point in resisting. Sam would get the details she was searching for, with or without my cooperation. There was no chance I'd get to sleep before recounting last night's escapade in graphic detail.

"Okay, okay. So, after you left us at the bar—" I began.

"Wait!" Sam interrupted, whipping her cell phone from her pocket, feverishly clicking away. Raising the phone to her ear, she held up a finger, clearly indicating she needed me to give her a moment. With little else to do, I slumped on the bed and relaxed.

"Ev!" Sam exclaimed. "You are *not* going to believe what happened last night!"

After a pause—presumably for Ev's response—Sam continued.

"I don't care what time it is in Hawaii, and you're coming home today anyway. Plus, your honeymoon is technically over—and trust me, you want to hear this. I'm going to put you on speaker."

One click and Ev's voice joined us in the room, "—and Hunter is making all sorts of unspeakable threats. This better be life and death."

"Megalicious tamed the one-eyed snake last night," Sam declared, "or did it tame her? Hmm, we'll decide once we get the details."

"She—come again? Meg, are you there?"

"Present," I answered like a student at roll call.

"Tell. Me. Everything. Who? How? Was it good?" Ev questioned in rapid succession.

"Westly-freakin'-Black," Sam replied on my behalf, "and it's all thanks to me."

"What? We hate Black! He tried to coerce you and he lied to Meg. What the heck is going on back there? I've been gone for a week and it's Armageddon!" Ev said. "You two are lucky we are booked to leave today, because Hunter would flip if I had to cut our honeymoon short because of you."

"Dial it back, mama bear. Let me catch you up before you jump on your crazy horse and come charging in, mucking up all my hard work," Sam scolded. "First, Black may have pushed me to settle, but with time to process, I'm not sure his argument was off base. Second, I don't think Wes realized Meg had confused him with the nice-but-boring assistant DA, Mark."

"Sam..." I tried to interject to defend poor Mark, but she ignored me.

"Third, she isn't marrying Black, she's banging him...and let's be honest, if you weren't married to your hottie hubby, you'd be all over what Black has to offer—as would I. The man is incendiary. The perfect GQ bad-boy. Every girl should take a walk on the dark side before settling down in the light. Since you and I missed out, now we get to experience the fantasy courtesy of Megs!"

"I'm not convinced, but what's done is done," Ev said neutrally.

We sat in silence for several moments. I, for one, was unsure if it was my turn to speak—with Horny Helen and Cautious Cathy, one could never tell.

"He *is* dazzling, in the quintessential heartbreaker way," Ev finally declared, cutting the last threads of tension.

"Amen, sista!" Sam exclaimed. "Okay, let me bring you up to speed. Wes bought the townhouse next door. He moved in the day we returned from Hawaii, came knocking on his neighbor's door to get the number of the maintenance office and—POW!—Megalicious answers. She gives him a piece of her mind, he denies all wrongdoing, insults are exchanged, yada, yada, yada. Now for the good stuff! We went to The Stop last night and who was there? That's right, you guessed it...Black!"

"Wait, he was at the Stop and Griffin didn't kick his ass out?" Ev interjected.

"Ehh, we talked about the whole Black situation a few times and he agrees that the guy was doing his job—albeit a slimy job—and neither of us thinks he was trying to con Meg. He even agreed that Black is the right kind of guy to use if all you want is to get your rocks off."

"Wow, Griffin was analyzing Black's sexual prowess and appeal? I'm having a hard time visualizing that one," Ev pondered. I couldn't blame her...I was there for the conversation and it was still mind-bending.

"Oh, my man is *very* secure in his sexuality. Although he wasn't really commenting on Black's hotness, more so his suitability to be used, abused, and discarded without guilt."

"Gotcha," Ev said.

"If you're done interrupting...so Black is at the bar and approaches. I encouraged him to show Megikins the time of her life—after verifying he could deliver the goods, of course—then threatened death by dismemberment if he hurts her. The two of them talked for about three minutes before putting on a display of public affection that nearly required intervention from the fire department. We're talking a blisteringly hot, epic make-out session in the middle of The Stop. Even *I* was uncomfortable watching—okay, that's a lie...I watched and it was awesome. Then he carried her out of the bar, tongue still down her throat, with Meg clinging to him like a baby chimp."

"Ugh! I miss all the good stuff! Dammit," Ev said, followed by a low grumble in the background. "Sorry, babe...you're the bestest stuff—wouldn't trade a minute of our honeymoon for the world—but it still bites that I missed

Meg's dramatic dry-hump-at-the-Stop moment. Continue," Ev said, addressing us again. "Wait, Hunter says that Meg should wring him dry, but be careful not to convince herself Black's something he isn't. He doesn't want to have to resign from the FBI for committing homicide if Black breaks your heart. Don't get me wrong, he'll do it, but he rather likes his job—so keep your head on straight."

"Aww," Sam and I said in unison. "Love you too, Hunter!" I added sincerely.

"Alright, Ev, you're up to speed…Meg, the floor is yours."

Here goes nothing…

"It was a fantastic night—for the most part—and I'm glad you persuaded me to enjoy myself, Sam. No regrets," I finished, knowing there was no way they would let me get away with such a homogenized answer.

"Ha, ha, ha. You're hysterical. Now give us the nitty-gritty details…hold nothing back. I want specifics, unless it wasn't as stellar as your exhaustion would imply," Sam goaded.

"Oooh, does she look well-used? Is she rockin' the one-night stand hair? Snap a picture and text it to me. Damn, why am I in paradise when all the action is at home?" Ev shouted through the phone.

A quiet click sounded before I knew it.

"You be the judge; the picture is on its way," Sam advised Ev.

"One sec…" A chime carried over the line. "Got it," Ev paused, likely examining the evidence. "Hell yeah! Girl, you look rode hard and put away wet! Good job, Black. Now start again and leave nothing out."

I sighed. After a year of similar antics, I should've been immune to their insanity, but it still caught me off-guard on occasion. Don't get me wrong, I loved Sam and Ev dearly and was grateful beyond words that they cared so much about me. But, dang, those two were a handful! Hunter and Griffin were in a category of men all their own for handling these crazy women.

"Alright, alright. He carried me to the car and teased me all the way to his house. We went straight to the bedroom and made out. He took a trip down south, but things got a little...complicated—"

"Explain complicated," Ev said while Sam asked, "Complicated how?"

"It felt amazing—the man really is gifted—but I couldn't, you know...finish. It was messing with my head and I made him stop—actually, I kicked him away."

"I would have paid to see that," Ev interjected, and Sam nodded her agreement.

"I tried to leave but he refused to let me, insisting I explain. I did—full disclosure—he took it as a challenge and got back to business. He must have spent an hour stroking and worshiping my body before he made any real effort to bring me to orgasm—it was extraordinary. Then he returned south and claimed victory. Can I just say...Ho. Ly. Shitballs! I swear my mind short-circuited and I was nothing more than a giant ragdoll for about ten minutes afterward."

"Told you the big O was real! Yep, I'm definitely saying 'I told you so,'" Ev teased.

"Well, you were right. Once I was able to form semi-coherent sentences, he offered to prove I could also have a vag-gasm. Let me tell you, my lady bits will be singing his praises and sending me chocolates for the next decade, at least. He did things I didn't even think were physically possible. His body is beyond perfection. And Wes, Jr...that not-so-little man should have odes and sonnets in his honor—or at least some dirty limericks. Let's just say the man is exceedingly blessed. Ginormongous! Anyway, we were up most of the night getting down. When I woke up this morning, I said thanks, kissed him goodbye, and left. End of story."

I couldn't believe I just catalogued my first orgasms in graphic detail—evidently Sam was rubbing off on me.

"I need a cold shower!" Sam declared.

"Um-hmm. I second that," Ev added. "Are you going to see him again?"

"I don't know. I think we had an unspoken agreement that it was a one-time thing. It was stupefyingly fantastic, but I don't want strings. And while he feels the same, it makes being neighbors a little too convenient. I'm not looking to develop a habit...know what I mean?"

"I can see where you're coming from with the neighbor thing. If one of you decides the thrill is gone but the other is still looking to play 'what's in my pants,' it could get awkward," Sam offered supportively.

"Exactly! It was truly a once-in-a-lifetime night, and I don't think we could replicate that kind of magic anyway. Sometimes it's better to hold fast to the memory so it doesn't tarnish," I said, confident in my choice.

"I concur," Ev said, validating my feelings. "Next item on the agenda for our impromptu meeting: where are we meeting tomorrow for dinner? It's been waaaayyy too long since I've seen you girls. Seven days without estrogen is like an eternity!"

"Everyone should come here for dinner tomorrow. I have a new recipe and I need guinea pigs," Sam said, chuckling sinisterly.

Ha! As if Sam ever cooked anything that wasn't delicious. After years of recreational and therapeutic cooking, she'd recently enrolled in culinary school with the encouragement of Griffin. She'd always have her bachelor's degree to fall back on, but her passion has always been cooking—even when she didn't know it.

"I'm working, but I can be home by seven," I shared.

"Hunter and I will be there by seven, too," Ev confirmed.

Plans set, we bid goodbye to Ev, wishing her a safe trip home.

"Now that you've spilled your guts, I'll let you get some rest," Sam said, placing a motherly kiss on the top of my head—never mind I was the older of the two of us.

"Thanks, Sam. I'm really lucky to have you in my life. I don't know where I'd be now without you."

"Pssht. You'd be fine, just leading a substantially less interesting life—an orgasm-free life. Actually, you're right...I totally rock!" With a fist pump to salute her greatness, she slipped from my room as I slipped into sleep.

Chapter 13

"Friendship is held to be the severest test of character. It is easy, we think, to be loyal to a family and clan, whose blood is in your own veins." -Charles Eastman

Westly

More than twenty-four hours had passed since Meg left my house, and I'd yet to see or hear from her. I spent my Friday in court, trying every trick in the book to tame my dick when frequent memories of her circulated through my mind. Needless to say, my balls were aching and my nerves were tattered. If the jury believed I had a hard-on for the middle aged, overweight forensic accountant I questioned—despite the awful comb-over he was sporting—there was no way I'd win the case. Every time I gained an ounce of control, Meg would saunter back into my consciousness and wreak havoc.

We'd made no plans to meet again, nor were any promises exchanged, but I wasn't done with her. Whether she realized this fact or not was immaterial—I would have her again. One taste was not enough to satiate my hunger for her. I needed weeks to explore all of the ways I wanted to debauch her, maybe months to realize every erotic fantasy...twice.

God, I nearly choked when she told me she was unable to climax. It was hard enough to believe she'd never come, but her embarrassment was too evident for it to be a lie. It was sad, actually. That she was convinced something was wrong with her was ludicrous.

Meg oozed an instinctive sensuality, completely without artifice. Her every response was honest and unrehearsed. No overdramatized moans or screaming. No obnoxious shrieks or flailing. I swore women watched entirely too much porn, replicating the dramatized orgasms they saw on-screen, believing that's what a man wanted. Hell no! A real man wanted a woman to fall apart for him in *her* way, not feigning pleasure that's so transparent the actress might as well be reading the phone book while wearing a muumuu. Not, Meg—she was a snake charmer beguiling me with her spell of authenticity.

That is what Meg gave me—100% pure Meg and 100% participation. She never lay there like a lump, waiting for something to be done *to* her, or for me to be done. Even when I was feasting on her, there were small caresses that let me know she was with me. And when I was inside her, she gave everything. She rode me hard, working my cock like a prize winning bull rider despite her lack of experience on the rodeo circuit. She reached for her own satisfaction unapologetically but cared equally about mine.

No, I wasn't done exploring her body. I hadn't memorized every nuisance yet, and I needed more of her sweetness on my lips. I wasn't done feeling her pussy grip my cock like a vice, milking me until I was wrung dry. Shit, I hadn't even felt her lips wrapped around my cock yet. I wasn't done. Period.

The best part—that's a lie, the second best part—was that I liked her. When we weren't fucking or napping, I liked listening to Meg and trying to figure her out. She was innately good and had a subtle innocence that was beguiling without being cloying. Nonetheless, she was complex. She honestly didn't want commitment, but she seemed starved for connection. Her words and deeds reflected her integrity, though her eyes were shadowed with hidden darkness. It was obvious there were secrets locked deep within that she was unwilling to share.

A huge part of my professional success was determined by my ability to read people, to ascertain their motivations and detect secrets and lies. Meg set all my alarm bells ringing, but not because she was inherently dark. More so, it was like a darkness had been planted inside her and allowed to grow unchecked. It was independent of her spirit, but she was forced to carry its burden.

She was a mystery, wrapped in challenge and ribboned with secrets.

She was the Rubik's Cube I was going to solve.

I debated stopping by Higher Yearning but didn't think she'd appreciate being propositioned at work. With great effort, I resisted the urge to track her down, giving her a day I didn't want or need. Now it was time to reengage, to entice her back to my bed while the memories of pleasure were still fresh in her mind. My efforts would be far more effective if her body was still sensitized from my pillaging.

The nagging question remained...how to make my approach? My advantage was in directness mixed with seduction. She'd consistently responded to both, one addressing her mind, the other her body. A candid invitation with whispered reminders should entice her to crawl beneath—or over—me again.

Sam advocated our tryst, championing me as the perfect 'fuck buddy,' which made her a resource not to be ignored. If I approached Meg with Sam nearby, she might support my cause. The tiny spitfire was my secret weapon, a steamroller to any resistance. My best opportunity to speak with both would be at Sam's house—all I needed was an excuse.

An hour later, inspiration struck. Armed with a plan, I headed to the shower to get ready for my impromptu 'date.'

Window-stalking yet again, I waited until Meg's car returned before heading over. Jumping the low hedges between our homes, I walked to their door with confidence, prepared to handle whatever the spunky ladies threw my way. A few knocks and the door swung open—clearly I hadn't planned for all contingencies.

"What do you want, Black?" a bronzed Hunter asked, not bothering to mask his big-brotheresque disapproval.

I sighed to myself, suppressing the overwhelming desire to plow through the obstacle before me. Nothing with Meg ever came easily, and most of the time it was a part of her charm. But in the case of the FBI agent currently barricading the door, it was a pain in the ass!

"Good to see you, too, Agent Charles. I understand congratulations are in order," I said, attempting to smooth his ruffled feathers.

All I received was a blank stare.

This guy must be fantastic in an interrogation room. I wanted to confess and I had yet to do anything wrong—at least in my opinion.

"Is Meg home?" I inquired after a lengthy stare-down.

I would have bet a year's salary he was about to shut the door in my face when lady luck intervened.

"Babe, who's at the door?" I heard Everleigh question as she approached. "Well, well, well...if it isn't Westly Black—in the *flesh*." The innuendo was impossible to miss—it was obvious the girls had been gossiping.

"Hello, Everleigh. Congratulations on your marriage. I'm sure you were a stunning bride."

"Hunter, love, why don't you step back so I can invite Wes in. You're giving the impression he's not welcome," Ev cooed to her husband, waving a red flag before the bull.

"He's not," Hunter grumbled beneath his breath, earning him a hard smack on the bicep.

"Move, you big lug, or I'll move you myself. You know I can do it. Remember in Hawaii when you tried to block me from taking a bath and I—"

"Stop right there. Black does *not* need the details."

Resigned to his loss, Hunter stepped aside, allowing Ev to open the door fully in invitation.

"We were just about to sit down to dinner, would you like to join us?" Ev offered solicitously. "Sam cooked so it's guaranteed to be delicious."

Foreboding warred with anticipation. Joining the feisty group of my not-so-biggest fans for dinner would give me the opportunity and time needed to slide back between Meg's silky thighs. On the other hand, I smelled a set-up. Despite Griffin's neutral greetings at The Stop and evidence that the women had let go of past grudges, I suspected each would relish the prospect of making me squirm. Had I mentioned that nothing—*nothing*—came easily where Meg was involved? And twisted as it was, I loved it. The game. The challenge. It was invigorating.

"I'd love to crash the dinner party, since my plan to invite Meg and Sam to dinner is scrapped," I accepted, entering the house and following Ev to the kitchen.

"Sam, do we have enough food for one more?" Ev asked.

Still facing the stove, Sam replied, "Of course, you know I always make leftovers for the guys. Who's coming to dinner?" She turned around and caught sight of me standing beside Ev. "Ohhh, this is going to be fun! No one tell Meg, let's surprise her when she comes down from changing. If she's dressed in the damn yoga pants and t-shirt, it'll serve her right."

Yoga pants and a tee sounded perfect to me. They clung to the places that mattered most and were easily removed. Sam, however, looked truly outraged by the prospect so I kept my opinion to myself.

Griffin entered the kitchen with another dispassionate nod, followed by Hunter whose glare exhibited far more contempt.

"Hey stud," Sam shouted while ladling soup into bowls, "get our guest a drink."

"As you wish," came Griffin's reply, while Hunter countered with, "Hey, what are Ev and I, chopped meat?"

"No, you are family. I don't have to fetch you drinks. You get off your firm derrière and get it yourself...and grab Ev's while you're at it," Sam shot back.

"Do you see what marriage has done to me? I used to win all of these little exchanges—now Sam and my wife have both schooled me in under ten minutes," Hunter playfully griped.

"True...but would you change it?" Griffin asked.

"Not for my life."

"Exactly!" Griffin said, then smiled good-naturedly, "So do as Lo ordered and get Ev a drink. Wes, you want red or white with dinner? I suggest white."

"You're the expert," I returned, grateful for his amiable tone. Perhaps my suspicions had been a temporary bout of paranoia. Hunter was the only one discontent with my presence, but he seemed to be coming to terms, accepting he was outvoted.

"All right, everyone sit down, dinner's ready. Wes, you take the left seat by the window. Megawatt, get your butt down here!" Sam finished, her voice echoing thanks to the vaulted ceiling of the adjoining great room.

"On my way," Meg's voice returned, accompanied by the sound of her steps on the stairs. "Sorry, I had to shower. I spilled chocolate sauce all over me. I was—"

"Hello, beautiful. I would have been happy to help you clean up the sticky mess. Maybe I should inspect you after dinner to ensure you didn't miss any spots," I greeted her, taking a moment to absorb her beauty. Even in a t-shirt and the stretchy black pants all women loved, she was stunning.

"I...you..." she paused, shaking her head as if trying to clear her vision. "You're here. Having dinner. With," she glanced around the table, "everyone."

"You don't mind, do you?" I asked, structuring the question with the correct answer.

"Um, no? I mean...why would I? I was just surprised to see you after..." She cleared her throat nervously. "Anyway, of course you're welcome to join us. We're neighbors, after all. But, uh, how is it you wound up joining us?"

"He came over to invite you and Sam to dinner. I invited him to join us instead," Ev explained with a mischievous twinkle in her eye. Maybe my concerns weren't unfounded.

"Oh. Okay," Meg said, shifting from foot to foot, still anchored several feet from the table. The only empty seat was conveniently beside mine.

Enjoying her discomfort more than I probably should, I patted the vacant seat, "Come sit down, the soup smells delicious."

With one more scan of the table, Meg shrugged and sat down beside me. Feeling particularly devilish, I leaned closer to her and whispered, "Are you okay, Meg? You seem a little tense." I lingered in her space, forcing her to respond with the same intimacy.

"I'm fine. Just a crazy day at work. Although I'll admit I was thrown when I found you sitting down with the gang for dinner," she confessed before pulling back, only to close the distance again and whisper, "Are you sure you're up for this? I don't think you know what you've gotten yourself into."

"Nothing I can't handle," I replied, full of self-assurance.

"We'll see," came her cryptic reply.

"Everyone eat. You have carrot soup infused with ginger, a goat cheese island, and crispy crouton rafts," Sam explained.

I loaded my spoon and savored the first bite. *Damn, the fireball could cook!*

"It's spectacular, Sam," I praised sincerely.

"Oh, don't I know it. You all better love this. I won't even tell you how long I spent juicing carrots and ginger root."

The kitchen remained quiet for several minutes as everyone enjoyed their first course. Making a tactical decision to score points with the women, I stood to gather the empty bowls and then carried them to the sink. I wasn't above sucking up with the right incentive.

"Kiss-ass," Hunter mumbled when I collected his bowl.

Griffin and Sam delivered plates of pasta with kale pesto, sliced chicken breasts, and toasted pignolis. Once again, the kitchen was as quiet as a graveyard while we inhaled the flavorful dish.

When the table was cleared, Sam served key lime cheesecake while Meg poured coffee for everyone—except herself. When I raised my eyebrow in question, she winked, returning a few moments later with a cup of hot chocolate and several squares of dark chocolate on a plate.

"I'll taste Sam's dessert because it will be delicious, but for me, it's all about the chocolate. No coffee or tea—either Lindt Dark Chocolate with Sea Salt or hot chocolate. Sometimes both," she added with a mischievous smile.

"A chocoholic. Interesting. This is definitely a fact I can put to good use in the future," I teased, reaching under the table to squeeze her thigh playfully. When she didn't react, I left my hand in place while she recapped her day at Higher Yearning for Ev's benefit. When she launched in to sales figures, I slowly slid my hand up her leg, encroaching on her center but stopping a millimeter from the sweet spot.

Her breath caught momentarily, but she quickly regained her composure to answer Ev's question. I was gloating internally until she surprised me by slouching ever-so-slightly in her seat, forcing my fingers to meet her core. With the subtlety of a super-spy, she rocked her hips against my hand, gaining the friction she desired.

My plan to arouse her into an undeniable state of desperation was an epic backfire, because now I was every bit as tortured as she—and my response to her was far harder to disguise. Thankfully, everyone seemed content to continue our conversation around the dinner table.

"Why don't we move to the couches and get comfortable? I'll take care of the dishes later, Lo," Griffin suggested, a smirk threatening. *Bastard!*

Everyone agreed readily and began to move toward the overstuffed couches.

I was screwed.

With few options, I untucked my shirt and followed the crowd into the great room, hoping that no one would notice my wardrobe alteration. This hope was quickly dashed by Meg's self-satisfied grin, Hunter's scowl, and Griffin's snicker. Directing my attention to the source of my predicament, I glowered at Meg with a silent promise of retribution. Evidently, the threat of punishment was appealing because the minx winked in return.

I sat beside my temptress, pressing close, tormenting us both.

"Hey, Black. What's it like protecting the bad guys every day?" Hunter asked snidely. "Is it rewarding when you help a rapist go free?"

My blood pressure shot through the roof. I was going to tear the condescending douche to pieces with my bare hands. As my muscles tensed for action, Meg clutched my hand in hers, soothing my blazing temper.

"For a law enforcement agent, you're remarkably eager to toss accusations without collecting the facts. I guess that's a common problem for you self-righteous types. I should be grateful—it makes my job so much easier when you jump to conclusions and focus on what you want to see versus the truth." I paused to ensure I had captured the attention of the room. "I have *never* defended a rapist, domestic abuser, pedophile, or any of the other heinous criminals you'd like to link me with. Do I represent individuals and corporations with questionable practices? Perhaps. Are my clients guilty of embezzlement, tax fraud, and bribery? I don't ask, but usually not, according to a jury of their peers. They pay obscene amounts of money to get themselves out of hot water, but I wouldn't be able to keep them from boiling if you '*good guys*' did your jobs. I operate within the constraints of the law to defend my clients. The judicial system doesn't work if I don't exist—prosecutors and defenders are required."

"I hear a lot of rationalization and justification. You walk a very thin gray line between right and wrong. The balancing act would strain anyone's conscience, provided they have one. Do you sleep easily at night?" Griffin asked bluntly, but with less animosity than Hunter.

I was getting double-teamed—raked across the coals in retribution for Sam's suffering. Did I deserve their censure? No. Would I take it for Meg? Yes. If her friends banded together against me, there was no way she would give me the time of day.

"Do you sleep easily, Griffin? Have you ever wondered if the liquor you served led to a fatal accident when the patron that 'seemed fine' swerved into oncoming traffic? Do you worry that the abrasive 'regular' whose twenty you accepted might have gone home and beat his wife and kids?" I asked steadily, without emotion. "And Hunter, you sleep well with Ev wrapped up in your arms? You're not haunted by the serial killer you didn't catch? How about the suspected rapist you questioned and believed was innocent, only to catch him red-handed a few months later? What about when the chain of custody is compromised and a suspected terrorist walks off scot-free?" I let my questions resonate for a moment. "It's very easy to paint me as the villain, to make me the butt of your jokes. Point your fingers and judge me to your heart's content—just don't forget to turn a mirror on yourselves when you're finished with me. I may not be a paragon of virtue, but at least I'm honest with myself, and I never pretend to be anything other than what I am."

My phone rang, saving me from further admonishment. "Excuse me for a minute, I need to take this," I said to no one in particular before exiting to the front porch.

"This is Wes. What can I do for you?"

*"Don't have sex, man. It leads to kissing
and pretty soon you have to start talking
to them." -Steve Martin*

Meg

"What the hell was that? You guys said you were okay with Wes. *You* were the ones who invited him to dinner. Was it all a set-up so you could verbally flagellate him? I mean—seriously—that was vicious! Both of you are better than that stunt you just pulled. I expected more of you," I finished, disappointed in the ones I loved.

Saddened, I rose from the couch with the intention of tracking down Wes to apologize.

"Hold up, Meg," Hunter pleaded. "It's not what you think—at least, not entirely. We had a plan," he added, gesturing to Griffin.

"Oh you did, did you?"

"I think you guys better explain what scheme you're working. I have to agree with Meg, you both crossed the line," Ev scolded.

"I second that," Sam echoed.

"Hunter and I discussed it before dinner," Griffin began. "It was one thing when you were using Black as a take-and-toss. When he showed up here this evening, that elevated things to hook-up territory. I know you don't intend to get into a relationship, Meg, but proximity and sex can often lead to one. Hunter and I agreed that if Wes wanted to continue sniffing around and enjoying your company, he needed to prove himself worthy of your time."

"Exactly," Hunter chimed in. "We decided to push his buttons and see how much he would take in order to have you. If he can't stand some tough questions, then he doesn't deserve your time. It was a litmus test. Plus, we've all assumed that our initial reactions to him were wrong and he didn't intentionally hurt you and Sam, but we don't know for certain. This was the easiest way to verify he's not an evil bastard—he's just a lawyer," Hunter added with a chuckle.

Sam, Ev, and I all exchanged looks.

"It *was* kind of sweet in a twisted big-brother way," Ev decided.

"I should have known Griffin wouldn't let any guy near our Meggie without careful screening," Sam added.

"I appreciate your concern, but you took it too far. Whether he's screwing my brains out or he's just the attorney who represented the Varbecks, your actions were extreme. You both owe him an apology."

They nodded their agreement, but neither appeared truly contrite.

"Good. I'm going to find him," I announced, but Ev stopped me with a hand on my arm.

"They may have gone about it the wrong way, but their intentions were good. Don't go after Wes. Wait here and see if he returns. If he does, then continue on your merry way. If he doesn't, then don't waste your time."

I considered her point and found no grounds to argue. Ultimately, Wes was wronged and the guys would have to apologize, but if he couldn't handle a little heat, then he didn't deserve my fire.

Returning to my place on the couch, I listened as Sam distracted us all with funny stories from culinary school. Five minutes passed at a snail's pace, forcing me to acknowledge that Wes was not going to return. I couldn't blame him, but I was far more disheartened than I should have been. Not good. Maybe it was for the best he slinked off quietly. After only one night, I was entirely too eager for him to return and prove himself.

Resigned that my tryst with Wes had come to an end, I rested my head on the back of the couch and closed my eyes for a moment to savor the memories that would remain.

"I'm sorry, Wes."

My head popped up in shock as Hunter's words registered in my brain.

"I overstepped. I wanted you to justify your career and prove yourself worthy of Meg by doing so under hostile conditions. Last year when everything was coming to a head with Sam, your intentions were good even if your approach wasn't. We all understand that now. I justified my right to test you based on that history. I was wrong," Hunter finished, approaching Wes with his hand extended. "I still think you're a cocky bastard—completely unworthy of Meg—but I don't believe you're ethically bankrupt...maybe just a little cash poor."

Wes shook Hunter's hand, looking as shell-shocked as I felt. Hunter's apology was more thorough than I'd anticipated. My faith was restored.

Not to be outdone, Griffin picked up the torch.

"I agree. You made a number of valid points, which I'm embarrassed to say I've never considered. Despite the snide jokes—which will persist because you're an easy target—you have a job to do, and it's a job that needs to be done. I'm not sure what led you to choose criminal defense as your specialty—other than the money—but you have more character than a lot of the sleazeballs out there."

Griffin extended his giant mitt, which Wes accepted solemnly. Again, my faith was renewed in the men I loved and respected.

"I appreciate the apologies," Wes responded graciously. "There was some truth in your words as well. I have to walk a fine line to represent my clients to the best of my ability without breaking the law. Most people—the ones with a strong moral compass—would find my job abhorrent. I don't struggle as much as I probably should," he said candidly. "And we can all agree Meg deserves much better than me. But I can give her what she needs for now and I won't hurt her. She and I are on the same page."

"Would that be a page out of the *Kama Sutra*, or do you have a different handbook?" Sam asked, straight-faced, breaking the tension as only Sam could. "I have a few books I could lend you two if you need help."

"Samantha, I could write the book on the topic of sexual positions and lend it to *you*, I'm that good," Wes replied, staring at me intently.

My whole body responded to the promise in his stare. I wanted that promise. I wanted it *now*.

"Wes and I need a to talk about a few things," I announced, turning toward him, "Do you want to go to your place?"

"Subtlety is not her gift," Ev whispered to Hunter, loud enough for everyone to hear.

"If that's not the woolly mammoth calling the yeti hairy, I don't know what is," Hunter shot back.

"Did you just call me a yeti?" Ev asked in a voice filled with warning.

"I believe I called you a woolly mammoth," Hunter said, clearly missing the danger.

"You do realize you pledged your life to me ten days ago. I have decades to make you regret that comment."

"Angel, I pledged my life to you almost two years ago. It was the day I permanently inked my body for you. You just didn't know it," Hunter said with conviction.

"He totally won that point," Sam called like a referee.

"Oh, yeah," I replied, an eager spectator.

I could see Ev had been moved by Hunter's declaration, but our reminder of her most recent defeat restored her focus. We really shouldn't take such pleasure in riling up these two, but it was hard to feel bad when the entertainment factor was off the charts. Not to mention, verbal warfare was foreplay for them so there really were no losers.

"Are you claiming that your vows and a tattoo grant you the right to compare me to every hideous beast in the wild kingdom?"

"Not unless you specifically make the comparison first," Hunter qualified.

Ev stood frozen, clearly outmaneuvered by a conversation the rest of us were not privy to. Hopefully Hunter would fill us in.

"When I asked during our honeymoon what your favorite part of married life was, did you or did you not—my beautiful wife—tell me it was the fact that you no longer had to shave unless you felt like it. In fact, I specifically recall you saying, 'I'll be a woolly mammoth come winter and you are still legally obligated to love me.' I believe you finished with a sinister chuckle. So you see, I was just repeating your warning to mentally prepare myself."

"Thank god he's not with the DA's office—he'd be hell on my win stats," Wes said, earning a laugh from everyone, except a still-pouting Everleigh.

"You promised in our vows to let me win on occasion," she complained.

"And you promised not to make it too easy for me," Hunter countered.

"Nevertheless, you called me a hairy beast. Now you need to soothe my wounded pride. It's your husbandly duty."

With unparalleled speed, Ev was draped over Hunter's shoulder and halfway to the door. Hunter's *thanks for dinner* was barely audible over Ev's shrieks of feigned indignation.

"I think we'll make a less dramatic exit," Wes said, still laughing at Huntleigh. "Thank you for a delicious meal, Sam, and your hospitality. Griffin, it takes a big man—pun intended—to apologize to a prick like me. Thanks."

Wes twined our fingers and led me to the door as I called my goodbyes to GriffLo. We strolled to his home at a leisurely pace that belied my insufferable need to tear the clothes from his body.

With unexpected gallantry, Wes held the door open, allowing me to enter first. We stopped in the foyer, each taking measure of the other as if gauging whether we had the same goal in mind.

I licked my lips, impatient for his kiss.

Fuse, meet powder keg—boom!

My back was pressed against the wall and legs in the air before I knew what hit me. My t-shirt was whipped off and tossed aside, followed quickly by my favorite lace bra. Yoga pants were stretched to the limits as he tugged one leg free while keeping me levered against the wall. Too frantic to care, I left the other pant leg dangling comically from my ankle. It was lucky I hadn't bothered with panties because they would never have survived.

In less time than seemed humanly possible, Wes' pants were down and the condom secured. He didn't bother to check if I was ready as the answer was obvious. Entering me with one long, powerful stroke, I wiggled to adjust and assist his advance. A breath later, he was pounding into me with raw hunger, his merciless penetration just on the right side of pain.

I devoured his mouth, seeking more of him, wanting him in every part of me all at once. My orgasm built with swift ferocity. I clawed at his back, trying to find purchase to meet his thrusts with the same passionate force.

He chanted my name like a mantra, as if reminding himself I was real and not imagined.

My name on his lips was the last push needed to send me careening over the edge into an abyss of euphoria. I rode the waves of completion as his body tensed. A final thrust and he joined me in paradise, whispering my name one last time.

His arms supported me as he repositioned my body, carrying me with ease to his bed and tucking me under the covers. A few minutes later he joined me, nestling close as I fought the pull of sleep.

"What's happening with us is special. It won't last forever, but it's rare and undeniable. I can't make you any promises and I know you don't want them. Can we explore what we have until it runs its course? I'm not done with you—it will take more than a few nights to get you out of my system, and I'd like to enjoy that time without a predetermined expiration date we arbitrarily set for ourselves."

He was offering me the best of both worlds—life-affirming sex and companionship without the risk of expectations. I could surrender to his pull without guilt or regret.

"No expiration date sounds perfect. I will warn you that I'm moving when the semester finishes—I guess that's a deadline of sorts—but we'll probably be done long before then."

"You're moving out of Sam's? Why, is Griffin moving in?"

"No, Griff has his own house near Huntleigh's. When they move in together, Sam will most likely move in with him. It's just time for me to get my own place and stop mooching off of Sam," I answered with a version of the truth.

Wes looked skeptical, clearly trying to decipher the real reason for my move. *Dammit!* Why did I open my big mouth? I should have just smiled and said 'sounds perfect.' I didn't owe him a timeline.

"Are you planning to move into Hensley's resident apartments?"

"Heck no. They charge an arm and a leg for those. I found a studio off-campus for half the price when I started grad school," I said casually, still skirting the truth.

"Sam seems happy with your current arrangement. Why leave?" he probed.

Why, oh why, was I whatever-this-was with a lawyer—cross-examinations sucked!

"There are some issues that require my attention back home. I've been putting it off for a while, but it's time to deal with them. I'm taking a leave of absence from the Ph.D. program until I have it all sorted out."

"You're dropping out?" he asked, his shock evident. The reproach in his words prickled.

"No, I'm not *dropping out*—I'm taking a leave of absence. I'll finish my doctorate as soon as I'm able. If I can't come back to Hensley, there are other programs."

"If you quit now, you'll never finish. I've seen it happen a million times. What is so critical that you would waste all the time you invested and risk your future?"

"How dare you?" I answered angrily. "Just because you've screwed me a few times doesn't mean you get to question my life choices. You may know my body, but you don't know *me*. It doesn't matter how many times you make me scream your name, you have no idea what I will or will not do in the future—or what I'm capable of. I'm leaving," I announced as I rose from the bed. "Thank you for the orgasms, but as great as they were, they're not worth subjecting myself to your uninformed assumptions."

He followed me from the bed, scooting by me to block the exit.

"I want you, and I've enjoyed every one of the orgasms I've given you. Without a doubt, I know your body and I'd like to get to know it better. As hard as it is for you to believe, I also like *you*—independent of your body—which is why, despite the drama you just threw at me, I'm blocking you from leaving instead of pushing you out the door. Any other woman would have been history by now," he said earnestly. "You think I know nothing about you? I know your reaction is a result of your fear that I'm right. I know you evade questions you don't want to answer, which are any questions that skim below the surface. I know you wouldn't give up your studies unless the situation was dire, yet you're pretending whatever you're facing is nothing more than a minor inconvenience. I may be arrogant and self-centered, but I'm not ignorant or blind." His face softened as he continued in a gentle voice, "There's something magnetic about you, Meg. I've felt your pull since the first time I saw you, and I haven't been able to escape it since. I may not be your—or anyone's—forever guy, but for right now I'm yours. Whatever you're facing, I want to help. You don't have to lay it all out for me, but you have to open up a sliver...just a glimpse beneath the surface. That is, if you want what I'm offering."

"If only it were that simple...I don't want to lie to you or tell half-truths, but you have no clue what you're asking of me. You want me to flay myself open for you to poke and prod—would you do the same? What's beneath your surface? You promote the image of a shady attorney. You revel in your reputation as a self-centered asshole. You proudly declare your roguish, commitment-phobic lifestyle. Is that the real you? It may be in part, but I've seen another side, too. To gain access to my psyche, you'll have to return the favor."

I was certain he would shoot me down—the intent to dismiss my challenge was written on his face.

"Okay," he said with resignation. "Ask me anything."

It was an unexpected boon that I couldn't ignore. Unfortunately, I didn't know enough about him to target my questions for maximum potency. Instinct would have to guide me.

"Why are you a defense attorney? You describe yourself as a necessary evil and defended your ethics against Hunter and Griffin's assault. But based on the contempt with which you regard your clients, I can't imagine criminal defense was the specialty you intended."

"Of all the questions to ask, you pick the most challenging to answer. I should have known," he said with a melancholy smile. He led me to the bed where we sat side by side in silence.

"Where to begin? There is no simple answer so I'll have to explain the history," he said as he rose to pace.

"When I was young, my mom had an affair. It completely destroyed my father. Something in him broke that never healed. He was a great man; honorable, smart, and hard-working, which is why I still can't understand why she risked everything for a meaningless fling.

"My mom stuck around for a while and tried to make it work—for my sake, I guess—but our family was never the same. A couple years later, my dad was diagnosed with a severe case of multiple sclerosis. He never had a period of remission like some MS patients. It was a steady decline that was painful to watch, even in the early days. I guess Mom didn't love him—or me—enough to stick around when the going got tough. 'For better or worse, in sickness and in health' apparently didn't hold much weight for her. Not that I should have been surprised, since she'd already broken her vow of fidelity.

"Anyway, I was twelve when she left. Dad qualified for disability and social security, along with basic in-home services through Medicaid. They sent a nurse, who taught me everything I needed to know to take care of him, from how to properly assist him in and out of the wheelchair to how to administer his meds...she even taught me the proper way to bathe him when he could no longer manage it himself. Money was tight, but I learned to stretch a dollar and I kept us fed. By fifteen, I was more his nursemaid than his son. I worked my ass off in school to earn every scholarship imaginable and graduated high school at sixteen—my goal was to finish school and get a secure job with benefits ASAP. I worked my way through undergrad in three years and earned my JD from NYU by the time I was twenty-two. After acing the bar exam, I landed a position with the Suffolk County District Attorney's office and finally had proper insurance coverage. I petitioned the courts to have my father legally declared a dependent adult and then battled with the insurance company to have him instated on my plan. The coverage, along with my salary, allowed me to provide a better level of care for the last year of life. He passed away just after my twenty-fourth birthday."

I longed to comfort him but he shook his head, letting me know the story wasn't finished.

"I loved working in the DA's office and I was making a name for myself. My record of wins was unprecedented and my methods were aggressive. It didn't exactly endear me to my coworkers but they had to deal with me—I was too good to get rid of. I've never been a knight in shining armor—more like the dark knight caked in mud and gore—but I started out in the DA's office determined to prosecute criminals and protect the innocent. It was fulfilling and I had no plans to leave, however what I plan and what life throws my way are rarely one and the same.

"About a year after my dad died, my mom showed up out of the blue. I hadn't received so much as a birthday card in over ten years, yet there she stood telling me she'd been diagnosed with an aggressive form of breast cancer. Of course, she had no insurance, no money to her name, and no one to take care of her. She'd heard through the grapevine that Dad was gone and I was 'doing well for myself' and decided it was my duty to help her. She cried and offered a myriad of half-hearted apologies until I explained there was nothing I could do to help her. I couldn't fight for dependent status because she would never qualify, as she was still physically autonomous. The last of my dad's medical bills hadn't even been paid off at that point, so I certainly wasn't rolling in dough that I could loan her to live on. She eventually left, only to return six months later, knocking at death's door. There was a treatment the doctors swore would give her a chance, but Medicaid wouldn't cover it. God—I didn't want to let her in my life and I sure as shit didn't feel obligated to take care of her, but I couldn't *let* her die, knowing I had the power to prevent it. I may be a lot of things, but I wouldn't become a monster.

"I needed money—a lot of it and fast. My signing bonus with Cauldwell, Rueger & Stein, coupled with the correlating salary bump, provided the means I needed. The treatment saved her life, as promised, but it didn't cure her. She continued to be ravaged by the cancer, forcing me to put her in an assisted living facility last year. It's a nice place and they take care of her, but it's ridiculously expensive. The monthly fee is more than the mortgage on my townhouse.

"The financial burden keeps me with CRS, but at this point, I don't know where I would go if I left. The DA's office wouldn't want me after a stint on the 'dark side.' They barely tolerated me before—now I'm enemy number one."

He walked back to the bed and flopped on his back next to me. Sharing his story had been taxing—it was clear in the lines carved on his usually smooth face.

"You're a good man, Wes, despite your claims to the contrary. I can't imagine the struggles you faced as a child—the sacrifices you made for your Dad. And what you did for your mom...no one would have faulted you for slamming the door in her face," I shared, awed by the man and all his story revealed.

So much lay beneath the polished veneer that appeared untouchable and immune to emotion. He let the world believe he was callous and unscrupulous because he didn't give a damn what people thought of him—and perhaps because a part of him wanted to be impenetrable. It was easier to allow others to believe the worst instead of fighting to prove otherwise, exposing a vulnerability to friends and enemies alike.

He was the antithesis of every man I'd ever met—good or bad. A rare breed that was content to play the antihero while hiding a river of nobility so pure it cleansed his soul of the filth that surrounded him.

Today I learned the truth about Westly Black.

He was a liar and a deceiver, masquerading as something other than himself, because the veiled reality was...

Wes.

Was.

Good.

Chapter 15

"The truth is rarely pure and never simple."
-Oscar Wilde

<u>Westly</u>

Sharing my past with Meg hadn't been as difficult as I'd expected. It was unpleasant and mildly embarrassing—after all, who wanted to admit their own mother didn't want them...or that they 'sold out' for the same derelict's benefit? Can you say *chump*?

Opening the vein was an acceptable price, however, if Meg would reveal a fraction of herself in return.

"Quid pro quo," I prompted, earning me an exasperated breath.

"This is so unfair," she griped, "your deep dark secret is that you are essentially good."

She averted her eyes, but not quickly enough. The trepidation and sorrow glowed like high beams on a moonless night. Whatever she was hiding was the source of deep shame. Did she worry her confession would change the way I perceived her? There wasn't anything she could tell me that would make me send her away. I was prepared to tell her as much when she finally spoke.

"I ran away from my family on my eighteenth birthday. I won't say 'home,' since it never was, and the specifics of what drove me to leave are immaterial. All that matters is that it wasn't a healthy environment, so I fled. With no money and only one friend thousands of miles away, I was completely alone and petrified. I knew they would look for me, and if they found me I'd be brought back. Luckily, a good Samaritan took pity on me and helped me reach my old friend, Jay, without discovery. Jay took me in for a few months and helped me find my footing. He managed to— and I'm invoking attorney-client privilege for this part— buy me a new identity and establish a history. Everything about me is based on a lie...my name, social security number, school records, employment history—all of it. I'm a liar and a fraud."

The disgrace emanating from her whole being was heartbreaking. She may have broken the law by purchasing a false identity, but she wasn't using it to plunder someone's bank account. Something forced her into hiding, the new identity a necessary evil to ensure she remained hidden and untraceable. However, none of this explained the level of shame she was displaying. I held my questions, hoping she would continue.

"I worked off the books as a waitress, saving every penny. Jay wanted me to stay, promising to protect me, but my family knew of him. Eventually they would make the connection and find me with him. When I left, he gave me Bessie—my car—and a pay-as-you-go phone. All he asked in return for his help was that I call him if I ever found myself in trouble.

"I slept in my car until I reached New York and then stayed in shelters most nights. I found another waitressing job and continued to save money while I established residency in New York under my assumed identity. After a year, I applied to community college and attended classes around my work schedule. Two years later, I earned my associate's degree and transferred to Hensley University to complete my bachelor's. On-campus housing was crazy expensive so I found a tiny studio and lived alone, working every minute I wasn't in school to pay tuition and rent. One of my sociology professors championed me and helped me obtain grants for Hensley's Ph.D. program, which allowed me to work only one job while in school.

"Ev stole me away from the campus coffee shop to work for her at Higher Yearning, which is how I got to know Sam, Griffin, and Hunter. You know Sam was nearly kidnapped, I presume? Well, they kind of adopted me into their ragtag family after the shooting. Everything has been fantastic—the best time of my life—but I can't stay past the end of the year. It's time to move on.

"So now you know. The only other people who know that much about me—besides Jay—are Sam, and Ev, who dragged the truth from me with the assistance of Captain Morgan—he's a relentless interrogator, that one. I haven't even told Griffin or Hunter, although I'd be naïve to assume the girls didn't spill at least some of my story. Please— *please*—don't say anything to them about my leaving. I'll tell them when the time is right. I don't want to spend the time I have left fighting with them about the inevitable, and I *definitely* don't want them trying to wade in and 'fix' my messes," she implored with so much desperation it stole my breath.

I was certain there were huge pieces to her story that had been omitted, not the least of which was what had driven her to run away. However, it was abundantly clear that she would not delve into the subject and now was not the time to push for more. If I did, she would run and never look back.

Her struggle to survive as a young woman, alone without resources, sent chills down my spine. No doubt the simple, sanitized account she gave me bypassed countless precarious situations. I prayed nothing horrible had happened during those years, especially the ones spent homeless and living in shelters.

As I replayed her story in my mind, all I could think was...*how the hell did she do it?* How did she not only survive but thrive? She accomplished more than most, even though the deck was stacked so heavily against her it was a miracle she could stand upright. Which led me to two nagging questions that had to be asked.

"I have two questions, if that's okay—then I'll distract you from the past," I teased, hoping to reduce the tension in the room.

She gave me a stiff nod, reluctant but willing.

"Clearly something was wrong with your family situation, and it wasn't safe or healthy. You made the right choice—the only choice—by leaving. So why do you seem ashamed about leaving?" I asked bluntly. We were both naked, physically and emotionally, at the moment. Being anything other than direct was insulting.

She didn't respond immediately, obviously debating if she would answer and weighing her words.

"I wasn't the only person living in the unsafe and unhealthy environment. When I ran, I did so alone because it was the only way to gain my freedom. I left the others behind and the guilt gnaws at me. What's worse, after all this time I never returned for them. I can think of a thousand excuses for why I haven't returned, but that is all they are...excuses. You want to know why I look ashamed?" she asked, clutching her hand to her chest, eyes filled with sorrow. "Because I am a selfish coward. I hate myself for abandoning them."

It was worse than I'd feared, both the situation she ran from and the guilt she carried. It would be difficult to dissuade her without details, but I couldn't let her continue on her path of self-loathing. It was a painful road that could take you so far from yourself you may never find your way back.

"Obviously I don't know specifics; hear me out anyway. From what I gather, you left alone because you *couldn't* bring the others with you—not because you didn't want to bring them—correct?"

She nodded her agreement.

"You've been hiding out of fear for seven years, that's how bad the situation is with your family. If you returned for the others, is there any chance you would succeed?"

She shook her head in the negative, averting her eyes from mine.

"Did you ever contact anyone to intervene after you left...police, social services, whomever would be appropriate?"

"Yes, it was the first thing I did after leaving. I called the sheriff's office. I also told the social worker that helped me leave town."

"Then, Meg, you've done everything you could possibly do. Even if you sacrificed yourself, the odds that you would succeed in helping them are slim to none. You have nothing to be ashamed of. I know you don't believe me, but you need to find a way to let go of your guilt. It's not justified and it's eating you alive."

She nodded, not in agreement but to confirm she heard me. My words would not be enough to unravel the knot of emotions strangling her. She needed to find the truth herself—to see herself clearly.

"Second question—"

"You just asked me about ten questions, buddy," she interrupted with the first glimmer of humor I'd seen in the last hour.

"No, I asked question one, you answered, and the subsequent questions were riders."

"Such a lawyer," she muttered before regally waving her hand, granting me permission to continue.

"Second question...why do you have to leave by the end of the year? What's changed?"

She looked away again, unwilling to answer.

"Meg, please answer me. I swear on my life I will not repeat a word you say to anyone—ever. You can't keep everything bottled inside indefinitely. Life will shake you up and then you'll explode like a can of Coke you didn't know had been dropped just before opening. Please."

I waited for-*fucking*-ever while she debated if she would answer.

"They've found me," she said, barely above a whisper.

"What?" I asked with forced calmness.

"I received an email in my student account a few hours before I ran into you at The Stop. Somehow they figured out I'm at Hensley. Don't ask me how...I have no clue. If they don't know exactly where I am, they will soon. I spoke to Jay and he agreed that they would probably hold off for a little while to give me a chance to return home willingly. If I don't, they'll come here to find me. I can't let that happen, so I have to leave before they arrive."

I tried to wrap my brain around the fact that she glossed over this *very* pertinent detail. What else had she left out? Was her life in jeopardy, or was it a matter of an overzealous family that had stifled a young girl to the point she bolted? I couldn't see the big picture with so many pieces of the puzzle missing.

"How can you be sure you have until the end of the year?" I asked. It was one of the missing pieces that nagged at me.

"I can't, it's an educated guess. I'm positive I have a few weeks before their patience runs out...beyond that I can't be certain. It's a gamble, but I'd like to finish the semester and arrange the leave of absence so I have the possibility of returning or transferring. I'd also like to celebrate the holidays with everyone—one last memory to take with me."

The idea of her leaving didn't sit well. Our time together shouldn't have to end until we were both ready. And if the concern I felt for her was any indication, I would need more than a couple of months before I could stand to let her go.

"There has to be another way," I said futilely.

"There isn't. I can't be here when they arrive and pull everyone else into my mess. It wouldn't be fair to them."

"I'm sure everyone—myself included—would be happy to help, no matter what the mess."

"But I don't *want* help. Not if it means all of you being compromised. And don't even think about going behind my back to enlist anyone else. You promised."

The situation was more than a mess, it was a shitstorm—the aftermath of a category five hurricane. With no means to right the wreckage at the moment, only one question remained. Though I had more than exceeded my allotment, I hoped she would answer.

"What's your name? Your real one."

"I can't answer that."

I didn't like it, but I accepted her answer in light of everything else she'd given me tonight.

"Come here," I said, pulling her closer, needing to hold her. "I want to tell you it will be okay, but I might be lying."

"Don't lie to me, Wes...don't ever lie to me," she whispered fervently. As her body finally relaxed against mine, she accepted the comfort I offered freely. "It will be what it will be. For now, let's stick to the plan and enjoy our time together. Nothing in life is guaranteed. You may wake up in the morning and decide you're done with me. All we can do is live in the moment and treasure what we *do* have, not focus on what we don't or may never have."

Her advice was sound; I wish I could take it. Despite agreeing to our plan for no-strings fun, I was feeling the threads securing themselves. It wasn't a completely unpleasant feeling, but it was entirely unfamiliar. After countless women, faces, and bodies I could barely remember and names I never bothered to learn, this desire to *know* her was disconcerting yet undeniable. Reminding myself of our arrangement didn't help—our pact now sounded shallow and jaded. A quiet voice in the recesses of my mind—the one I rarely listened to—was cautioning me to do something, to intervene despite my promise.

I needed time to work through the quagmire and find a solution that satisfied all parties involved, and that wasn't going to happen tonight. With Meg—ugh, I hated calling her that now that I knew it was a lie. With my beautiful girl lying in my arms, I let go of everything else and held on to her.

Chapter 16

"God grant me the serenity to accept the people I cannot change, the courage to change the one I can, and the wisdom to know it's me." -Author Unknown

<u>Meg</u>

Four weeks had passed since the night Wes and I exchanged pieces of our souls—even in my head that sounded cheesy, but there was no truer way to describe what we'd shared. When I awoke the next morning still wrapped in his embrace, he made love to me with a tender sincerity that changed everything I'd ever learned about sex. Gone was the fierce lover who claimed my body as his prize. In his place was a man who used his body to tell me I mattered...to him I was valuable. Even amongst my friends there was a part of me that questioned what I brought to the table. Wes convinced me without words that when I was gone, he would remember me and never be the same man for having met me. It was the start of an undefined relationship, not labeled or qualified. Because we didn't need classification...we only needed each other for as long as we had.

In the weeks that followed, we hoarded time, spending every free moment together since time was a commodity in short supply. Wes understood that I needed to be with GriffLo and Huntleigh as much as I did him, and because he cared, he ensured I got what I needed. He appointed himself the group's unofficial social director, a strange role for 'the new guy' to claim, but his position went unchallenged. Group texts were sent to establish dinner dates, hang-out sessions at The Stop, and he even went so far as to plan elaborate outings involving the use of his company's skybox for a NY Giants game. If anyone questioned the increased frequency of organized 'group time,' they never said a word.

'We were a family, and families spent time together whenever possible,' Sam said. 'There will be points in our lives where it's hard to wrangle everyone into the same place on a regular basis. Life gets crazy and we're all pulled in a thousand different directions, so when that bitch cooperates, we take advantage.'

On his mission to help me collect as many memories as possible, Wes found himself the sixth 'orphan' adopted into the clan. Watching him bond with the guys—a ritual that centered around sports games and teasing us girls—was a highlight of many of my days. Thanks to our heart-to-heart, I was able to see how much these new bonds meant to him and how desperately he needed to feel connected. Like the rest of us, he needed a family.

Some of the funniest moments arose while I watched him experience Ev and Sam unfiltered. For a man who had encountered his fair share of female attention, he was surprisingly surprised by their antics, often finding himself at a loss for words. The first time Sam overshared about an impromptu sexploit her and Griffin had engaged in earlier in the day, Wes was left choking on his ill-timed sip of wine. He learned an important lesson the rest of us had mastered: do *not* consume beverages while Sam is speaking. You never knew what she might say next.

After a few weeks—and as his comfort with the group grew—he began to wade into debates with Ev and Hunter, often taking the point, leaving both uber-competitive debate connoisseurs beside themselves. For that feat alone, he'd found a lifelong brother in Griffin.

In the evenings, we found our way back to his bed, where we would make love like it was the last time before cuddling and talking about everything and nothing...just being together. Despite my best efforts, I was falling for Wes. I saw what very few were permitted to see because he had given me the magic decoder ring, and each night another tiny piece was revealed.

He continued to question me about my past and what my plans were for the future, but he never pushed me when I redirected the conversation. The only time we fought was when he pressured me for my real name. It was the same conversation each time.

"Beautiful, what's your real name?" he'd ask. He hadn't called me Meg since I told him it wasn't my name.

"I can't tell you that," I'd reply, time and time again.

"Why not? What are you afraid I'll do...track down your family?"

"No, I trust you not to do something as harebrained as that. I just can't tell you. I wish I could, really I do. You can ask a thousand times a day and my answer won't change," I'd patiently explain.

Frustrated, he would retreat to his home office for a little while to work, and when he returned, the strife was forgotten. But even these exchanges endeared him to me. They were evidence that he cared and it bothered him to have anything between us.

Every moment of that month—when past and future were held at bay and there was only now—my life was idyllic. I could almost pretend it would go on forever, this deep sense of happiness and belonging. However, like so many hard-learned lessons, the past intruded to remind me this joy wasn't my destiny.

It was a typical Wednesday morning, shortly after returning from Wes', when I logged into my email to verify the appointment time for a meeting with my graduate advisor. The email awaiting me was one I'd been dreading but was certain would come. Bile climbed my throat, burning my tongue, as I fought the reflexive gag. I needed more time...I was supposed to have more time. *Dammit!* I wasn't ready to leave them...I wasn't ready to leave him.

My terror mounted by the second until it was hard to breathe or think. *Get a grip,* I commanded myself. This was not the time to fall apart. I had to confront my fate, regardless of how much I dreaded it. A sip of water helped clear the bitterness from my mouth, and I counted breaths until they became slow and steady. Under control and braced for what was to come, my finger hovered hesitantly over the touchpad before finally opening the message. Immediately, I wished I could unsee its warning.

There was something diabolically effective about the single word communications, as if the point were so profound no other words were necessary. The word this time: *punishment.* I realized that Jay and I had been correct—they had been waiting for me to return. I also believed this message was meant as a scare tactic to force me back, a final warning before they took action. Thankfully, I had a little more time.

Tomorrow was Thanksgiving and my finals would be completed in two weeks, officially marking the end of the semester. I knew in my bones they wouldn't come for me for several weeks, maybe even a month. I had to plan for the worst and hope for the best. During my meeting today with Dr. Mesina, I would petition for the leave of absence and file the necessary paperwork. After Thanksgiving, I would tell everyone I had to return home after my finals ended to take care of some issues. It was still up in the air if I should leave immediately following the tests or push my luck and stay for Christmas. I had a little time left to decide so I pushed the question from my mind, needing to focus on my current objectives.

Parking in the lot adjacent to the sociology building was exceptionally easy with no classes in progress, courtesy of the holiday break. I hustled into the building and navigated the corridors until I reached Dr. Mesina's office door. Her voice beckoned me in and I sat down, making myself comfortable in a plush armchair.

Dr. Mesina was a stunning woman, and while her age was likely in the low-fifties, she didn't look a day over forty. She was always stylishly dressed in designer labels and accessorized to perfection. I believed her husband was in commercial real estate, and from the looks of it, business was good. I didn't value material possessions—as I'd never had many—but her wardrobe and top-dollar haircut were enough to cause a fleeting pang of longing for such luxuries.

After slipping her reading glasses from her nose, she looked at me with a somber expression. To say I didn't get the warm fuzzies from that look would be an understatement.

"Meg, we need to talk. Some information has been brought to my attention in regards to the veracity of the case studies and interview data you've used to support your doctoral thesis. It doesn't look good. Not only is your thesis contingent upon your cited evidentiary documentation, the implication that you falsified or manufactured witness interviews to support your position is grounds for expulsion from the program.

"We've known each other for nearly four years, and despite the evidence provided to me, I find it hard to believe you created false reports just to further your thesis. I'm going to give you a chance to explain, but before you begin, I will tell you what I still tell my children to this day: don't even think about lying to me. I can handle the truth, but deception or omission will earn severe consequences because a) you lacked the integrity to admit your mistake and b) you are disrespecting me with the assumption that I can't discern the truth. Remember, I'm older and wiser...there is nothing you could do or think of doing that I haven't already done, considered, or witnessed. Now, is there anything you want to tell me?"

Her eyes bored into mine, urging me to tell the truth, the whole truth, and nothing but the truth.

Cornered, I could either throw away my years of education and refuse to answer, or I could risk sharing the truth with my professional idol. I would like to say it was an easy decision, but my integrity came at a very high cost.

"I'm presuming the document in question is a witness statement and interview from the Oregon assessment—specifically, witness number seven," I clarified.

"It is. There was also a minor discrepancy in a correlating witness statement from field personnel in the Oregon office," she confirmed.

"Witness statement number seven isn't manufactured, it is one-hundred-percent authentic—the problem is in my documentation, Dr. Mesina," I began but was forced to stop when my throat fisted closed and tears stung my eyes. I cleared my throat and blinked rapidly before trying again. "Dr. Mesina, witness statement and interview number seven are mine. She, the subject, is me. I confess that I withheld this fact, but not because it's a lie. I didn't document and appropriately source the report *because* it is the truth. I didn't want anyone to know. I'll admit it is one of the key documents referenced in my thesis, but the arguments presented would stand without the inclusion of the statement."

"Then why include it?" she interrupted.

"Because it is a truth that deserves to be shared. Because it is the best and most comprehensive illustration of my thesis that exists. I didn't choose the document to support my thesis. I chose the thesis because I lived what was in the document. My passion for sociology and particularly my specialty of study stems from my own experience. I knew I was treading in a gray area by not disclosing that I am a case in point—that my personal story was being used to support my positions. But isn't that true of most theses? Everyone is a product of their environment and the arguments they make will be shaped by personal experience. We all strive for impartiality, but it is impossible to be completely detached from our own unique points of view. It's not unheard of for a sociologist or anthropologist to immerse themselves in their field of study to better understand their subject and clarify their arguments and theories. What I did was no different. I know I should have disclosed my direct connection to the citations, but can you understand my position? In my shoes, would you want to expose yourself in that way to your colleagues and in journals? I don't want to change my field of study, Dr. Mesina. I believe in the research I'm doing and that my findings will be instrumental in developing new programs that are desperately needed. However, if the cost is parading myself before a panel of my peers and publically declaring myself— I don't think I'm strong enough to do it."

She was silent for a long time in contemplation.

"And the secondary document?"

"The only alteration of the field statement was the removal of my name. You can contact the office and speak directly to the witness to verify everything I'm telling you."

Dr. Mesina steepled her hands and studied me intently.

"This is a very complex issue, Meg. I need to think about it further and consider the ramifications of allowing you to continue drafting and ultimately defending your thesis as it currently stands. I may choose to consult with others in the department, but I will not breach your confidence and disclose that the statement is yours personally. You've bent the rules to the brink of breaking, but technically, I don't think you have violated any part of the school's honor code. As such, you will not be expelled, but we will meet after the holidays to discuss how to proceed with your thesis. Agreed?"

"Umm..." I faltered. "For the most part, yes, I agree, and thank you. However, I was hoping you would support me in taking a leave of absence."

If not for the seriousness of the request, her look of shock would have been comical. Clearly, my request was unexpected.

"For how long?"

"I'm not sure," I said, squirming uncomfortably.

"Even without the outstanding issue of your thesis, you have to know I can't support your petition without just cause. This is one of the premier graduate programs in the country and you have substantial grant assistance that would be held for you. Unless you can provide me with a persuasive reason, I can't justify preventing another student in need of grant assistance."

Nothing was ever easy. *No-thing*.

"They've found me...my family," I started to explain but paused at Dr. Mesina's gasp. All I could do was nod in agreement. "Since you've read my witness statement and interview, you understand the implications. I've received email messages to my student account from them, warning me to return or face the consequences. I have a few weeks— at most—before they come here in search of me. I should be able to finish my finals, but after that...I have to leave here for a time. I can't let them find me, especially not here. I have no idea how th—"

"The FBI. That's how they found you. When your thesis went before the review board for preliminary assessment, several professors raised concerns about the implications of the university sitting on these statements until you publish. To be frank, I have to agree. I understand you contacted local law enforcement when you first left, but given the relationship to your family, it was ineffectual.

Someone from the professorial panel must have tipped off the FBI and provided a copy of your thesis. I didn't know. It wasn't until Monday that they contacted me with questions regarding the accuracy of the documents provided. That is how I found out there were discrepancies. I'm so sorry, Meg. You should have been advised, but no one could have imagined *you* were one of the subjects and therefore at risk."

She gazed out the window, lost in thought for so long I began counting ceiling tiles.

"I'm going to remove the ridiculous hat they make us wear at graduation and don my 'mom hat' instead, okay?"

I nodded.

"I'm concerned for you, Meg—for several reasons. You are taking a big risk remaining near campus to finish your finals. Furthermore, the likelihood of you ever finishing your studies are infinitesimal if you're on the run. If you were my child, I would tell you it's time to stand and fight. You've been evading and hiding too long, and even if you are able to slip away from them again, it's only a matter of time until they catch up to you. The FBI is already curious. I'm certain they would be interested in hearing what you have to say."

"I'll think about it," I promised. "I've been so focused on surviving for the past seven years, it's difficult to imagine anything other than running."

"I will support your leave of absence for a period of one year, should you decide to go. However, if you decide to stay, I have a proposition for you. Other than the immediate danger, my primary concern is your well-being. What you have lived through and subsequently endured after escaping has shaped you, as it would anyone. In many ways, you are probably stronger and more resilient than ninety percent of the population. But there are scars too, I'm sure. The fact that you are willing to jeopardize years of hard work and your entire scholastic career to prevent the truth from being revealed...that is not healthy. You can't thrive if you are closed off from the rest of the world, hiding who you truly are."

It was my turn to stare out the window, swallowing the pain her words inflicted, primarily because of the truth they held. I was beginning to understand how stilted my perception was, largely as a result of my confession to Wes and his concern for me.

"Here is the deal," she continued when I offered no response. "If you begin seeing a therapist immediately, speak with the FBI, and remain at Hensley, I will pledge my support in every way possible. I'll personally defend the continuation of your thesis as it was submitted and assist you in implementing your paradigm in cooperation with the FBI and possibly the CIA, as I believe your work has global applications that would interest both organizations. I'll stand by your side and deploy all of my professional and personal resources to make your goals a reality. I believe in your work, Meg. You are brilliant and insightful, yet it's your intuition and ability to empathize based on your experiences that will make your model a success."

Overwhelming gratitude engulfed me.

"I don't know what to say."

"Say yes. If you leave, you'll never stop running. If you stay, you'll have a chance to live," she said, reducing my disastrous life and difficult decision to a very simple either/or statement.

Unbidden, Wes' face flashed through my mind. If I stayed, I would have more time with him. If I ran, there would be no more treasured moments with Sam, Ev, Griffin, and Hunter. If I remained, I could pursue my career goals with the support of Dr. Mesina. If I left, I could probably kiss all of my hard work goodbye. If I fought, I might be able to help the ones I left behind and countless others. If I disappeared, I would be helping no one but myself.

"Okay. Yes! I'm going to stay. I'm going to stand and fight, like you said. I'm going to fight for myself and the others, and I'm going to prevent anyone else from suffering," I declared, scared but more alive than I had ever felt outside of Wes' arms.

"Good! I'm proud of you, Meg."

Reaching into her desk drawer, she pulled out a business card and handed it to me.

"Dr. Cynthia Veritus is the therapist I want you to see. Call and make an appointment ASAP. She's a professor here in the psychology department, but she also has a private practice. I'll call her too, to let her know she should be expecting your call and make sure she knows she's donating her time...she owes me a favor."

I looked down at the card and blinked.

"Um, Dr. Mesina, there's just one problem."

"What is it, dear?"

"I know Thia...socially. I've played poker with her," I added to make sure my level of familiarity was crystal clear.

In a day full of surprises, I should have anticipated her answer.

"Even better! Call her when you get home. Now scoot. I have to get home and make sure my husband remembered to pull the turkey out of the freezer last night. Otherwise, he's the one who's going out to scour the island for thirty pounds of turkey that's not frozen."

"A kiss is a lovely trick designed by nature to stop speech when words become superfluous." -Ingrid Bergman

Meg

Filled with a new hope for my future, I exited the sociology building and walked to my car. Eager to share my news with Wes but knowing what I needed to do first, I hurried back to Sam's to phone Thia, a call I was less than eager to make. I liked Thia—a lot, actually. She came over for dinner once and soon after joined the guys for a monthly poker tournament. Occasionally, the rest of us girls would participate, but the guys were vicious competitors with no mercy, even for their women. The best player of the bunch, however, was Thia—the woman was cutthroat once the chips were on the table. It was this social relationship that made me hesitant to see Thia professionally. Sam still visited her as needed for 'maintenance,' but their professional relationship preceded their friendship. Regardless, if my chance at personal happiness and scholastic success was contingent upon spilling my guts at her office, nothing would stop me.

The house was empty when I arrived, providing much-needed privacy for my call. Ripping the bandage off as quickly as possible, I grabbed the portable phone and plopped on the couch. Expecting to leave a message, I was startled when she answered on the first ring.

"Meg, I'm so glad you called. You can't imagine how long I've been wanting to get my hands on you. Frankly, my patience was running out. I told Sam if she didn't make it happen sooner rather than later, I would be forced to initiate guerilla tactics. Had I known Dr. Mesina was the key to success, you'd have been straightened out months ago."

"Umm, hi, Thia," I said stupidly, at a loss for words. Was I so transparent that she'd identified my need for help over a few shared meals? Furthermore, was my need for intervention so substantial that my friends would plot behind my back? I was unsettled and embarrassed.

"Get out of your head, Meg. We all care about you, and to answer the question you've yet to ask directly—yes, it was obvious you need someone to talk to. You're not wearing a neon sign that screams 'dysfunctional,' but the frequency with which you evade all conversations focused on you is concerning. You're also a terrible liar, and when pushed for personal details, you lie...poorly. It's part of the reason why you're crap at poker....you can't bluff worth a damn."

"Oh," was my even stupider reply. Knowing she'd been *studying* me for several months was unnerving. What other insights had she ascertained while analyzing me?

"Going to have to do better than 'oh' when you come to the office on Monday at eleven. Well, it was lovely talking with you—so glad you called. Happy Thanksgiving to you all and I'll see you in a couple days. Bye."

Before I had the chance to form a single coherent thought, Thia had hung up.

What the hell just happened? I felt like I'd just stepped off a tilt-a-whirl ride—slightly nauseous and completely out-of-sorts. The sessions with Thia would either prove to be the best thing ever in terms of moving forward and building a life, or the time might turn out to be a giant waste, like the money spent on a ride that made you pray for death then puke.

I walked over to Wes' house, ringing the bell and knocking impatiently, excited to tell him my decision.

The door swung open, revealing a defined chest and lickable abdominals. My excitement was replaced with crippling lust, which drove me to grab him and pay for the show with a kiss that left no doubt as to the naughty thoughts he'd inspired. When I finally pulled back, Wes' smile stole my already thready breath.

"If this is the standard response, I will remember to remove my shirt before opening the door from here on out."

"The thin cotton sleep pants aren't hurting matters either," I encouraged.

"Duly noted. How are you, beautiful? Did the meeting with your advisor go well?" he asked, sounding genuinely interested in my reply.

"That's what I was so excited to tell you...before *you* got me all excited. Come on, let's sit down and I'll tell you everything."

He led the way to the great room, where we snuggled close on the couch. The hope that had begun to take root after my meeting with Dr. Mesina blossomed in the warmth of Wes' arms. I would have been content to remain silent, savoring the moment, but Wes' interest was piqued.

"Tell me everything."

"Okay. After discussing some minor concerns she had about my thesis—no big deal, by the way—I asked her to support my petition for a leave of absence. Needless to say, she was not pleased. She pushed me for my reasons and I explained that my family was searching for me and close to discovering my whereabouts, and that I didn't want to be found. Understandably upset by my disclosure, she encouraged me to contact local law enforcement if I was concerned for my safety. When I hesitated, she promised to throw the full weight of her professional standing behind my thesis, help me publish, and ultimately assist in finding ways to implement my research if I stayed. It was very persuasive and an amazing opportunity."

"Did you accept?"

"Not right away. She also asked if there was any other reason I could think of that would be worth the risk of standing to fight for my independence," I said cautiously.

"What did you tell her?" he asked, squeezing me tighter against his chest.

"I told her there was a man who I would regret leaving behind—that my time with him hadn't run its course, and my fear of staying wasn't as strong as my desire to be with him," I said, stretching the truth slightly about my conversation with Dr. Mesina but not my feelings.

"Are you saying what I think you're saying?" he asked in a tone I couldn't decipher.

Was he ready to be rid of me and didn't want to hurt my feelings, or was he containing his delight until I provided confirmation?

"If you think I'm saying that I'm staying, then...yes."

There was a long pause and my patience had run dry.

"Well? Aren't you going to say anything? If you're ready to end things, just say so. It's not like you're the *only* reason I'm staying. There's Sam, Ev, Griffin, and Hunter. Not to mention, the implications for my professional goals," I said, growing more agitated with each word.

When he laughed, I had no choice but to dig my elbow deep into his rib cage, causing him to grunt in pain. Good—he had it coming! Wrestling my arm away from his tender side, he rolled us until I was pinned beneath the heavy mass of his hard body, preventing any further assaults. My anger receded with the tender expression staring down at me. He placed a chaste kiss on my lips before finally speaking.

"Nothing would make me happier, beautiful. I've been keeping a 'how to make her stay' list for a while now. You don't want to know some of the desperate and depraved ideas I've considered to keep you with me," he teased before kissing the tip of my nose. "I'm not ready for us to end yet. I may never be. I still can't promise you forever—people change their minds every day. I'm sorry to say that my mom is living proof of that. But if how I feel now is any indication, you may grow tired of me long before I grow weary of you."

I had never experienced love in any form before meeting Sam and Ev, and what they gave was the love of both friends and sisters. Griffin and Hunter soon followed, offering me the love of brothers. In return, I loved each with my whole heart. Thanks to them, I had finally experienced what it was to love and be loved in return through the bond of family.

What I felt for Wes was different. I didn't know if it was love, because it was unlike what I felt for Huntleigh and GriffLo. There was a depth of emotion and desire to be with him that was so strong I was overwhelmed at times. I thought of him all the time...did I tell Wes this? What would Wes think of that? What is Wes up to? I wonder if Wes will do that thing with his tongue tonight? It never ended. I never wanted it to end. Was that love, the type with a capital 'L'? I didn't know. If I were *in* love, would I even have to ask? It seemed to me that love would be an undeniable, all-encompassing feeling that left no shadow of doubt.

Perhaps what I was feeling was the seeds of love or its first bud.

I wanted to deny the possibility, because Wes had been clear from the start that love was not on the table and never would be. I'd made a pact with him to never seek a commitment, and it would be unfair to change the rules this late in the game. Therefore, I was going to have to contain the burgeoning feelings and keep my emotions in the box where they belonged. Whatever Wes was able to give me was more than I'd ever expected, wanted, or deserved. I would be content and never ask for more than he offered.

"Are you going to leave me hanging?" Wes asked, his eyebrow raised in playful warning.

Evidently, I had been lost in thought longer than I realized.

"No, I'm going to do this..." With no further warning, I showed him with my body what I felt in my heart. I didn't need words or clearly defined emotions, I just needed him inside me in every way possible. His touch reached through my skin and sinew until it found the very essence of my being—a soul-deep contact that inflamed my mind, body, and heart until I was a blazing inferno that only he could contain or quench.

"I need you, Wes—please—take me, take it all," I begged, overwrought with emotion.

Heeding my plea, he efficiently divested us both of our clothes, leaving them strewn across the floor. Moments later, he slid inside me, my body offering no resistance, only welcoming acceptance. His strokes were measured, intended to build a gradual climb we could savor. The unhurried pace allowed us to hold one another instead of clinging frantically. Our kisses were long and searching, a slow exploration executed with finesse and passion. I trailed my fingertips down his back in reverence, cherishing the response of this man who had grown to mean so much to me.

We lost track of time, or perhaps it no longer existed when two souls left their shells to fuse as one. I never wanted the clock to resume its countdown, unable to let go of the profound connection we were establishing. Yet like a sunset in all its splendor, the end was inevitable.

"Come for me, beautiful—don't make me fall alone," Wes whispered urgently against my lips.

Together we fell—eyes locked, bodies entwined. It was one of life's rare moments of perfection.

"I have something for you," Wes said after a few minutes in comfortable silence. "Provided I can find the will to get up, that is."

There was nothing I wanted or needed more than to be wrapped in his arms, but I withheld my protests when he rose from the couch. He headed into the kitchen and returned with his hands behind his back. My curiosity stirred.

"Some people like a cigarette after..." he trailed off, perhaps having the same difficulty I was with calling what we'd just shared 'sex.' "I thought this was more appropriate for you."

In his hands was a Costco-size case of my favorite dark chocolate with sea salt. It was a gift that said, *'I know you and I think about you when you're not with me.'*

He pulled a bar from the box and handed it to me with feigned solemnity and ceremony. Laughing, I tore into the package and popped a square in my mouth. *Mmmm, so damn good.* He was right, it was the perfect post-whatever-that-was treat.

"That's a lot of chocolate you have there, Black," I teased playfully.

"I figured I should have a supply here to keep you from running home in the mornings to get your fix."

Wow! That was just...wow.

"Thank you, Wes. It's the perfect gift. I feel bad I didn't get you anything."

He paused, lost in thought.

"What's your real name, beautiful?" he asked with a quiet vulnerability.

"I wish I could tell you—really I do—but I can't answer that question."

He nodded sadly and returned to the kitchen. I had hurt him with my denial after what we had just shared. I wanted to tell him—to explain—but his question opened a can of worms I wasn't ready to confront. A quiet voice in the recesses of my brain cautioned that I had once again chosen poorly, allowing my fears and regrets to silence me. All I could do was hope that the cost of my mistake wasn't more than I could afford to pay.

Chapter 18

*"Hearts will never be practical until they are
made unbreakable." -Wizard of Oz*

Westly

I woke Thanksgiving morning holding the woman that had
me tied me up in knots. There were no strings in our
arrangement—no, these were nautical-grade ropes wound
in complex loops that only the most seasoned salty dogs
could tie. Instead of waning, my desire for her grew each
day, and it was more than just her body and its siren's call
that beckoned me to ruin—it was all of her. Knowing the
danger, I continued to sail straight into the rocky shoreline
where destruction lay in wait.

I was a fool to continue on the current course. She was
hiding something from me, not the least of which was her
name. More than a month had passed where we'd shared
my bed nearly every night. If I wasn't at work, I was with
her or on my way to her. She invaded my thoughts during
the day and starred in my dreams every night. There was
no doubt I was becoming addicted to her, dependent on her
smiles, laughter, and climax to find the same for myself. I
should be paralyzed with fear at the myriad emotions she
inspired, yet I welcomed them, certain my growing

attachment mirrored her own. If not for the secrets she was resolutely withholding, I would be tempted to classify what we shared and the emotions it invoked.

But the secrets were there, taunting me with the knowledge of all I didn't know.

My frustration had not been enough to discourage me from her or accepting anything she was willing to give. I'd promised myself I would allow her more time to reveal what was behind the curtain; I would be patient because the pull between us was too strong for her to resist eventual surrender. However, her refusal last night struck a blow that still stung. After what we'd shared—what the hell do you even call what passed between us last night?—after giving more of myself to her than any other woman, her wall remained firmly in place, which was unbearable and mildly insulting.

Still, with the exception of the secret-colored elephant in the room, everything about her was everything I never knew I wanted—or needed. I would yield for a few more weeks before renting a wrecking ball and backhoe to demolish the motherfucker separating me from all of her.

Smiling at the thought, I slipped my hand into the nightstand to grab her morning chocolate. Another example of this beautiful girl's perfection...her morning addiction didn't require me to get out of bed to satisfy. Speaking of satisfying, I reached back into the nightstand to snag a condom. After all, it was Thanksgiving—time to show my woman how *grateful* I was.

Seated at the dining room table, I glanced to the front door for the third time. Surely more guests were expected given the obscene amount of food covering the table and sideboard, as well as a folding table Sam insisted Griffin set up (and cover in a decorative tablecloth) to capture the overflow.

"Everything looks and smells incredible, Sam," I praised, my mouth watering. "I'm not sure where to begin."

"Everyone knows it's the sides that make Thanksgiving dinner worth eating. Start with the obligatory turkey and gravy, and then move on to the good stuff," Sam instructed.

Serving bowls passed hands and plates were loaded until even their rims were obscured. Various sounds of appreciation filled the room. The six of us ate until pleasure turned to pain.

"Dammit, I ate too much! It hurts...it hurts," Ev whined pathetically.

Ever the boy scout, Hunter pulled a small bottle of Tums from his pocket and placed it in front of her, causing her to squeal in delight.

"*This* is love. Are you watching this girls? A man who has antacids at the ready," Ev advised sagely.

"Anything you need, Angel, I'll always have your back. You know I can't stand to see you in pain," Hunter returned with a wicked glimmer in his eye that Ev missed.

"Oh, puh-leaze! Hunter Charles, you're a sly one," Sam scolded with a smirk. "Ev, my sweet naïve, Ev. Wake up and smell the Tums! He wants your tummy to feel better because he plans on throwing you over his shoulder—per usual—and doesn't want you to puke on him. The man reeks of ulterior motive."

Ev cast a warning glare at her husband while addressing her friend, "Sam, my husband is far too intelligent to resort to such rudimentary ploys. He would *never* put his desire for sex above my well-being. Isn't that right, honey?"

"Absolutely, Angel," Hunter replied with mock innocence that didn't escape Ev's notice.

Much like her husband, Ev's eyes held wicked intent.

"In fact, I'll bet my husband spends the night pampering me, knowing how uncomfortable I am. He'll probably rub my feet, fetch me coffee, run a bath, and tuck me into bed...never a thought of sex in his mind. He'll be far too concerned with tending me to focus on lovin'."

Hunter choked back his laughter. I had become accustomed to the linguistic warfare between the two, but it was still fun to watch. Ev clearly thought she had Hunter cornered, but something told me he would once again best her. The only question was *how*.

"Of course, my love, whatever you need. I'll remind you later tonight when you're begging for me that I can't because I'll be far too concerned with tending to your *other* needs."

The man was good—*very* good. It was not the first time I rejoiced in his choice of profession. I would have hated to wind up across the aisle from him in a courtroom. I'd still win—of course—but there was no doubt Hunter would make me work for it.

"I'm afraid you won the battle but lost the war that time, Ev," Griffin teased, high-fiving Hunter across the table.

The rest of the evening passed with easy conversation, laughter, and delicious desserts.

In bed that night, I realized it was the best Thanksgiving I'd ever celebrated. These new friends, who were quickly becoming family, and the woman in my arms were what I was most thankful for this Thanksgiving.

Black Friday arrived and much of the day was spent lounging around my house. By early afternoon, we were ready to venture out while carefully avoiding all shopping outlets. In search of entertainment, we decided to see the latest Marvel superhero flick, which proved to be a winning choice as we both left the theater bemoaning our lack of superpowers. Despite the tub of popcorn we'd consumed, our stomachs were growling a duet by the time we returned home.

"Why don't we head to Sam's place and nab some of Sam's leftovers," she suggested. We'd both been too full to consider bringing anything home last night, a decision we'd regretted throughout the day.

"Have I mentioned lately how brilliant you are?" I praised.

"I'll take that as a yes," she razzed, heading next door.

As she searched for her keys in the duffle bag she claimed was a purse, a man approached us without Meg's notice. Not wanting to alarm her, I blocked her view with my body while tracking the intruder's approach, prepared to protect my woman by any means necessary. Although not a black belt like Hunter or colossus like Griffin, I could hold my own. When the unknown trespasser was within striking distance, I balled my fist and adjusted my stance for optimal impact.

"Hey babe, I came to check on you, but it appears you already have a bodyguard," the man joked.

Babe—who the fuck was this guy to call *my* girl 'babe'?— spun around and gasped, not in fear but excitement, followed quickly by a stern look.

"Jay! What are you doing here? I told you not to come; it's not worth the risk."

"You're worth any risk, babe! You know that. Why don't you introduce me to your friend and then invite me in?"

"Her boyfriend's name is Wes," I offered with no subtlety. This guy was pissing me off with his '*babe*' and '*I'd give my life for you*' bullshit. "You'll receive an invite once you explain why you showed up unannounced, how you knew where to find her, and how you got past security at the front gate."

"You need to dial it back, dude. It's one thing to protect our girl—"

"She is not *our* girl, she is *my* girl. You'd do well to remember that," I interjected fiercely, unwilling to let the point go unaddressed.

"*Whatever*. The guy at the front gate let me pass when I explained I was surprising my sister for her birthday. PS, you need to talk to the head of security...it was way too easy getting in here. Miss Hides-a-Lot told me she was at Hensley. With the help of a friend, I obtained her address by *peeking* into the university's online billing records. PS, you need to talk to Hensley about their computer security. As for why I didn't call first...she doesn't have a freakin' cell phone, other than the pre-paid *I* gave her years ago, which is never turned on. PS, get *your* girl a freakin' cell phone."

"I don't need *you* to tell me how to take care of *my* woman. Where the hell were you when she was completely alone and struggling for the last seven years?" I accused, not bothering to mask my hostility.

"If she'd let me, I would have been by her side protecting her every minute of the last seven years, so don't you fucking question my concern for her, Johnny-come-lately. You weren't the one there to help pick up the pieces when her piece-of-shit husband finally scared her enough to give her the courage to run, and how do I know you'll be there when he finally shows up to claim her!"

The world stopped spinning on its axis, causing a dizziness so intense I feared I would pass out. I must have heard him wrong—there's no way she was married.

No.

Fucking.

Way.

Casting my eyes toward her, I saw it...the guilt.

My head shook with denial as I stepped away from her, unable to bear her nearness.

"Jay," she whispered, "can you give us a moment?"

"Shit, I'm sorry, babe. I didn't realize—"

"It's not your fault, but I really need a minute with Wes," she gently urged him.

"Yeah, sure. I'll go sit in my car for a few minutes. I'll be right there," he gestured to a car I hadn't noticed across the street, "if you need me."

He quietly walked away, running his fingers through his hair and mumbling to himself about his big mouth stirring the pot.

"Wes—"

"Is it true? Are you fucking *married*?"

She nodded, tears filling her eyes.

"And you didn't tell me? I told you, the only—*only*—moral I cling to is that I never sleep with another man's woman. You knew how strongly I felt, yet you let me do it anyway. No, not his woman, his motherfucking *wife*. Jesus Christ! Who the hell do you think you are? My mother *destroyed* my father and our family with her cheating, stealing my childhood from me. But you didn't care, did you? You let me do the same damn thing. Shit, you turned me into her!" I yelled, unable to lower my voice. The pain threatening to bring me to my knees was too great to be contained.

"Wes, please, you don't understand, it's not—"

"Stop! Nothing you could say will make any of this okay. You lied to me. You made me into a co-conspirator in your adultery. You made me fall—" I stopped, unwilling to consider the thoughtless words that were trying to escape. "You are not who I thought you were or who you pretend to be. We're done. I don't want to see you again—as far as I'm concerned, you don't exist."

I heard the chest-wracking sobs as I stormed away, but I was unmoved by her show of emotions. The sound of a car door slamming caused me to glance over my shoulder in time to see Meg collapse and Jay run to scoop her up into his arms. *Whatever...let him have her.*

My heart squeezed, but I told the fucker to mind its own business. I was as pissed at it as I was at her.

I slammed the front door with enough force to shake the pictures we'd hung on the walls not long ago. When I reached my office, I grabbed a bottle of Jim Bean and proceeded to drink straight from the bottle.

How could I have been so stupid? I knew she was hiding something, yet I buried my head in the sand instead of insisting on the truth. Fuck, she wouldn't even tell me her damn name! She was probably afraid I would use one of the firm's private investigators to run a background check and uncover the truth. *Married.* I'd been sleeping with a married woman all along. My stomach churned and I debated if a trip to the bathroom was in order. Once I was confident the popcorn would not be making an encore, I raised the bottle to my lips again.

She seemed so real...so perfect for me. Maybe that was the answer—she was too perfect for me. The only way a girl could be the realization of all my fantasies was if she was *trying* to be...faking it to lure me into her web of deceit. None of it was real.

Whatever her aim, she had failed. I discovered the nasty truth courtesy of *Jay's* slip, and I was once again free. I didn't need her to complicate my life and turn my perfectly orderly world upside-down.

I examined the bottle in my hand to find it half-empty. *Good.* A few more swigs and this night would be nothing more than a fuzzy memory.

Tomorrow, I would go out and find the hottest piece of ass in the bar, take her home, fuck her brains out, and forget about the last six weeks. I knew I wasn't cut out for this relationship bullshit—I'd been trapped, but not anymore. Time to remind myself who Westly Black was, because he certainly wasn't the sentimental, pussy-whipped little bitch I'd been lately.

I passed out a short while later, my dreams haunted by the sight of the stranger I thought I knew crumbling to the ground in a heap of despair and regret. Awake, I was able to ignore the scene, but in my dreams there was no escape.

Chapter 19

"Friendship is certainly the finest balm
for the pangs of disappointed love."
-Jane Austen

Meg

I awoke on the couch, my mouth cottony with dehydration. Given the river of tears I'd cried throughout the night, it was no surprise. My throat burned and chest ached from the violent sobs I couldn't suppress, and if the stinging of my knees and palms were any indication, I suspected both were scraped during my fall. All in all, my body felt like shit, which was appropriate seeing as how that was my exact emotional state.

Wes was lost to me, of that there was no doubt. The abject horror and self-loathing on his face when Jay mentioned I was married were enough to cripple me. Shame and regret swallowed me whole and the tears returned in torrents.

"Babe, I'm so sorry. I didn't mean to screw everything up. I was angry and didn't think before I spoke," Jay apologized—yet again.

"It's not your fault, Jay," I said through my tears. "I did this. Me! There is no one else to blame. I told him the bare minimum because I'm a coward. It wasn't that I was hiding the marriage...I could have explained that and he *may* have understood. Then again, maybe not—it's a sensitive subject for him. I didn't want to explain the marriage because I would've had to explain everything that led to it and followed after. I wasn't ready to go there...I may never be," I said, heartbroken and dejected. "This is *exactly* why I don't do relationships. There comes a point when the other person wants to really know you, to have you open yourself up for their inspection so they can understand what makes you who you are. Do you know what the problem with that is, Jay? Do you?"

He stared at me uneasily, my show of temper obviously unsettling him.

"I'll tell you...I don't fucking know who I am, because I'm *no one*. Nothing! I'm Meg Adeio—empty."

"I never should have let you pick that stupid last name," Jay muttered.

"Why not, it's apropos, isn't it? I'm only now beginning to understand myself, who I am and who I want to be. It's been seven years and I still struggle to see myself as anything more than a tool," I quietly confessed. "I'm so riddled with shame and remorse, there are times I can hardly breathe. Most of my life is defined by regret, and every time I find a sliver of happiness and peace, my past returns to steal it away or I make yet another bad decision and throw it away."

I wrapped my arms around myself, trying to find comfort that wouldn't come.

"What if Wes was my chance? My one and only chance at love and happiness. What if he was my redemption?" I asked, pausing to reflect on my own impulsive questions. "Oh god...what have I done?"

I dissolved into hysterics, my body shaking uncontrollably, trying to purge the realization and subsequent agony by force. It was too much...after all I'd survived and years living in disgrace, I'd finally reached my breaking point. Everything I'd sacrificed and every tiny step I'd taken to move away from the past meant nothing. I was once again undone by a man—only this time it wasn't being bound to a man that broke me, it was being unbound from the only man I wanted.

I lay on the couch, nearly catatonic, without the will to fight because the small candle of hope inside me had been extinguished. Throughout my life, I'd always believed things could be better. If I tried, worked hard enough, and made amends, then maybe—just maybe—I would find peace. That hope drove me onward when freedom seemed impossible.

Hope warmed me as I slept in my car on cold winter nights. Hope fed me when I was starving and had no money for food. Hope fueled me when I was beyond exhaustion at the start of a double shift.

And now hope abandoned me—following Wes as he walked away like a well-trained puppy on the heels of its master.

"Jay, thank you for checking on me. You've been a true friend and I'll always be grateful. I hope you know none of this is your fault. The blame for everything is on me." I stood and hugged him tightly. "But it's time for you to go. I don't want to chance them seeing you with me. I'll keep in touch by email and I promise to get a cell phone."

"Babe, I don't feel right leaving you. No offense, but you're a mess—and I don't just mean the red nose and puffy eyes. Everything is twisted in that pretty little head of yours and I understand why, but you need to untangle that shit before it strangles the life out of you."

"I will. I'm actually going to talk to someone on Monday," I said, my voice flat and lifeless, even to my own ears. "So thank you for your concern, but you can—"

"Look, we can continue to argue for the rest of the night, but I'm not deserting you when you're hurting. Go find the most depressing playlist on your laptop, sit down, and mope quietly while I question your taste in music," he ordered uncompromisingly.

"Jay—" I began, but he cut me off...again.

"Babe, I'll stay until you fall asleep. I know you're worried for me, but I'm worried for you. This is the best deal you're going to get. Take it."

My strength depleted, I complied without further argument. Heart-wrenching music drifting through the house, I collapsed on the couch beside Jay, who held my hand, reminding me I wasn't alone.

"You don't have to worry about me. I'll find a way...I always do," I tried to reassure him.

"And you'll always have me at your back, you know that. All you have to do is call," Jay whispered.

He fell silent while I succumbed to the mind-numbing agony, torturing myself by replaying every moment I'd shared with Wes like a movie in my mind's eye. It sharpened the knife in my heart, plunging it deeper, which I welcomed as penance.

I punished myself for hours until my mind could take no more and forced my body to sleep. But there was no escaping Wes' look of betrayal, even in my dreams.

I awoke to the voices of Sam and Ev, who I could tell were nearby. When my eyes opened, I found they were not only nearby, they were sitting on the couch...watching me. Nope, not creepy at all.

"She's waking up," Ev whispered.

"It's about time," Sam complained, "I was afraid we would have to call the doctor. What do you think is wrong with her? She looks like death warmed over."

"I don't know, but it can't be good."

"Uh, guys, I can hear you, regardless of how corpse-like I appear," I informed them.

"You can talk. That's good, because you have some explaining to do, missy," Sam warned.

"Don't wanna," I griped like a petulant child, pulling the covers over my head.

"Oh, no you don't," Ev said unsympathetically, forcefully exposing my face. "I know that look. I saw it in the mirror when Hunter broke my heart, and I saw it on Sam when her and Griffin were apart. Am I jumping to conclusions or is

Wes in need of a beatdown? I'm overdue for a good ass-whooping."

"Nope, his ass is mine. I warned him if he hurt you, they'd never find his body. I don't break my promises," Sam corrected Ev.

"Guys, I appreciate the concern, although no one will be kicking anyone's ass...or dismembering them. Wes and I broke up, but it wasn't his fault. He didn't do anything wrong."

They exchanged doubtful looks.

"Then what happened?" they asked in unison.

How did I word this as to not invite further questions? With these two, it was an impossible feat.

"My oldest friend, Jay, was in the area and stopped by to surprise me last night. He and Wes didn't exactly hit it off, and Jay—in a bout of verbal diarrhea—inadvertently told Wes I was married. Wes freaked out because his cardinal rule is no married women—ever. To make matters worse, he'd told me as much and I still didn't confess. He ended it on the spot and said he never wanted to see me again."

"You're married?!" Sam shouted.

"I was young and it was sort of like an arranged marriage. I told you I left my family because they were controlling and I wanted freedom...*he* was a part of the equation."

"Holy shit," Ev mumbled.

"So...you're married," Sam repeated, as if the concept was impossible for her to grasp.

"I guess. Maybe not. I've been gone over seven years. He could have had me declared dead, for all I know."

"Wait, are you saying you just up and left without warning?" Ev questioned. It was obvious she was trying to make sense of the fragments of information I'd provided over the past year, along with my new revelations.

"Pretty much. If I'd told them, they would have tried to stop me and that wasn't an option. I had to go—for my sanity."

"Why do I feel like there's a whole lot you're still leaving out? I'm having a difficult time picturing you walking out on your husband without a word of explanation, simply because you wanted a different lifestyle," Sam assessed. "That's not you."

"Well, apparently it is, because that's what I did," I said defensively.

"I don't believe it," Sam countered.

"Well, you should because it's the truth," I said vehemently.

"But not the whole truth," Ev said calmly. "If you're not ready to share more, then say so. Don't paint yourself as an indifferent bitch, because neither of us will believe you."

"That's all I can say—for now. My life before coming to New York was...complicated. It's not a time I like to think about, but I recently realized that in order to move forward, I have to put the past behind me. I'm actually meeting with Thia on Monday. Hopefully, after a few sessions I can sort out some of the mess inside me, then I'll be able to talk about it with you guys. It's not that I don't trust you, it's just hard for me to go back there in my mind."

"See, *that* I can understand," Sam said with approval. "In fact, I'm willing to give you three sessions before I start pestering you for answers."

"How magnanimous of you," Ev said, bumping Sam with her shoulder.

"Yes, it is," Sam agreed, the jest seemingly lost on her. "Okay, no more talk about who's to blame or why—for now. Let's get you downstairs and we'll start the all-important breakup ritual. Ev, you get the chocolate and wine, I'll grab the junk food, and Meg, you find the saddest, most gut-wrenching chick-flick available on-demand...something that makes you say, '*at least I'm not that person.*'"

We each accomplished our tasks and then gathered on the overstuffed couch to watch the movie.

"Thank you," I said, my voice brimming with appreciation. "I love you guys."

They hugged me in a strange Meg sandwich, returning my sentiment before we commenced the relationship-mourning ritual.

While the pain had not receded—not even an iota—at least I didn't feel alone. For that I was grateful.

Chapter 20

"Friendships are the family we make—
not the one we inherit." -Salman Rushdie

Meg

 Walking into Thia's office Monday morning was my battle in slaying the dragons of my past. At least that's what I tried to convince myself while sitting in my car, seriously contemplating the merits of driving until I crossed the border and losing myself in the vastness of Canada's northern territories, where surely no one would ever find me.

 No sooner had I shut the front door behind me than Thia's voice summoned me into the adjoining office. I left the elegant waiting room with a final glance at the door, thinking of Canada's Nunavut territory and the practicalities of becoming an Inuit. Realizing I didn't have the disposable income to invest in an arctic-grade parka, I bid farewell to the fantasy and entered Thia's inner sanctum.

 "Meg, I'm so glad you made it. I texted Sam this morning to place a bet on if you'd show or run. You cost me twenty bucks already, so I hope you make this session worth my while," she said as she squeezed my hand in greeting.

Thank goodness I was accustomed to Thia's off-beat humor or I would be parka shopping now, budget be damned.

"At least Sam will be happy when I get home. She's likely planning how to spend that twenty already."

"No worries, I'll just win it back from Griffin at the next poker night."

I sat down on the comfortable, tan loveseat while Thia sat across from me in a navy wingback armchair.

"Today's goal is to establish why you're here and determine how we will proceed. I'm not going to be digging around in your head today...at least not much," she said with a wink.

"Okay," I replied pathetically.

"I don't often know my patients—socially—as well as I do you, which could theoretically pose a therapeutic challenge. But seeing as I don't actually *know* you, we should be fine. Then again, no one actually *knows* you, do they? Not even yourself."

It was quite the opening remark. Thia neatly summarized the crux of my predicament with a mixture of accusation and understanding. The question seemed rhetorical so I didn't bother to answer.

"Don't worry, if you ask and answer the hard questions, then by the time I'm through, you will know exactly who you were, who you are, and who you want to be."

"I'd like that," I answered earnestly.

"We'll see. Everyone believes they want self-awareness but very few people can truly face themselves with honesty. Most everyone has a skewed sense of self—some focus on only the best, others only the worst. There is a small section of the population who internalizes and accepts blame for circumstances beyond their control, ultimately wallowing in self-loathing and feelings of ignominy. Is that an apt description of anyone you know?" she asked, looking at me pointedly.

"You have to know that some of those people aren't incorrect in their personal assessments. There are bad people in the world, Thia. And there are people who may not be bad themselves but attract evil to them like a disease that they absorb and carry with them, infecting all the innocents they come in contact with," I argued.

"There's a diagnosis for people who feel as you've described—avoidant personality disorder or AvPD."

"Is that what you believe I have?" I asked, dreading her answer.

"Hell no! You certainly display *some* of the traits associated with AvPD, but to diagnose you as AvPD would be trivializing the condition and minimalizing those that are afflicted with it."

"Okay, then what's wrong with me?" I asked, mildly disappointed that Thia didn't label me with the condition. Not that I wanted to have AvPD, but any diagnosis seemed like a step closer to fixing what was wrong with me and somehow it would be comforting to know I wasn't the only one suffering.

"Without the full disclosure of your past and the secrets you keep, I hesitate to make a definitive statement," Thia said with a glimmer in her eye. I smelled a set-up, but like Roger Rabbit, I just had to knock.

"Give me your best guess."

"In psychological terms, I would say there is absolutely nothing wrong with you...other than the fact that you have your head up your ass," she said in a sweet tone that belied her words and message.

"What? That's your professional assessment? Your diagnosis is that I have my head up my ass? Should I bend over so you can pull it out?"

"Don't be ridiculous...you're the only one who can extricate your head from your anus."

"I can't believe people pay you for this," I griped.

"They do—a lot, in fact. But seeing as you aren't the one footing the bill, you hardly have grounds to complain." After a pause, she continued, "What would you call a beautiful, intelligent woman who has proven herself to be compassionate and giving, who is surrounded by people who see this in her and love her, who has—by all accounts— fought tooth-and-nail for every achievement in her life, and who has survived some unknown ordeal that she won't discuss in order to protect those she loves, but despite *all* evidence believes herself to be 'a carrier of evil that infects all the innocents she comes in contact with?'" she finished. "I'd say that remarkable young woman has an affected sense of self, likely stemming from childhood and/or specific traumatic events. I would also say her self-perception is so warped that she does, in fact, have her head up her ass."

"You don't understand. There's so much you don't know about me. If you knew, you wouldn't be so quick to defend me against myself," I said sadly.

"Then tell me, Meg. Tell me and we'll find out who's right. I'll even bet you twenty bucks when all is said and done that you'll be the one agreeing with me."

"I can't, Thia. I don't know if I can do what you're asking. I've spent my entire adult life lying and hiding in order to survive. I'm not sure I can face my shame."

"You face your shame every day, regardless of whether the emotion is merited. You face your past with each evasion and half-truth you force yourself to tell to protect your secrets. You think you're hiding from your past, but you're not—you're hiding from the present by wrapping yourself in the past. It's time to confront your past and live in the present, otherwise you have no future."

I said nothing, too struck by the truth of her words.

"You're here and not running this time. That tells me you're ready. Am I right, Meg...are you ready?"

I thought about my answer, wanting to be sure I could follow through with the commitment I was making, knowing this was my last chance.

"Yes. I'm terrified but I'm ready. I just don't know where to start."

"Well, you're in luck because our time's up. You have an entire week to figure out where to start. In the meantime, you have homework. I understand Dr. Mesina has promised to support your academic pursuits with the contingency that you contact the FBI regarding the potential threats you're facing. Assignment one: call the agent Dr. Mesina has been in contact with. Assignment two: from now on, when one of the people you trust asks a question, you *must* give them an honest answer...no evasion or redirection. Assignment three: find a trait you admire in the people you love that you also possess. Write it down because you're going to have to share with me next week. Got it?"

"Geeze, Thia, I have easier homework in most of my graduate courses," I joked.

"That's because you sociology types are lightweights. It's the psych department that does the hard work," she teased, the classic psychology/sociology struggle for supremacy raging on.

"Har, har. You headcases only have to focus on one mind. We have to consider the collective conscious from small groups to the entire global population. Yet who gets all the cool TV shows? The head doctors, that's who," I said, laughing along with her. "Thanks for doing this, Thia. For caring enough to drive me nuts."

"My pleasure—and I mean that quite literally. I'm going to enjoy watching you squirm, now that I don't have to pretend you've actually evaded me when I ask a question," Thia said, looking far too enthusiastic for my comfort.

As I walked out, she shouted a final command.

"Meg, one more thing...eat! You're too skinny. Tell Samantha she needs to be home a few more nights a week to up your caloric intake. I know Griffin is a tempting distraction, but she's falling down on the job. Be sure to tell her I said so."

After leaving Thia's office, I headed to Higher Yearning for my shift, which proved to be a mistake as I was so caught in my head after our session that I screwed up virtually every order. Thankfully, Ev was in the office—still catching up on paperwork after her honeymoon—and immediately recognized my dilemma.

"I'm thinking we should switch your day off to Mondays until further notice," Ev suggested kindly without pointing out the obvious reason for the switch. "Also, I noticed the stockroom took a beating while I was away. I know you're supposed to be at the counter, but do you mind tackling that disaster zone and I'll cover the front until Jamie comes in?"

"Sure thing, if that would help you out, boss lady," I said teasingly, both of us knowing she was saving my ass, not the other way around.

I spent the rest of the day cloistered away, reorganizing. It was a task that occupied me just enough to keep the thoughts at bay, yet my foggy brain wasn't required to function above a kindergartener's competency—in other words, it was perfect.

Pulling into Sam's driveway after a draining day, I was pleased to see Griffin's car in the driveway. I was used to solitude, but I missed GriffLo when they weren't home. Having to adjust to life without Wes was crippling—not only the agony of missing him but the return of my loneliness.

As if conjured by my thoughts, Wes pulled into his driveway as I exited my own vehicle. I paused, hoping against all odds he would do something—*anything*—to let me know he still cared...that there was some small chance at reconciliation. That hope was crushed beneath the wheel of his car as the garage door opened and he drove straight in without so much as a glance in my direction. Glutton for punishment, I remained frozen in place, waiting to see if he would come out of the garage to talk with me. My answer came in the form of the garage door closing noisily. My already battered heart absorbed another hit. How many more would it take before I was down for the count?

I trudged inside, defeated and hopeless. Wes had proven true to his word—I no longer existed in his world. Unfortunately, he not only existed in *my* world, he was the epicenter of my happiest memories and now the primary source of my anguish and regret. Was that to be the sum of my life...an endless string of regrets and suffering caused by my own hand?

"Megaleena, is that you? Dinner's about to be served, so don't bother going upstairs," Sam called from the kitchen.

Collecting what little remained of my strength, I made the Herculean effort to paste a smile on my face as I walked into the kitchen, where the attentive eyes of GriffLo greeted me.

Taking an unusually tactful approach, Sam said, "You look...a little worn out."

Leaving her post at the stove, she came over and hugged me with all of her pint-sized might. It was a rare display of physical affection, which said more about her degree of concern than words ever could.

When she released me, Griffin offered his own show of support with an affectionate shoulder squeeze.

"Are you sure I can't kick his ass for you?" Griffin asked, undoubtedly prepared to walk next door should I consent.

"You can't. He didn't do anything wrong. The blame for this is on me. If anything, it's my ass that needs to be kicked. I hurt him, Griffin...badly. I took something from him thoughtlessly and betrayed his trust. It might not have been intentional on my part, but that doesn't lessen the impact of what I've done."

"There's no reason for me to teach you a lesson when you're already beating the crap out of yourself. Relationships are hard and people make mistakes. He may be justified in his anger, but he should have given you a chance to explain," Griffin surmised. "And you should have trusted him enough to be honest. You can't have a relationship if you keep yourself divided, only sharing the parts that are easy to love. That's true for family, too," he added, a gentle reprimand.

"I know...and you're right. I wish I had taken the risk earlier and given him the opportunity to decide for himself. Instead, I decided he couldn't love the whole of me, so I only gave him the best parts—the ones he wouldn't reject."

"If he can't accept all of you, choosing you in spite of your flaws and mistakes, then he doesn't deserve you," Hunter's voice answered from behind me.

I hadn't heard Huntleigh enter, but it appeared we were having a family dinner.

"You made a mistake, Meg, but you're not alone," Hunter continued. "We've all had our moments. I kept the truth from Ev for reasons I thought were justifiable and almost lost her. Griffin lost his cool and nearly lost Sam. I'm smart enough not to list Ev and Sam's mistakes when they're in the room," he joked, winking at them over his shoulder, "but we've all been where you are in our own way.

If Black is the right man for you, he'll come around. You just need to be sure if he walks through that door, you're ready to open the ones you've got locked up inside you."

I nodded, because it was all I was capable of in the face of such understanding and acceptance. Their unconditional love and support was a balm to my aching soul.

"After some debate, we've all agreed to give you a few weeks to work with Thia before we push you for answers. But consider yourself warned...we intend to push unless you start to give," Ev advised.

"We've made our mistakes with you too, Meg," Griffin said, picking up the baton. "You were left to your own devices because we were afraid to scare you off if we got too close. In hindsight, treating you like a skittish kitten was not the right approach."

"Knocking hasn't worked," Sam interjected, "so you either open the door or the battering ram is coming out. No more excuses. It's time to trust your family to love you, regardless of your past. The past is just that...past. Yes, it shaped who you are today, but have you failed to notice that we love who you are today? And in case you've forgotten, I have impeccable taste. Have you seen my man? Or my closet?" Sam finished, making me smile. "Enough of the mushy stuff, time to eat."

As the group headed for the table, Hunter snagged my elbow and spoke in a hushed tone, "You need to decide if you want me involved in whatever you have going with the FBI in Oregon. My director has asked me to be the local liaison between you and Hensley, but I stalled him. I haven't looked at the file yet, Meg. I know virtually nothing, which was no easy task...but it won't last. Whether I take the lead on this or not, I'm going to hear things. I wanted to give you the time to come to me by choice, but this is beyond my control. How involved to you want me to be?"

I knew it was coming. When Dr. Mesina mentioned the FBI, I had no doubt that Hunter would—at some point—discover everything. It was unavoidable.

"There is no one at the FBI I would trust more than you to handle the case," I answered sincerely. "I wish I had explained everything personally, but that was my decision. Read the report, investigate, do whatever it is you have to do...you have my blessing."

"I'll have to interview you," he said, making sure I understood exactly what I was in for.

"Okay, just let me know when you need me," I confirmed.

"And not to be a dick, but you'd really be doing me a favor if you filled everyone else in, sooner rather than later. I can't breach the investigation or your confidence by sharing any details, but those three are not going to care about protocol when it comes to you. So help a guy out, will ya?" he said with a smirk, which I returned with a smile and nod.

As we walked to the table to join the others, I noticed Ev's questioning eyes silently grilling Hunter, but he said nothing—just as he promised. Looking around the table at my family, I was overwhelmed with love for each of them and appreciative of their understanding and patience. But I knew that patience had an expiration date. I didn't want to lose them like I lost Wes, so I would do what was necessary to keep my family. Soon, I would tell them my story...the whole story.

Chapter 21

*"When a guy goes to a hooker, he's not
paying her for sex, he's paying her to leave."
-Author Unknown*

<u>Westly</u>

Tuesday night I found myself in an upscale bar near my
office, surrounded by the finest liquor and women money
could buy. They may not be hookers, but make no mistake,
every one of the *ladies*—a term I use loosely—were for sale.
They gravitated to me for the cost of my Burberry suit as
much as my good looks.

At least they were upfront about their motivations,
which is more than I could say for some people. *Fuck!* No
matter how hard I tried, my mind continued to circle back
to her. If the tightness in my chest and the knots in my
stomach weren't reminder enough, I also had to contend
with the torture of my twisted mind finding random
connections between her and *everything* I saw and heard
throughout the day.

I was tempted to call out sick and take an impromptu
vacation to warmer climates. Maybe if I put enough
distance between us, I would be able to prevent her from
invading my every waking thought, as well as my dreams.

In the four days since I learned the truth, I hadn't bothered to leave the house, other than for work. I spent Saturday morning window-stalking Sam's place to see when the big-mouthed jackass left. Then I tortured myself for hours, wondering if he'd spent the night inside her beautiful, deceitful body. The torment finally ended when Jim Bean saw fit to tuck me into bed.

On Sunday, I persuaded Ry to come over and distract me from said window-stalking, which he succeeded in doing by coercing me to explain in female-worthy detail precisely what had happened. When he suggested I may have been impetuous in my dismissal and should have allowed her to explain, I threw his ass out of my house. Then, I window-stalked until the night gave way to morning, forcing me to leave for work.

It was time for a new approach to move past the betrayal. The goal was to bring a girl home and screw her until I passed out from exhaustion. A simple, time-honored plan. All that was required was that I select the most energetic woman available to help me accomplish this mission. I looked around again, uninspired by the options, but not willing to throw in the towel. I selected a woman at random—or as random as picking someone who was the exact opposite of the woman who broke your heart could be—and made my approach.

"Hello, I'm Westly Black. Can I buy you a drink?" *Blah, blah, blah*. I went through the motions: compliment, casual touch, asked her about herself, pretended to listen, casual touch, dropped the name of my firm and the type of car I drive, her turn for a less-than-casual touch, and finally...

"Would you like to join me at my house for a nightcap?" *Blah, blah, blah*, she agreed, I settled both our tabs, and we're off.

"Oh my, you are a big boy," she said appreciatively as we entered my development. She would know since her hand was on my dick as the words left her mouth.

Yes, I was hard, but not because of *this* woman. Any female hand on my dick after said dick has been completely neglected for four days would make me hard. I was relieved when we reached our destination because she stopped petting me to study the exterior of the townhouse, enabling me to hide the fact that my 'big boy' was rapidly deflating as he became aware that the hand making nice with him wasn't his old friend from next door. *Traitor*.

Regardless of my mind and cock's rebellions, I was determined to bang...Regina, Rose, Roxy—what *was* her name? I couldn't remember, but it wasn't required information to proceed.

I stopped in the driveway and threw the car in park, needing to get the show on the road. When I exited, I noticed she made no move to join me. Rolling my eyes, I walked around the car and opened her door. As she stepped out, whatever-the-hell-her-name-was rubbed against me like a bitch in heat before grabbing my head and shoving her tongue in my mouth with less finesse than the dog to which I'd just compared her. I could only assume she intended for the kiss to be provocative, but instead it was desperate and sloppy.

With no clue how I was going to pull this off, I distracted myself from her exaggerated moans, trying to find a solution. My plan was to get Betty-Lou-Screw off with my fingers and then take her doggy-style, in hopes that shoving her face into the mattress would allow me to forget who I was with. I could fake it if needed, but a little cooperation from Wes, Jr. was necessary for my plan to succeed and thus far he was being a temperamental little shit.

The never-ending kiss finally ended when a car door slammed *very* nearby.

Against my better judgment, I opened my eyes and immediately wished I'd been born blind. Ten feet away, devastation written across her beautiful face and tears cascading from her empress-green eyes, stood the only woman I'd ever truly cared for. Like a car accident on the side of the highway, I couldn't look away from the wreckage.

Feelings of guilt and remorse surged through me, but I beat them back, unwilling to allow *her* that power over me. I'd done nothing wrong. I was a single man choosing to enjoy the company of a woman in the privacy of my own...driveway. I owed no explanation or apology for my behavior. Frankly, *she* should feel guilty for watching us like some creepy Peeping Tom. Unwilling to back down, I held my ground until *she* finally broke eye contact and ran inside like the hounds of hell were in pursuit.

"Who was that?" seriously-what-is-this-chick's-name asked.

"Just some girl who's staying with my neighbor," I answered coarsely.

"She looked really upset." God, this woman was the anti-wood. The Viagra counter-pill.

"Didn't notice," I said as I grabbed her hand and tugged her toward the front door.

"Really? You were looking right at her. How did you not see she was crying?"

Was this woman completely oblivious? Hello, earth to whoever-the-hell-you-are, I don't want to talk about her!

"I was too disturbed that she was watching us in a private moment to notice much else. If I was staring, it was in shock, and because I was expecting an apology for her voyeurism."

"Poor baby, did the weirdo neighbor scare you? Don't worry, Raquel will make it all better."

Raquel! *That* was her name— it was just on the tip of my tongue.

"Why don't we go to your bedroom and enjoy the nightcap you promised. You can show me what you're hiding in your pocket," she said, slipping her hand into said pocket. "I'm hoping it's a sucker...I have a bit of an *oral* fixation."

Come on! Was she kidding me with this routine? This made porn movies look like Oscar contenders. To make matters worse, she was now attempting to work my flaccid cock through my pocket, which was doing little other than chafing me.

"Does this big boy need some extra special attention to come out and play with Miss Raquel?"

She dropped to her knees and reached to unzip my fly. *Oh hell no.* I trapped her hands in mine and hauled her to her feet.

"Look, Raquel, you are a special woman, but it isn't going to work. It's not you...whiskey dick, you know how it is," I said in my best 'aw, shucks' voice. Clearly, she was buying my line of crap because she nodded with a sympathetic smile. "Why don't I drive you back to your car and we can pick up where we left off another time?"

After an awkward thirty-minute drive in which I was forced to hold Rhianna's hand to prevent her wandering paws, I was finally rid of her. I even managed to avoid her Labrador tongue with a well-timed cough *directly* in her face that would have made me feel bad if her hand had not once again been cupping my balls.

Women! I swear they only had one thing in mind.

I thought the drive back from the bar was the longest of my life, but the return trip home proved to be infinitely worse. Without the distraction of Peggy Sue I-grab-you to divert my attention, my mind was left to its own devices, which doggedly returned to the desolation I'd unwillingly witnessed earlier. Each tear coursing down *her* beautiful, stricken face replayed in mental IMAX, clawing at my resistant heart.

But why should her devastation be my cross to bear? She was paying the price for her own sins...if she couldn't handle the cost, it wasn't my problem. I did nothing but play the fool. Despite my lack of experience, I'd performed admirably as her...*boyfriend*, an admission I may not enjoy but it was the truth.

I'd spent the past six weeks as someone's boyfriend. I shuddered at the thought. Yes, I might have enjoyed the position courtesy of my ignorance—ignorance is bliss, after all—but the blinders were now off, and all that remained was the harsh reality of betrayal.

In spite of the betrayal, seeing her pain caused a visceral response to shield her—even from myself. And wasn't that a kick in the balls. She'd used me, forcing me to violate my principles and making me into the person I most despised, and still the instinct to protect her roared inside me.

Ry's admonishments replayed for the hundredth time. Was he right? Had I been too hasty in my anger, not allowing her to offer any explanation? *Was* there any explanation that would lessen her treachery? I couldn't conceive of any reason that would justify her duplicity...but what if—?

No, I wouldn't let Ry's compassionate nature or Meg's too-little-too-late admissions sway me from the facts. It didn't matter that my guileless heart still believed in us, nor would I consider the shrieking protests of my gullible soul. My only ally was my intellect—the only one I could trust to be logical and objective.

Finally home—again—I parked in the garage and headed to my office, where a fresh bottle of Jim awaited me, ready to replace Ruby as my companion for the night.

A fifth down and even my mind turned on me. Flashes of memories plagued me, forcing me to relive every second of happiness with Meg. Soon there were so many seconds they became minutes, then hours—time filled with tenderness, amusement, warmth, and peace that I would never have again. Each recollection brought me one step closer to madness, my psyche overwrought with all I'd lost...or perhaps never really had.

On the brink of insanity—and possibly alcohol poisoning—a melody played, evoking a forgettable conversation from several weeks ago. Unable to place the song, I focused on the conversation, trying desperately to remember in my compromised state. The song had come on the radio and I recalled Meg telling me it was her most and least favorite song ever. I must have asked why because she'd told me it could have been written for her...about her. She'd said she loved the song itself but hated what it represented. After her confession, she'd changed the subject, distracting me from the lyrics before I could gather the meaning. I'd intended to download the song later to understand why she connected to it, but I'd forgotten until now.

What was the damn song? It was a megahit, one of those songs you couldn't escape on the radio or TV, in shopping malls and elevators—it followed you like a stalker you were actually happy to see. I stumbled to my laptop, googling the 'top ten hits of the year' and there it was. I pulled up YouTube and searched for the song with lyrics, turned up the volume, and sat back.

"Demons" by Imagine Dragons

As I listened to the voice of the lead singer filled with pleading caution, the words on the screen spoke volumes. Though I was certain countless people had listened to the song and related, a large group probably claimed it could have been written about them, thanks to the cryptic lyrics that allowed for personal interpretation. However, *her* response to the song was primitive, as if the words originated from the essence of her being.

I replayed the track several times before muting the computer to focus solely on the words. She had shared something profound about herself with me through this song. In her own way, she was confessing unnamed sins, counseling me to proceed with caution, and begging me to help her find a way past the darkness she carried.

A small fissure formed in the ice surrounding my heart. Whether the lyrics were an accurate representation of her or simply a reflection of how she saw herself, the parallel she felt was a kick to my gut.

I closed my laptop, more confused than ever, unsure of what the revelation meant...if it meant anything. What did this new insight change? Nothing. She was still married. She had still deceived me. Why then did I wish I had given her the opportunity to explain?

With more questions than answers, I downloaded *"Demons"* to my iPod and headed to the guest bedroom in hopes I would actually sleep tonight if I avoided a bed riddled with her scent. I placed my iPod in the dock and set my newest addition on repeat.

Yeah, I was a glutton for punishment.

Chapter 22

"It's hard to let go of something you never really had, but even harder when you know it's everything you ever wanted."
-Author Unknown

<u>Meg</u>

Wednesday morning began with a stiff neck, courtesy of a night spent on the bathroom floor. My stomach churned uneasily despite its emptiness. The immediate, violent physical reaction to seeing Wes with that whore had taken its toll—even the thought of my beloved chocolate set off a wave of nausea. The only good news in the melodrama that was my life came between bouts of dry heaving. I could say beyond all reasonable doubt that the sole source of my illness was Wes' public indecency, not an unexpected bundle of joy. Considering the state of our relationship and my life in general, that was a significant bullet dodged.

A groan escaped as I pulled myself upright with the aid of the vanity. Ugh! I had no idea what time it was, but I was grateful classes had ended last week and finals didn't begin until next. That provided the necessary time to recuperate before my evening shift.

I plodded arthritically to my bed with a new appreciation for the elderly while gingerly laying my weary body down. The alarm clock on my nightstand helpfully informed me that I could resume sleep in a more customary position for another four hours. At least that was the plan...as soon as I convinced my mind to power down instead of replaying the live-action soft-core porn I'd witnessed last night.

My stomach clenched at the unbidden memory. Clearly mind and stomach were not in agreement and I was the rope in their game of tug-of-war. All *I* wanted was the oblivion of sleep where, if lucky, blessed blackness awaited me.

First, I needed to purge the emotions instigating the mind/body turmoil if I had any hope of sleeping. I needed music to serve as an outlet and offer temporary relief. Collecting my laptop from the desk, I recalled a cover of "*Wrecking Ball*" Griffin had recently shared with me. I lay on my bed, eyes closed, and listened to the emotive duet sing the story of my mistake. Thankfully, by the fifth repeat I was finally able to lose myself in sleep. Unfortunately, my unconscious mind wasn't ready to let go.

In my dream, I could see myself pulling into Sam's driveway, the headlights illuminating a couple locked in a heated embrace, their bodies undulating in pursuit of pleasure. The beams clearly displayed another woman's fingers threaded through the thick chocolate brown hair I loved. They were so lost in the erotic scene that I parked and exited without notice. Instead of escaping to save the last vestiges of my sanity, I was rooted to the asphalt, unable to look away. Every second was another lash of the whip across my battered heart, shredding scar tissue that riddled the surface until fresh wounds appeared and deep ruby blood ran freely. The pain was excruciating, robbing me of breath and thought. My mind roared for me to run, to save myself from further punishment, but the insidious darkness within me reveled in my suffering, forcing me to stay and bear witness. The darkness condemned me, whispering sinister words, reminding me that my deceit provoked his actions. I gave him to the woman with a hand down his pants and her tongue down his throat.

I felt the tears spill from my eyes, flowing down my face unchecked, the only external proof of the agony within. A sob broke free, reminding the couple to my presence, but they still made no effort to separate. Impassive caramel eyes finally met my own, his emotionless state yet another blow to an already broken spirit. So quickly and easily he felt *nothing*—I had been replaced.

Finally finding my feet, I sprinted inside, barely making it to the bathroom before my body found another method of demonstrating my suffering.

I awoke covered in sweat and tears, gasping for breath and clutching my chest as if applying pressure to actual physical wounds. Shaking as I rose, eager to wash the remnants of the dream/memory from my body, I vowed to never sleep again.

A chime alerted me that a customer had entered, and I hustled from the supply closet, my arms laden with accompaniments for the self-service bar. It was near closing and I wanted nothing more than to finish the nightly checklist and officially end the day. I wasn't eager to head to Sam's for fear of running into Wes, but I was in no condition to be exposed to the public. Years of experience had taught me how to firmly affix a mask of normalcy, but the same mask that once comforted me now felt restrictive and irritating.

Quickly emptying my arms, I took my place behind the counter, surprised to find a familiar face smiling back at me.

"Mark," I said, shocked. "What a surprise! How are you?"

"I'm great, Meg. It's been a while. I called a few weeks ago but didn't hear back. Is everything okay?"

"Yeah, sorry about that. Between work and classes, not to mention my thesis, I've been swamped. I kept meaning to call you back and then something else would pop up."

I was stretching the truth to its limits, but I didn't know what else to say. A few weeks ago I was happily lost in Wes, relegating Mark to nothing more than a distant memory.

"What can I get for you?" I asked, trying to distract myself from my guilt with routine.

"I was actually hoping for a date."

"A date?" I parroted in shock.

He chuckled.

"Yes, we've been on them before and enjoyed ourselves," he teased. "The district attorney's office is having a holiday party the Friday after next—the twelfth—and I was hoping you'd join me. Those things are dreadfully dull without a companion, and I could think of no one I'd rather spend an evening with than you."

I desperately searched my mental calendar for a conflict that would prevent me from joining him. Mark was a very nice man, but Sam was right when she said there was no spark between us...at least no spark for me. Mark, I suspected, would disagree. With no real or plausible excuse prepared, I had little choice. Plus, my guilt that I'd ignored him without any explanation or return call prevented me from declining.

"That sounds nice. Thank you for thinking of me. Of course, I'd be happy to join you," I said with faux enthusiasm.

"Excellent! I was hoping you'd be free. It will be a great night and we'll have plenty of time to catch up. I've missed you, Meg."

I smiled cordially but not heartily, which he didn't seem to notice.

"Absolutely," I replied, avoiding his 'missed you' comment like the plague.

"I know you need to close up shop, so I'll leave you to it and call you next week to finalize the details," he said, leaning in to place a kiss on my cheek before departing.

How did I find myself in these messes?

"Sam," I called out as soon as I entered the house.

"In here," she replied from the great room.

I found her on the couch with a book in hand, one finger raised in the universal sign for 'just a minute.'

"Done," she said, closing the book with a flourish. "That was some hot stuff right there. I'll lend it to you."

I swear, Sam was a 'lady porn' pusher. A purveyor of all things smutty. The modern day literary Hugh Hefner for women.

"You'll never guess who showed up at Higher Yearning tonight," I said with confidence.

"Wes? Did you guys make up? Oh, yay! This is such good news," she rambled on, not giving me an opportunity to correct her incorrect assumption.

I sucked in a pained breath, trying to regain my enthusiasm at sharing the bizarre events of the evening.

"Umm, no...to all of it. Actually, I ran into Wes last night."

Sam's eyes widened with hopeful anticipation that needed to be squashed. I quickly added, "He wasn't alone—and when he saw me, he acted like I was invisible. He's done with me, Sam," I said miserably.

"Why didn't you call me? You shouldn't have been alone after witnessing his manwhore ways. God, you poor thing! What a jackass. It's been less than a week, a little soon to be flaunting new pu—"

"I know," I interrupted, unable to bear thinking about the skank again, "but that was always the risk with him living next door. As much as it hurts—and it hurts like a *bitch*—he's entitled to move on. I'm just surprised he's moving on so easily...and quickly," I muttered, the rapid replacement still burning. "But it was bound to happen sooner or later. He's a no-strings guy—always has been, always will be."

I hoped I sounded like the mature adult I was pretending to be, because on the inside I was a two-year-old throwing a wailing temper tantrum of epic proportions.

"No strings, my ass. That man was strung up tight as a submissive at a sex club while you were together. You hurt him, he got spooked and ran—typical man. Trying to make the hurt go away by banging the first Barbie he finds—

typical man. Pretending you don't exist so he doesn't have to reconsider the biggest mistake of his life—typical man," Sam paused, deep in thought. "It really is a wonder we're not all lesbians. Think about it. Who wants to deal with the typical male bullshit?"

"What about Griffin...or Hunter?"

"I said 'typical man' and neither of them are anything close to typical—they are exceptional. That's not to say they don't occasionally have 'typical man' moments, but those are few and far between, which is why we keep them around," Sam explained. "Are you okay?"

"No," I answered honestly.

"Are you going to be?"

"Will I live? Yes. Will I ever get over him? Probably not. Will I find a way to be happy without him?   I don't know...maybe."

"You love him," Sam surmised. It was not a question, it was a conclusion.

"I don't know, maybe. I've never been in love before. I feel like someone gutted me with a rusty hunting knife, and when I saw him with that bimbo, I wanted to blind myself and perform an at-home lobotomy after cryogenically freezing my heart until science found a way to remove the pain of losing the person you want most. Is that love?"

"I actually think that's the textbook definition, so yeah, I'd say you love him," Sam verified my worst fear.

"Great—story of my life. I never wanted love, never looked for it, even went out of my way to avoid it by hooking up with the king of all no-strings playboys. And what did I do? Fell in love with the bastard, then drove him away with my fears and omissions."

"I'd say you're being overly dramatic, but that's actually a pretty apt description of events."

I nodded my agreement and slumped to the couch in defeat.

"You need to be distracted?" she asked as she headed toward the kitchen.

I nodded again, but she must have been watching me because she continued, "Can do."   Returning from the kitchen, she handed me an entire bar of chocolate and a glass of wine. "So who came into the shop tonight?"

"Mark. Totally out of the blue. He invited me to his office party on the twelfth. Weird, right? I wanted to say no, because I wasn't into him before and I'm definitely not up for anyone now. But he mentioned I hadn't returned his calls and then I felt guilty, so..." I trailed off.

"So you said yes and are now going on a date with boring Mark, the ADA," she sighed, shaking her head. "Megalicious, I've heard of getting back on the horse, but you're going from stallion to pony. Not exactly an upgrade."

"I'm not riding any horses. I've thrown my spurs away. Burned my cowboy boots. Buried my hat. This is a guilt date, not the start of a new relationship," I explained.

"No—this is Mark wanting to take you to bed and bore you to death."

"He can *want* until the cows come home, but this bovine is not on the auction block. I'm off the market—permanently."

The rest of my week was spent at the library, lost in books and journal articles in preparation for next week's finals. I wanted to ace every test to prove my worth to Dr. Mesina and the rest of the faculty, especially following the controversy regarding my thesis. This goal required complete focus while studying, which also happened to provide my only escape from the ache in my still-bleeding heart.

It had only been a few days since I'd witnessed the cruelest revenge any woman could suffer—immediate replacement. Perhaps my expectations were too high, but any hope that the tidal wave of misery would recede was soon dashed. In fact, my suffering increased each day, the loss becoming more pronounced. The lacerations on my heart festered, multiplying the pain ten-fold and preventing healing.

The only grace I could claim was that I had not seen Wes since Tuesday's fiasco. I knew he was fucking away his memories of me in the arms of a bevy of bimbos, but at least I wasn't witness to any more of his trysts.

By Friday afternoon, I hit the proverbial wall, unable to absorb one more fact or figure. I headed home for what I was sure would be another fruitless attempt at sleep, surprised to find Hunter's car in the driveway when I arrived. There was no doubt as to why Hunter was at Sam's house during working hours—my time had run out.

I'd avoided poor Hunter like the plague this week. I wasn't naïve enough to believe my success was a result of skill or luck, but rather his patience, which had seemingly run out.

"Hi, Hunter," I called as I entered the house. "I see you've tracked me down. Took you long enough," I taunted impishly.

"You know damn well I was allowing you to come to me when you were ready," he replied from the great room.

"How's that working for you so far?" I jested as I approached the couch.

"About as well as I anticipated," he said, placing a kiss on the top of my head.

It was yet another uncharacteristic display of affection from one of my friends. Oh, they were plenty demonstrative with one another, but they usually curbed their inclinations for my benefit. Unaccustomed to affection, hugs from friends felt unnatural and made me self-conscious. It would seem the gang had decided it was time for exposure therapy.

"Let's sit down. There are a few things we need to talk about," Hunter began. Once I was seated, he continued, "I know your finals are next week and I'm concerned that delving into the past might interfere with your performance. After speaking with the Assistant Deputy Director, we've agreed to postpone the official interview until the Monday following your exams. I've made sure Ev schedules you off for Monday through Wednesday of that week, and Sam called Thia to make sure she could move your appointment to the afternoon after the interview."

I stared at him, mouth gaping like a fish on the line.

"I may have taken some liberties given our personal relationship," he continued, an acknowledgement of his actions but not an apology.

"I'm not sure how to respond to this," I said, completely flustered by his invasion of privacy but touched by his concern and care. Certain his heart was in the right place, I decided to focus on his alpha-male version of nurturing. "Thank you for trying to make this easier for me. It was...thoughtfully intrusive, but I appreciate the effort."

"Good, I was hoping you'd see my intentions instead of my methods," he said with an all-too-pleased smile. "The reason I'm here today is to let you know I've read the reports and interviews the FBI obtained from Hensley—yours included."

The silence echoed yet I said nothing.

"Hun, I had no clue and I hate myself for not helping you sooner. Why didn't you come to me? You had to know I was your best chance at lasting freedom and setting the situation to rights. Don't you trust me?" he asked, visibly wounded by my silence.

"Hunter, of course I trust you. I'm sorry I didn't come forward sooner. I was afraid for myself, and I didn't want to put any of you at risk either. Deep down, I knew they'd find me one day. But if anything had happened to you guys because my family—"

"Do *not* call them that. They are not your family—we are," Hunter interrupted, fiercely claiming me as one of their own. My throat tightened and tears threatened to fall from the love and acceptance he offered.

"Yes, you *are* my family, and if they had hurt any of you I wouldn't have been able to live with myself. I was trying to protect everyone—especially you, because I knew you wouldn't rest until you *fixed* all of my problems and that would put you on their radar."

"I can see where you were coming from," he acknowledged my point, "but you were dead-ass wrong.

We were all at risk as soon as you became a part of our lives, even when you were only an employee of Higher Yearning— I see that face, step back on the platform, away from the guilt train," Hunter ordered, correctly ascertaining my reaction. "What do you think would have happened if they'd shown up to take you back and one of us was around? It doesn't matter if it occurred a year ago or today, the results would be the same: Ev would end up dispatching every Krav Maga defense move she could think of, Griffin would have another 'Hulk' episode, I would have shot the bastards, and Sam...I loath to think what Sam would have done. There would have been no stopping us in our defense of you. The only difference is—had we known—we would have been prepared. We were all lucky that they didn't arrive earlier. With surprise on their side, someone might have been seriously injured...and we've all had enough time in and around hospitals."

Holy shit! How could I have overlooked the risk I'd subjected them to by keeping them ignorant of the threat? What a fool! If anything had happened...I couldn't even bear to think of it.

"You're right. I never thought about the danger of you all *not* knowing. I'm sorry, Hunter, it seems every time I try and do what my heart says it right, I make the situation a hundred times worse," I confessed, the tear that had threatened finally falling.

"No, you don't, hun. You did the best you could and you survived when you had no choice but to do it alone. Your *only* mistake was not asking for help when it was finally available to you. We love you and we *want* to help you—up until now, none of us knew how, other than to accept you as you were and hope you'd open up eventually. But everyone's patience with waiting has run out, so you can expect a full-on assault to break down those walls. Keep in mind, all of their plotting is well underway and they don't even know an eighth of what I do. I don't envy the unadulterated TLC you're going to receive once you 'fess up—if you thought they were bad after you were shot, you ain't seen nothin' yet."

"Oh shit," I groaned, recognizing the truth in his words.

"For my part, I've already started the necessary paperwork to establish your identity—your legal identity," he chided teasingly, "and you'll need to decide if you want to keep the name 'Meg Adeio' or not."

"Do I have time to decide?"

"A couple weeks. The FBI will have to finalize your interview, which will be included as supporting documentation to the petition to establish your identity."

"Thanks, Hunter—for everything."

"Fear cannot be banished, but it can be calm and without panic; it can be mitigated by reason and evaluation." -Vannevar Bush

<u>Meg</u>

The weekend passed in a blur of studying and overly solicitous friends. Hunter's prediction was spot-on; Sam, Ev, and Griffin may not have known details, but they knew something substantial was happening beyond just my breakup with Wes. Ev suspected Hunter was in the know and I'm not sure who I pitied more, Hunter or myself—though at least Hunter could hide out at work when the heat was on.

There was no escape for me. Sam stuffed me full of food, Ev brought me chocolate, and Griffin observed me with astute eyes, occasionally asking an insightful question that begged an equally insightful response. I was never alone in the house, and when I tried to escape under the guise of needing more index cards for review purposes, Ev magically produced a list of *much needed* office supplies to justify accompanying me. I suspected Hunter alerted the crew to be vigilant without offering specifics.

The weekend was full of so many expectant looks and long pauses mid-conversation, it was verging on comical. It was obvious they were starved for my secrets and the hunger was growing ravenous. Several times I caught Griffin whispering sternly to Ev or Sam, which I deduced was him urging them to exercise patience—*not* generally one of their strengths.

I was forced to put my foot down when Sam tried to escort me to Thia's office for my appointment. It was a beautiful Monday morning in spite of the overcast skies, and for the first time in three days I was blessedly alone. Even the daunting prospect of baring myself to Thia didn't rain on my parade...until I approached the door to her office.

At that point, trepidation consumed me. My hand trembled as I reached for the knob, the tremors making it nearly impossible to turn the handle. After several inelegant fumbles, I managed to enter the waiting area, where I stood like a statue despite Thia's calls for me to come in.

I couldn't do it.

I couldn't unearth the skeletons I'd long ago buried. I couldn't withstand the shame and degradation stemming from the first eighteen years of my life. Without the fleshy cover of the last seven years, what remained was vile and abhorrent and—if exposed—would cost me the respect and love of those that mattered most.

I couldn't do it. Not if the cost was exposing my true self to my new family and risk losing them. I'd rather live a lie than be alone again.

Suddenly, I was unable to breathe, my chest tight and pained like I had been struck by a freight train. Clawing at my neck to fight the choking sensation that overwhelmed me, my heart rate increased beyond anything I'd ever achieved during my most intense workouts. I was dizzy and near fainting when the realization struck that I was going to die. Unable to breathe or call for help, there was nothing I could do to prevent the inevitable. Death would come for me—as I always knew it would—and I would face it, scared and alone. It was no more than I deserved after the life I'd led, but my countless regrets would follow me to the grave, where we would lie beside the skeletons I had buried.

Distraught, I didn't hear or notice Thia's approach until she ushered me into her office and sat me on the couch.

"Meg, I want you to hold your breath while I count back from ten. When I reach one, you're going to take a slow, deep breath until your lungs are completely full and then exhale, slowly and completely. Ready?"

I nodded franticly, my mind latching onto the simple instructions, my body complying until we had repeated the exercise three times.

"Good girl. Keep breathing, just like that. Deep breath in, filling your lungs completely, slow exhale out. I also want you to count back from one hundred by threes in your mind...100, 97, 94...there you go, keep going."

Drenched in sweat and shaking near convulsion, I struggled to maintain the deliberate, even breaths but found the distraction of counting helped. My heart returned to its normal rate after several minutes passed, but in its wake was a skull-splitting headache and bone-deep exhaustion.

"What was that?" I asked hoarsely.

Handing me tissues to address the tears streaming down my face, Thia gently patted my back.

"That was a panic attack," she replied definitively. "A textbook example, actually. How were you feeling today before coming to the office?"

"Great. I was enjoying the alone time after being smothered with love and concern all weekend. I didn't feel anxious until I was about to enter the office and then..." I trailed off, embarrassed by my freak-out.

"And then you were forced to confront the reality of why you're here. What were you thinking during the attack? It's clear the trigger was your apprehension about opening up in our session—again, completely typical and nothing to be embarrassed about. To be frank, it's so ordinary I'm almost disappointed in you. I had such high hopes that you would pose a challenge. You know, break up the monotony every therapist is subjected to day in and day out," she said, shaking her head. "Everyone has a case of I-am-a-mess-and-no-one-could-ever-love-me. You'd be shocked by how similar all you humans are. So much unwarranted pain, shame, regret, and anger...although I shouldn't complain.

If people didn't torture themselves with misplaced guilt or blame themselves for circumstances beyond their control, I wouldn't have a shiny new boat to enjoy during the summer. But I digress...where were we? Right, you were about to tell me what was running through your mind during the panic attack."

I blinked in shock. My head hurt too badly to fully process everything she'd just said, but I'm fairly certain there were several none-to-subtle messages directed at me in her *random* tirade.

"It's a bit fuzzy now. For the most part, I was terrified. I thought I was dying."

"Textbook. What about immediately before the thoughts of dying?" she prompted.

"I was getting ready to leave. I can't do this, Thia. I can't take off the mask and show what's beneath. They won't want me anymore...they won't love me. You don't understand. I don't want to lose them...I can't be alone again. I can't, I can't, I—"

"Shh, you're fine, Meg. Let's take another deep breath...good, hold it...and let it out, nice and slow. Good...now again," Thia coached.

Several breaths later, I felt the tightness in my chest ease slightly and the tension in my shoulders soften. Grabbing more tissues from the box, I proceeded to wipe my soggy face—yet again.

"I am going to make you a promise; we will *not* talk about your past today or whatever it is you are afraid to share. Moreover, if you give me a few minutes to assign your homework, I'll let you head home to rest—you're going crash hard after the adrenaline rush from the attack. Deal?"

Immediately calmed by her promise not to delve into my past, I nodded quickly before she could change her mind.

Thia's throaty chuckle told me she was onto me.

"For your homework, I want you to think about the following before our next appointment...wait, when is your last final?"

"Wednesday afternoon," I answered.

"Okay, I want you to think about the following before our appointment this Wednesday at seven pm. Also, I'm going to text Griffin and Sam to come get you—it's not safe for you to drive at the moment. Deal?"

I didn't think I had a choice in the matter so I nodded my agreement.

"Good," Thia said, already mid-text.

"Here you go," she said, handing me a notebook and pen. "I wouldn't want you to forget anything, so jot these down:

1. Who told you that your life is less valuable than anyone else's?
2. Who told you that you are unworthy of love?
3. You're allowing these lessons to govern your life, relationships, and future. Have you ever considered if the source is trustworthy?

Thia paused, allowing me to finish writing down her rapid-fire questions before resuming.

4. What might you gain personally, professionally, and psychologically by discussing your past with me to understand how it has shaped you and to what degree it influences your future?
5. What do you stand to lose by discussing your past with me?
6. Do you truly believe Sam, Griffin, Everleigh, and Hunter will abandon you if they learn what you've been hiding?

"Before you answer the last question, I want you to remember something...every one of your friends has made mistakes in their lives and has regrets they must face each day.

7. Don't you believe they can empathize with what you're going through, accept, and—if necessary—forgive you, just as they've learned to forgive each other as well as themselves?
8. Haven't they already proven their steadfast commitment to you?

9. What more must they do to prove they are worthy of your trust?

"One last question before you hitch a ride home with Griffin and Sam," Thia added.

10. What have you sacrificed by not disclosing your past to the people who care about you?"

After saying goodbye to Thia, I met Griffin and Sam out front.

"Hi, guys, thanks for coming to get me," I said tiredly.

"No problem," Griffin replied breezily. "Sam will drive your car and you can ride in the truck with me."

"No!" Sam protested. "She can ride in her car with me."

Obviously, my mode of transportation was a point of contention.

"Lo, we talked about this," Griffin replied firmly, a tone rarely used when addressing Sam.

"I'll be good...promise," she said sweetly, noticeably changing tactics.

"You're always good, love, but the temptation is too great. Just think of it as a preventative measure," he replied, unconvinced by her promise. "Meg, we're under strict orders to take you home to rest, and..." he continued while giving Sam a warning look, "*not* to question you about your session with Thia."

Ah, it all made sense now. Griffin didn't trust Sam not to push me for answers, which in all fairness was a valid concern because Sam *had* to have all the answers so she could get busy fixing the problem.

"Fine, ride with Mister I-don't-think-Sam-has-any-self-control," Sam said to me before turning her attention to Griff, "and you...you'll see *exactly* how much self-control I possess tonight."

Sam snatched the keys from my hand and hugged me tightly against her petite frame before climbing into Bessie and slamming the door.

"Wait for me to follow you," he called to Sam through the open car window. "Meg's car is, uh...vintage—you know how temperamental vintage cars can be," he added with an apologetic smile.

Despite my fragile mental state, I laughed at his floundering attempt to call Bessie a piece of shit without calling her a piece of shit. I was going to have to order a bumper sticker this week: 'I'm not a POS—I'm *vintage*.'

Sam didn't acknowledge Griffin's request, although I was fairly certain I saw her flip him the bird from the corner of my eye. But she didn't drive off, so I assumed she intended to comply.

Once Griffin and I were buckled in and on our way, he spoke, "I'm not going to ask you to share anything—I promise—but can I share with you?"

"Of course," I responded immediately.

"Did you know I meet with Thia on occasion?" He glanced at me in time to see my head shake. "I thought not. There are times I struggle with my guilt from Sam's attack. I get a horrible case of the 'what ifs'...what if I'd gotten off my ass and asked her out sooner? What if I'd listened to my gut and called the police the night Heath assaulted Ev at The Stop? I review every detail of the months leading up to Sam's ra—attack, contemplating the vast number of small actions or decisions on my part that could have saved her. The regrets pile up until I choke on them, suffocating in remorse."

I opened my mouth to tell him that he couldn't have known and he was in no way responsible for Sam's rape, but he stopped me.

"I know what you're going to say—it's not my fault. But it doesn't matter if you, Ev, Sam, or the whole freaking world tell me I'm not to blame. I blame myself. I'm ashamed that I allowed the woman I love—the woman who will one day be my wife and the mother of my children—to suffer, and regardless of what anyone says, I *know* if I'd made different decisions, the outcome may have changed. I live with it every day, Meg. Late at night, when I hold Lo close and try to calm her after a nightmare—I hate myself. When I see the pain in her eyes as she shares her story as a spokeswoman for RAINN, trying to help other survivors find hope—I hate myself.

"Sam will tell you I'm her hero, and as much as I love how *she* sees me, it's not how *I* see me. Every day I fight to keep the regret and self-loathing from winning. But if I allowed the remorse to control me, I would leave Sam to punish myself for my failings—I would destroy my entire life and one chance at true happiness.

"It came to a point where I had to decide if my regrets defined me, or if the man I *could* be deserved a chance at happiness despite the mistakes of the man I've been."

To hear Griffin's pain for what Sam suffered was not a surprise, but to learn he still held himself personally responsible for events so far outside the scope of his control was shocking. He had no cause to carry the weight of blame on his broad shoulders, yet he grappled with his guilt daily. I wouldn't classify myself with Griffin—my culpability was far more tangible—but I could identify with his struggle to live with remorse.

I reached out and took his massive hand in mine, gently squeezing it to convey my understanding and support, while adding two more questions to my homework list: Did the woman I was becoming deserve her chance at happiness despite the mistakes of the girl I was? And if so, could the person I am now love the woman I could be enough to forgive the girl I'd been?

"The truth is, everyone is going to hurt you. You just got to find the ones worth

suffering for." -Bob Marley

Westly

"Jesus, you smell like a fucking distillery," a disembodied voice grumbled, several decibels louder than was strictly necessary. "Yeah, I'm talking to you, asshole—time to wake up and buy me breakfast for rescuing your ass last night."

I had no clue what he was talking about, but I'd happily give him a twenty to buy himself breakfast if it meant he would go away.

"I'm too old for this shit," Ry complained with a grunt as the mattress went vertical and I plummeted to the floor. "Get up, shower, breakfast. Now."

"What are you doing here? How did you even get into my house?" I asked, disoriented from the mother of all hangovers and Ry's *assistance* getting out of bed.

"Dude, that's how bent you were last night...you don't even know where you are. You're at *my* house, motherfucker. By the way, thanks for that three am wake-up call. You have three minutes, then I'm tossing you in a cold shower—clothes on. You can take me to breakfast soaking wet for all I care, but we're riding in *your* car."

Threatening my baby did the trick. I dragged myself to the shower before swiping gym pants and a Henley from Ry's room. No way could I put last night's clothes back on my body—the mixture of whiskey and expensive perfume was nauseating to my already sensitive stomach.

"Please, help yourself," Ry said, gesturing to his clothes. "I'm not sure what worries me more, the thought that you also borrowed my briefs or that you may be going commando in my pants."

"Commando. I tried your briefs, but they were too small for my package," I retorted, smirking. "I guess it's true what they say, built guys tend to overcompensate."

His look said more than any words could have communicated. Ry was beyond confident in the quality and efficacy of his junk.

"Take me to the diner and feed me, then you can explain what the hell you think you're doing," he ordered, to which I uncharacteristically complied.

Sitting in a booth by the window, I watched as Ry added an obscene amount of RedHot to his double-portion turkey and egg-white omelet. I sipped orange juice between small bites of a plain bagel in deference to my compromised state. Whoever said a greasy breakfast cured a hangover was full of it. The twisted bastard probably just wanted to make other dumb shmucks suffer along with him.

"Alright, we're here and I have my food. Care to explain to me why you were fall-down drunk last night? And for the record, that was not an expression—I had to drag your ass all the way to bed last night because you were too toasted to walk."

I shrugged, not wanting to discuss the cause of my recent venture in binge drinking. I'd already given her enough headspace to fill ten city blocks; I didn't have the intellectual real estate to spare one more square foot.

Ry eyed me across the table before putting his fork down.

"Let's get one thing clear—you called and dragged my ass out of bed so I could play nursemaid to your incoherent, oversharing self. I learned things about you and sweet Meg that I can never unlearn," he said, causing me to wince. That name wasn't hers—wasn't real—but Ry didn't need to know that. "You invited me into the middle of your implosion, so cut the crap and start talking."

I sighed, debating the probability of getting out of this conversation—*zilch*.

"I hooked up with a girl last week and brought her home. Meg saw us and took it hard."

"Did you sleep with the barfly?" he asked directly.

"No, I couldn't...not after I saw the look on her face. Even though there was no reason for me to feel guilty," I added defensively. "It's not like we're together."

"True," he said without further commentary.

"Ever since, I've been obsessing over every detail, trying to fit the puzzle pieces together. But it's like I have two different puzzles mixed together and none of it makes sense. Is she the amazingly sweet, fun, caring girl I spent the last six weeks with, or is she the lying, manipulative bitch who put her desires ahead of my principles?"

"You'll never be able to answer that question unless you talk to her, which I distinctly recall pointing out last week before you tossed me from your house," he reminded me testily.

"Sorry about that, I wasn't in the right headspace to hear you at the time," I apologized. "The problem is, I'm not sure I *want* to hear what she has to say. I still want the girl I thought she was, but the glimpses of the *other* Meg—no thanks."

"You can't love someone unless you accept all of them, even the parts you don't like. She's not a buffet where you get to pick and choose what you want and leave the rest. If there is a part of her that's a deal-breaker for you, then there's no future," he said sagely. "*But*...you reacted without getting the details first, which is why you're questioning the decision after the fact—there's still so much you don't know. If you want to stop going nuts—and drinking like a frat boy—you have to talk to her and get the facts to reassure yourself you made the right choice."

I nodded my agreement, "But what if I made the wrong choice?"

"Then, my friend, you're screwed. That stunt with the bimbo last week..." he finished with an exaggerated whistle. "Not some of your best work."

"Thanks," I responded sarcastically.

"Just speaking the truth. And, brother, lay off the booze. With or without your girl, Jim Beam is not a friend to hang out with every night."

"Thanks, Ry...for everything," I said with sincerity.

After dropping Ry back at his house, I headed home to prepare for court the following day. Several hours passed lost in case law when my cell phone rang with 'Hunter' displayed across the screen. I debated ignoring the call, in no mood to hear another sanctimonious lecture, but decided to answer seconds before voicemail would have picked up.

"Black," I answered coolly, preparing myself for the inevitable confrontation.

"Wes, how are you doing? Haven't heard from you in a while," Hunter replied amiably.

I pulled the phone from my ear and double-checked the screen. Yep, 'Hunter' was still clearly displayed. *Huh.*

"Hey, Hunter, good to hear from you. I'm alright, just busy with work. How about you?"

"I've been better. I'm working a tough case right now, you know what I mean...one of those cases that feels really personal—it's a bull's-eye straight to the heart. Of course, we're all working overtime trying to help Meg out...she's in rough shape, man. Breakups are always tough, but it's especially difficult when she knows she's the one at fault."

It was confirmed—I was officially living in the Twilight Zone. Not only was Hunter talking to me like we were still friends, but he was talking to me about Meg *and* acknowledging that she was the one who screwed up.

"Wes, you still there?"

I cleared my throat, trying to find my voice.

"Yeah, I'm here. I've had cases like that when I worked in the DA's office...the ones that follow you home. I hope you get your guy."

No way was I touching his Meg comments.

"Thanks. Hey, we wanted to invite you to poker night on Friday at Griffin's house. It'll be Griffin and me, plus another friend, but we need a fourth. You in?"

"Umm, I'm not sure. I had tentative plans with a friend—"

"Bring him...or her. The girls won't be there, if that's a deciding factor," he volunteered, saving me from having to ask.

"Alright. Sounds like a plan. What time should I be there?"

"Eight o'clock work for you?"

"Yeah, that's perfect. Thanks for the invite," I said, truly grateful. Provided this wasn't a set-up for a beat down, I was relieved to learn the friendships I'd formed with the guys could extend past my time with Meg.

Friday night arrived quickly and I was surprised by the nerves plaguing me as I knocked on Griffin's door. The man in question answered and ushered me in with the same friendly demeanor to which I'd become accustomed. Maybe this wasn't a set-up.

"How are you, Wes? Glad you could make it," Griffin asked as he led me into the kitchen where Hunter and an attractive, middle-aged woman were seated.

"No girls? I asked Hunter.

"I'm not a girl, I'm a woman...usually. Tonight I'm one of the guys. I don't subscribe to typical gender roles, unless it pertains to cutting the lawn or taking out the trash," she said breezily.

"Wes, meet Thia, an old friend," Griffin introduced. "Watch out, she'll bleed you dry 'til there's nothing left if you don't keep your guard up," he stage whispered.

"I'd listen to him if I were you," Thia confirmed. "I've been known to make grown men cry."

Hunter chuckled and muttered something to the effect of *'and not just at the poker table,'* but I couldn't be certain.

Thia was quirky yet had an authoritative demeanor in a very informal way. I liked her and feared her in equal measure, because I suspected that she was the smartest person in the room but didn't need to flaunt it.

"Alright boys, sit those tight tushies down and let's get this show on the road. My money's burning a hole in your pocket."

We all settled in with cards and beers in hand, playing with focus as we felt one another out. It wasn't until the fifth hand that the trash-talking began, and then it was no holds barred.

When Hunter refused to call Griffin's bet, Thia scolded him, "Dammit, Hunter, why did you even bother to come tonight if Ev refused to take your balls out of the lock box she keeps them in and return them to you on loan?"

"You've got it all wrong. I gave my balls to Ev before I left the house tonight for safe-keeping, because I knew you would bust them until they were black-and-blue," Hunter immediately countered, leaving Griffin and I rolling with laughter.

The goading and barbs continued as the pots climbed higher. With a pair of fours in hand, I folded, having already pegged Thia's tell when she had a winner as well as Griffin's when he was bluffing.

"Why the hell did we even invite him? He keeps taking my money and then pussyfooting away when there's any risk to his pile-o-chips," Griffin complained.

"Never would have guessed he was a cheap bastard," Hunter agreed.

"Hey, now...I'm not cheap, I'm sensible. Just 'cause you two goons throw money around like it grows on trees doesn't mean I have to refill your coffers. Try a little restraint, gentlemen," I returned, enjoying the banter.

"I appreciate a man who knows how to manage his money," Thia interjected. "It's hard to earn and easy to piss away. The financially secure learn that lesson young...or they learn to use their *assets* to increase their assets—either way works."

"I don't know, Griffin...maybe Wes is such a tight-ass at the table so he doesn't have to seduce some sugar momma tomorrow night to pay the mortgage. He is awfully pretty," Hunter razzed.

"That he is, but I think the explanation is much simpler—he's afraid to put too much out there because he may lose something he can't get back," Griffin theorized.

"Ah, so you're one of the guarded types who doesn't want to play the game unless the odds are stacked in your favor. Risk gets too high and you fold. It's a sound strategy, keeps you safe and you never have to worry about losing big," Thia summarized. "Then again, sometimes you have to go all in to win the big pots, but that takes balls the size of coconuts."

"You'd know, Thia. No one in this room has balls as big as yours," Hunter said.

"Laugh all you want, lawman. I'm content to have the biggest pair in the room, just surprised the lot of you aren't feeling emasculated by my presence. I've lived long enough to know when the potential reward is worth any risk. I thought you fools had already learned that lesson the hard way, but maybe it was luck, not brains...or balls."

Griffin and Hunter exchanged knowing looks, clearly understanding her reference. I, on the other hand, was lost.

"New guy here. You lost me, Thia."

"Ah, I forgot you weren't around when these two seemingly exemplary men lost their women and were too blind or stubborn to put it all on the line and win them back," Thia explained before muttering *'idiots'* under her breath. "Can you imagine Hunter without Everleigh or Griffin without Samantha? Not a pretty picture, I assure you. Hunter would never find another woman who challenges him like Everleigh and inspires the same level of friendship and passion. And Griffin...I don't even think he's capable of loving a woman other than Samantha. It's like he's hardwired exclusively for her."

"I can see all that," I said, wondering how we veered so far off course into relationship territory. This is what happens when women play poker. We should still be talking about balls or calling each other names.

"It's true," Griffin seconded. "If I hadn't given Hunter a kick in the ass, he would never have gotten Everleigh back. He was too busy whining about missing her and worrying that she would never forgive him after he lied to her and pushed her away. It was pathetic. It took a month and regular injections of common sense before he finally manned up," Griffin shared.

"And you're one to talk," Hunter countered. "You were too busy singing sappy breakup songs and beating yourself up to win your woman back. Sam had to come *herself* to knock some sense into you. Left to your own devices, you would still be sitting on stage, lamenting the one that got away...not your best cover, by the way," Hunter said, shaking his head as if Griffin was a disappointment to all mankind.

"I did not cover that song," Griffin defended.

"Might as well have," Hunter returned, then exchanged a high-five with Thia.

"Back to my original point," Thia said, reclaiming the conversation, "you two lummox came exceedingly close to losing the grand prize because you were playing it safe. I don't generally associate with feeble-minded wimps—unless they pay me...a lot, and then let me whip their asses into shape—so don't start regressing on me."

I leaned toward Hunter and quietly asked, "Is Thia a professional dominatrix?"

He doubled over, laughing so hard his entire body shook. When he finally sat up, he was wiping tears from his eyes.

"Holy shit! I needed that. I owe you one, man. Although my appreciation is offset by the mental image you just conjured—I could have lived without that."

"I'll take that as a no," I said, feeling ridiculous for having asked but still believing it was a possibility.

"Nah, she's a teacher at Hensley, which is how we all met."

"That is decidedly less exciting than my guess," I said chuckling.

"But now that you've mentioned it, I wouldn't put it past her," he said with a wink.

"What are you two laughing at?" Thia asked.

"Nothing," we answered in unison, sounding like schoolboys caught talking in class.

She gave us a skeptical look but changed topics, "What are the girls doing tonight?"

"Lo and Ev were helping Meg get ready and then going to see a chick flick," Griffin answered.

"Get ready for what?" I asked before my brain could stop my mouth.

"Umm," Griffin stalled, shooting Hunter a 'help me' look.

"Don't look at me...you opened the door, now you're the one who's walking through," Hunter said unsympathetically.

"And the plot thickens," Thia chimed in dramatically.

"She was invited to an office holiday party, so the girls were helping her get all dolled up. Lo was excited to have a human Barbie and Ev was in charge of keeping Lo in check," Griffin answered, obvious in his efforts to subtly steer the conversation from Meg to Sam and Ev.

"Whose office party?" I asked, annoyed.

"Just that lawyer she goes out with sometimes...oh, the other lawyer, not you obviously," Griffin added sheepishly.

Something in the 'aw shucks' delivery pinged my radar. Tonight was a set-up after all, just not the type I'd been anticipating. The relationship talk, the betting analogies...it was all crystalizing in my mind. I would have called them on the ploy immediately, but their trap had sprung and it was effective. I couldn't drop the line of questioning until I had the answers I sought.

"Which lawyer?" I asked.

"Mark, from the DA's office. Oh, that's right, you probably know him from work. He seems like a good guy...treats her right and all that."

I ignored the bait. "How often do she and *Mark* go out?"

"I'm not sure exactly," Griffin said evasively. "I know they've been out several times. It's usually just dinner and a movie. This party is the first real 'couple' type event."

It was getting harder to ignore the worm wriggling on the hook in front of me, but I persevered. "Were they dating while she and I were together?" I asked through clenched teeth.

"No," Griffin and Hunter said in unison without hesitation. I looked expectantly from one to the other, knowing there was more to the story.

"He invited her the day after she saw you with your new *friend*," Griffin said, shaking his head, clearly disappointed in me. "It had been several months since their last date and frankly, I was surprised she said yes. I'm guessing she needed a distraction."

"Men!" Thia interrupted.   "She didn't need a distraction...that's a typical coping mechanism for *men* after a breakup. Meg needed someone to make her feel desirable and sexy after coming face to face with her replacement."

Thia was *not* helping. My temper was rising from simmer to boil.

"I think you're right, Thia. Sam did mention she was going to stay here tonight so Meg could have the house to herself," Griffin said, winking in Thia's direction.

I was clinging to sanity by a thread, unable to speak as angry as I was.

"Yeah, Ev made me stop at the drugstore on the way to Sam's to get *supplies* for Meg, just in case. You know Ev, always the mother hen."

5, 4, 3, 2...

"You know what they say, the best way to get over a man is to get under a new one," Thia said, striking the final blow.

1—blast off!

"Are you fucking kidding me? You're all sitting there joking about Meg screwing someone—who I know, I might add—like it's no big deal. What the hell? And PS, Mark-freaking-Stuart is a two-faced sleazeball who would sell his mother if it benefited him."

"*Is* it a big deal?" Thia asked. "You broke up with her and have been seeing other people. She's doing the same. I don't see the problem."

Who the hell was this woman and how did she know everything about me? I looked to Griffin, who was studying the table intently, then to Hunter, who was equally enthralled with the ceiling. *Son-of-a-bitch!* These two were worse than women—I should buy them a jumbo-sized box of tampons and a collection of chick-flicks.

"You don't see the problem? We have unresolved issues! There are still conversations to be had and decisions to be made. She can't just go and sleep with that shmuck before we have a chance to talk."

"You've had two weeks to talk, but you haven't. Furthermore, you slept with someone else while trying to figure things out. What's good for the goose is good for the gander," Thia said, further enraging me.

"I did not! I couldn't get it up *before* Meg saw the barfly pawing me, and I took her home as soon as Meg left," I said, pausing to catch my breath. "Whatever you may think of me, I'm telling you...Mark Stuart is a wolf in sheep's clothing. If he's set his sights on Meg, then he has an angle—something that benefits him, and trust me, it will be at Meg's expense. In the end, Meg will gain nothing."

"Other than an orgasm?" Hunter asked flippantly.

I lost my mind. It flew away to a remote locale, where it could enjoy a siesta.

"Don't you dare talk about Meg that way! You have no idea what you're saying, motherfucker. Christ, you're supposed to be like a brother to her. I can't even stand to be in the same room as you right now," I shouted my reprimand. "You know what, screw you guys—I'm going to find Meg and warn her, since you all are too busy enjoying her impending suffering."

"Griffin, where's my twenty? You know the rules—all bets must be settled immediately upon completion," Thia said with a smug look on her face.

"You're betting on what? My reaction? Did you make that shit up so I'd be forced to admit there are unresolved issues? Twisted pricks. You had me going for a minute. I actually believed you," I said, my relief palpable.

"Unfortunately, no," Hunter answered with genuine regret. "I confess we brought it up to test the waters—see if you two were really over—because we all agree you and Meg need to have a conversation, but we stuck to the truth...for the most part."

"We *may* have over-embellished Meg's enthusiasm, and I don't think she intends on sleeping with Mark," Griffin added hastily.

"Her intentions are irrelevant," I replied hostilely.

"Are you saying he'd force her?" Griffin growled, jumping to his feet.

"No, I don't think he'd use force, but he wouldn't need it. He's a manipulative parasite who will do or be whatever it takes to get what he wants. He'll find her weaknesses and insecurities and exploit them. I've seen him do it before, professionally and personally."

"Then what are you still doing here?" Thia asked. "Go crash the party."

"That's the best advice I've heard in a long time," I said as I walked out the door.

Chapter 25

*"No man, for any considerable period, can
wear one face to himself and another to the
multitude, without finally getting bewildered
as to which may be the true."*
-Nathaniel Hawthorne

Meg

Worst. Date. Ever.

I walked into Sam's and set the alarm while kicking off
the heels she had crammed my feet into despite being a size
too small. With a sigh of relief, I headed to the kitchen to
grab an unopened bar of chocolate. Oh yes, I planned to eat
the entire bar tonight—I'd earned it. I had, after all,
endured the...

Worst. Date. Ever.

As I headed for the couch, I caught a glimpse of myself
in the window—what a waste. Sam and Ev had outdone
themselves transforming me from a duckling to a swan.
And hours of effort for what? A disingenuous hypocrite
who thought I could be bought like a two-bit hooker and
used to further his career. One thing was for sure, Mark
Stuart learned a lesson tonight in the dangers of
manipulating the wrong woman.

The evening started well enough. He arrived on time with a dozen roses and a pocketful of compliments. We drove to Taglio's on the Sound while exchanging pleasantries without incident. He helped me from the car and walked me into the restaurant like any proper gentleman should do. And that was where 'well enough' ended. From our arrival at Taglio's until I climbed in a taxi to return home, it was a steady descent into hell.

I'd always believed Mark was a nice guy—albeit a bit dull—and after several dates I thought I knew what to expect. I failed to take into account the Jekyll/Hyde effect when surrounded by his coworkers and boss. In the new environment, his mask came off and I had my first opportunity to see what lay beneath, which was repellent to any sane human being with even a modicum of social consciousness.

The passive-aggressive elitism and bigotry was shocking from a representative of the state sworn to uphold the law with blind justice. *Blind, ha!* All the man saw was color, religion, socio-economic status, gender...hell, any method of generalizing or stereotyping was welcome. His holier-than-thou attitude and self-righteous diatribes verged on delusional.

What was most astonishing was how quickly the mask slipped in place when local lobbyists, charities, or community outreach organizers came to introduce themselves. It took everything in my power to bite my tongue and persuade myself not to kick him in the shins. I succeeded admirably until dessert, when his commentary degraded beyond my ability to remain silent.

While I was treated like an accessory throughout the night, very little of his negativity was directed at me. However, when dessert was served and I requested hot chocolate in lieu of coffee, he nudged me under the table before advising the waiter to give us a moment.

Apparently, Mark wasn't satisfied I had received his message, so he then proceeded to patronize me in front of our tablemates, "Meg, sweetheart, it's best to order one of the options provided. These poor waiters have a job to do, and it would be a shame if your special request distracted them from their other responsibilities and ultimately cost them their position. Remember, low-wage workers are often more susceptible to errors and distraction as a result of their shorter attention spans. Why don't you relax and I'll order your dessert."

My nails dug into my palms with such force I was certain there would be crescent indentations visible for days. Still feeling the urge to scream, I bit my tongue until it was numb with pain. Despite the many indignities of the evening, I was determined to maintain my composure. Just because my date was an embarrassment didn't mean I had to embarrass myself.

My resolve nearly crumbled when the waiter returned and Mark ordered me a trio of berries with vanilla ice cream. *Vanilla!* We had been on at least five dates and each time I'd ordered the chocolatiest item on the menu for dessert. Did the man pay attention to anyone other than himself?

When the conversation turned to the 'where are they now' of previous co-workers, I knew trouble lay ahead. As I suspected, the conversation eventually turned to Wes.

"Westly Black," Mark said with disgust, "is still over at Cauldwell, Rueger & Stein, which is exactly where he belongs. Lou, you do you remember what it was like when he was at the DA's office? Every day was a waiting game to see what stunt he would pull next. Rumor has it he left because they were about to fire him...something about losing a motion that nearly freed a pedophile. There should have been an investigation into his conduct as I suspect he was accepting bribes from the defendants' families all along."

"Really, did he lose that often?" I asked with mock innocence.

"No, his win record was the highest in the office—that should tell you something right there," the man across from me answered spitefully.

"That he was good at his job?" I asked flatly.

"A little *too* good—impossibly good," the man replied, heavy with implication.

"There are many intricacies in our profession," Mark condescended, "It's possible for an unscrupulous person—such as Black—to twist evidence, coach witnesses, or manipulate the system in various other ways in order to guarantee a conviction. On paper, everything might look clean, but behind the scenes, we see the manipulation."

"So which is it? Either Wes is selling out to help the defendant avoid conviction or he's abusing the system to gain a conviction. You can't accuse him of both...one results in a win, the other in a loss," I argued calmly.

Mark's face reddened with anger—or possibly embarrassment—at my critique before his peers. *Tough shit!* The self-righteous ego mongers had spent the entire night flaunting their compete lack of social conscious and absence of principles. None of them knew anything about Wes beyond their jealousy of his success.

"*Wes?*" Mark asked suspiciously. "Do you know Black *personally*?"

When I refused to react to his inference, he offered me a demeaning smile.

"Now I understand...you think you know him. You've spent time with the snake and took a bite of his apple."

It would be more accurate to say that the snake took a bite of the apple—specifically, *my* apple—but I didn't bother to correct him.

"Meg, I hate to be the one to tell you this," he started, the callous fervor in his eyes contradicting his words, "but you deserve to know to truth. You are but one in an exceptionally long line of women Black has deceived into his bed. Despite what he has led you to believe, Westly Black is a depraved narcissist who will discard you once you've fulfilled your purpose—the *only* purpose he has where women are concerned."

"Oh, thank goodness. I was only using him for sex or else your character assassination would be very distressing," I tossed out casually as I stood. "It has been an enlightening evening, if not a pleasant one. I'll see myself home...and Mark, don't bother calling or showing up at Higher Yearning. I won't be serving you *anything*."

The last square of chocolate dissolved in my mouth as delicious and necessary as the first, removing the residual bitterness from my tongue left by the...*Worst. Date. Ever.*

It was hard to believe the Mark I was with tonight was the same man I'd broken bread with previously. There was a definite possibility he suffered from multiple personalities. The only other explanation was that the Mark I'd dated previously was an impostor, and tonight's Mark was the genuine article. Who'd have guessed that the bumbling, gentle—though somewhat boring—attorney I'd known was a ruse that masked a self-important, ignorant, and ethically bankrupt manipulator?

Experience had taught me this type of man was the norm rather than the exception, so I didn't know why I found it surprising. Men, or people in general—but men especially, in my experience—were apt to project whatever image gained the confidence of those around them in order to secure their own interests, regardless of the destruction left in their wake. They were masters of manipulation and deceit, bending those around them to their will until the unsuspecting victims eagerly submitted, always to their detriment.

Perhaps that was what most appealed to me about Wes—his willingness to project an image that colored him in the worst light in order to achieve goals that were to the benefit of others. Ultimately, the only person suffering from Wes' deception was himself.

Wes...I couldn't escape him. He had already occupied copious amounts of my mental hard drive over the past two weeks, tonight only proving how profound a mistake I had made and how great the cost. I'd sacrificed my first taste of happiness for secrets that only brought me sorrow.

Each day I hoped for a sign he was softening, willing to give me one more chance to explain. Losing Wes—or rather, the promise of what we could have been—was the impetus to change. Terrifying though it may be, the prospect of resurrecting my skeletons for his inspection was infinitely more tolerable than abandoning our potential.

What could I do to force him to acknowledge me? How could I capture his attention and his ear? My desperation was such that nothing was beyond consideration, yet he hadn't even provided the opportunity to humiliate myself for his benefit. He was either never home or exceptionally good at avoiding detection. All the grand gestures I'd considered—and even one that I attempted—went unrealized without their intended recipient present. Last night, after listening to *"Say Something"* by Great Big World on repeat for over an hour, inspiration struck, leading me to his lawn with my laptop raised above my head, reenacting John Cusack's epic boom box scene. It might have worked had he been there to hear it.

My chocolate gone, music was next on my agenda in hopes of erasing the disastrous night from my memory and deterring regrets from consuming my every thought. Halfway up the stairs, the doorbell rang, demanding my attention. Nevertheless, fear of who might be on the other side of the door kept me rooted in place. Bravery be damned, I resumed my climb, intending to hide under the covers until the unwanted visitor was gone and morning arrived.

"I know you're in there. Open the door!" the disembodied voice ordered.

Wes.

Heart in my chest, I ran down the stairs, disarmed the alarm, and flung the door wide open. Sure enough, he was there, looking beautiful as ever.

"Where is he?" Wes asked harshly.

"He, who?" I asked, perplexed. "Griffin is at home with Sam," I finished, guessing who *'he'* was.

"I know where Griffin is, I just left him. Where is *Mark*? I swear to God, if he's in your bed right now, I'm going to tear him limb from limb," he said menacingly. "How could you fall for his act? You have no idea the type of man he is—you deserve so much better."

"Can we rewind? Seems I've missed the opening scene and now I'm not following the plot. Mark is not here. I left the condescending ass with his belittling buddies an hour ago," I explained, hope swelling at his show of jealousy. "Why? Did the idea of him in my bed—*eww*, by the way—bother you? Maybe make you a little...jealous?"

"*Jealous*?" he parroted. "No, I wasn't jealous—covetous, possessive, and homicidal would be far more accurate descriptions. Why would you agree to go with him tonight?"

"When he asked, I felt guilty about ignoring his calls for several months, which he was kind enough to point out—manipulative jerk."

"Are you seeing the pattern here? You plus guilt equals bad decisions," he said, concern in his tone.

"You don't know the half of it," I muttered to myself, but unfortunately, he heard me.

"Tell me...I will never know unless you open your mouth and give me some of those precious secrets you're stockpiling like an end-of-days survivalist collecting canned foods."

Didn't I spend the last hour longing for this precise opportunity...why then was it impossible to speak? I could do this—I *had* to do this. Telling Wes my story *might* cause me to lose him forever, but keeping my secrets would *absolutely* kill any chance with him.

"Can we sit down?" I asked, stalling. "My feet are killing me and this may take a while."

His discerning stare said he was onto my ploy. *Oh well, it was worth a shot.* Leading the way, we entered the great room and sat on opposite ends of the sofa, facing each other. Wes rose from the couch to grab a blanket from the back of the loveseat and draped it over my legs, which were extended on the couch.

"You looked cold," he explained.

Reseated on the couch, he took my left foot in hand, massaging the balls of my feet with a firm pressure that relieved the lingering pain I'd endured all night.

"Wearing heels can be torture if you're not accustomed to the position—or so I'm told," he said sympathetically.

Realization dawned...

Wes was stalling *for* me, giving me time to gather my thoughts. Courage was a fickle friend, always around to boast when there was no need, yet fleeting when needed. Luckily, courage's cousin 'desperation' showed up in his stead.

This was my last chance with Wes—I was certain it was now or never.

Here goes nothing...

Chapter 26

"Love takes off masks that we fear we cannot live without and know we cannot live within." -James Baldwin

Westly

Patience was not one of my limited virtues, making the wait torturous. She was trying, that much was obvious, yet seemed unable to find the words...or perhaps not knowing where to begin. Accustomed to leading the witness, I asked the question that had plagued me for months, hoping to finally obtain an answer while providing her a starting point.

"What's your name, beautiful?"

"I can't answer that," came her familiar refrain. My hand froze mid-rotation as I dropped her foot like it was on fire.

Seriously? After everything—knowing this was her last chance—she still wouldn't answer the fucking question! Why did I waste my time? Because I was a glutton for this girl's punishment.

"Wait!" she shouted in panic. "Let me explain, please—*please*, don't walk away again."

Offering a nod of approval, I relaxed my tensed muscles.

"I can't tell you my name because..." she paused again, averting her eyes, "I don't have one."

Say what? My brain came to a screeching halt, unable to process four simple words.

"That's not possible," was the only reply I could manage.

"In most circumstances, you'd be correct. But in my case, you're patently wrong."

"Would you care to explain?" I prompted.

"No...but for you, I will," she stated simply. "I was born in a small town near the borders of Oregon, Washington, and Idaho, surrounded by national forests and rural roads. It was very isolated, yet only a four or five-hour drive from Portland, Seattle, and Boise."

She stopped again, the halting recollection of her story exhausting my patience. She obviously needed help. "So you grew up on a farm?"

"Kind of...I guess you would call it a compound. It was completely self-sufficient and required minimal contact with the outside world. Life was basic; no electronics or phones were permitted for the general population of the community."

"Wait, are you Amish?" I asked, attempting to fit the pieces together.

"No, the Amish are an enclave of ultraconservative Christians whose beliefs are compatible with major Protestant denominations. Unlike where I come from, they do not require their members to pool their finances, nor is their faith centered on a single human authority."

"What does that mean?" I asked, frustrated with her roundabout responses.

She signed, resignation painted across her face.

"It means the Amish are a recognized and accepted religious sect—a Christian denomination—whereas I was raised in what you would refer to as a cult."

She fell silent, obviously awaiting my response. Too stunned by her admission, I said nothing. Then the rambling commenced.

"Although *cult* is a heavily debated term due to the intrinsic negative connotation and subsequent discrimination, which ultimately led to a movement in the 1990's toward the term 'new religious movement.'

Sociologically, a cult is a religious or other social group with deviant and novel beliefs. From a purely academic standpoint, the term has no positive or negative association; it is merely a classification. Now, the term *destructive cult* is what most people mean in the colloquial or pejorative use of *cult*. *Destructive cults*, including religious extremist groups and terrorists, are likely to cause loss of life among their memberships or the general public."

"That was a lot of information, beautiful. I'm still trying to process the *'I was raised in a cult'* part, so I don't know if I'm ready for a sociology lecture yet."

"Sorry, it's my field of expertise—when I get nervous, I start spewing facts to fill the silence."

"Let me make sure I understand. You were raised in a cult, but a cult is not necessarily bad...just an atypical religion, except when it's considered *destructive* as is the case with religious jihadists or whackjobs like Charles Manson."

"Exactly, except Charles Manson's 'The Family' was one of the few cults without strong religious themes, which made it the exception not the rule. David Koresh's 'Branch Davidians' would be a closer comparison," she replied with a slight smile, clearly proud of my grasp of her explanation.

"So which type was it...your cult?" I asked, knowing the answer.

"It's *not* my cult," she began defensively before catching herself. Gentling her tone, she continued, *"To Ieró—The Sacred* began nearly a century ago as a novel faith, blasphemous by Christian standards, yet borrowing portions of the vernacular and calendar from the Greek Orthodox tradition. While *To Ieró* existed well outside the box, it was completely localized and in no way destructive. It evolved, the dogma growing more controversial and radical to the point of fanaticism—still it wouldn't have met the criteria to be deemed *destructive*. However, the microstructure of the enclave underwent an abrupt mutation approximately twenty years ago, though the change in doctrine went unnoticed by most of the followers. The changes were insidious at first, eventually becoming toxic, until finally graduating to lethal. It was the epitome of every horrific cult generalization by the time I ran. I can't begin to imagine what has transpired in the last seven years," she finished sadly.

"Okay, I can understand why you may be embarrassed by your upbringing and the family you were born into...but beautiful, you have nothing to be ashamed of. So what if your family is crazy—maybe even evil? That doesn't mean you are. Who cares if you weren't given a name when you were born? You picked one for yourself, which is even better. I'm curious, how did you decide on 'Meg'? Also, how the hell does anyone know who they are talking about or to if no one has a name?" I asked, my questions all over the place, courtesy of the vast number of thoughts running through my mind while processing what she'd disclosed thus far.

"If only it was as simple as you're making it. Yes, it's an embarrassment to come from a crazy family, but that isn't the source of my shame. Countless others are the product of criminals, rapists, drug addicts, and the like—that doesn't make them fruit of the same tree. Each person has a choice, I know that. Family may shape an individual, but it does not determine exclusively who they are or will be. It's the choices I've made that bring me shame, not the DNA within me. I promise you I deserve every moment of guilt and remorse that gnaws at my soul—I've earned them all," she confessed, tears filling her beautiful green eyes. "As for my name, or lack thereof, I was the only member of my generation not given a name. When Jay created my new identity, he needed a name but I had no ideas. He picked 'Meg'—it was a tongue-in-cheek selection that I didn't find particularly funny, but the damage was done. I provided the last name."

"You know what my next two questions are going to be."

She nodded, "Adeio—or άδειο, in Greek—means 'empty.' It seemed fitting. Jay was inspired by my position—or you might say title—in *To Ieró* when he named me 'Meg.'"

"I'm assuming your nameless state and title are linked, but care to tell me what your position was?"

"Yes, my potential standing at conception dictated I not be named. When my potential was *realized,* I was referred to as *The Omega*...o-*Meg*-a, get it? It wasn't funny then and it's not now, however Jay's intentions were good."

"Beautiful,   *'potential   standing'*...*'potential realized'*...you keep giving me glimpses that don't amount to a full picture. I'm trying to be patient—to understand what you're saying—but it's nearly impossible with only fragments of information. Furthermore, nothing you've said explains your self-abhorrence and disgrace. And we haven't even touched on the fact that you're married, for fuck's sake, nor why you withheld that pertinent piece of information."

I sighed wearily, at the end of my rope. Without grasping the scope of her issues, I couldn't ask the right questions to pry her open. It was like picking through an Olympic-sized swimming pool full of flash drives, hoping to find the one with the document you needed—an impossible feat.

"Just what? Lay it all at your feet—every secret, mistake, regret, and shame, on display for your inspection. If I introduce you to my demons, what then? You try to exorcise them, or run away in fear? I loved the way you looked at me before, like I was something to be treasured. Even after Jay told you I was married, you still look at me as if I held some value. I've never had that, Wes...there have been days when the only thing that made me believe I was of any worth was the fact that *you* believed it. Forgive me for not rushing to destroy that look and lose what little respect you may still hold for me."

"Holy shit, woman! I've tried to be supportive and give you time, but enough is enough. The Mr. Nice Guy approach isn't working, so I'm going back to my roots," I near shouted. "You can't have a relationship of any kind with *anyone* if you won't let the other person know you. Not the façade or lies—you. It took guts to leave and attempt to live in a completely different world with nothing, not even a name. Where the hell is that backbone now? If you left to escape the life you were trapped in and the girl you didn't want to be, then why do you insist on still being her? Face that girl and her secrets, take responsibility for any sins that are yours—and only yours—figure out how to atone, then move the fuck on. Keeping yourself locked away to obsess over every sin you believe you've committed is nothing but a means to punish yourself. Stop playing the damn martyr and fight! Fight for us. Fight for your friends. And if nothing else, fight for yourself."

"You should really consider a career as a motivational speaker...or maybe a therapist," she replied sarcastically.

"Last chance, beautiful. The clock's run out so you have to decide. Keep your secrets or take a chance. What'll it be?"

"Wes, I'm trying, I swear I am, but I don't know what to say...or how to explain."

"Just tell me your story. All of it, from beginning to end. I'm *begging* you."

"The truth does not change according to our ability to stomach it." -Flannery O'Connor

Meg

"As I said, I was born in Oregon," I began shakily. "No, wait...the story starts before that. In *To Ieró*, there is always an *Alpha*—the incontrovertible, omniscient leader who is an incarnation of Theós, or God. He is revered to the point of worship, never to be questioned or doubted. While *To Ieró* is governed by strict traditions, mores, and laws, *The Alpha* can spontaneously alter or contradict the norms at any time without question. Each *Alpha* is born of the previous *Alpha* and his *Omega*. When the current *Alpha* dies, the new *Alpha*—his son—ascends as leader, at which time Theós, who lay dormant inside, is awakened. The new *Alpha* then recognizes his *Omega* and declares her publicly. He leads and she follows, eventually birthing the next *Alpha*.

"When I was in utero, the Mánti—or seer—Malachi prophesied I possessed the potential to be *The Omega*," I explained with a skeptical look that told him I thought the whole concept was preposterous. "Traditionally, two or three infants in each generation are divined as possessing the potential, however no other was foretold after my conception—lucky me," I added sarcastically. "Seeing as I was a foregone conclusion, I was treated as *The Omega* from birth—given no name, and with rare exception, not addressed directly by anyone other than my mother or *The Alpha.*

Forcing the familiar tidal wave of loneliness and segregation aside, I continued.

"As potential *Omega,* my sanctity was preserved at all costs. *To Ieró* believes that the incarnation of God is transferred from *The Omega* to the fetal *Alpha*-to-be. Supposedly, an *Omega* is born with the dormant Theós within herself, and to protect Theós she—the vessel—must remain unblemished by external forces. For this reason, I was raised in near isolation without love or affection for fear either would establish a sense of worth that would corrupt my purity. It was imperative that I only conceive of myself as an object with no innate value, since only that which I safeguarded was of worth. Ultimately, I would pass the treasure to another and my usefulness would end."

For the first time, this detail captured my attention. What happened to *The Omega* after giving birth? No present or past *Omega*s lived amongst *To Ieró* that I was aware of. Were they sent away, separated from their young children? A horrible suspicion took root—what did one do with the packaging after the toy was opened? Too disgusted for further contemplation, I resumed my story.

"You have to understand, my own mother was a fervent believer. She was overjoyed to learn she possibly carried *The Omega* as it elevated her standing in the community and would provide additional resources to the household. Women, with the exception of *The Omega,* were married to *To Ieró* as a collective—the wife to all as the children of these unions were the children of all.

"It never occurred to my mother to treat me any differently than she would an antique box. I was provided the necessities for physical survival, but I was not nurtured or loved because one doesn't not love an object. The dynamics set the stage perfectly to produce an obedient, docile little girl who would grow into a perfectly biddable

Omega. Had I acted out or exhibited a strong sense of self, it would have been regarded as a sign of corruption, causing me to be shunned and banished from *To Ieró.*

"Growing up, no reaction from my mother was the equivalent of praise. If I received acknowledgment in any form, it was a mark of disapproval, resulting in swift punishments that deterred future mistakes. Punishments ranged from the withholding of food, should I make eye contact, to physical discipline for egregious errors such as speaking to anyone other than my mother. The first time I met Jay, my mother was bringing me to the meeting hall for a blessing. Jay was only a few years older than I was, and he smiled and waved like most kids would do. It was the warmest, kindest interaction I'd encountered in my five years of life so I impulsively returned his wave. In order to cleanse me after an act of individualism and defiance, I was required to undergo a purification ceremony."

The little girl within was screaming for me to stop, but I had opened the door and there was no closing it now.

"Do you know how *To Ieró* purifies a five-year-old *Omega* for waving...at a young boy, no less? They remove the fingernails from the offending hand with a consecrated tool that amounted to a scalpel and pliers. The nails grew back after several months, but the lesson wasn't so easily forgotten."

I shuddered at the memory, involuntarily touching my nails to assure myself they were where they belonged. To this day, I couldn't stomach a manicure or anyone with tools near my nails.

"I officially ascended as *The Omega* on my tenth birthday. Nothing horrific happened, but I made a promise that day. Before the congregation of *To Ieró, The Alpha* stared into my eyes and confirmed he saw Theós present and unsullied. He then ordered me to kneel before him and kiss his feet, not rising until he instructed. I did as he commanded because it what was expected of me. After twelve hours on my knees, I was permitted to stand—with assistance. Having proven my commitment and obedience, my mother was permitted to tend the wounds on my knees before the rite continued. Finally, *The Alpha* asked the question eagerly anticipated, *'Are you The Omega, keeper of Theós and vessel of my heir?'*—I said, *'yes.'*"

Anxious to provide explanation for my grievous error, I continued.

"It was a promise I didn't fully understand, the ramifications of which were impossible for my ten-year-old mind to comprehend. I sold my soul in exchange for *change* with the ardent belief I was gaining something of value...a better life, a purpose—acknowledgement. I was wrong, of course. So fucking wrong.

"But the worst part, Wes—the source of countless years of self-loathing—it was *my* choice. I accepted the position carelessly, so desperate for affection that I willingly surrendered my life. What a pathetic, hasty fool I was."

Appalled with myself, I rushed on to avoid the culpability that always followed my memories.

"In truth, the decision was never mine—my future had been established long before that day. Now I understand that I was only provided the *illusion* of choice. They zealously believed I carried Theós, which in their minds justified every conceivable heinous act to force my compliance. Still, I will never know how the outcome may have differed if I had said *'no.'* Even now, I am haunted by nightmares where I'm screaming at the little girl I used to be to choose differently...pleading with her to be smarter than I was, to understand the consequences of her decision.

"That was my first mistake...many more followed. Shall I continue the story, or have you heard enough?" I asked, certain he would run for the hills. "I understand if you want to go, Wes. Everyone has baggage, but I have a cargo freight loaded with storage containers, filled to the brim with knock-off suitcases from China."

I looked up from my hands for the first time since beginning my story, expecting to see disgust—instead I found compassion.

"Beautiful, you made me wait this long...no way am I letting you off the hook that easily. Come here," he said, gathering me in his arms and dragging me into his lap before tucking the blanket around us both. When we were snuggled in close, he continued, "I have no clue what to say to all of this, though I suspect that was the easy part of your story. For now, I'll just hold you so you know that even if you had to endure these experiences alone, you're not alone now. I'm here, and I'm not leaving. Finish your story, baby."

His hand rose to cup my head, which rested against his chest. After placing a kiss on my crown, he gave me a gentle squeeze, encouraging me to continue.

"Little changed after my pledge, except *The Alpha* would visit me on occasion. Our conversations were brief before he dismissed me. It wasn't until later I ascertained that his visits had little to do with me. Despite my position, *To Ieró* customs dictated he could not take me until my seventeenth birthday to ensure Theós had optimal conditions to transfer to any child conceived. During the years between, my mother served as my sexual surrogate."

Wes gasped in shock, causing me to chuckle. Why I found this humorous was a mystery, although it may stem from the knowledge that his head was likely to explode before I finished if that tidbit elicited a reaction from him.

"On my twelfth birthday, I was working in the vegetable garden behind our home when Jay showed up. He was hiding in the cover of trees not far from where I was working and threw pebbles at me to covertly gain my attention. I hadn't forgotten the pain I'd endured six-and-a-half years earlier, but it had faded enough and my loneliness was so intense that I threw caution to the wind and inched my way nearer. I worked at the furthest edge of the plantings so he crept to the nearest section of forest until we were separated by only fifteen feet. He didn't say much more than 'happy birthday'—I didn't say anything at all—but he kept me company and offered his silent support. It was my first taste of friendship and the first gift I'd ever received.

"After his first visit, Jay came to see me several times a week. Most of my days were spent working in the garden or—March through November—tending to the land, making it easy for him to approach me unseen. Thankfully, our cottage was the most isolated in the entire community, deliberately chosen for my mother and I to ensure limited exposure to anyone.

"For four years, Jay kept me company. At first, he remained silent with only a greeting or farewell—I later learned he was allowing me to become comfortable in the presence of another person, especially a male. After a couple of weeks, he began telling me elaborate stories. Some were about imprisoned princesses and their attempts to escape, others were of knights rescuing the damsels in distress, and still others chronicled a strange world with schools and people who thought for themselves and enjoyed freedoms I'd never even imagined. Those years were the closest I came to happiness before moving to New York.

"In four years he never came closer than ten feet, yet it was the most affectionate relationship I'd ever experienced. He introduced me to the concept of the individual—in short, he introduced me to *me*. Through his stories, he fostered the development of dreams and aspirations. I cherished his friendship, our time together being the only ray of light in my otherwise dreary existence.

"Several days after my sixteenth birthday, my mother noticed me 'talking to myself' and came to investigate, since time spent in contemplation was strictly discouraged. When she approached and realized I wasn't alone, she dragged me to the meeting hall and told *The Alpha* what she'd discovered. Jay was immediately banished from *To Ieró*. He was twenty years old without a penny to his name. I can't imagine what he must have gone through to survive—all because of me. His compassionate heart cost him the only family—deranged though it was—he'd ever known. You want to know why I am ashamed? Well, there's another reason...my desperate need for connection cost Jay dearly, yet despite the price he paid, there's a part of me that can't regret those years and the gift he gave me—how selfish am I?

"After Jay was sent away, I was forced to undergo another purification. I was locked in a windowless closet for forty days and forty nights with only bread and water as subsistence, and I saw and spoke to no one for nearly six weeks. When I was finally released, I was brought before *To Ieró* to confess my wrongs and beg forgiveness from each member by providing an offering of myself. Each member shaved a section of my hair, representing the removal of the stain on my vessel. Once *The Sacred* finished, they each offered their tribute to *The Alpha*, burning my hair in a copper bowl at his feet. When the hair was reduced to ash, it was mixed with water and autumn crocus, a concoction I was required to drink as my final act of penance and cleansing. The potion triggered a violent sickness that lasted days, leaving me feeble for weeks.

"Despite my suffering, Jay's punishment was far worse than my own—or so I thought at the time. Later, I learned he had been planning to leave for years, his stories of princesses and knights intended to plant a seed that he hoped would flower into a desire to escape with him. Jay's skill as a mechanic allowed him to leave *To Ieró* several times a month to obtain parts and tools needed to maintain *The Sacred*'s farming equipment. During these trips, he fell in love with freedom, slowing building friendships with the outside world. Biding his time, he saved the little money he was allotted each month, as well as pay earned from odd jobs accomplished during his time in the city.

"All that remained of Jay was a piece of paper with his name, an address, and phone number that had been left in a small bottle at the edge of the garden where I worked. He must have found a way to sneak back and leave it for me after his banishment. Without the means to contact him, I assumed the message was intended to give me peace in the knowledge that he had somewhere to go. The scrap of paper became my most treasured possession, a reminder that I once had a friend—I once hoped and dreamed, if only for a short while.

"Life changed with Jay gone—the color leeched from my days and my hope dwindled until nothing remained but pain and loss. Looking back, I can see I was depressed. Although it wasn't a concept or term I was familiar with, it was one I felt intensely. A penetrating, bone-deep loneliness consumed me, causing the girl that Jay had awakened to retreat, slowly withering away until the numbness returned. I once again became the robot I was created to be, continuing mindlessly throughout the next year.

"It wasn't until my seventeenth birthday that I once again felt *something*—although they were not the feelings I would have chosen. I ascended and officially assumed my place as *The Omega*, accepting the role ambivalently and the responsibilities that followed. On a raised dais, before my mother and the watchful eyes of *To Ieró*, I surrendered my virginity to a man eighteen years my senior and for whom I held little regard.   It wasn't making love or sex...hell, it wasn't even fucking—it was ritual and mechanical.   I   wasn't   prepared—physically   or emotionally—for the act, so it hurt on every level. The *only* commendation I can give *The Alpha* is that he didn't enjoy my suffering—nor did it dissuade him. But he was not a sadist.

"Luckily, the traditions of *To Ieró* dictated that I be given forty days between each '*receiving'* to provide a sanctified environment for a child to take root.   During my '*cultivating,'* I was left in relative peace and *The Alpha*'s needs were attended to by countless surrogates amongst *The Sacred*.   Mercifully, his chosen worshipers were all willing, although some were barely seventeen," I paused to shake my head in disgust. "He is a truly vile creature."

I collected my thoughts before continuing with my tale, not risking a glance at Wes' face for fear of the disgust I would see.

"When   biology   confirmed   that   his   effort   was unsuccessful, the ritual was repeated before *The Sacred*. The second attempt proved fruitful—at first. I miscarried in my fourth month, which was an acceptable loss as Theós does not pass to the child until the seventh month. The loss provided a reprieve for two months at the insistence of the midwife.

"There was concern that my miscarriage resulted from my indulgence in '*contaminated thinking,'* which led *The Alpha* to move me into his home, where I could be properly supervised at all times. For the most part, I was ignored, doing my part by remaining silent and virtually invisible during my stay—as was expected of me. The unforeseen byproduct of this arrangement was my exposure to the inner workings of *To Ieró* under *The Alpha*'s leadership. As primary *counselor, The Mánti̱* often visited to share his visions and prophecies with *The Alpha*, as well as advise about various issues facing *The Sacred* community. During these meetings, I went unnoticed while garnering more awareness and secrets than I'd ever thought possible.

"I'd often suspected that *The Alpha* was not following in the footsteps of his predecessors as exactingly as law would dictate, but *The Alpha* was the law so any abnormalities went unchallenged. Without careful scrutiny, most would have overlooked the inexplicable fortune befalling *To Ieró* under *The Alpha*'s reign, attributing the prosperity to the virtuousness and obedience of the community. Yet from my position within his household, I discovered the truth...*The Alpha*—or this *Alpha*, at least—was a fraud. A charlatan professing the beliefs of *To Ieró* and purporting his divinity, while violating the tenets of the faith, breaking his covenant with Theós.

"The influx of wealth toted as proof of *To Ieró's* divine compliance were, in reality, profits for the production and sale of crystal meth. *The Alpha* spent years learning to make meth, establishing conduits for distribution and selling to the top dealers in the neighboring three states. *To Ieró's* location was the perfect base for manufacturing...off the grid in an established *'religious community'* with no history of trouble or complaints. The self-sustaining agricultural efforts of *To Ieró* were well-known, enabling *The Alpha* to secure the necessary ingredients without raising alarms. So the supposed 'incarnation of God' was actually peddling drugs indiscriminately to anyone willing to pay, and no one outside his inner circle was the wiser.

"I was at a loss for what to do. The guilt of doing nothing ate at me, but every action I contemplated was thwarted. I knew none of *The Sacred* would stand against *The Alpha*—he was their god, above reproach. There was no phone accessible to me, and I was supervised like a child with a tendency to wander.

"Desperate for a solution, I took greater risks, eavesdropping in hopes of gaining information I could use to access a phone or escape. The last conversations I overheard revealed *The Alpha* had planned and experimented for over a decade before positioning himself as one of the primary meth suppliers in the Northwest, going so far as to kill his father—the previous Alpha—to gain control of *To Ieró* in pursuit of his goals. The man is a sociopath and a killer.

"My attempts at stealth must have failed because he grew suspicious of my lingering about when company was present. I had no doubt he would punish me severely—or worse, kill me—when he discovered all I knew. Time was running out, yet I remained isolated with no plan for escape.

"A stroke of luck provided by a small chemical fire in his workshop finally presented the opportunity to sneak away. I hid in the back of a box truck filled with meth, bound for Boise. During the four-hour ride, I strategized my course of action upon arrival. Having never left the compound, my knowledge of the outside world was sparse at best, and I didn't know who was safe or how far *The Alpha*'s reach extended in the area.

"Since Jay was the only person I trusted—despite our two-year separation—my plan was to find my way to wherever he was. Thankfully, I had memorized the address and phone number he'd left for me. When the truck arrived at its destination, I remained hidden until the two *Sacred* were distracted, then ran for my life. Well over an hour later, I stumbled into a doctor's office, begging to use the phone. The receptionist denied my request and insisted I leave before she was forced to call the police.

"Crestfallen, I exited, determined to visit every office, store, and restaurant I could find until successful. A woman followed me out of the doctor's waiting room, offering me her cell phone, which I gratefully accepted. Before connecting, she explained that she was a social worker for the State of Idaho and recognized a girl in trouble when she saw one. Still unsure of whom I could trust, I simply nodded and dialed the number Jay had provided. I nearly cried when an unfamiliar man's voice answered the phone—I'd gambled my one chance at freedom on my only friend's willingness to help...and he wasn't there. Jay's name slipped from my lips, but I received no response. I was about to disconnect when the man said, *'Oh my God! You're her, aren't you? The girl from Oregon. Holy shit! He's going to freak. Hold on, I'll get you Jay's number, just don't hang up—he'll kill me if you do.'* After a moment, the man returned, rattling off ten digits that I forced him to repeat five times until I was certain I'd committed the number to memory. The good samaritan gestured to the phone as I pressed 'end,' granting me permission for a second call before I had to ask. Fingers shaking, I dialed the number, anxious until Jay's voice finally came over the line.

"All it took was his name from my lips and he was ready to hop on a plane to retrieve me. After a brief debate, we agreed it would be best if I left town immediately, which precluded Jay making the trip to accompany me. Air travel was impossible as I had no identification, so it was decided I would travel by bus. After speaking with the Good Samaritan, Jay told me we could trust her and instructed me to tell her my story, as well as call Oregon State Police before boarding the bus.

"My Good Samaritan, Wendy, drove me to the bus station, paid for my ticket to the tune of five hundred dollars, and listened to my story. Just before boarding the bus, Wendy lent me her phone to call the police and report the felonious activities at *To Ieró*. I left an anonymous tip detailing everything I knew and hung up with the reassurances the police would investigate.

"Two days, two-thousand miles, and four buses later, I arrived in Greensboro, North Carolina, where Jay was waiting to greet me."

Chapter 28

*"The greatest happiness of life is
the conviction that we are loved;
loved for ourselves, or rather, loved
in spite of ourselves." -Victor Hugo*

<u>Westly</u>

Thirty minutes—that was how long it took to discover her secrets and the source of her shame. Thirty minutes of gut-wrenching, soul-shredding, mind-bending honesty that left me feeling violated on her behalf. Too many emotions fought for supremacy, tangled together, feeding off one another until it was impossible to separate or process. Hell, I needed therapy after listening to her story—experiencing such trauma through her eyes was harrowing. Nausea sat heavy like a boulder in the pit of my stomach as I fought to contain my desire to be sick. No way could I risk her misinterpreting my visceral response as a reflection upon her rather than what she'd survived. I knew enough to know she would internalize my reaction as a judgment against her instead of empathy *for* her. As if on cue, she confirmed my intuition.

"I've already told you what happened once I reached Jay—*for the most part*—so there you have it. Now you know everything," she finished stoically, before adding, "I understand if you want to leave, Wes. You signed up for a good time, and my life is the antithesis of uncomplicated fun. "

Her arms tightened around my middle as she spoke, the physical communication contradicting her words. She wanted my acceptance and understanding even when she couldn't give it to herself.

"Oh, beautiful, you've always been complicated—it's one of the things that attracted me to you," I teased in an attempt to lighten her spirits and convey my acceptance. "I won't lie to you, that was a whole lot of fucked up you just shared, but it's fucked up that happened *to* you, not because of you." I immediately raised my hand to halt her dissent. "As desperately as you want to tell me this is all your fault, every ounce of the guilt and shame you carry is complete bullshit. I know you believe it—because they did a damn good job conditioning you to feel accountable for *their* actions—but that doesn't make it true."

Craning my neck awkwardly, I looked down at her until she met my eyes. *Shit!* She didn't believe a word I' said—not that I was surprised. But she would...one day she would recognize that the sick bastards who abused her were responsible for the wrongs committed at *To Ieró*. I would make sure my beautiful girl finally saw how incredibly strong and brave she'd always been. There would be no doubt in her mind as to the phenomenal, tenderhearted, *good* person she truly was. If it took the rest of my days to achieve, so be it. At least I would die with the knowledge I had succeeded in restoring what was taken from an innocent. It would be the one exceptionally noble act of my life, perhaps redeeming my stained soul.

"I see we have work to do," I declared, mostly to myself. "There is no way I can undo eighteen years of habituation in one night, but I can start now and will keep working until we've unbound all the chains they've bound you with, however long it may take—weeks, months, maybe even years. You *will* be free, and not just physically...in here," I said, gently tapping her temple with my finger.

Opening her mouth to speak, I placed my hand across her lips, circumventing her attempt.

"Nope, you don't get to talk yet, the floor is still mine."

Shaking her head in what appeared to be mild exasperation, she pulled my hand away, yet remained silent. I counted it as a victory—the first of many. After all, I always won.

"That was entirely too much information for me to process in such a short time, some stated outright and much implied. Off the cuff, I have a few questions and observations that warrant discussion, so how about you stay in my arms where you belong and be a cooperative witness?"

I felt her nod against my chest as I organized the facts and my suppositions.

"This is by no means the most important conclusion of what you just shared, but you, my beautiful girl, are not married."

She said nothing, so I continued, "You had no civil ceremony, no marriage license could have been obtained as you have no legitimate identity, and your *'religious ceremony'* is irrelevant given your age at the time it occurred. Furthermore, you were under duress. Legally, you never consented to marry and ethically, the entire agreement was a travesty. One item off the 'to-do' list."

Her laughter shook my torso and raised my spirits. It had been far too long since I'd heard the music of her mirth. *God, I'd missed her.* The absence was like losing a limb...you would learn to live without it, but you would never be the same, the phantom pains haunting you until your dying day.

In a short time, she had become a vital part of my life...the center of my universe. Realization hit like a Mack truck going one hundred miles per hour, downhill, fully loaded with gold bars—I loved her. I was *in* love with her. I'd never understood the distinction, yet it was now crystal clear and utterly necessary. *In*, because she was inside of me, now an integral part of myself that I couldn't separate. *Love*, because while I cared for her as a friend and as a person, it was more. I loved every part of her; the easy and complex, the painful and the tender, the past and the present. I loved the parts of her she hated in herself because they made her who she is. I loved her entirely, accepting her burdens and sorrows as my own, along with her joys and triumphs. I loved her in a way that made me a better man—a man willing to sacrifice anything for his woman to ensure her happiness and safety. She tempered my selfishness until it was selflessness, distilled my bitterness into hopefulness, and exchanged my emptiness for completion.

Well, that was unexpected—and might I add, poorly timed. The comprehension of my feelings for her and their depths was begging to be spoken, however such a revelation felt inappropriate given our conversation. I would have to hold my tongue—for the moment—until the right time presented itself.

Pushing aside my life-altering insight proved to be a Herculean feat, but my girl didn't need words of love at present—she needed a reality check.

"Beautiful, you've had seven years since leaving those whackjobs to find your own identity, to learn about the great big world that existed beyond the isolated compound, to build a life and a future for yourself...and you've achieved all of that admirably. What you've accomplished with virtually no assistance or support verges on the miraculous. There aren't words for how proud I am of you. *Truly*. But—"

"Why does there have to be a *'but'*? I really liked the direction you were headed. Can't we stay on the *'oh, beautiful, you are a gift to all mankind'* train of thought?" she interrupted sassily.

Thank God! My girl was fighting her way back from the darkness—even now. *So damn strong!*

"But," I continued, playfully nudging her, "in seven years, with all the knowledge and experience you've attained, it never occurred to you that the shame and guilt you are lugging around is just one more lie they fed you...one more trap you have to escape?"

"Wes," she began to say, but I interrupted her—again.

"Sorry, I'm not going to listen to your, or rather *their*, regressive thinking. We are moving forward, over that mountain of remorse and self-loathing, even if I have to strap you to my back and carry you, kicking and screaming. Got it?" I didn't bother to wait for a reply. "You feel guilty you *'chose,'*" I said with finger quotes and a heavy dose of sarcasm, "to become *The Omega*—bullshit! You said it yourself...you only had the *illusion* of choice and at ten years of age, you weren't intellectually or emotionally equipped to stay home without a babysitter, let alone commit yourself to marriage."

Something clicked—I saw it in her eyes—a piece of their filth was chipped away. Impatient to capitalize on the fracture, I continued.

"You feel guilty Jay was banished—complete crap! You admitted he had been preparing to leave for years, and I'll bet if you asked him...no, scratch that—I'll bet you *have* asked him and he said it was the best thing that could have ever happened to him. Did he tell you to stop apologizing and let it go?"

She looked at me sheepishly before nodding to confirm my suspicions.

"Exactly. The only other source of guilt I can fathom you claiming is that you've failed to out *The Alpha* to the community and stop his drug cartel."

"Don't trivialize my responsibility to protect innocents," she snapped, attempting to rise despite my vice grip.

"Relax, baby. No need to turn into a hostile witness," I joked, trying to smooth her ruffled feathers. "I'm not trivializing the seriousness of the situation, just trying to help you understand that you are assigning blame unjustly. Was there anything you could have said or done while still at...*To Ieró*," I struggled to pronounce the unfamiliar name, "that would have convinced the followers that their leader was a homicidal sociopath?"

"No," she supplied simply.

"And you called in an anonymous tip to the cops as soon as you were given an opportunity. You did everything in your power to help those left behind in the cult and prevent

The Alpha's meth from being sold. Furthermore, I would be remiss in my defense if I didn't point out that those you are concerned with protecting are hardly *innocents.* The people buying the meth are addicts who have made and continue to make the choice to use. I'm not saying they aren't in need of help or worthy of compassion—even I'm not that big of an asshole—but if you cut off the supply from *To Ieró,* the dealers will buy from another supplier and the users will still end up using," I outlined the harsh reality. "As for the other members of the cult...I understand most were probably born into the society and don't know any other way of life, *but*—what type of person with any moral compass can stand and watch a five-year-old have her fingernails pried from her hand without intervening? There may be psychological explanations or sociological justifications for their inaction, but their obligation and responsibility to act on your behalf is far greater than any you have to them now. They remain at *To Ieró* by choice or ignorance; you were physically abused and tortured. Many words come to mind to describe *'The Sacred,'* but innocent is not one of them."

My temper was high, anger coursing through my veins as I thought of what she'd been subjected to and the bystanders who had failed to intercede. In the heat of my rage, I wanted to burn the entire godforsaken compound to the ground with everyone over the age of eighteen locked inside.

"Wes," she whispered as she brought her hand to cup my cheek, "thank you—for so many reasons, thank you."

The kiss she bestowed was both reverent and loving in equal measure—it melted me. With restraint worthy of sainthood, I pulled back from the kiss before it could escalate, my body protesting raucously.

"There's one more thing I have to confess," she said nervously.

Dammit! Would the hits ever stop coming? I loved this girl—nothing she could say would change the depth of love I felt for her, but she was a magnet for trouble. It wasn't her fault, I knew, yet loving her would always be wrought with challenges, courtesy of her propensity to attract messes.

"Okay, I can do this," she murmured, offering herself a pep talk. "Since we first met, I've held a lot of opinions and theories about the type of person you are—most of them *not* good. For that, I'm sincerely sorry, because most of my assumptions proved wrong. You are a good man, compassionate and honest..." Looking in my eyes and straight to my soul, she continued, "I love you, Westly Black. I didn't want to, and didn't even believe it possible— but it's true...I'm utterly and irrefutably in love with you. It's okay if you don—"

"*Thank God,*" I thought aloud before pulling her closer, grazing my lips against hers delicately. Without retreating, I spoke the words that had been pleading for release, "I love *you*, my beautiful, strong, challenging girl." Her mouth parted as she gasped in shock, causing me to chuckle. "If you're surprised, imagine how I feel—it was a scandalous realization that I, a heartless asshole, was capable of love. Several months ago, I told you I only excelled at two things—sex and the law. I propose an amendment to my statement, your honor."

"Proceed, counselor," she returned, playing along perfectly. *God, I loved this girl.*

"I move to amend the record to add 'loving you' as my third area of expertise. Although I may not have mastered the subject as of yet, I fully intend to make doing so my life's work."

"Motion approved...in fact, I *insist* on it."

Chapter 29

"Jealousy is the fear of comparison."
-Max Frisch

<u>Meg</u>

"Is Jay the other guy you were with?" Wes asked unexpectedly, shortly after our declarations of love. "You said you've only been with two."

Hesitating—to assess my options—I decided the blunt approach would serve me best.

"Yes, he was," I responded directly.

An incomprehensible utterance preceded his reply, "More than once?"

Well, that was specific!

"Geeze, Wes! Would you like an account of his technique and which positions he attempted? You already know he didn't *get me there*, so at least I can avoid that invasive question."

"Okay, that was uncharacteristically clumsy of me. I was endeavoring to find out if you were...*intimate* the other night, without being offensive. It appears I misspoke," he admitted contritely. "The jealousy has been gnawing at me for weeks. We weren't technically together at the time, so I have no reasonable complaint—still, I need to know so I can let it go."

Unbidden, the Disney song *'Let It Go'* played in full stereo inside my head. Dammit, would I ever be able to hear that phrase without being held musical hostage? Regardless of how much I enjoyed the song when I first heard it, that tune was now the bane of my existence—an inescapable ditty that would torment me for hours.

Wes cleared his throat, "Still waiting...please tell me that space-out wasn't a result of you revisiting your time with Jay. I may be secure in my abilities, but knowing you're thinking of him *like that* when I'm with you is a mindfuck I can't handle."

Laughing at his idiotic assumption, I teased, "Green is not a good color on you, Black."

"*Beautiful*," he warned.

"Yeah, yeah, yeah...keep your pants on—for now," I winked saucily. *Dang, it was fun messing with him.* "I was actually contemplating the efficacy of epic movie songs for torture applications at Gitmo."

He looked at me with a *'oh shit, she's lost it'* expression that indicated I should have kept that particular musing to myself. *Ooops!*

"No, *darling*, I didn't sleep with Jay the other night. I did, however, coat him in a layer of snot and tears that likely forced him to chuck his t-shirt," I said, unable to mask my amusement.

Wes nodded, appearing slightly mollified, "Do you love him?"

"Yes," I answered honestly, his look of distress spurring me to clarify ASAP, "but not the way I love you. I love Jay the same way I love Griffin or Hunter...like a brother. You have to understand, he was the first person to show me any kindness. The risks he took to humanize me and later provide a safe place for me to find my bearings...he knew the dangers, Wes, but he stuck his neck out to help someone he barely knew. He'll always have a place in my heart for what he's done, but that place is small compared to the vast territory you've claimed."

"So you love him like a *brother*, but you slept with him?" he said, his tone accusatory and riddled with doubt.

"Hey, Mr. Hypocrites-'R'-Us, are you serious? Did you love the bevy of barflies you screwed? I understand you're jealous—it was almost cute until you started being an asshole," I snapped, annoyed by his suspicion, yet a part of me understanding his position. There was a distinct difference between banging a random stranger and sleeping with someone you had emotional ties to—not that I would admit it when he was being a prick. "I'm going to explain—although you don't deserve it—and then you are going to move on and never bring it up again. Got it?"

His only response was a jerky nod. Evidently, someone's head was still crammed up his super-fine ass.

"Jay didn't want me to be alone so soon after escaping. He wanted me to remain in North Carolina with him, but fear for his safety prevented me from staying. When I refused, he offered to come with me. I wouldn't let him abandon the life he'd built for me, so again I declined. The night before I left, he played the only card he had left— seduction. I knew what he was doing, but I was also curious about what sex was like outside of the microcosm of *To Ieró* and *The Alpha*. Deep down, I believe Jay knew sleeping together wouldn't change anything, yet his need to protect me compelled him to try every tool at his disposal."

Wes' humorless bark of laughter interrupted my story, causing me to raise an eyebrow in question.

"Don't be naïve, beautiful—he wanted you...still does. He may have had good intentions to justify his actions, but the bottom line is he wanted in your pants and grasped at any excuse possible to grant himself permission. You underestimate how captivating you are."

"*Whatever!* We slept together, but there was no fire and I couldn't...you know. Jay's no fool—when we finished, he knew the connection wasn't there and never would be. After explaining—yes, *he* had to enlighten me since I didn't know *anything*—what sex was supposed to be like, he took the time to reassure me that I would find the right man one day who would provide a safe place to explore sex and find the satisfaction I was missing," I paused, blushing at the memory. "Are you hearing me? Poor Jay, who despite his best efforts was unable to get me off, had the birds-and-the-bees talk with me! He took the time to comfort me and answer my questions, reassuring me that there was more to sex than what I'd experienced. You want to know why Jay will always be special to me? In a moment when most guys' egos would have blamed me for the crappy sex, Jay focused on my needs. Then, he honored my wishes and let me go the next day without making the situation awkward and with the assurance he would always be a friend I could turn to."

Releasing an exasperated breath, I continued, "I'm not *in* love with Jay, and I never have been. Frankly, I don't think he's ever been in love with me either. He wanted to save me—and yes, he was attracted to me, I'm not an idiot— but he knew the spark was missing."

Wes was quiet for an exceptionally long minute before his laughter filled the room, continuing until he was forced to wipe moisture from his eyes.

"Are you seriously telling me that *Jay* had to have the sex talk with you...*after* he failed to score the touchdown. Damn, this is good stuff—might even make the top ten list of emasculating moments."

The dirty look I threw his way left no question as to my feelings regarding his pleasure in Jay's suffering.

"Come on, beautiful...I know he's been a good friend to you, but even *you* have to admit that is fucking ironic."

I couldn't help but giggle. Replaying the scene years later with new perspective, it was ludicrous. We smiled at each other until a thought arose that stomped my merriment to smithereens. "What about you and Miss Public Indecency? I hardly think you have grounds for jealousy," I finished bitterly.

"Ah, I'm not the only one battling the green-eyed monster. Not so fun when the shoe's on the other foot, is it?"

My elbow connected with his ribs before he had time to prepare. "*Ouch.* Dammit, beautiful, your elbows are lethal weapons."

Good! He had it coming—I was the one who had a front-row seat to the Wes and Miss Slutty McSlutterson's live-action porno.

"To answer your question, no, I didn't have sex—of any kind—with...with...whatever her name was.   Evidently, you've bewitched Wes, Jr. and he will only respond to your siren call."

"Well, at least one of you had his head on straight," I admonished, secretly pleased with his admission.   "Now, can we stop talking about sex with other people? It's killing my warm fuzzies."

"I'm sure I could distract you from such unpleasant thoughts. For example, I have never officially made love to you," he said while rising to his feet with me secure in his arms. "An oversight I'm about to rectify."

"As long as you're not planning to *rectal*fy, I second that motion," I joked salaciously.

His surprised laughter was music to my ears.

"No...not tonight at least," he said with a wink. "It seems you've been spending entirely too much time with Sam in my absence, an issue I plan to thoroughly address.   Then again, I'm beginning to see the personal benefits of girl time."

Having reached our destination, he placed me gently on the bed and undressed me carefully and deliberately, like I was made of glass. With each article of clothing removed, our mood shifted further from naughty nettling to cherishing caresses.

Naked before him in every way possible, I returned the same attention, dotingly removing the fabric that hid him from me. With each exposed inch, I worshiped his body, conveying my desire to connect with him at the most fundamental level of our beings.

Equally exposed, he covered me with his body, engulfing me in his warmth and presence. The embrace was safe and familiar like...home. Never having had a real home, the feeling was not instantly recognizable—yet once identified, it was undeniable. Wes was the home I had searched for and tried to build for myself. In my journey since escaping *To Ieró,* I had found a family, filled with the love and acceptance of friends. However, until now, I had remained homeless.   Soul-deep recognition brought forth unparalleled peace, causing tears of joy to form.

"What is it, beautiful? Why are you crying?" he asked, his voice full of concern.

"You—you're my home. I finally have a home, Wes," I whispered with conviction as a quiet sob escaped.

"Yes, baby. I'm your home and you're mine—always. Through any storm, I will give you shelter. When you're broken or damaged, I'll repair you. In the cold, I'll warm you, and when you get too hot, I will be the one to cool you down. And if trouble comes, I will protect you at all cost—with my life if necessary," he pledged solemnly. "I love you, beautiful...all of you. Even the parts about yourself you hate are miraculous to me," he whispered. With those final words, he slid inside me, breaching the barrier of skin to find the heart of me.

He captured my hands in his as he slowly raised them next to my head, interweaving our fingers to cement our connection. We kissed as if it were our only source of sustenance—nibbling lips and sliding tongues, we feasted on one another endlessly.

Our pace was slow, allowing us to relish every miniscule sensation together. I felt his pleasure as keenly as my own—every muscle contraction in response to my touch, every throb of desire, every pulse throughout his body in time with his heartbeat.

His body slid against mine sensually, further arousing my sensitized skin until I anticipated each glide of his muscled chest as much as the thrust that followed. I moved with him in perfect counterpoint, my legs woven around his, keeping us connected from our threaded fingers to the tips of my toes.

Each time I raised my hips to meet his stroke, tiny explosions of light on the backs of my eyelids rewarded my efforts. Finally breaking our kiss, he nipped at my neck before teasing my earlobe with barely-there kisses.

"You're killing me, baby. I could get lost inside you for days, wanting nothing more than the feeling of you wrapped around me, squeezing me like you'd rather die than let me go. Every inch of your soft body pressed against mine...there is nothing in this world that's better."

Untangling my legs to hitch them higher around his waist, I locked my ankles behind his back, clinging tightly as his rhythm picked up speed. My core clenched, alerting me that I was nearing the precipice. The air around us charged with an inexplicable energy, the intensity of which elevated our lovemaking from passionate joining to something that would be indelibly etched in our memories.

Desperate for all of him, I pulled my hands free to grip his head, pulling his lips to mine with urgency. Understanding my need, he grasped my hips tightly, working me harder with equal parts power and finesse. The additional force and twist of his hips detonated the nuclear orgasm he had built, and I exploded with a ferocity that left me shaking with involuntary muscle spasms. He followed closely behind, whispering words of love before unintelligible groans of completion. His body remained stiff, every muscle contracting for long minutes as the after-effects of his own volatile orgasm subsided.

When his body finally relaxed, he fell to his side before rolling on his back, taking me with him and draping me across his body like a favorite blanket on a cold night. Neither of us spoke for several minutes, each lost in our own thoughts...or perhaps trying to regain the ability to think.

"What was that?" I finally asked, breaking the companionable silence.

"I think that was making love...on steroids—no, jet fuel. Whatever it was, I want to do it again in about an hour, and then again an hour later, and...hell, let's find a way to do nothing but that forever," he suggested.

"An interesting idea, but I believe the only profession that would be compatible with your plan would be a career in porn—and I'm not up for cameramen in the bedroom. Plus, we'd have to eat at some point," I explained reasonably.

"Mmm, food does sound good. What mountains of food does Sam have hidden away for Griffin?"

"Dunno, and the kitchen is *sooo* far away," I pouted.

"Luckily, you have a man who loves you to tend to your every need. I'll go forage for sustenance while you rest up for dessert."

After a delicious dinner of leftover Chicken Rustica with grilled veggies, Wes and I relaxed in bed, enjoying gentle touches and innocent kisses while we snuggled.

"This is amazing," I finally said, breaking the silence. "Just lying here with you—it feels so...right, like we've been together for years. Isn't that weird?"

"Weird or not, I wouldn't trade this time with you for anything. It's like you said, being with you is home, and I haven't had a home since before I can remember. Thank you for giving me that gift, beautiful."

"You're welcome, but I think it's me that should be thanking you," I said quietly.

His only reply was a dismissive *Pssht*.

"Have you met Thia?" he asked abruptly.

"Hello, non sequitur," I chuckled. "Yes, several times. She's a friend of GriffLo, and I guess mine too. Actually, she's my therapist now...it was one of Dr. Mesina's motherly conditions in support of my work."

"Wait...Dr. Mesina? Do you mean, Dr. Rosalia Mesina?"

"Yeah, she's my academic advisor. I've told you about her several times—weren't you listening?" I asked, teasing...mostly.

"You've told me plenty about your academic advisor and I remember it all, but you *never* used her name. I guarantee it," he said with unerring confidence. "I can't believe I didn't make the connection myself," he muttered while laughing. "*Damn*, this is going to be fun. Ry is going to lose it when I tell him."

"Tell him what?"

"Do you remember me mentioning my best friend Ry?" I nodded.

"Ry—Ryland Mesina. Dr. Rosalia Mesina is his mother and the closest thing to a maternal figure I've ever had. *Holy shit!* She is going to have a field day with this. She's been riding my ass to settle down for years. I think she goes to church every Sunday just to light candles for my '*poor lost manwhore soul.*'"

"You have got to be kidding me! I feel like I should break into a chorus of '*It's a small world after all.*'"

We both laughed at the coincidence, Wes securing my promise to meet Ry next week.

"Why did you ask about Thia?" I questioned, backtracking to our previous topic.

"I played poker with her tonight. She's...I'm not even sure what to call her—eccentric, maybe? I liked her, even though she pinched every chip I won off Hunter and Griffin. Plus, I'm almost positive poker night was a cover for group therapy, of which I was the star tonight."

"That sounds about right. If the powers that be decided we belonged together and we weren't *fixing* the problem at an acceptable pace, there is nothing they wouldn't do. They are a devious bunch, and with Thia at the helm—*geeze*, they could probably take over the world or solve the Middle East conflict. I'm glad they used their powers for good."

"So am I, baby. I would have found my way back to you regardless—my stubborn pride was already weakening—but their intervention was welcome," he admitted.

"Agreed," I smiled. "But whatever you do, don't *ever* repeat that to any of them—it's the equivalent of granting permission for future meddling."

"I wouldn't mind meddling if this is the result," he said, hugging me closer.

"You say that now. Have you already forgotten Sam's lack of boundaries?"

I felt his exaggerated shudder. *Exactly, buddy!*

"Point taken. Silent gratitude it is," he conceded. "I'd like to take you out for dinner tomorrow night—our first official date."

"We've gone to dinner before," I said in confusion.

"Yeah, but that was 'hanging out,'" he replied with finger quotes. "I want to take my woman out to dinner and show her off," he finished with a wink.

"Well, by all means, flaunt me, baby!"

"Here's all you have to know about men and women: women are crazy, men are stupid. And the main reason women are crazy is that men are stupid." -George Carlin

Westly

Dressed to impress, I picked my girl up at Sam's and drove her to my favorite restaurant, Thai House, for our first date as an official couple. I checked all the boxes: brought flowers, opened car doors, pushed in her chair—yes, I was kicking ass at this boyfriend thing.

Since she'd never eaten Thai, I selected a few items for us to share and our waitress also suggested her favorite dish on the menu.

"Beautiful, you don't have to clear your plate if you're too full," I said, laughing, as she groaned in pain while trying to squeeze the last bite of spicy eggplant into her overloaded tummy.

"But it's sooo good, and I want Ashley to know how much I enjoyed it."

"Who the heck is Ashley?" I asked, at a loss. *Did I even know an Ashley?*

"Ashley...our waitress—the one who recommended the eggplant," she said, sighing dramatically when I scanned the restaurant, trying to identify the server in question. "Cute girl with blond hair, fixed in one of those awesome side braids everyone is wearing."

Nope, I had nothing. I shrugged, unsure why I cared in the first place.

"Hey beautiful, can I ask you something?"

"You can ask me anything, Wes...I may even answer you," she quipped.

Obviously, Thai made her feisty, which would benefit me later. Note to self: bring home a take-out menu.

"You said you hate the name Meg. Have you considered what name you're going to give Hunter for your identification papers?"

The curiosity was killing me. Rarely did people get to select their own name, and I couldn't help but wonder what she felt represented who she was—or rather who she wanted to be.

"I've narrowed down the list, but he promised I had a few more weeks before committing. It's a tough decision...I want something that represents me but still sounds pretty. Plus, I want to have an easy nickname."

"Okay, are you going to tell me what you're considering?" I prompted.

"Nope, I want you to be surprised. I'm not telling anyone 'til I've decided. Otherwise, all the differing opinions will make it impossible."

"My opinion doesn't count? What if I hate it? I'll be forced to repeatedly call out a name I despise every time we make love. Think of the potential trauma," I argued.

"Oh, poor baby," she mocked. "I'm tempted to name myself 'Christopher' just so you have to cry out a man's name every time you come."

"Oh, you're evil...wait a minute, why do I sense Ev and Sam are behind this particular suggestion?"

"Because you're astute," she teased, confirming my suspicions.

"You ladies need close supervision on all future playdates," I declared, happy for an excuse to crash girls' night and spend more time with my woman. Having just gotten her back, I wasn't ready to play nice and share just yet. Maybe in a year or two...*nah!*

We arrived back at my house and decided to watch TV before bed, both of us too stuffed to do much else.

"Do you mind if I borrow your laptop to check my email?" she asked. "I've been waiting on a message from Dr. Mesina."

"Go for it."

Snagging my computer from the coffee table, she began to click away while I headed to the kitchen to grab us drinks. A few minutes later, her horrified gasp had me running to her side.

"What is it, beautiful?" I asked as calmly as possible.

Without speaking a word, she turned the screen so I could see.

"You have to help me out here, baby. I have no idea what I'm looking at," I reminded her.

"It's from *him*," she replied shakily. "It's another email warning."

"What does it mean?" I asked, still unsure what the hell it said. To me, it was nothing more than a strange image that could almost pass for a tattoo.

She pointed to the bottom image as she explained, "This is the sign for *The Alpha*—like his signature. They are the Greek letters for alpha and omega intertwined." Pointing to the top picture, she continued, "This is the symbol for *The Omega*...see, it's *The Alpha*'s symbol upside-down. It's supposed to reflect *The Omega*'s subservience and lesser status." Then, she pointed to the strange letters in the middle of the message, "And this means 'sacrifice.'"

"Okay. I'll admit it's rather creepy, but what does it actually mean?" I asked, not understanding the significance of the email but suspecting there were implications I was missing.

"It's a threat. He's telling me time has run out, and if I don't return he will force me to sacrifice something I treasure to appease Theós. I don't know what, specifically, but he's capable of anything. It wouldn't surprise me if he hurt my mother in the hopes it would cause me to return."

"You're not going back there, not for any reason," I ordered, "but especially not for the woman who birthed you. Christ, she even makes *my* mother look like 'parent of the year.'" Screw women's lib, I'd cuff her to me before I let her face that monster again. *Hmm*—cuffs—the plan had merit! "I know you're scared, beautiful, but I promise you are safe here. The FBI is involved and we are all on the lookout. You're not going to be left alone for a second."

She quirked her head to the side as if studying a foreign specimen.

"You're getting awfully comfortable issuing orders. I've got my eye on you, buddy. Don't think because your BFFs with *Hunter the Hun* and *Griffin the Gladiator*, you can start bossing me around. Luckily, I agree with you. It's safer to have them come for me—now that you and Hunter know the dangers—than for me to return to *To Ieró*."

"*Hunter the Hun* and *Griffin the Gladiator*? They are going to love that," I laughed. "What does that make me?"

"*Westly the Wicked*," she said suggestively before *forcing* me to prove precisely how wicked I could be.

Chapter 31

"We can only bend so far before we break."
-Author Unknown

Meg

A week passed in relative peace with no further emails to taunt me. As Wes promised, I was never left alone, which helped me relax and control the panic that threatened.

Monday, I met with Hunter and provided my official statement to the FBI regarding the living conditions and treatment of those living at *To Ieró*, as well as the crimes being perpetrated by *The Alpha*. Reliving my time as *The Omega* became easier to bear each time I told my story, as if each recounting passed a bit of my burden to the listener, allowing them to help me shoulder the load.

Hunter was professional throughout the interview, but the telltale twitch in his right eye, coupled with his clenching and unclenching fists, indicated how deeply affected he was by my experiences. He paused several times for breaks, although I assured him I was okay to continue.

"It's not for you, sweetheart. I'm the one who needs a breather," he'd responded candidly.

After providing copies of the messages I'd received and explaining their significance, Hunter assured me the FBI would take the threats seriously, cooperating with local police to initiate drive-bys using both marked and unmarked squad cars. When we finally finished, he asked that I return to the New York field office to answer any additional questions that arose upon investigating the information I'd provided thus far. Of course, I agreed, willing—no, *needing*—to help in any way possible.

The drawback of remembering was the nightmares that plagued my sleep. Every night I became the young girl I'd once been, reliving the worst moments of my life with agonizing realism. Yet each night, Wes was there to comfort me, beating back the monsters that lived in my dreams with love, understanding, and when all else failed…distraction.

My sessions with Thia continued. After once again detailing my past, she picked up where Wes left off, helping me identify erroneous thoughts that had resulted in me accepting blame where I held none. As Sam had warned, Thia's therapeutic approach was jarring but effective. She found ways to push me past my past, giving me the tools to break down the walls *To Ieró* had constructed around my individuality and temperament.

In our session on Wednesday, Thia pushed me to have the inevitable and long-overdue heart-to-heart with Sam, Griffin, and Ev that I'd successfully avoided thus far. After that, she moved on to her second favorite topic…my name.

"So, CG—" Thia said with a poorly contained smirk.

"Thia, *dammit,* I've asked you not to call me that! One slip around Sam and I'll be stuck with the nickname for life. It's not the most flattering moniker, you know."

"And I've told you, I'll stop calling you CG just as soon as you pick a name to be called. I refuse to call you '*Meg*' because it references '*The Omega.*'"

"But CG is just as bad," I argued.

"Mmm, perhaps," she replied, pretending to contemplate my grievance. I wasn't fooled. "At least it's not directly connected to that godforsaken title. CG is new and has an indirect association. Plus, it has a certain... *je ne sais quoi.*"

"*Not directly connected?* Are you nuts?" I barked in frustration. "Thia, you're calling me *'Cult Girl'*...in what universe is that not directly connected to my past?"

"Well, *Cult Girl*—that's a mouthful, CG rolls off the tongue—*The Omega* is something you were forced to *be*, whereas *Cult Girl* is nothing more than a description of where you lived and your experiences. Do you not see the distinction?"

When she put it that way, how could I miss the difference? Thia was right—I reacted to CG because I didn't want people to know about my past. I was embarrassed, afraid of an intolerant and ignorant society who would assume I chose to join *To Ieró* willingly, then judge me accordingly. Discrimination against former cult members was a harsh reality for those who escaped and attempted to reintegrate into the 'normal' world. Nevertheless, I was not adopting the name *Cult Girl*—or CG, for that matter—but the significance between CG and *The Omega* were completely different.

"Fine, call me CG for now...as long as you don't explain the acronym to anyone," I granted.

"Only until you decide who *you* want to be. Pick a name and I promise to respect the choice and use it. If you're getting hung up on finding something with profound meaning, then go ahead and just pick a name that sounds pretty or badass—I'd go with badass, personally, like 'Shakira.' And don't let your fear of the future or criticism from others keep you trapped in the past. This is *your* life...make the choice to live it fully."

Thia was right...again—*damn it was annoying*—and I knew it. It was time to move forward in full measure, not hiding behind a fake name, false history, and half-truths. My friends had exhibited more patience than I thought them capable of, out of respect and concern for my well-being, but the time was fast approaching. If I didn't initiate the conversation, they would soon demand answers. It was time to *wo*man up and trust my family to support me—without judgment—as they've always done.

With more fanfare than I would have preferred, our motley crew assembled for dinner with the knowledge I was finally going to have "the talk" with Sam, Ev, and Griffin. Wes was thrilled as he considered it another step in my journey to heal, also believing the added support of the trio would provide further fuel for progress. Hunter nearly kissed me with gratitude, anxious for an end to Ev's incessant grilling—although I noticed his complaints didn't include the sexual feats she was using in the hopes of tiring him to the point of exhaustion, resulting in a slip of the tongue. Yes, Sam felt the need to share in great detail the evil plots afoot as confessed by Ev.

Wes and Hunter remained in the kitchen as I retold my story, close enough to come to my aid if needed, yet far enough that they could spare themselves from reliving my past again—*wimps.*

During my account, Ev cried silent tears, Sam threatened to castrate *The Alpha* and kick my 'good-for-nothing-bitch-of-a-mother's' ass, and Griffin tested the strength of his grip on his thighs, which I suspected would be black and blue the following day.

"I'm sorry I didn't tell you sooner," I said nervously, "You all mean the world to me...you're the only family I've ever known. I didn't want you to look at me differently, to see me as weak and broken. You are all so strong. Ev, you fought off Heath when he attacked you, Sam, you survived the rape and clawed your way back, to the point where you are now helping others do the same, and Griffin...you're the one we all turn to when we need someone to hold us up or talk us down. You're the strength we all count on. Each of you is this remarkable, inspirational person who has overcome challenges and mistakes, only to come back stronger. It's a lot to live up to. You all cast a big shadow that I've been content to hide in."

"Time to see the sun, girl," Griffin said definitively. "You deserve the warmth on your face as much as anyone else in this house."

"Hell yeah," Sam added, "After what *you* have survived and the strength it took to claw *your* way free, you deserve more than just a few rays. You need to move to a tropical island where man-servants are at your beck and call, bringing fruity drinks, lathering you with sunscreen, massaging your back, and—"

"I'm still here, Sam," Wes interrupted, walking into the room. "The private island and fruity drinks are all good, but I'll be the only man-servant keeping her company."

"Then you better call your travel agent and book the vacay ASAP, because if you leave the planning to me, there will be boy-toys a plenty."

Sam winked at me as Wes flipped open his phone, typing away like a man possessed while stringing together an impressive combination of curses.

"They are so easy to control, it almost takes the fun out of it," Sam whispered to me.

Ev came over and hugged me before sharing, "Sometimes it's easier to accept what we have instead of reaching for what we want most, because the risk of losing everything is daunting," she glanced in Hunter's direction before continuing, "but I can promise you that claiming your life, embracing your family, and loving that man," she said, pointing to Wes, "is worth the risk. You've earned your happy ending, paid for by blood, sweat, and tears...now it's up to you to reach out and grab it."

An epic group hug followed that left me misty-eyed and immensely grateful for the gift each of them was in my life. I still wasn't sure if I deserved them, but I wasn't going to let them go.

"Hold on a sec," Sam said as Hunter and Wes joined us on the couches. "What the heck do we call you until you pick a name?"

I groaned aloud, sick of this conversation before it even began.

"I don't know, whatever you want. I'll pick a name soon, I promise," I said, stalling. There was no name that felt right. Perhaps Thia had a point—I needed to figure out who I was and wanted to be before I could name me.

"Too bad we didn't get to meet Jay when he visited. He sounds like a good guy," Ev said, saving me from the name game.

"He is. Actually, he reminds me of Griffin a little, minus the muscles and Viking vibe," I shared. "Maybe he'll come back to visit—and bring his girlfriend," I said while delivering a pointed look at Wes, "once the FBI does their thing."

"Absolutely. He can stay in your room," Sam said impishly, having caught my sharp look at Wes, earning a growl from my man. "What? She'll be at your house, won't she?"

"Damn straight," Wes confirmed vehemently, "right where she belongs."

Friday afternoon, I arrived home after my shift at Higher Yearning to find Hunter's car in my driveway. Foreboding rose, swift and acute, causing me to hasten my steps. As I entered the house, I found Wes and Hunter in the midst of a heated exchange that abruptly ended at my appearance.

"Babe, what are you doing here? Aren't you supposed to be in court?" I asked Wes, shocked at his presence when I knew he had spent the entire week preparing for today's hearing.

"I got a continuance, don't worry," he said dismissively. "Come sit down, beautiful, we need to talk."

This wasn't going to be good.

Turning my attention to Hunter, I asked, "Is it my mother?"

Wes quickly approached, taking my hand to guide me to the great room. It didn't escape my notice that Hunter failed to respond to my inquiry. Wes sat next to me on the sofa while Hunter settled on the loveseat to my left.

"Beautiful—" Wes began, but Hunter interjected, "Man, *please* trust me on this. Let me tell her."

Wes nodded, clearly unhappy but willing to give Hunter the floor.

"I have some bad news," Hunter stated the obvious. "The FBI's regional director contacted me because one of our witnesses was found dead after failing to show for a follow-up interview. I'm so sorry, sweetheart—Jay was killed last night."

No. No, no, no, *no—NO!*

This wasn't happening. There was a mistake. Jay lost track of time while working on a car and would call the FBI to apologize any minute.

"He can't be. You've made a mistake," I said to Hunter with conviction. "You're wrong."

"I've spoken to the Special Agent in charge and reviewed the crime scene photos—there's no mistake. I know how close you were, honey. I'm so terribly sorry."

"No!" I screamed at the top of my lungs, jumping to my feet, crowding Hunter as I jabbed my finger in his chest. "You *promised* me he'd be safe when I gave you his contact info. You *promised* the FBI would protect him, just like they are protecting me. Lies...you lied to me and now Jay is dead, and it's all your fault."

I pounded on his chest with my fists, calling him a liar with each blow, as the tears fell in torrents down my face. But nothing could wash away the pain. My heart screamed its denial, refusing to accept the truth that my first friend— *my savior*—was gone...murdered by the man who claimed to be a god and my husband. I didn't need to see evidence to know the truth: *The Alpha* had ordered me home, I disregarded him, and he warned me that my defiance would require a sacrifice in restitution.

I gasped.

"It's *my* fault. If I'd returned to *To Ieró*—" I whispered, collapsing into Wes' prepared arms before I could finish the thought. "Jay's dead because of me. The email...it was me or him, and I chose me. I might as well have killed him myself. Selfish, murderous bitch."

Cries of raw agony poured from the center of my being as grief burned through me like battery acid, corroding everything it touched. There was no escape, no relief from the torturous grief. I embraced the pain, welcomed it like an old friend, because I deserved every moment of soul-flaying agony.

My throat burned with screams of anger that wouldn't stop tumbling from my lips. I clawed at my chest, desperate to reach the heart that bled with unstaunched anguish, needing to touch the sorrow as if it were a material object.

Voices echoed through the fog of my misery, unrecognizable yet familiar.

"Get her fucking hands, Hunter, before she does any more damage to herself."

"I'm trying, man. She's flailing like...God, I don't even know."

The voices faded but gentle hands wiped my face, stroking my head tenderly.

No! I didn't deserve comfort. The compassion hurt more than the grief—compassion fed the guilt. Frantic to escape the white-hot flame of responsibility, I struggled to break free of the binds restraining me, kicking, clawing, and biting anything that came in contact with me.

"...call Thia."

"...dead...breakdown..."

"Griffin, we need you..."

"Beautiful...please, baby...love you so much...not your fault...."

Time lost all meaning and eternity claimed me in an ocean of fiery regret.

A sharp pain captured my attention, then...

Chapter 32

"People are like dirt. They can either nourish you and help you grow as a person or they can stunt your growth and make you wilt and die." -Plato

<u>Westly</u>

Covering my beautiful girl with a blanket, I stared at her face, which was covered in anguish even in sleep. Needing to connect, I kissed her forehead to reassure myself she would return from whatever hell she was currently trapped in.

"What the hell did you give her?" I asked Thia with far more hostility than was warranted, but my fear and frustration needed an outlet.

"Lion tranquilizer—why, do you think that was the wrong choice? I didn't have any of the usual human stuff on hand," she shot back.

"Thia, I'm not in the fucking mood for games," I cautioned.

"And I'm not worried in the slightest," she said sarcastically. "Let me ask, did either of you two idiots think to call me *before* you dropped that nuclear bomb on our girl like she was Hiroshima? Oh no, you morons with your *zero* years of professional training had it under control. You were so prepared, you didn't even bother to call Griffin, who would actually be a doctor of psychiatry by now if he hadn't decided offing a psychopathic rapist was a more noble cause. God save us all from good intentions!"

"Thia—" Griffin said, undoubtedly attempting to intervene in our verbal berating. But Thia was having none of it.

"*Shh*! You're the only one in the room not currently on my shit list, Griffin. Let's keep it that way," she advised before returning her attention to Hunter and me. "At least Griffin had actual training and clinical hours under his belt when he waded into Sam's recovery. He *knew* what he was doing, whereas you know-it-alls with hero complexes had nothing but confidence and ego. What on earth were you thinking? Don't answer that—you weren't, obviously, or CG wouldn't be knocked out on the couch, battling a heavily armed battalion of guilt."

"We knew it would be tough for her to accept," Hunter explained, "and were prepared for her guilt, but this was *way* beyond ordinary guilt, Thia. She kept saying she killed him—over and over. There was no breaking through."

"She's only just let go of twenty-five years of misplaced guilt, which is no small feat. Yes, she was doing exceptionally well, but this loss would be difficult for anyone to confront. Without preparation or professional guidance, the news served as a reminder of all the guilt she'd recently released, which increased exponentially with the addition of Jay's death."

"Jay's death is not her fault. He was cooperating with the FBI, and odds are that sick bastard would have come after him no matter what," I argued for no purpose other than it felt good.

"She's feeling appropriate guilt in regards to her friend's death," Thia said, holding up her hand to stop my objection. "Like it or not, his connection to her and *To Ieró* resulted in his death. Is that CG's fault? Of course not. But feeling guilty that his relationship with her was the *'cause'* of his death is natural. With time, she will see that it was Jay's choice to reach out to her when they were young, help her again after she fled, and most recently, cooperate with the FBI. She *will* achieve that level of understanding and clarity; it will just take a little time and a lot of hard work."

Helplessness was a brutal emotion—anger, scorn, hatred...those were more tolerable companions. As I sat next to my brave girl, heart aching for her loss and pain, I realized this was what love was—feeling another's emotions as if they were your own. Crying with them, laughing with them, smiling with them, and hurting with them. It sucked! It was also the result of the most intimate and fulfilling connection I've ever had, and one that I could no longer live without.

With nothing to do to make it better, no way to fix her problems or heal her as she slept, I remained at her side and did the only thing I could—I just loved her.

"Wes?" she said in a hoarse voice, reaching for my hand.

"I'm here, beautiful."

"Tell me it was all a bad dream," she asked, more fragile than I'd ever heard her.

"I wish I could, baby."

Her silent tears fell until the pillow was stained with the evidence of her grief in the form of large, dark circles. Gathering her in my arms, I held her close, offering the love and forgiveness she needed from me that she wasn't willing to grant herself.

"He is a monster," she said with absolute conviction.

There was no need to clarify who *he* was. I wanted nothing more than to find her monster and slay him, ensuring his cruelty would never touch her again.

"I'm an apple," she said randomly.

Shit! Was she having another breakdown? Where the hell was Thia when I needed her?

"I like apples," I replied stupidly, because really, was there a correct response to that declaration?

"No, you are missing the point. I am an apple, like in *Snow White*. I'm poison, ruined...rotten! The evil king dipped me in his cauldron of filth and contaminated me. Now everyone that comes near me is in danger of being infected—or worse, *killed*."

Although Disney was not my area of expertise, I was fairly certain it was an evil queen. Nevertheless, her point was clear...and completely off-base.

"Beautiful, if you are an apple, then it is one that brought nourishment to a starving man, not toxic but life-giving. It destroys me to hear you say these things about yourself because they aren't your words, but those of the evil king."

"I spent the majority of my life rolling around in filth, of course I'm rotten!" she snapped impatiently. "You can't see me clearly because you love me."

"Yes, I do love you—*all* of you—flaws included. However, the guilt has to stop because it is tearing you apart and driving you crazy."

"How do I stop? You say it like it's just that easy. Stop—*poof*—all better. That's not how it works, Wes."

"You change your perspective. You are an apple, not poisonous but nourishing. It is that simple. You change your perspective and—*poof*—the guilt is gone."

"You don't understand! You're surrounded by filth all day long, but you are a river of goodness. Underneath the dirty image you project, you are clean and pure."

"In what universe are you the dirty, corrupt one and I'm the pure, innocent one? Do you even hear yourself? What you're saying is ridiculous," I nearly shouted. She was driving me nuts with her faulty logic. Her self-assessment was so skewed it was nearly impossible to see up from down. "Okay, you are an apple. Yes, you grew amongst shit, but that waste fertilized you—made you stronger and sweeter than most apples could ever dream of being. Maybe some of the filth still clings to you after being forced to spend years in the muck, but, baby—it's only on the outside. What's beneath the apple's skin is untainted. All you need is a thorough washing, maybe a little elbow grease, and you will scrub that grime away to reveal the most beautiful, perfect apple I've ever seen."

She was quiet for a long time, but I could tell she was contemplating my words carefully. A small push and I might be able to sway the jury in my favor.

"Love, I've never lied to you. Before there was even an 'us,' I confessed to you all of my faults and weaknesses. You have to decide who you trust: the man who loves you and has always given you the truth, or a man who has proven to be a monster and a liar. Each of us has told you who *we* think you are, now you choose who to believe—it's up to *you* to accept who you are."

Another stretch of silence greeted me. I held my tongue with great effort, knowing she needed to reach the verdict on her own.

"Then you are water," she said vehemently. "I am an apple and you are the water. I'm covered in filth and you are an expert filth remover. You cleaned me until I could finally see what was hidden beneath the layers of lies and manipulation. You, Westly Black, are my essential element—the water I need to survive and thrive."

Before my beautiful girl, I never expected to be on the receiving end of someone's profession of love. But if I was forced to imagine it, such a declaration would *not* have included apples or water—*shows you what I know.* Her heartfelt words resonated profoundly, opening a previously undiscovered compartment in my heart that she filled completely.

"I'm happy to be your water, baby. Actually, I'm honored."

She nuzzled her head beneath my chin, holding me tightly as if I were her favorite stuffed animal. Slowly, I felt the tension leave her body and she drifted back to sleep.

More than a week had passed since we learned of Jay's death, and my girl was once again clawing her way out from under the mountain of blame. Regular appointments with Thia, combined with the acceptance and support the gang provided, fueled her progress faster than I'd anticipated. As much as I wanted her to be *'all better'* instantly because it hurt to watch her struggle, I understood that confronting her past and sorting through the jumbled, misguided thoughts that dominated her mind would take time. Nevertheless, the demons that lived inside her were receiving eviction notices daily. As each packed their bags and left, the vacated space was filled with the love we provided. Visible changes in her appearance were evident; her shoulders stopped tilting forward as if burdened by an unbearable weight and the bleakness in her eyes lessened until it was an occasional appearance versus a constant companion.

Despite the progress she was making, there was no doubt the grief was still fresh, a wound that would heal slowly, leaving a scar in its wake. Thia reminded me this was a natural, healthy part of healing after a loss, encouraging me to engage my girl in conversations about Jay that evoked memories of the good times they had shared. It was an unfamiliar role, yet I did my best to provide a safe place for her to grieve and remember.

Christmas came and went quietly, none of us in the mood to celebrate. We split off to spend a quiet evening alone as couples on Christmas Eve before gathering together Christmas morning for brunch at Griffin's house. It was a lazy day, tinged with sadness but buffered by the company of friends who were family.

As my girl continued to heal, Sam spent every free minute cooking obscene amounts of food that she insisted my beautiful girl eat, under threat of force-feeding should she refuse. Seeing her plight, I took to swiping bites from her plate when Sam's gaze was turned, which earned me a smile each time.

Ev took charge of distracting my woman's when she needed a break from introspection, accompanying her to Higher Yearning for short shifts, followed by trips to the dojo for Krav Maga classes. Ev swore the best way to release frustration and free up head space was beating the shit out of weighted dummies—or better yet, one of the unsuspecting male volunteers.

Griffin watched my beautiful girl like a hawk, swooping in each time she showed signs of being overwhelmed by emotion to guide her through her feelings, encouraging her to express her concerns or regrets so they could dissect them together. He was Thia's surrogate at the house, ensuring my girl's psychological care and progress continued to gain momentum instead of regressing.

Hunter continued to work with her on the FBI's investigation into *To Ieró*, *The Alpha*, and Jay's murder, keeping her apprised of significant developments. The updates appeared to have a substantial effect on her disposition. After each debriefing, she appeared calmer and more at peace, for which I was grateful. She told me that her contribution to bringing *The Alpha* to justice helped to alleviate some of the guilt caused by Jay's death.

As Jay had no family—outside of the cult that had banished him—we held a small memorial in his honor to allow her to say goodbye. While my meeting with him was brief and the rest had never met him, we all paid tribute to the man who had our gratitude for the care and protection he showed our girl.

The days passed quickly, each dawn bringing new challenges with well-earned victories. Though coated in sadness, our time together cemented the bond we shared, our relationship now tempered in the fire of adversity and the water of revitalization, forever changing us individually—and most importantly, together.

New Year's Eve arrived along with bitter cold and biting winds. Huntleigh joined GriffLo at The Stop, where Griffin would have to ring in the New Year. My girl and I decided to stay in, enjoying a quiet evening to celebrate the year's end and in anticipation of the year to come. We made plans for upcoming holidays and birthdays, and I even persuaded her to join me for a vacation during spring recess. It was our first time looking to the future after living in the past, which I counted as one more victory.

As the clock ran out and the ball dropped in Times Square, I was inside the woman I loved, proving with my body that she was where my years would begin and end from that day forward.

Sleep clung to me like a wet blanket as the first morning of the New Year arrived. My internal clock neglected to recognize it was a holiday, which would have provided the luxury of sleeping in if my body had complied.

Hmmm...there was one surefire way to exert energy that would entice me back to sleep—and I never had to leave the bed. Ready to introduce my girl to this stroke of genius, I reached for her—stretching farther until I found the edge of the bed. Opening my eyes, I listened for sounds of life in the bathroom. Hearing nothing, I sighed with regret—evidently it would be necessary to get out of bed in order to enact my plan.

Heading for the kitchen where her chocolate stash resided, I was surprised to find the room empty until I noticed that the stash in reference was gone. Laughing at the rate with which she consumed those bars, I grabbed my fleece from the closet, zipping it over my bare chest, and headed next door to find my woman. It was immediately clear that my fleece was insufficient protection against the frigid cold, causing me to sprint like an Olympian while cursing the cold. *Fuck! Was there nothing the woman wouldn't endure for her morning chocolate?*

I knocked, knowing the door would be locked as we remained on red alert for rogue cult kidnappers. When no one answered, I rung the bell, estimating the likelihood it would be heard in the shower—slim to none. *Shit!* Dashing back to my house, I grabbed the spare key for Sam's, then ran like a bat out of hell before finally gaining entrance. Sneaking up the stairs like a super-spy in hopes of surprising my girl, I was shocked to find her room and bathroom empty.

Dread and denial washed over me. *No! She wouldn't dare.* Glancing around her room to take stock, I noticed several dresser drawers were ajar. *Don't you even think about it*, I mentally threatened as I approached her laptop that sat open.

Clicking the touch pad, the computer came to life and an image illuminated the screen.

καθαρισμός

Examining her desk, I found a piece of paper with a single word handwritten across the page... *'Sorry.'*

Chapter 33

"Oh yes, the past can hurt. But you can either run from it, or learn from it." -The Lion King

<u>Meg</u>

Two days, 2,200 miles, one train, and four buses later, I arrived in Boise, Idaho at the same terminal I had left from almost eight years earlier. I'd spent twelve hundred of those miles staring out the window, contemplating what Wes was doing and wondering if he could ever forgive me for leaving him. The question was moot as the likelihood of me making it back to him was infinitesimal. Would he—or any of the others—understand why I left? Would they see that I had no choice?

Wes...how did he come to mean everything to me after only two and a half months? We hadn't even been together a full semester, yet my love for him was undeniable. All I had been looking for was to experience sex in a healthy, typical fashion—to find the pleasure everyone else seemed to enjoy.   Never once did I want the emotional entanglement of a relationship, nor did I believe I was capable or worthy of that depth of love. Then, Wes came along and gave me everything I wanted—and more—in terms of physical satisfaction, as well as everything I never dreamed I needed.

Months ago, if I'd been pressed to describe my ideal Prince Charming, Westly Black—or who I thought he was—would have been the opposite in every way. He'd fooled me into believing the same lies the rest of the world held true—that he was an arrogant, selfish, egotistical, immoral, greedy asshole. That wasn't to say that he didn't have his moments of arrogance...he definitely did. Although it could be more accurately described as excessive self-confidence in his abilities, which he usually proved was warranted. However, the rest of my assumptions were wrong—*so, so wrong*.

Wes was actually the valiant knight in not-so-shining armor. He was content to let the world perceive him in the worst possible light, partly because he didn't give a shit what anyone thought about him, but also because it protected him from being hurt. Yet underneath the asshole façade was the man I'd grown to love with every molecule of my being—a man who conquered my body, fought to breach my barriers, patiently peeled back my layers, pushed me to confront my past, forgave me after I'd withheld the ugly truth, and cared for me when I was broken. He accepted me and all my challenges with love and enthusiasm, finding ways to show me that I mattered to him instead of offering empty platitudes. His thoughtfulness was displayed in the small gestures that proved each day *I* was what he treasured most.

With Wes, I never doubted where I stood, never questioned if I was enough, and never worried about who I was supposed to be. He let me be me, even when I wasn't sure who *me* was. In him, I found the home I never had, my safe place to let go of the burdens I could no longer carry and finally find rest. Leaving my home, unsure of when or *if* I would return, shredded me, but it was my turn to protect him. If I succeeded in vanquishing my demons, I would return to him and be the home that *he* needed and deserved—the home he spent years hiding from but desperately craved.

When the final email from *The Alpha* arrived New Year's morning, I knew what had to be done. It was the only option left. Jay's murder had made it abundantly clear that *The Alpha* would stop at nothing to bring me back and protect his secrets. *To Ieró* was coming for me unless I returned immediately and submitted to *his* will—purification.

Reading the word on my computer screen was enough to nauseate me. Having been subjected to several such *cleansings* in the past for comparatively minor infractions, I shuddered to think what awaited me at the compound. Such thoughts led me to question what had been plaguing me for the last one hundred miles of my journey...*what the hell was I thinking?*

Bravery...such a noble concept, one would think it should come easily in the face of evil. Yeah, not so much. I recalled reading a quote from Ambrose Redmoon in my freshman year literature class that said: *"Courage is not the absence of fear, but rather the judgment that something else is more important than fear."* That about summed it up. Terrified didn't even begin to cover how I felt about returning to *To Ieró*. Had there been any other option, I would have jumped on it. But my need to protect those I loved outweighed my trepidation, especially after losing Jay.

Jay—my first friend—the man who stuck his neck out for me, time and time again. Words could not adequately describe the pain of losing him. Even during the years following his banishment from *To Ieró*, I'd found comfort in the knowledge that Jay was out there...that somewhere in the world there was one person who cared about me and saw value in a lost, broken girl. The contact information he'd left for me was a promise that he would never stop caring, a pledge that he would always be there when I needed him. During his absence, that promise had sustained me, offering the only glimmer of hope in my otherwise dark existence.

After I'd escaped, he fulfilled his vow, protecting me and providing refuge, giving me the temporary security and acceptance I needed while adjusting to an unfamiliar world. He never asked for repayment and never made me feel like I was a burden. He encouraged me to grow and move on, to let go of the past and embrace the potential that lay before me.

And now he was gone...

Why did he have to be a hero? I should have known when Hunter asked for Jay's contact information that my overly devoted friend would jump at the chance to remove the threat *The Alpha* posed to me. How could I have failed to realize that Jay would once again try and fix my problems in order to provide a safe environment for me to live?

It was what he always did. Even as a little boy, he recognized the hurt I carried and reached out to me. When I was a lost adolescent with no clue how dysfunctional my life was—how *warped* I was—he found a way to reach me, enlighten me, and give me hope.

He gave me everything he had to give, and in my heart, I knew there was nothing he would have denied me because he loved me in a way that few would ever experience. For a time, he may have believed there was a romantic component to that love, but I knew better. Jay loved me like a parent should love their child, consistently putting my well-being before his own. He accepted me at my worst, taught me about the world and my place in it, and then let me go when it was time to fly on my own. He never stopped worrying about me and was always there to support me when needed, but he respected the value in me finding my own way. Though we shared no blood, he was family—I only wish I had understood what that meant before I lost him. Instead of having years to thank him for all he'd given, I was left with memories to cherish and regrets for all that was left unsaid. My only comfort was in attaining the justice he deserved—this was why I had to go.

Leaving New York was the hardest choice I'd ever made, but sadly, there was no alternative. Had I remained, *To Ieró* would come after me and inevitably one of my well-intentioned loved ones would have intervened—stupid, reckless, wonderful fools were liable to get themselves killed. I would *not* lose anyone else!

So here I stood in front of the Boise Greyhound bus terminal, waiting for one of *The Sacred* to come and collect me like the Prodigal Daughter—except this daughter didn't return of her own volition. Although, I doubted the poor toadie picking me up was aware of my duress. Like everything else, *The Alpha* manipulated the situation to suit his endgame. *Bastard!*

Images of torture and inhumane conditions swirled through my head, causing the panic already suffocating me to spike sharply. While focusing on my breathing, I reminded myself what I had already endured and survived in *his* efforts to break me—he'd done his worst, yet I had prevailed. This time would be no different. After all, I'd already sacrificed my first friend and abandoned the love of my life...what else could he take from me?

Chapter 34

"It is easier to forgive an enemy than to forgive a friend." -William Blake

<u>Westly</u>

"Hunter, I swear to God, if we don't do something today other than sit in meetings, planning for every contingency, I will steal your gun, shoot you in the kneecap, and go haul her out myself," I threatened for the umpteenth time.

"What is with you and my kneecaps? Every promise of violence manages to include them," he replied glibly.

I was going to kill him. Not figuratively—literally.

"It's been almost three days! How can you sit there calmly without concern for her safety? The stupid, brave woman sacrificed herself for us, yet you sip your coffee and click away at that computer without a care in the world. Do you know how infuriating it is? Huh, do you? It's fucking mind-numbingly aggravating!"

"Wes, man, you need to relax. You're bound to have an aneurysm before we have a chance to storm the castle and save the day at the rate you're going," Hunter said. "I know you're worried...I am too. But I've already confirmed through video surveillance at the Greyhound terminal in New York that Meg traveled by bus. We may not have identified her exact route, but it would have taken two—almost three—days to get to any of the major cities near *To Ieró*. We—" he paused to offer yet another reprimanding look, my trip to Oregon remained a point of contention, "beat her here by at least a day, so forgive me if I take this time to actually *prepare* for her rescue instead of going in half-cocked and jeopardizing her life, along with those of every other member of the cult."

"God, you are a pompous prick—and they call *me* an asshole," I muttered. "I understand the logistics...why do you think I've been so patient up until now?"

He scoffed, "*Patient*? I'm buying you a dictionary for your birthday. You have not exhibited one shred of patience since calling me at six am, New Year's morning... *'Hunter, she's gone! She went back to those fucking KoolAid-drinking nutjobs because she's trying to be a goddamn martyr. Grab your fucking gun and meet me at JFK Airport in forty-five minutes or I'm leaving without you,'*" he said in an unflattering impersonation of my voicemail. "I had to have the damn TSA prevent you from boarding the plan until I arrived to collect your impulsive ass. Again, I know you're scared shitless—I understand, I've been there, too—but we aren't moving on *To Ieró* until we confirm she is inside *and* have all equipment and personnel in place to ensure her safe extraction. We are assuming she's already inside, but we can't be certain she was in any of the trucks that have arrived over the last twenty-four hours. If we go in hard and our assumption is wrong, she'll be gone with God-knows-how-many abductors and we may never find her. So, sit your ass down, shut your mouth, and let us do our jobs. You're here as a favor—don't take advantage or I'll cut you out of the loop and you'll really suffer the wait."

Biting my tongue until it bled, I withheld the scathing reply that was dying to be voiced. Hunter's ability to disassociate from the situation to objectively evaluate each course of action before selecting a strategy was sensible—only it irritated the fuck out of me. If our positions were reversed, I knew I would be the one playing the consummate tactician. However, it was *my* girl that had willingly walked into unfathomable danger to protect me and our friends.

It didn't take a rocket scientist to decipher her reasons for sneaking away in the middle of the night. She'd decided in her guilt-addled brain that the only way to protect the rest of us from Jay's fate was to sacrifice herself. If this were an action flick, I'd think her heroic—in real life, I wanted to spank her ass for carelessly tossing her life away.

Gathering the remains of my sanity, I finally spoke. "I need to get her out, Hunter—soon, as in yesterday. I can't live without her."

He sighed heavily. "I know, Wes," he sympathized. "This is exactly why I didn't want you to come to Oregon. The movies make my job look like one dramatic showdown after another, but the reality is far less exciting. Most of the time is spent acquiring intel, then planning the *least* dramatic maneuver to obtain our objective—in this case, bringing your girl home safely while obtaining the necessary evidence to put the bastard behind bars for life. The hurry up and wait is unbearable for everyone. But I assure you, it's almost time. Just hang tight a little while longer. I promise we will bring her back to you."

His promise wasn't enough to assuage my riotous emotions—fear being the predominant one—but it was as much as Hunter or anyone could offer.

"Special Agent Charles," a female agent said while entering the office we occupied, "we just received infrared images that indicate everyone at the compound is now located in the central building—something is definitely going down. Tech is working to establish audio feed, but there's no chance at visual confirmation beyond satellite and infrared. The surrounding land is too densely wooded and the main building is in the heart of the compound. Do you want to send ground recon to confirm the girl is present before sending a full unit in?"

"No, hold off on the solo recon—we don't know if there are any warning systems in place that will tip our hand. I want to go in hard and fast when the time comes. We will give tech a few hours to attempt audio verification before moving in."

A few hours—*is he insane?* There was no way I was waiting one hour, let alone several, now that everyone was assembling for '*something.*' And I knew exactly what that '*something*' was. Hunter's communications expert was able to translate the email—not that there was much to it. Other than the alpha and omega symbols, there was only one word...*purification.*   Undoubtedly, *The Sacred* were gathering in the meeting hall my girl had described for her '*purification*' ceremony.   The   thought   made   me simultaneously   want   to   vomit   and   punch someone...anyone. Hunter was currently my primary candidate.

"No," Hunter abruptly declared.

I turned to find him staring directly at me. "Huh?"

"Whatever you're thinking—don't. If you take one step out of this office, I'll lock you in an interrogation room until I have your girl back home in New York," Hunter threatened convincingly.

"I'm not waiting hours for you to *try* and get audio in that godforsaken shithole in the middle of nowhere. It's a waste of time...a Hail Mary pass. Stop following some bullshit protocol to cover your ass and worry about saving my woman, or I'll do it my own fucking self!" I shouted, my frustration spewing forth.

"Calm down, you impatient ass. Not that I owe you any explanation, but I'm not trying to '*cover my ass.*' I would put my career—not to mention my fucking *life*—on the line to bring her back safely. The voice transmitter should already be in place if she's in there; tech just needs to identify and boost the signal. Then we'll have audio, which will give us a clearer picture so we can formulate an entry strategy that minimizes the risks to your girl."

It was not the answer I wanted, but his logic was persuasive. If a few hours would provide the necessary information to ensure her safety during the rescue, I would find a way to muddle through. The audio would—

"What did you just say?" I asked calmly.

Hunter released an impatient breath before replying, "Which part? I've said a lot in the last ten minutes."

"The audio—you said if she was there, the bug was in place," I led.

Hunter looked away, not meeting my eyes.

Son-of-a-BITCH!

That motherfucker knew...he *fucking knew* she was going to leave.

"Wes, you have to understand...she was our best chance to take this guy down. And she would have come on her own after what happened to Jay. It made sense to use her—"

The punch came as a total shock or I have no doubt he would have deflected my efforts. As it was, he was on his ass, rubbing the cheek which would be marked with the evidence of my fury by tomorrow. Stepping forward, intent to continue his well-deserved beating, the fucking Karate Kid somersaulted away from me before springing to his feet. Undaunted by his display of skills, I swung for his chin, hoping for a knock-out. He deftly averted my fist but failed to capture me.

"I'm going to beat your traitorous ass until even your own mother won't recognize you! And if anything happens to her, Hunter, I'll put you in the ground," I vowed.

"*Jesus Christ!*" he bellowed, once again thwarting my attempts to introduce my fist to his face.

Changing tactics, I landed a blow to his stomach, which earned me a satisfying grunt of pain. However, I lost my advantage as proximity allowed him to slither behind me and snake his arms around my waist and neck. Fully restrained in his constricting embrace, I yielded—temporarily.

"If I let you go, will you settle down enough for me to explain?" he asked, breathing heavily.

That he would imply there was any reasonable explanation for his betrayal was enough to reignite my temper, resulting in an elbow to his ribs. It was a good hit considering my limited range of motion.

"*Dammit!*" Hunter barked in pain. "If you don't stop, I'm going to start hitting you back instead of just avoiding you. Also, you're the one who's going to answer to Ev for all my bruises. I'm going to release you now...do *not* try to hit me again," he warned as he released me before mumbling, "*Hot-headed asshole.*"

"Unless you're about to claim temporary insanity, save your breath. Nothing you say will convince me you didn't choose the best course of action for *you*, not my girl."

"It was the best choice for everyone involved. If you manage to find any objectivity, you would see it was the *only* choice. After Jay died, she was pushing me daily for updates, begging me to let her help, offering to come back here and wear a wire...anything. I tried to dissuade her, to convince her we had everything under control. She wouldn't listen. In her mind, it was *her* job to bring *The Alpha* down—her redemption.

"When she threatened to return on her own without any support, I caved. There was no doubt in my mind that she would have followed through, Wes. We had been working another angle that didn't involve your woman, but she would've blown the plan to hell if she'd waltzed back into the thick of things without our knowledge. I made the unbelievably tough call and brought her on board—if it were anyone else, you would have done the same.

"For the record, the plan was to bring her back under *controlled* conditions in about two weeks. She jumped the gun after receiving the last email and took off without notice. She obviously left the email open to alert us of the change in plans—still, she was lucky the majority of the groundwork had been laid or it would have taken longer to mobilize."

"And if it were Ev...if our roles were reversed, would you have made the same decision?"

"No, but I wouldn't have had the presence of mind to see the forest through the trees. I would have fought it tooth and nail, and meanwhile, Ev would have charged in alone like freakin' Joan of Arc, leaving me scrambling to clean up the mess," he answered unequivocally. "You also would be in the back of an ambulance by now if the shoe were on the other foot."

"Exactly," I returned, my anger still simmering, on the verge of boiling over.

"Look, hate me when we get home if you need to—for now, you have to trust me. We have the same goal, and whether you believe it or not, the same priorities."

"Do you understand how this could set her back? What he will subject her to? She may not survive this time," I said in desperation.

"Or, this may be *exactly* what she needs to move on. There's no way to know until the dust settles. Regardless, I wasn't taking any chances. Thia will be here in the next two hours, ready for her after the extraction."

"Oh," I replied, unable to find words of gratitude through my apprehension.

"It will all work out—you'll see," Hunter calmly promised.

"You'd better be right...for both our sakes."

*"Your pain is the breaking of the shell
that encloses your understanding."*
-Khalil Gibran

<u>Meg</u>

Time was a fickle crook, stealing seconds when you wanted to hoard them like treasure, then stuffing your pockets with the thieved hours when you wished you could give them away. There was no doubt returning to *To Ieró* was a gamble that could potentially cost me everything. At the moment, my sanity—possibly my life—seemed the most likely forfeits. My only remaining hope was that Hunter would gain the necessary proof to imprison *The Alpha* for the rest of his miserable life. If sacrificing myself would ensure no other women would suffer as I have and no other man would die as Jay did, the cost would be bearable.

However, *The Alpha*'s attempts to bend me to his will were testing my ironclad determination to survive. My threshold for pain was exceptionally high given my upbringing, but time had increased his creativity and honed his skills for inflicting pain.

He wasted no time upon my return, calling *The Sacred* to the meeting hall as he prepared for my purification ceremony. By the time they answered his demand, I stood—naked—in what amounted to a kiddie pool with my arms and legs knotted to a wooden frame that had been secured to the ground. Tied in the 'X' position, my body was completely exposed to the community, which was unpleasant but not a unique experience. What caused my heart to pound and palms to sweat was the unknown torture he planned to inflict.

Ever eager to hear himself speak, *The Alpha* launched into a long-winded declamation outlining the importance of following his leadership for the spiritual fulfillment and prosperity of *To Ieró*. He effectively painted me as a threat to the eternal souls and livelihood of the community, adeptly justifying the *need* for the extreme measures being taken during my purification. Planting the seed of responsibility for any and all misfortune that befell the compound during my seven years of absence ensured none of *The Sacred* would stand against *The Alpha*'s inhumane treatment of me—after all, I was just *The Omega*, a container...a vessel, if you will.

As I listened to his propaganda, it amazed me that I once found him persuasive and charismatic. While I'd continued to believe in *The Alpha's* deity until I learned of his treachery seven years ago, I had lost faith in the dogma of *To Ieró* and my supposed position long before that. Jay revealed to me my own humanity and his stories opened my eyes to the falsehoods I'd been fed. The passage of time and experience provided additional clarity that allowed me to see *The Alpha* in his full-Technicolor evil glory.

Drifting in a stream of consciousness, I lost track of his rhetoric until he finally turned to face me while the community chanted, '*Purify her that Theós may thrive. Purify her that The Alpha to come may thrive. Purify her that To Ieró may thrive.*'

He raised a hand to silence *The Sacred* before speaking, "My spirit is heavy with the burden of responsibility as I, Theós incarnate, enact my will for the protection of *To Ieró* and the sanctity of *The Omega*. Yet, for you—my sacred chosen—I bring righteous fire to cleanse this vessel of its contamination so that Theós may come to be realized in my heir."

The Alpha approached me with a sinister smile meant only for my eyes. Once near, he leaned in to place a kiss on my crown as he whispered, "You can't imagine how much I'm going to enjoy this. I've fantasized about the retribution I'm about to deliver for far longer than I'd expected."

I shuddered at his exultant pleasure in the suffering to come—*my* suffering.

With great ceremony, he mixed the contents of two glass vials in a bowl. I stared at the vials he returned to the table, trying to read the labels—50% glycolic acid and 50% lactic acid. I recognized the chemical names from Sam's girls' night facials. *Was he giving me a facial?* I knew it was a ridiculous thought, nonetheless a giggle escaped.

The Alpha's head snapped up to catch me still gazing at the glass jars. The cunning smirk he returned communicated more than words ever could. Whatever his plans entailed, they would be slow and painful. He nodded to Malachi, who presented a small brush with an ornately carved handle.

"Let the fire of Theós cleanse the stains upon this vessel. Let my anointing purify *The Omega*—the beginning and the end—restoring the sanctity that has been lost."

Laughter threatened at the first stroke of the brush. It tickled as he painted the clear solution across the skin of my chest, above my heart. I was tempted to make a snide remark about his skills in the art of torture slipping as the first tingles nipped at my skin. He continued to cover my chest and stomach as my skin began to sting painfully. As *The Alpha* coated my legs and arms, the burning sensation was enough to cause me to pant, searching for relief. By the time he had smeared the liquid fire over my back, tears threatened to fall. When he walked around to once again stand before me, raising the brush to my face, my composure showed the first signs of strain.

"Please, no. Stop this—you don't have to continue. I've learned my lesson, I promise," I lied.

"Hmm—" he murmured as if seriously contemplating my request. "I don't believe you."

Without further ado, he slowly spread the devil serum over my face and neck.

It was impossible to know how much time passed—it felt like years. The pain escalated as he painted a second layer of chemicals across every inch of skin. My entire body trembled as the agonizing fire devoured my flesh like the demons of hell. Tears poured down my face in salty rivers, dripping onto my exposed breasts, highlighting my vulnerability.

To my shame, I would have promised almost anything to bring an end to the scorching blaze. Blistering pain wiped my mind clean of all thoughts, and all that lived within me was brutal, unrelenting hurt.

Without warning, ice cold water was dumped over my head, followed by bucket after bucket of the blessedly torturous liquid that squelched the fire before revitalizing the ache.

"*Oh god*, let it end. I can't...*I can't,*" I begged senselessly to *The Sacred* observers. A few averted their eyes, but most watched unsympathetically.

"Don't worry, Omega, I am not an unsympathetic God. I will let you rest for a few hours before we begin again," *The Alpha* announced viciously before exiting the meeting hall.

Free from his watchful eye, I proceeded to welcome the darkness that threatened, eager for its peaceful oblivion.

I came to slowly, pain radiating from every pore. Flexing my arms, I tested the bonds that confined me to the wooden frame—they offered no leeway. My joints ached from the excessive time spent in an unnatural position and my neck was stiff from hanging limply during my '*nap.*' However, those aches were trivial when compared to the scorching burn of my skin.

Afraid to look at the damage my body had incurred, I kept my eyes screwed tight while offering myself a pep talk. Courage in place, I opened my eyes and looked down.

Holy fucking goddamn son-of-a-bitch!

My skin was bright red—like the worst sunburn in the history of sunburns—with small yellowish patches that were beginning to ooze. I was hideous. Vanity was never my weakness and a few scars wouldn't phase me, but the extremity of the damage was alarming, forcing me to acknowledge the possibility of permanent disfigurement if the *cleansing* was repeated.

I had prepared myself for many possible outcomes when persuading Hunter to let me return to *To Ieró*, but not this—permanent disfigurement I had not anticipated. Even the pain surpassed my expectations, a foolish mistake given my history with the *purification* process. Time had dulled my recollections of the severity and creativity of *The Alpha's* punishments.

Sucking in a deep breath, I exhaled slowly, visualizing the panic and pain exiting my body. I focused on my purpose, the reasons I subjected myself to this living hell— justice, protection, and redemption.

Justice for Jay, who had sacrificed his life by protecting me—trying to take down the same man I now sought to imprison.

Protection for my new family in New York— surrendering myself to prevent their interference when *To Ieró* came for me.

Redemption for all my mistakes—an act of bravery and sacrifice that would wash away the guilt and shame I'd carried for so long.

Guilt and shame, the two emotions that had ruled my life for so long. Every choice I'd made since childhood was shaped by the two. They stifled my growth like large trees blocking the sun from a fledgling plant.

Returning to the compound yielded new perspective I may never have obtained otherwise. Now the blinders were removed and I saw the truth. *To Ieró* was not real...it was a bubble, isolated from the rest of the world in which one man—one *bad* man—controlled the thoughts and actions of everyone. The backward ideology that had served as the foundation of the community for nearly a century was further polluted under the unchallenged rule of a corrupt leader.

Guilt was a powerful tool, wielded expertly to ensure my compliance. If I defied *The Alpha*, misfortune would strike, be it dying crops or sick animals—the blame would rest solely on me. In retrospect, I could see that these adversities were purposeful, intended to induce the remorse that prevented me from repeating undesirable behaviors. With my newfound objectivity, I could see how my compassion for others was used against me.

The Sacred were not permitted to challenge *The Alpha*, yet they needed a target to direct their disappointments and frustrations. As *The Omega*, I was the perfect scapegoat for the community to pile their blame upon. I'd learned to take responsibility for any and all hardships *To Ieró* faced, accepting the community's condemnation as penance for my supposed shortcomings. I was Pavlov's dog—my reactions were not natural or an intrinsic part of me. I had been trained to respond in a specific way to the benefit of *The Alpha*.

Holy Shit! I was born and raised to serve *The Alpha*, trained to be what he needed, and when I finally ran, I continued to live as he'd taught me. Despite my efforts and years of progress, I'd never truly escaped, allowing him to control my life from 2,200 miles away.

Enough! I would not give him another second of my hard-won freedom. He would never dictate my emotional responses again.

I felt like Sleeping Beauty waking up after years of slumber, completely unaware of the life and happiness she had missed. Not anymore—this Aurora was ready to start living. *Hmm...*Aurora—Rory, for short. If memory served, Aurora meant dawn, the beginning of a new day, or in my case, a new life...a new me. Jay introduced me to *Sleeping Beauty* all those years ago while trying to teach me about life and myself through stories. The name was a perfect tribute to his friendship.

In that moment, I became Aurora—Sleeping Beauty awakened, the dawn of a new life, the princess finally freed.

The irony was not lost on me that weeks spent searching for a name to claim myself and symbolically move on from my past was finally fruitful in the same place it all began.

Giving up was not an option. I would endure until Hunter arrived with the FBI to rescue me. I would accomplish my mission and see *The Alpha* behind bars, finding justice for Jay and myself. And when all was said and done, I would return home and win back the heart of my prince.

Chapter 36

"Those things which are precious are saved only by sacrifice." -David Kenyon Webster

Westly

"We have to move," Hunter ordered urgently to the agents in the room.

Whatever he heard through the headphones from the recently established audio connection inspired a reaction that caused my blood to run cold.

"What's going on?" I asked, anxious for an explanation.

"Not now, Wes. Stay here with Special Agent Welch—I'll have her update you as the situation progresses."

"What fucking situation?" I snapped, unwilling to be dismissed like a petulant child.

Hunter ignored my profanity along with my request for details, "Someone find Thia—Dr. Cynthia Veritus—she just arrived in the building, escort her to the trucks...she rides with me."

I moved to intercept Hunter as he exited the room but was obstructed by a 'by-the-book' redhead in FBI standard attire.

"Sorry, Mr. Black, you'll have to remain with me per Special Agent Charles' instructions," she said in a no-nonsense tone.

"Look, Agent Welch, I appreciate that you're trying to do your job, but right now you are standing between me and my girl. If you don't extract yourself from that precarious position, I will steamroll you to get to her."

"You're so intimidating, Mr. Black," she replied sarcastically. "There is nothing you can do out there but get in the way. Sit down, try to relax, and I'll let you know when there is news."

She reached out to grab a chair, dragging it loudly if front of the door before sitting down gracefully.

"That's your big plan to deter me—sit in front of the door? Lady, I don't think you appreciate the lengths I'm willing to go to be by my woman's side at the first possible second. You have no clue what she's survived in the past, and none of us know what she's endured over the past few days. There is no way *in hell* I'm sitting this one out and waiting 'til you all bring her to me. I *will* be the first face she sees when she is free. If you think a hundred-and-thirty-pound FBI agent in a cheap plastic chair can stop me, you're in for a rude awakening."

"One-thirty, really? I may not own a scale, but I have been working out and trying to eat right. You know how hard it is when you're trapped in an office all day or stuck in a car on stakeouts to stick with a balanced diet? Impossible!" Although her smirk told me she was being deliberately obtuse, this woman was tap dancing on my last nerve.

"I don't give a shit about your dietary regimen! Move!" I snapped.

"Black, you want to know my plan? I'm going to sit here—maybe grab my laptop once you settle down a bit so I can be productive while I babysit—and I'm not moving until I receive the all-clear. If you lay one finger on me in an effort to break free, I'll arrest you for assaulting an officer and throw your butt in jail. Once Miss Adeio is secured, I *may* remember to drop the charges and let you out."

"What's with you agents and threatening to throw me in jail?" I grumbled before assessing whether or not she would carry through with her promise.

Based on her body language and unyielding stare, the answer was yes—she'd throw me in prison in a heartbeat and take her sweet time letting me out for the inconvenience. *Time to change tactics.*

"Special Agent Welch," I began respectfully, "may I ask your first name?"

"Delilah," she finally answered after considering my request.

"*Delilah*," I continued, "have you ever been in love—not trivial lust or comfortable familiarity but penetratingly deep, can't live without the other person love? That is what I feel for my beautiful girl. She softens my jagged edges, forces me to expose my heart, and inspires me to be a better man. Because of her I have a family, and in her I found my home.

"Now you have your assignment to keep me out of trouble, but I have a job to do too—I have to take care of the woman I love. If I can't be the one breaking down doors and pulling her out of that hell on earth, fine—but I *have* to be the one there to greet her when she's free because I can give her the care and support none of you can, the love and acceptance she will only allow me to give. *Please*—I'm not a man who begs, but I'm begging you—let me be what she needs me to be...what I need to be for her."

It was the most exposed I had ever been in front of anyone other than my love, yet I wouldn't regret my raw honesty given to a stranger. I would stand naked and profess my need for her in front of the world if it kept me by her side.

"I hate you for making me feel guilty, Black," she said before sighing dramatically. "*Fine.* I will drive you *near* the compound, but we will *not* approach until I receive word the premises is secured. Then—and only then—will you be permitted to go to Miss Adeio. Agreed?"

"Absolutely," I answered quickly before she changed her mind and rescinded the offer. I would agree to anything that brought me closer to my girl.

"You just lied to me, didn't you?" she asked, skeptical of an agreement so easily acquired.

"I promise to follow your orders to the letter," I said convincingly before mumbling under my breath, "until we get there."

"I know I'm going to regret this," she grumbled to herself.

Yep, she probably would.

An hour later, we parked outside the entrance to *To Ieró* amongst a fleet of black SUVs. The FBI's overt presence was not a good sign.

"I thought Hunter was planning a stealth infiltration?" I asked Agent Welch, concerned.

"Stay in the car," she commanded without addressing my question.

I watched anxiously as she approached another agent, listening carefully before glancing back at the vehicle where I sat. The look on her face said it all. Whatever plans had been laid were extraneous—circumstances had changed.

Quietly slipping from the car, I circumvented several agents before Welch noticed my absence and scanned the area looking for me. I ducked behind the nearest SUV in the hopes of escaping detection. I heard Welch calling out to me, asking other agents if they'd seen me, but my cover held. After a few minutes passed, I circled around the back of the vehicle and slipped into the surrounding forest.

There had to be another way into the compound. I remembered the story of Jay's secret return after banishment to leave a phone number for my girl in case she escaped. Walking deeper into the woods, I began to circle the perimeter of the fenced complex, studying the chain link for any signs of weakness.

My pace remained slow and deliberate as to prevent the FBI or *The Sacred* from finding me. The only plan I'd formulated thus far was to get to my girl and protect her— by any means necessary—until I could find a route to freedom. While my strategy left much to be desired in the way of details, I would improvise as I went. There was no question that infiltrating and engaging *To Ieró* on my own—an unarmed civilian with no combat experience—was less than brilliant. The place was surrounded by trained law enforcement officers far more qualified than I to launch a rescue mission.

However, I had one advantage over all the professionals inundating the area—I would give my life for hers. No questions, no hesitation...if it came down to it, I would die to save her.

After walking for almost an hour, I finally found a break in the fence near the extensive planting fields she had described—now lifeless in the midst of winter. Quickly making my way to an outcropping of buildings, I hid from view while assessing the area. In the distance, I spotted a large metal barn isolated from the rest of the buildings. I cautiously crept closer, my gut urging me to inspect the barn before moving to the meeting hall. Ducking into the woods, I approached the back of the structure, surprised to find a small group of men in a heated debate near the rear door.

Although less than one hundred feet away, the wind stole most of their words. From the snippets heard, I deduced *The Sacred* were divided about the proper response to the FBI's demand for entry. Most of the community remained in the meeting hall, apparently debating the best course of action, while *The Alpha*, unused to being challenged, had retreated to the barn.

"He's gonna do it again," the fat man said to the others.

Realizing the monster responsible for my love's lifetime of torment was so near, I couldn't leave. In fact, I snuck closer, stopping less than twenty feet from the men, enabling me to hear them more clearly.

"...and how much more can she survive? Did you get a good look when we moved her here?" the bald man asked the others. "I know we aren't to doubt his divine guidance, but—"

"Shh, don't even finish that sentence," the thin man interrupted. "She has brought this upon herself with her disobedience. Had she remained steadfast, our livestock and crops would not have faltered and our children would not be ill. If we wish to regain the favor of the spirit, there is no other way—he must purify the vessel to safeguard Theós."

"I know," the fat man added wearily, "but I wish there were another way. I can't bear to look at her."

What the fuck had they done to her?

My stomach lurched angrily at the prospect of my girl being harmed. There was no time to wait. Sliding my phone from my pocket, I texted Hunter my location with confirmation that my love was inside. I didn't bother to wait for his reply, which would have forced me to disregard his order to hold off until he arrived. It was plausible deniability, pure and simple—if I didn't read his command, I couldn't technically defy him.

There was no chance I could overtake three men on my own without a weapon, so I continued around the building in search of another entry point. On the north side, I found a set of windows—two of the few the building possessed— slightly ajar. Approaching surreptitiously, I peered in, surprised to find an industrial-looking kitchen. The pieces of the puzzle clicked into place. This '*barn*' must be the meth lab she'd described.

Easing one window open, I levered myself up and slid inside, climbing into an empty metal trough. I canvassed the room in search of a weapon, finding a small chef's knife as well as a hammer—they were better than nothing. I tucked the hammer into the waistband of my jeans but carried the knife.

Slipping from the kitchen, I followed the only discernible voices to the southwest corner of the building. I remained outside the door, listening without seeing to plot my entry.

"*Alpha*, you must listen to reason. The odds of loading and transporting all the crank out of *To Ieró* without detection are infinitesimal. Even if the FBI isn't guarding the back road, they will have aerial surveillance that will locate the box trucks with ease. Our best chance is to destroy the evidence along with the girl. If we stall them for a day, we have a chance to avoid felony prosecution."

"I will *not* sacrifice fifty pounds of street-ready crystal! Would you destroy one million dollars so easily if it sat in the room with us now? What you're suggesting is no different. A million dollars worth of product is not easily replaceable, Malachi. I tire of this conversation. After the media coverage during the Waco standoff, the FBI won't be eager to call attention to our present impasse. Send one of *The Sacred* to let them I know I'm in meditative contemplation of their request to enter our sacred ground and will go speak with them when I'm finished. In the meantime, I need to *purify* my errant wife. Bring me the brush, then you may leave."

I quickly ducked into the neighboring room, seething with rage but lucid enough to protect my advantage of surprise. With Malachi departing, the playing field was level—me against *The Alpha*—and a primal beast within me reveled in the prospect. I heard Malachi shuffle down the hall but remained hidden to ensure the coast was clear.

"No," the voice I loved shrieked in horror.

Instinctively, I ran from my hiding spot and charged into the room. *The Alpha*'s back was to me and without hesitation, I plunged the knife into the center, causing him to jerk in pain as something clattered to the floor. He stumbled away, yelling for help, but I was too consumed with my first glimpse of her to follow him.

"Help me. Please, Wes. It hurts...it hurts..." she whimpered.

My mind refused to process the sight before me. My beautiful, strong girl was nearly unrecognizable. Her entire body was an unnatural shade of fire-engine red and scaly patches of mustard-yellow skin were liberally scattered everywhere the eye could see, oozing and beyond painful looking. Tears poured from her eyes like they too were trying to escape her agony.

"Tell me, baby, how do I help? Tell me what to do," I pleaded for guidance, at a loss for how to proceed.

"Water. Water will stop it," she said weakly, on the verge of blacking out.

I scanned the room, locating a slop sink and bucket at the ready. The container appeared to be filled, but I didn't trust the contents. I sniffed the liquid but detected no scent before proceeding to dip my pinky finger below the surface. After several seconds without reaction, I scooped a palmful to my mouth and slurped—water. *Thank God.* Hoisting the prefilled bucket over my head, I carefully dumped the water over my beautiful girl's brutalized body, attempting to drench as much skin as possible without waste.

Her agonizing screams of pain and relief tore at my heart until tears threatened. I rushed back to the sink, twisting the handle for the cold water on as far as it would go while placing the bucket beneath the stream.

It would take a few minutes to fill even halfway, and all I could think was she needed to be cut down from the contraption that held her on display. I hurried to the corner where a wheezing *Alpha* lay, alive but in pain—good. Having no sympathy for his suffering, I forcefully rolled him to his side, jerking the knife from his back. He looked as if he were going to thank me for my effort, which would have incited me to stab him again, but I needed the knife to free my girl. Instead, I sucker-punched him—a perfect strike to the chin—knocking the sadistic bastard out cold.

I rushed back to her side to free her when her voice, barely above a whisper, stopped me in my tracks. "No, don't touch me. It hurts too much. Just water, more water..."

Retrieving the partially full bucket, I dumped its contents over her skin again. Shit, this process was too fucking slow. During each refill, I whispered words of love and encouragement, promising her anything her heart desired if she fought through the pain and survived.

There was no way to tell if her injuries were life-threatening or what else she had endured, so I chose to believe that, despite her unfathomable pain, she would live. I heard her grunt what appeared to be a request for me to come closer. As I leaned in, she whispered, "My name is Aurora," and then immediately passed out.

Seconds after she lost consciousness, a commotion down the hall caught my attention. Unsure if it was friend or foe, I held the knife at the ready, prepared to protect my gir—Aurora, with my life.

Hunter charged into the room, followed by a squad of the FBI's finest, armed to the hilt and ready for battle. He took one look at my gi—Aurora and shuddered. I knew she would despise being seen by so many in her current state, but I didn't dare move her. Instead, I stepped in front of her naked, abused body to preserve a small measure of privacy.

"I need a paramedic and ambulance for Aurora—now!" I snapped impatiently. "Send a few men to the kitchen to find containers to fill with water. We need to keep her wet. I'm not sure why, but it seems to be helping her."

Like the highly trained agents they were—or more likely because my tone brooked no debate—my requests for aid were answered instantaneously. An agent radioed for medical assistance while another group headed to the kitchen, and still others began inspecting the room.

I nodded to the corner where *The Alpha* was still unconscious.

"There's your guy. If you could get that bastard out of here...oh, and don't feel the need to be careful, but he was stabbed in the back before I knocked him out."

Hunter immediately commanded two agents to secure the '*suspect*' and have him assessed by the second medical team. The paramedic entered the room moments later, followed by the water-toting agents.

Everything happened at lightning speed from that point on. The agents investigating the room advised the paramedic that Aurora had likely been tortured with a mixture of glycolic and lactic acid. The medic immediately ordered the agents to continue flushing her skin with copious amounts of water.

"Will she be okay?" I asked urgently.

"Her vitals are good—she will live, but the pain will be intense for several weeks. We can manage her suffering at the hospital. It's too soon to tell about scarring. Given what

I see, I'd anticipate some degree of permanent damage, but that is only an educated guess."

I nodded to convey my understanding, relieved and infuriated in equal measure. The torture she had been subjected to was unimaginable—and worse, *avoidable*. I didn't dare dwell on either of these right now or I'd go mad.

As I watched the medic lather Aurora's skin with ointment, someone approached me from behind and placed a hand on my shoulder.

"I'm so sorry, man. So fucking sorry," Hunter apologized quietly, his voice full of sorrow and regret.

I shrugged his hand from my shoulder.

"I will never forgive you for this," I stated definitely.

"Neither will I," he replied, his voice breaking under the weight of his anguish.

Epilogue

"The harder the struggle, the more glorious the triumph. Self-realization demands very great struggle." -Swami Sivananda

<u>Aurora</u>

"Wes, love, we're going to be late!" I shouted from the front door of his house.

"I told you I'm not going," he called back from his hide-from-Aurora room, also known as his home office.

"That's your prerogative, but it really is a shame," I said, laying the trap. "Sam worked so hard dolling me up for dinner. She even made me wear these ridiculously high heels."

In a flash, he was at the top of the stairs, ogling me with masculine appreciation. *Men, so predictable!*

"Damn, you look amazing. You are always beautiful—you know that—but...*damn.* I can't wait to take you out of that dress later," he declared while surveying me again from head to toe, "but the heels stay on."

"As long as I don't have to remain standing in them, you have a deal."

"No standing for you—I want to feel those heels digging into my ass while you scream my name."

That was an offer I couldn't refuse.

He continued to stare hungrily, clearly weighing his options—although whether he was considering accompanying me or attempting to persuade me to stay, I wasn't sure.

"If you really don't want to come with me, it's fine, babe," I continued baiting him. "I'm sure Ev can find a nice FBI agent to join us at the table for dinner—the banquet hall should be jam-packed with law enforcement personnel."

"I know what you're doing," he deadpanned. "Unfortunately for me, it's working. Give me five minutes and I'll be ready."

"Love you," I cooed sweetly as he headed to the bedroom to change.

It was like taking candy from a baby—*waaaay* too easy.

Heading to the kitchen, I snatched a piece of chocolate before settling on the couch. Four months had passed since my rescue from *To Ieró*. It was a long, painful recovery—both physically and emotionally—but I was finally feeling better.

Working with Thia each week, I built upon the self-realizations I'd gained while at the compound, developing new thought patterns and emotional responses to break the oppressive and unhealthy conditioning I'd suffered at the hands of *The Sacred*. Guilt and shame were no longer my constant companions, only occasional visitors.

Without the weight of blame on my shoulders, I felt like I could fly. The range and freedom of emotions I was able to experience—without my focus directed toward old thought processes—was remarkable. The broken little girl inside me rejoiced having finally found a family who wanted her, and although there was still work to be done, I was light years away from where I began. The support and love Wes and our friends showered me with was the fuel to keep my progress train in motion. I felt good—*no, spectacular*—for the first time ever.

The physical recovery was a painfully slow process that I still struggled with. After two weeks in the hospital with hefty pain management narcotics, I was able to fly back to New York. Chemical burns were a *bitch*.

Wes never left my side, taking a leave of absence from work to care for me for the first month, much to his firm's chagrin. Although the circumstances were not ideal, the time together was a gift we both cherished after my ordeal. Countless hours were spent talking and learning the minute details of one another's lives, and we learned to communicate as a couple. Unable to have sex, our need to connect was fulfilled with words and emotion versus physical expressions of love. As much as I missed our lovemaking, the foundation of our relationship was infinitely stronger having been forged in the mind and heart instead of the body. Now when we made love, our experience was deeper and more profound.

It took two months for my open sores and scabbing to heal, leaving newly exposed skin that was extremely delicate. Thankfully, make-up had never been a priority as it was strictly prohibited during the first two months. Now, four months after the incident, I was nearly pain-free. I still was not permitted to expose my skin to the sun, which sucked since late spring was quickly turning into summer, but there was nothing to be done for it.

Luckily, I had very few permanent effects from the torture. My new skin was a few shades lighter than before, however it didn't appear 'weird' since the acid coated my entire body, producing a fairly uniform alteration. There were a few irreparable scars where selected patches of tissue healed slower than the rest, but the marks weren't dramatic and would fade with time. The only physical alteration that gave me pause were the streaks down my face, originating at my eyes. The tears I'd cried in pain neutralized the acid, which left the skin in the tracks of my tears less damaged. The difference was minimal, nevertheless, with the right lighting and no make-up, the naked eye could perceive the slightly darker streak on each cheek. At first, I despised the evidence of my ordeal, until Wes reminded me that they were badges of courage—proof I'd fought and won. For as much as I disliked the lines, Wes loved them because he claimed they reminded him of how blessed he was that I was alive.

Wes spoke with Dr. Mesina on my behalf and she rearranged my semester so I only had one online course—of which she was the professor—to accommodate my temporary disability. The remainder of the semester was dedicated to completing my thesis and working on the proposals and constructs that would one day be presented to the FBI and CIA for their use. The paradigm I'd hypothesized would allow law enforcement to identify and target potentially dangerous cults *before* activities escalated. It was profiling for cult enclaves that provided clear qualifiers and quantifiable risk factors that had never before been outlined and explored.

Wes' footsteps captured my attention and I met him by the front door, where he was waiting with my coat, scarf, shawl, and gloves.

"Thanks, babe," I said gratefully once I was fully covered.

"Anything for you, beautiful."

As we walked to the car, I knew it was time to bring up the big-ass elephant that followed wherever we went.

"I know I promised not to bring it up again—*I lied, by the way*—but you need to forgive Hunter. You are holding him responsible for *my* decision, which isn't fair," I gently nudged.

"When you can sleep through the night without nightmares or go outside without reapplying SPF 100 every hour, in addition to covering every inch of skin, then—and only then—I'll consider forgiving the prick," was his predictably grumpy response.

I sighed at the familiar conversation, not wanting to ruin our night by pushing further, so I dropped the subject—for now. However, my love was in for a rude awakening if he didn't come around soon. The girls and I had been hatching a plan for months to lock the men in a room together until they all sorted out their issues and moved on.

A smile spread across my face at the prospect. It was going to be so much fun teaching these alpha males a lesson.

"What are you smiling at, my beautiful girl?"

"Nothing...I'm just happy," I replied innocently.

"Are you—happy?" he asked, suddenly serious.

"Westly Black, you make me happier than I ever dreamed possible. Because of you, my life is filled with love and joy," I paused to kiss him gently on his plush lips. "There is no other man I want to spend my life with."

"That *is* good news. Since I'm never letting you go, I'd say you're stuck with me. I love you, Aurora White."

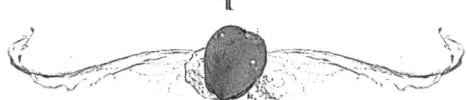

Dear Reader,

When I began the For You series, I intended it to be three novels: *Only For You, Pieces For You,* and *Temper For You.* Even as I began writing *Temper For You,* my plan remained the same. But as I continued to write, I met another character in need of a family, and we all know how much Sam, Ev, and the gang like to adopt.

I tried to ignore my new imaginary friends, but they were relentless. Therefore, I'm happy to share that the For You series will continue.

Book #4 will feature Special Agent Delilah Welch, and *damn* does she have a story to tell! Of course, we will also hang out with all our old friends to make sure they are staying out of trouble.

Additionally, my new series Broken Roads will launch in 2015. This series will focus on the Mesina family. If that name is ringing a bell you get an A+. Yep, the next series will include several characters you were introduced to in *Temper For You,* including Ry, Paris, and Dr. Mesina. I'm incredibly excited to share the stories of this dynamic, entertaining, meddlesome family with you all.

I'll keep you posted on Facebook, Twitter, my website, and whatever other newfangled social media site pops up.

Thank you so much for reading my book babies!

Love,
Genna

Acknowledgements

Adrienne, you know you've earned a special shout-out! Damn girl, *Temper For You*, would not be what it is without your thoughtful and constructive (← a euphemism for kickass) feedback. But what's more, you have been a true friend and shoulder to lean on over the past year. It is *"as if"* (lol, gotcha) the hand of fate stepped in and shoved my review request under your nose while shouting, "Read this book, biatch!" Can you imagine if you had ignored my email? I can't. I love you, girl! Thank you a million times for all your love, support, and honesty!

To My Roadies, you know who you are! When I began writing *Only For You*, I had a lot of goals and hopes, many of which have been realized. What I hadn't anticipated was that through writing I would meet so many amazing people that have grown to be my friends! You ladies have been my loudest cheerleaders, biggest pimps, most staunch supporters, as well as an infinite well of love, acceptance, support, and laughter. You make me want to get up and write every morning! Thank you for being you and for becoming my go-to girls, a safe place for me to be me. <3

I am blessed with the best beta readers in the world—truly—*the best*!!! Yes, those exclamation points were necessary to convey how spectacular they are. Many of you may not know this but an author's greatest asset—alongside a phenomenal editor--is a strong, passionate, opinionated, HONEST beta reader. Betas read a manuscript and share with the author their constructive critiques line by line, word by word. They are encouraging when warranted, and hard a$$es when necessary! They make you laugh and sometimes want to cry, but at the end of the day, they make an author stretch and grow until their story is the best it can be. Betas are the unsung heroes of any book, so now I sing your praises loud (and perhaps off-key). I love each of you and thank you from the bottom of my heart!

FYI, this is the EXACT same acknowledgment I put in *Pieces For You*, but every word is just as true now as it was then. I can't say it any better than last time, so I'll just repeat myself. There have been a number of cheerleaders who have encouraged me since I released *Only For You*, all of whom I adore. But there is one special chica who has been there to encourage, empathize, and make me laugh when I was having moments of self-doubt and self-pity. Jennifer, you can't take a compliment for shit, but you give them beautifully. You ask for nothing, but 'pimp' my work like a pro. I trust your book whispering, spidey-sense implicitly. Time and time again you've proven yourself to be a true friend, and I am so grateful for you. Besides, who else will laugh about HGSxM with me?

There are millions of editors in the world. Some are good, some are great, and a handful are God's gift to an author. Sheri, you fall into the last category. You are not only my editor but also my friend. I don't think anyone loves my book babies as much as you do. You treat each one like it's your own! You are my story soul-sister (that alliteration was just for you, Sher). Furthermore, you are one of the most interesting people I know...if I was kidnapped by terrorists, I think I would want you on the squad to come save me. I adore you for your mind-blowing editing skills, but more so for the sensational woman you are! Thank you...just, thank you! PS-I'm laughing that you have to edit this.

Last but not least, I must thank my family, specifically my husband and two boys, whose patience and support make it possible for me to chase my dream and give voice to the stories in my head. Thank you all for being my own personal heroes and cheerleading squad! Honey, without your help (and willingness to ignore the laundry that I never seem to find time to fold), none of these book babies would ever be possible.

About the Author

Genna Rulon is a contemporary romance author with a passion for blending comedy, tragedy, suspense, and hope to create her "book babies."

During her 15 years in the corporate world, Genna—inspired by her love of reading—fantasized about penning her own stories. Encouraged by her favorite authors, many of whom are indie writers and self-published, she committed to pursue her aspirations of writing her own novels.

Genna was born in California and raised on Long Island in New York, where she still resides, surrounded by the most amazing family and friends. She's married to a wonderful man who patiently tolerates her ramblings about whichever book she is currently working on—even feigning interest relatively convincingly! Genna is blessed with two little boys who do their best to thwart mommy's writing time with their hilarious antics and charming extrapolations.

All of Genna's books are brought to you courtesy of coffee and Disney Junior.

You can find Genna online at: www.gennarulon.com

Or you can contact Genna through social media:
    Twitter: www.twitter.com/GennaRulon
    Facebook: www.facebook.com/genna.rulon.author
    Goodreads: www.goodreads.com/gennarulon

For more breaking news, exclusive excerpts, and special contests, join Genna's fan page on facebook: www.facebook.com/groups/rulonsroadies

Genna would <u>love</u> to hear from you, and will personally respond to all messages! You can contact her via email as follows: genna@gennarulon.com

Be sure to join the mailing list for updates about future books, as well as giveaways, and other fun facts: www.gennarulon.com/guestbook.php

Other books by Genna

Only For You
For You Series - Book #1
published: September 17, 2013

"In its purest form love is self-sacrificing, eternal, selfless, enduring, truthful, forgiving, and indulgent. It also feels an awful lot like a kick to the stomach when you try to fight it!"

All Everleigh Carsen wanted to do was complete her final semester at Hensley University and begin the life she planned.

When a wave of violent crime seizes campus, Everleigh is persuaded by her best friend to attend a school sponsored self-defense seminar, where she meets volunteer instructor, Hunter Charles. After Everleigh's biting sarcasm induces Hunter to eject her from class, an explosive relationship is born.

Everleigh is determined to forget the striking man, but fate—that fickle shrew— continuously intervenes. Unable to escape him, she casts Hunter as her prime adversary. The only complication...Hunter is resolutely pursuing his vindication...by any means necessary. Verbal warfare ensues, and despite Everleigh's ingenious efforts, in Hunter, she has finally found her equal.

Only For You is a compelling tale of friendship, desire, and redemption—brimming with witty characters, intelligent dialogue, unexpected twists, profound sorrow, unfettered hope, and love's unassailable perseverance.

Pieces For You
For You, Book #2
Published: December 17, 2013

*"The phoenix hope, can wing her
way through the desert skies,
and still defying fortune's spite;
revive from ashes and rise."*
-Miguel de Cervantes

Samantha Whitney survived unimaginable tragedy only to discover she had been betrayed by a man who claimed to love her. Shattered, Sam spends months at a safe haven trying to piece herself back together. Ready or not, the time has come for her to return home.

As Sam struggles to resume a life that no longer feels familiar, she finds unwavering support in an unexpected, familiar face. Confronting Sam's raw emotions and open wounds head-on, Griffin manages to take two steps forward for every step she retreats.

But when Sam is once again threatened, Griffin must decide how far he is willing to go to protect the woman he wants...knowing the cost of her safety is the risk of losing her.

Pieces For You is a captivating journey of survival, healing, and sacrifice—teeming with honesty, humor, unexpected twists, and love's unsurpassed endurance.

Temper For You

For You, Book #3

Published: September 24, 2014

"Life is messy. Love is messier."
—Catch and Release

Meg Adeio has led a life of isolation—not by choice, by necessity—until one act of heroism forces her out of seclusion. Despite a past shrouded in mystery, Meg is "adopted" by an eclectic group of friends that become the family she never had. Life was good for the first time in...ever.

Or it was until Westly Black reappeared on her doorstep. She knew he was the last man any woman should give her time to—only good for one thing—yet a temptation no woman could deny. Wes might make her life messy, but Meg's eyes were wide open and she had it under control. At least she thought she did.

When past and present collide, loyalties are tested, forcing Meg to sacrifice her future to protect those she loves.

Temper For You is a gripping story of regret, deception, and redemption – filled with raw emotion, sarcastic wit, intrigue, and love's propensity to forgive.

Ever For You: A novella
For You, Book #1.5
Expected publication: Winter 2015

*"While all deception requires secrecy,
all secrecy is not meant to deceive."*
-Sissela Bok

Honor For You
For You, Book #4
Expected publication: 2015

*"Hard times don't create heroes.
It is during the hard times when
the 'hero' within us is revealed."*
-Bob Riley